EMILY BRADSHAW, who also writes as Emily Carmichael, has won three *Romantic Times* Reviewer's Choice Awards, five Affaire de Coeur Golden Certificates, and was a 1995 RITA nominee for Best Western. She lives in Illinois with her husband and four dogs, where she writes, vacuums dog hair from the carpets, and flies small planes.

RAINE CANTRELL won fourteen awards for eight novels including *Romantic Times* Best Civil War Award for *Tarnished Hearts* and Booklovers Romance of the Year Award for *Darling Annie* (both published by Topaz). She lives in Florida and, when not writing, rescues stray cats, studies history, and collects antiques. Christmas is her favorite time of year.

KAREN HARPER's most recent novels include *The Poyson Garden,* a mystery with Queen Elizabeth I as an amateur sleuth, and *The Baby Farm,* a romantic suspense about a midwife in modern-day Appalachia. A former English teacher, Karen and her husband divide their time between Columbus, Ohio, and Naples, Florida.

PATRICIA RICE was born in rural New York, grew up in suburban Kentucky, raised her children in small-town America, and now lives with her husband in rural splendor outside Charlotte, North Carolina. Ms. Rice has two children and a degree in accounting, which in no way explains her long list of award-winning contemporary and historical romances—unless one correlates them with a need for escapist fantasies.

JODI THOMAS is a two-time RITA Award-winning author. As a fifth-generation Texan, most of her twelve books (published by Putnam/Berkley) are set in her home state. She divides her time between Amarillo, Texas, and a cabin in Red River, New Mexico.

A Country Christmas

Five Stories by
Emily Bradshaw

Raine Cantrell

Karen Harper

Patricia Rice

Jodi Thomas

AN ONYX BOOK

ONYX
Published by New American Library, a division of
Penguin Putnam Inc., 375 Hudson Street,
New York, New York 10014, U.S.A.
Penguin Books Ltd, 27 Wrights Lane,
London W8 5TZ, England
Penguin Books Australia Ltd, Ringwood,
Victoria, Australia
Penguin Books Canada Ltd, 10 Alcorn Avenue,
Toronto, Ontario, Canada M4V 3B2
Penguin Books (N.Z.) Ltd, 182–190 Wairau Road,
Auckland 10, New Zealand

Penguin Books Ltd, Registered Offices:
Harmondsworth, Middlesex, England

Originally published in a Signet edition, November 1993.

First Onyx Printing, October 1999
10 9 8 7 6 5 4 3 2 1

Contents

A Husband for Holly
  by Jodi Thomas   7

Friends Are Forever
  by Patricia Rice   65

The Gift
  by Emily Bradshaw   134

A Time for Giving
  by Raine Cantrell   208

O Christmas Tree
  by Karen Harper   280

A Husband for Holly
by Jodi Thomas

Texas, December 23, 1865

1

LUTHER WALTERS grumbled at his lifelong friend, Samuel Stone, as they pulled a flatbed wagon onto the loading dock at Bryan, Texas. The sun was just coming up and they'd been driving half of the night, leaving Luther in no mood to be sociable. "I'm still not sold on this idea for a present for Holly. Too many unpredictables in this kind of deal, Sam."

Stretching his back, Luther spat a long stream of brown liquid and continued, "If this ain't the most hair-brained notion you've ever come up with, I hope my memory doesn't return enough to think of a worse one."

Samuel climbed carefully down from the wagon, favoring his left knee as always. He tossed the buffalo robe he'd used as a lap quilt into the back. "We agreed to get her something special, it being both Christmas and her twenty-first birthday." He pulled on the belt, which had insisted on sliding below his belly at every opportunity for more than fifty years. "So no use pondering what's done any longer."

"Yeah, but a husband?" Luther shouted remembering Sam's hearing problem. If we order our Holly a husband, she'll skin us both alive if she don't like him. What if he's a no account?''

"Stop worrying about 'what if' when we ain't dealt with the here and now. Besides, if he could read the ad, the feller's one up on us." Samuel waved at the stationmaster. "Mornin' Seth, you notice a man climb off the train a few minutes ago?''

The station manager looked up at the two aging cowhands and smiled before pointing to the end of the platform. "He's the only soul who got off this morning. Been standing there watching the sun rise ever since.''

Luther and Samuel looked down the empty dock. Standing alone waited a tall man wrapped in a wool coat. His Union blue hat was pinned up on one side in the manner of a cavalry officer, and finely tooled black saddlebags hung over one shoulder. His dark coat was pulled open to reveal a polished Army Colt strapped to his waist. Unlike the ragged Rebel boys they'd seen coming home, this soldier looked as though his uniform was new from boot to brim.

Luther grabbed Samuel, as if they were about to take a step closer to the devil himself. "Sam! That can't be him.''

Sam squinted hard into the morning sun trying to make out details of the thin stranger. "He's tall, just like his telegram said. Least we won't have to worry about Holly's kids being runts. Nice-looking feller, too, from what I can make out beneath that hat.''

Luther didn't decrease his hold on Sam's arm. "But it can't be him!'' The aging man was shaking his head so hard, his saggy chins fell a step behind the rest of his face. "He can't be Holly's present. That's a Yankee!''

Sam pulled free of his friend and moved forward.

Being raised in the Oklahoma Territory, he'd never been as fond of marking a man by his birthplace as most. "Pardon me, mister?" Sam shouted as he hurried toward the officer before Luther could stop him. "You wouldn't be Zachary Hamilton, would you?"

The stranger turned toward the two men and nodded once without speaking. At first glance, he cut a handsome picture with his dark hair and blue-gray eyes. But as Sam got closer he saw more, far more, maybe even more than he wanted to see.

The stranger's eyes were puffy with sleeplessness, and his high cheekbones hollow with thinness. His mouth was tight, as if he hadn't smiled in years. His stare had the coldness of one who valued nothing, not even his own life. Sam had seen what war did to some men, but he hadn't expected to see such total loss of a belief in dreams in a young man wearing Union blue.

Sam slowly offered his hand. "Nice to meet you, Captain Hamilton. I'm Sam Stone." He glanced at his partner. "And this here is Luther Walters. We're mighty glad you answered our ad."

Before either of the men could react, the Union officer before them crumpled, as if he were made of damp paper. He hit the platform with a hard thud that seemed to echo off the station house.

Sam dropped to one knee and touched Hamilton's forehead. "He's burning up." The old man lifted the officer's shoulders. "We'd best get him home."

Luther picked up Zach's feet. "Great! Not only did we get Holly a damn Yankee for Christmas, we got her a dead, damn Yankee."

Sam struggled with the body as they moved toward the wagon. "Look on the bright side. If we can get her to marry him before he dies, she'll be a widow.

You know how much higher widows are thought of around these parts than old maids.''

Luther shook his head in agreement. ''I told you from the first she wouldn't marry any man we had to order for her. She's got too much pride.''

''Well, it's too late to find her another Christmas present. We'll have to go with this one.''

They tossed Zach onto the dirty buffalo hide in the wagon bed with the same care they loaded firewood. Sam wiped his forehead and thumbed toward the town's only diner. ''Might as well eat breakfast. It'll take several hours to get him home. That is if he lives long enough for Holly to meet him.''

''Kill him is more like it.'' Luther laughed. ''If there ain't a man in the state who can tame her, what hope does a sickly Yankee have?''

Sam agreed as they disappeared into the town's only eating establishment.

2

Zachary Hamilton awakened slowly, one sense at a time, to the welcoming aroma of baked bread and freshly boiled coffee. He could feel the warmth of a fire crackling several feet away. A woman hummed softly from somewhere beyond the room. A feeling of being home blanketed Zach, and he didn't want to open his eyes. For the first time in years, he remembered a moment when he'd felt alive, when he thought there was good in the world. A time before the war between the states, a time before the prison at Andersonville.

Slowly, he forced himself to open his eyes, even though he knew the dream might disappear once he came fully awake. Huge railroad cross ties formed the ceiling of the room he was in, giving him the impression that this home had been built to weather any storm.

His hand gripped the quilts covering him as his gaze moved around the rest of the room. The large bed he lay in was against one wall, surrounded by a menagerie of furniture. Large hand-cut wooden pieces mixed with thin-legged French pieces. Lace brushed against animal hides in this large house that seemed to be missing inside walls to separate one area from another. Two doors cut into each of the far walls. One, Zach guessed, would be to the kitchen; the other, judging by the bolt, must lead outside.

In the center of the room stood a table set for four, with dishes as mismatched as the room's furnishings.

The humming stopped abruptly. "Evenin' '' came the clear sound of a woman's voice from the doorway leading into the kitchen.

Zach turned his gaze, but all words log-piled in his throat as he caught first sight of her. Leaning against the doorway was a young woman who seemed to belong in the room, for she was as mismatched as the china on the table. Her stance was wide, like a man's, with an old revolver strapped to her thigh, and pants three sizes too big belted at her waist. The white shirt she wore was drop-shoulder, making her slender build seem even smaller. Hair the color of a fiery golden sunset massed around her face and hugged her shoulders in a wild tumbling of softness.

She could be an angel or a devil, but one thing Zach knew: he'd never forget the sight of her. This woman was the kind to haunt a man's dreams.

With a sudden blast of cold air, the two men Zach had seen at the train station stormed through the outside door. Each was loaded down with branches of greenery.

The strange woman smiled warmly at the two old men, and motioned for them to take a seat at the table. Both men nodded toward Zach and took their chairs as the woman brought in a pot of coffee.

As she poured, she glanced toward Zach. "I told the boys I'd cook supper, then we'd see if you were dead." She moved toward him with a grace nature granted few women. Her slight smile told him she had no doubt he'd live. "Seeing as you're alive, I might as well introduce myself and offer you a cup. I'm Holly McCarter, and this has been my ranch since my father died six years ago."

Zach couldn't believe what he was hearing. He tried to remember how the ad he'd answered had read. Something about an old maid looking for a man to help her run a huge spread in Texas. He'd known at the time that the ad was no more than a strange advertisement for a husband, and he'd been just heartsick and drunk enough to answer it. But he must have been wrong; the woman before him would have no trouble finding a husband, and she was years away from being what he'd consider an old maid.

As Holly raised her hand to his forehead, their gazes met and Zach was hypnotized. Her eyes were evergreen. The color of the huge fir trees that grow deep in the forests of upstate New York. The color of peace.

"Everyone knows for a hundred miles around that there's always a meal offered on the McCarter spread," she said, "but we usually have our guests arrive conscious."

When Zach didn't reply, Holly glanced at the two old men filling their plates at the table. "He doesn't talk much, does he? Where did you two say you found him?''

Both Luther and Samuel seemed too preoccupied to answer, but Zach remembered his manners. ''Pleased to meet you, Miss McCarter. I met your friends at the station this morning.'' When she looked confused, he hurried to explain, ''You're nothing like I expected from the ad.'' How could he begin to tell her that he'd stayed drunk the entire train trip, dreading the sight of a woman who would have to put an ad in a paper to find a husband? How was he ever going to explain that he'd have sold his soul for a place where he could see the sun rise and set without a house in his line of sight? And she'd offered just such a place, for only the use of his name after hers.

Holly looked surprised. ''Ad?''

She tossed her hair back over one shoulder in a way that made Zach's gut tighten suddenly. Her beauty made him ache for something he'd never known he missed.

He glanced toward the two cowhands, but they didn't look his way. Both were shoveling down food as if they wouldn't get the chance to eat again for days. There was nothing left for Zach to do but face his future wife and iron out the details of their agreement. But he wouldn't do it without standing. He shoved his feet from beneath the covers, and was relieved to find his trousers still on. His feet hit his boots as he swung them off the bed.

Holly stood, none too patiently, as he pulled on his boots and coat. She knew something was up. She'd sensed it the moment she'd returned from the north pasture and found Sam and Luther tucking this stranger into her father's old bed, as though there were nowhere else on the ranch to put him. Luther and Samuel had been whispering for weeks, and they had disappeared entirely last night.

Now they were eating her cooking without complaint. Something they hadn't done in ten years.

She studied the stranger as he finished dressing. Despite his thinness, he wasn't bad-looking. It was not so much that his features were perfect, but more that there was a strength molded into his every bone. She could see it in the determined set of his jaw and the rigidness of his back. She might have found him handsome, if he hadn't been a Yankee.

He faced her with the stance of a seasoned soldier. "I'm Zachary Hamilton, and I believe I meet the qualifications in your ad. Before the war, I was a veterinarian by education, so that should cover the part about knowing horses and cattle. I'm under thirty, single, have all my teeth, and can read."

Holly's eyes darkened to indigo green. "What ad?" This time she turned her question to the two old men. "Either this man is crazy, or you two have been up to something."

Samuel and Luther jumped from their chairs and put the table between themselves and Holly, as if her question had been punctuated with war drums.

"Now, Holly," Luther wiped his mouth with his sleeve, "don't go gettin' mad. We didn't just find him, we sent for him. Thought it was a good idea. How was we to know the only man who answered the ad would be a Yankee?"

Samuel's head was bobbing in agreement. "We just wanted to get you something special for Christmas. And the war's over. And he don't look so bad if we could fatten him up a little. And . . ."

Holly advanced slowly toward the two men. "Are

you two trying to tell me you *ordered* this man for me?"

Zach couldn't help but laugh aloud. How could these two men possibly be afraid of such a slip of a girl? It was almost as ridiculous as the idea that they'd gotten her a husband for a gift.

To his surprise, the woman turned on him. "Stop laughing!" she demanded with eyes shining in anger. "I'll deal with you when I'm finished with these two."

Luther moved a step closer. "We can't take him back now. There's not another train until after Christmas."

Holly pressed her lips together until they disappeared. "How could you?" she asked so quietly, both men looked even more nervous. "How could the two of you place an ad for a husband? Did you think anyone who answered would be acceptable, like ordering a sack of flour?"

Sam saw his chance. "We thought we'd give it a try. After all, that's the way your dad found your mother, and a sweeter little French lady never lived. Luther and me figured it was worth another shot. Thought you might like the idea, 'cause there ain't a man in these parts to suit your fancy."

Luther nodded. "He ain't bad. He can even read, so the two of you can talk about those books you like."

"Did it ever occur to either of you that I might want to pick my own husband?" Her voice might have been calm, but her fists were planted firmly on her hips. "And when and if I do, it won't be a northerner. I want no part of even inviting a Yankee onto my property."

Luther didn't have an answer, so he fell back on the only tactic that worked when he had no ground to stand on. "Now, Holly, you know we promised your father we'd see after you like you was our own. You being motherless from birth. We did the best we . . . ''

"Out!" Holly shouted. "Both of you!"

"But . . .''

"Out!" She moved toward them, and both men ran as if they could hear a rattler's tail shaking.

They were out the door and gone before Zach could control his laughter.

With a fiery whirl, Holly turned on him. "How dare you take advantage of two dear old men?"

"Me!" He could see the anger in her eyes and the tightness around her mouth. She would run him through if she had a blade, unless he explained. "All I've done, Miss McCarter, is answer an ad. I thought you knew about their plan."

"I knew nothing of any ad or plan." She moved closer, a little of the anger passing from her face as she realized he might be just as much a victim of the old men's plan. "Let me make one thing crystal clear, Mr. Hamilton. I want no husband ordered for me. If I did, I'd pick him from sturdy Texas stock, not the likes of you. The war's over, so I'll grant you the McCarter hospitality—but nothing else. You must be as crazy as those two old men to think I'd go along with this."

Zach didn't defend himself. He couldn't tell her that he'd been starved in a Rebel prison camp for almost a year. Or that when he'd been last wounded in battle, he had caught a fever and had lain in the mud for three days waiting for death. "I assumed the agreement was tentative." He felt his muscles tighten in attention. "Pending on both parties' agreement."

"There was no agreement, Mr. Hamilton," she reminded. "I'll have no part of being married to a man ordered for me by my two absentminded old godfathers."

He nodded once, understanding her clearly. "No agreement."

Anger passed from her like a summer storm, leaving her more beautiful. "I'll pay you for the train ticket back."

"That won't be necessary." He could sense her nervousness, and suddenly felt sorry for the lady. This must be embarrassing for her. "I'll have the men take me back to town immediately."

When he passed her heading toward the door, she didn't even come up to the top of his shoulder; however, he had a feeling there was little this lady couldn't do.

"No," she said, her voice finally calming to a normal tone. "Sam and Luther are too tired after being up all night, and you must be exhausted as well. You're welcome to stay the night, and I'll drive you back myself come morning."

"Thank you," Zach glanced at the one bed in the room. "But . . ."

Holly caught his unvoiced question. "I'll sleep in the loft. I do most nights anyway. My father would come back from his grave to haunt me if I didn't show a stranger, any stranger, the McCarter hospitality. It, like the Christmas Eve party tomorrow night, is something he always insisted upon no matter what else was happening."

A silence fell between them, as wide as a canyon. Zach wasn't accustomed to talking with women, and she wasn't one for small talk. Without a word, they sat down at the table and began to eat, both very much aware of the other.

He noticed her hands were small, but calloused across her palms from hard work.

She noticed his manners were impeccable, and his slight smile warmed her to her boots.

3

"I've more steak in the kitchen—if you're still hungry?" Holly asked as Zach finished off the last piece of meat on the platter. She'd never seen one man eat so much at one time.

He looked slightly guilty. "I'm sorry. Do I look like I'm starving? It's only that I haven't eaten a meal since I boarded the train. The food in the shacks along the stops didn't seem worth the time to run and get. Now, I can't get full."

Holly smiled. "Don't apologize. I'm the worst cook in the state, and watching you eat my cooking is a treat. Folks usually make up reasons why they can't eat another bite." She stood and picked up the empty platter. "How about I fry you a few eggs to go with the last of the meat?"

Zach wanted to be polite and say, "no, thank you," but the thought of fresh eggs was too much to turn down. He followed Holly into the huge kitchen, and watched as she overcooked a half dozen scrambled eggs. While he ate every bite, she began hanging the greenery around the room and tying tiny Christmas bells to each branch. Without making eye contact, they found it easier to talk of ordinary things, of safe topics. She told him the story of how her father had built the cabin of railroad ties that had washed downstream. He described the train ride west. There was no talk of marriage, or war, or of him staying.

Zach couldn't help watching her move with a grace about her no amount of men's clothing could ever hide. He could almost see what her parents must have been like. Her mother small and dainty, her father strong and capable. She'd inherited the best from both of them. He'd never met a woman like her. A woman who could take care of herself, and who didn't seem to need or want a man to lean on.

As he finished the last of the coffee, he said, "I'm truly sorry about the mix-up over the ad, but I'm not sorry I came to Texas. This open land looks like as good a place as any I've seen to start over."

Holly didn't respond, and he wondered if she'd heard. Finally, she climbed down from the chair she'd been using as a ladder and asked, "Why *did* you answer the ad, Mr. Hamilton?"

Her question was too direct to be answered any other way. "I don't know. I spent most of the war dreaming of going home, and when I did there was nothing there for me. Even the woman I thought I loved didn't wait for me to return. So I took a few months leave before deciding whether to re-up, and then I tried to drink my troubles away. Not in the sloppy-town-drunk kind of way, but alone in one hotel room after another. Finally, I woke up one morning and didn't know what town I was in. I went downstairs, and there were strangers everywhere; no one I cared about or who even noticed me. So I bought a paper and ordered another bottle sent to my room. Before the bottle was delivered, I read your strange ad and decided any direction was better than the one in which I was headed."

Holly moved closer and sat down across from him as he continued, "I wanted a place away from people for a while." He couldn't tell a lady what it had been like in the Confederate prison camp with thousands of men on only a few acres. Just the smell had made most new prisoners sick for days. "I want to stand and

watch the sun rise and set every day of my life without
seeing people between me and the horizon.''

Holly jumped to her feet, as if she were the very
genie he'd called for. "Well, come on, Mr. Hamilton.
If you're up to a little ride, I'll show you the sunset
from the end of my spread before you leave. It's just
like you want to see, nothing but nature to color the
view.''

"After that meal, I think I could use a little exercise." With food under his belt, he could almost believe he could do anything. Maybe if he started eating
and sleeping regularly, the fever would stay at bay.

Zach grabbed his warm wool riding coat and headed
toward the door. He wasn't surprised to see Holly pull
a man's leather jacket from the peg. When he offered
to help her put it on, she pulled away without a word.

They walked out of the house into the yard of the
huge ranch. She yelled at one of the men to saddle two
horses, then turned to Zach. "This is my world, Mr.
Hamilton. We can ride about a mile west and watch
the sunset along the breaks.''

Zach looked around at the cluster of buildings.
Bunkhouses, barns, well house, all cared for properly.
The ranch was like a place he'd dreamed of for years. A
place large enough and far enough away from others
that it could be a little world unto itself.

Sam limped from the main bunkhouse so fast, he
looked like a top about to spin. "Howdy, Captain."
The old man smiled as though he was surprised to see
the Yankee still alive. "I didn't hear any yelling coming from Holly's house, so I figured she'd either killed
you or the two of you had made up.''

"Don't get any ideas, Sam." Holly stepped between
him and Zach. "We're just going for a ride. My

Christmas present goes back to town tomorrow. And don't try to tell me, you didn't hear me."

Sam looked disappointed. "Of course, Holly. If that's what you want."

"That's exactly what I want." A touch of anger colored her cheeks. "A husband for Christmas is about the worst idea you two have ever come up with."

A ranch hand led two horses from the barn, distracting her from any other comment. Zach moved to help Holly up, but again she skirted away from his touch. She swung into the saddle with ease atop a huge roan. "This is Cinnamon." The mane of the horse almost matched the color of Holly's hair. "I raised her from the time she first stood, and I'm the only one who rides her."

Zach nodded his approval of the horse and walked around her to the other mount. As he climbed into the saddle, his muscles strained from the lack of riding. Biting down hard on his bottom lip, he hid his discomfort.

"Have a nice ride." Sam smiled at them as if his mind were already moving onto another plan. "Some of the boys and I will carry in the Christmas tree while you're gone."

Holly kicked her horse into action. "You can ride, can't you Yankee?"

"I can ride," Zach answered as he followed, praying he could keep up with the little lady.

They rode west at a gallop and after a short distance, Zach felt his body responding to the feel of the powerful animal moving beneath him. The exertion seemed to build his strength as they rode over the open country toward a long line of low cliffs she'd called breaks.

She reached them first and encouraged Cinnamon to

follow the trail leading to the top. His horse followed, with Zach showing a little of the skill in horsemanship he'd learned in the cavalry.

As they reached the summit, the sun was just touching the horizon. Zach pulled up beside her, and watched as yellow gold spilled out across the land.

"It's fabulous!" he whispered. "The ground looks like it's on fire for miles."

"I know," she answered. "I've been riding to this spot most of my life to watch it. My dad told me the sun just drops from sight in the mountains where he grew up. One minute it's there, and the next, it's gone. But here the sun spreads out and puts on a show, as if it doesn't want to die. And after the sun disappears, the clouds still glow with its light, as though remembering the warmth for as long as possible."

Zach could never remember seeing such a magnificent sight. The thought that she could watch it daily almost made him jealous. "Thank you," he finally said, "for sharing your sunset with me."

"You're welcome," she answered, reluctantly turning her horse back to the path toward home.

As they rode among the shadows, he finally broke the silence. "Why wouldn't you allow me to help you into the saddle back there? Or on with your coat in the cabin?"

"I'm not in the habit of having someone help me do anything."

Zach took a deep breath and dove into what he had to say. This wasn't a woman who'd give him a second chance, so he might as well be direct at his one try. "You know how you said your father had rules he followed, like hospitality and a Christmas Eve party?"

"Yes." She slowed her horse, intrigued.

"Well, where I come from, we have a few rules

also. My mother was a fine woman, and she'd have had my hide if I didn't offer to assist a lady on or off a horse, or help a woman into her coat with the proper amount of manners.''

"I'm not helpless," Holly started. "I'm able to . . .''

"Being able has nothing to do with it, Miss McCarter. It's a matter of custom, nothing more.''

Holly was silent. No one since her father died had reminded her of her manners. Not Luther, or Sam or anyone else around the place. Whatever she said was fact, and no one questioned her. She wasn't sure she liked this Zachary Hamilton, but she couldn't help being intrigued by the idea that he wasn't the least bit intimidated by her.

"I'll not be pampered." She raised her chin and looked straight ahead.

"I wouldn't dream of it." He couldn't seem to keep the corner of his mouth from lifting slightly. "But would you consider allowing me to pay you the common courtesy when we return, for my dear departed mother's sake?''

"I might." Holly kicked her horse. "If you're there when I reach the barn.''

Zach was beside her in a heartbeat as they raced toward the barn's glowing lanterns.

Minutes later, Sam's smile reached all the way to the laugh lines around his eyes as he watched Holly slide from her saddle into Zach's waiting arms. They only touched for a moment, but Sam felt the earth shift in his world. He slapped Luther on the back, and suddenly decided that he believed in Christmas magic.

4

Holly watched Zach build the fire in the huge corner fireplace while she warmed milk for hot cocoa. He was not an easy man to read. He seemed to have enough pride for several men, yet he'd answered an ad to be anybody's husband. Since their ride, conversation had flowed calmly between them, light with laughter and flavored in honesty. He was, and always would be, a stranger she'd met for a few hours, but she felt she could learn from this proper Yankee with his good manners and true stare.

She didn't need a gypsy palm reader to tell her something was wrong with her. She'd known it from the time she'd turned fifteen and Sam had dragged her to a barn raising and dance. Holly wanted to giggle and whisper with the other girls, but she had no idea what they were laughing about. If there was a barn to be built, it seemed more practical to grab a hammer and climb. The men at first had been shy around her, but by the time the barn was completed, they'd welcomed her as one of their own. Only when the dance started, not a one welcomed her as a dance partner.

As Holly filled the cups with steaming cocoa, she made up her mind. She'd talk with this Zach Hamilton, and learn how she should act. It would be no great embarrassment, for he'd be gone tomorrow morning, and she'd never have to face him again.

"Thanks," he said, as he stood and took one of the mugs from her hand. "I don't remember the last time I had a cup of cocoa."

"It's one of the few things I fix that I don't burn." Holly tried to sound relaxed. She curled cross-legged on the floor in front of the fire. The smell of evergreen blended with the aroma of burning pinion. This house, this room was the only place Holly felt comfortable, and even tonight the stranger before her couldn't take away that feeling.

Zach took a sip. As the warm chocolate slid down his throat, he glanced around the room. "The men picked a fine Christmas tree. It's as high as the ceiling, yet not so wide that it takes up too much space. They must have worked all the time we were gone to get up the rest of the greenery. There's even mistletow over every doorway."

Holly nodded, remembering how every year the hands took all the furniture out of the huge room and invited the neighbors over for Christmas Eve. The cook in the bunkhouse would make gingerbread, apple turnovers, and taffy for the children. Most of the wives would bring other candies and cakes, until the kitchen table bulged with the banquet. "We'll decorate the tree with cookie stars and ribbon rings. There'll be lots of talking and laughing and even dancing tomorrow night in this room. It'll be days before I'll stop smelling evergreen and candles, but it's a McCarter custom dating back to when there were only a few families within traveling distance."

Zach relaxed in the chair close to the fire and crossed his long legs in front of him. "You'll dance all night with the many ranchers and cowhands from these parts?"

Holly knew her time of honesty had come. If she didn't tell him the truth now, she'd never get any instructions. She'd spend the rest of her life ranch talking with men and never know how to talk romance. "No." She lifted her head, as if daring him to laugh. "I don't own a dancing dress or know how to dance, even if I did. I learned a long time ago to only do things I'm good at. Dancing isn't one of them, so I'm satisfied to watch.''

Zach leaned closer. The longing in her green eyes made a lie of what she said. ''Would you like to learn?'' he asked.

''You'd teach me?''

''For showing me your sunset, it's the least I can do.'' Zach stood and bowed low. ''May I have the honor, Miss McCarter?''

Holly lifted her hand. ''You may,'' she whispered, feeling more afraid than she had facing down wild mustangs. ''If you promise not to tell anyone I'm wasting my time so foolishly.''

''You have my word.'' His strong hand closed around hers and pulled her to her feet. Slowly, as if he were testing her seriousness, he moved in front of her. He lifted her left hand and placed it on his shoulder. ''I'll count, and all you have to do is follow.''

He counted to four over and over while they moved about the room, and Holly slowly relaxed. Dancing wasn't as hard as she'd thought it might be. His sure hand guided her and steadied her when she faltered.

''Why have you never danced before?'' he asked without stopping. This might seem a foolishness to her, but it was pure pleasure to him. There'd been a time in his life when he'd never thought he'd hold a woman and dance again.

''No one ever asked me,'' she stated flatly, wishing she had another reason to give him.

''I find that hard to believe,'' Zach responded.

Suddenly Holly planted her feet wide and refused to move another step. ''I'm not in the habit of lying, Yankee.'' Anger sparked inside her like lightning striking a dry prairie. No one in her life had ever even hinted that she might lie. She knew men in this country who would kill someone for saying such a thing.

But Zach's anger rose to meet hers on equal ground. ''And I'm not in the habit of being referred to constantly as 'Yankee.' Do you think you could use my name now and then when you're yelling at me, so I'll know you're mad at me and not the entire upper half of the country?'' His voice was calm, but she had a feeling his wrath was just as deadly as her own.

Before either of them could move, the door swung open, and Sam hurried inside. ''Wind's getting up, Holly, you want me to . . .'' He froze at the sight of Holly in Zach's arms.

She pulled away from the stranger, trying to act as if her being in a man's arms were not the eighth wonder of the world Sam appeared to think it was. ''We'd best move the horses into the corral by the barn. I don't want them spooking again.''

''I'll help.'' Zach moved with her to their coats.

''No, Yank . . .'' Holly hesitated. ''Zach. I don't need a man helping who doesn't know his way around the grounds after dark. The corral can be tricky. You stay here. I'm capable of running a ranch, even if I can't dance.''

She knew he would've argued if he'd known her better, but a guest on an unfamiliar ranch had no choice. She appreciated his offer. ''Sam, you stay here, too. With that bad knee of yours, we're liable to be pulling you out of the mud.''

''All right.'' Sam was already taking off his coat, as if he'd known he'd be staying behind. He touched his knee, which always seemed to give him trouble when any work appeared after sunset. ''I need to talk with this here young fellow anyway.''

Zach stood silent as he watched Holly pull on her

coat. He could still feel her in his arms, and her fresh smell lingered, if only in his mind. He wanted to stop her, but he knew she was doing what she did every day of her life—the only thing she seemed to feel comfortable doing: being a rancher.

When Zach finally turned back to the fire, Sam had made himself comfortable in the only chair. "I know what you're going to say, old man, and there's no need." Zach wanted to make it clear to Sam before the old guy started giving him warnings and threats. "I realize I'll be sleeping under the same roof as Holly, but I assure you I'm a gentleman, and she has nothing to fear."

Sam hooted with laughter so loud, Zach was worried about the man's sanity. When finally he quieted down, Sam shouted, "Son, it wasn't Holly's safety I was worried about; it was yours! You can bet that if you do anything to displease her, she'll have you tied to the hitching post come morning."

Sam shifted the tobacco in his mouth and looked toward the door. "I best get going." He shoved himself from the chair. "Consider yourself warned. Don't dance with the devil's daughter unless you can take the heat." He slapped Zach on the back like he probably wouldn't see the man alive again.

As the door slammed behind the old man, Zach folded into the chair and ran his fingers through his hair. He was too tired to think about anything. It seemed a million years since he'd watched the sun rise at the train station. For the first time in months, he fell asleep without the taste of whiskey in his mouth or the memory of the war on his mind.

The fire was low when he heard the door open. He didn't move while Holly took off her coat, gun belt, and boots. She'd been gone for hours, but she looked as fiery and beautiful as before.

Keeping one eye open slightly, he watched her tiptoe across the room to a huge wardrobe. She glanced his direction, then satisfied he was asleep, unbuckled her belt.

Zach felt guilty for spying on her, but he couldn't bring himself to move and announce that he was awake. The gentleman in him told him to keep his eyes closed; the man in him wouldn't allow it. He knew there was nowhere else to get undressed that was as warm as this room.

The wool trousers slipped from her hips to the floor with a soft plop. Her oversized shirt hung almost to her knees, hiding all but a quick glimpse of her legs. She pulled her arms into the shirt, and he thought she was going to pull the huge garment over her head; but instead, she began unwrapping a long strip of white cotton from around her chest.

Zach had heard his mother talk of women binding their breasts when they wanted to stop nursing babies, but he'd never known a woman to do so otherwise.

When she finished, Holly tossed the binding in a drawer and put her arms back into the shirt. Tiptoeing over to where Zach sat, Holly gently covered him with a blanket. "Good night, Yankee," she whispered.

For a long moment she stared at him, and then, convinced he was sound asleep, she leaned forward and lightly brushed her lips against his. "Thank you for my first dance and my first kiss."

Her lips were the feather light of a wish across his mouth, but they sparked his mind with longing.

She was on the second rung of the ladder to the loft when he stopped her. "Wait!" Zach closed his fingers over her hands, resting on either side of the ladder.

Holly almost lost her footing. "You're awake!"

He could feel her hands trembling beneath his, but her eyes were afire with challenge. The wind had blown her hair wild and free, while the night's chill had stroked a blush into her cheeks. Her beauty could never be captured in a painting, he thought, for the artist would have to hold the fire in a sunset and the wonder of a forest in winter to do her justice.

"I didn't mean to startle you." Zach could barely make words form, his heart seemed to be pounding in his throat. "I had to stop you before you were gone for the night." He couldn't let her just walk away after the way she'd touched him. "Why did you kiss me just now?"

Holly's cheeks burned, but her chin didn't lower a fraction. "If you're looking for an apology, you'll wait 'til the prairie floods."

"I'm not wanting an apology; I'm wanting an answer. Why did you kiss me just now?"

"Why did you act like you were asleep?"

Zach leaned an inch into the ladder, pinning her between him and the wooden rings. "I've heard folks in Texas are hospitable, but I don't believe that includes a good night kiss to every stranger spending the night."

Holly twisted to face him. "And I've heard folks around these parts call a kiss a 'Yankee dime.' "

Zach couldn't help but laugh. "Tell me why you kissed me, Holly."

She looked as if she longed to swear, but she answered, "I just wanted to know what it felt like to kiss a man. You'll be gone tomorrow, and then if anyone ever asks me if I've been kissed, I can say yes without lying."

"So you thought you'd practice on me until a man

you think is right for you comes along?'' He couldn't hide his smile. He could tell by her face that he'd guessed the truth.

''Maybe,'' she answered.

''Don't you think you should get your money's worth on that 'Yankee dime.' '' He leaned closer and lightly brushed her lips.

Until she'd kissed him, he hadn't thought there'd be a chance of him ever being this close to her. But the touch of her lips had changed his mind.

''Kissing is like dancing,'' he whispered against her cheek. ''All it takes is a little practice.''

''And you'll teach me?'' She moved her head so that his lips brushed across her cheek. ''Then you'll be gone tomorrow, and no one will know of the lessons?''

''If that's the way you want it, pretty lady,'' he answered, having trouble putting words together when all he could think of was touching her lips again.

Very slowly he leaned against her, pressing Holly back against the rungs of the ladder. His mouth opened slightly as he tasted her full bottom lip.

''Put your arms around me,'' he ordered gently.

''Like this?'' she asked with her hands on his shoulders. He could feel her tremble, but knew it was more from adventure than passion.

''No.'' Dear Lord, she was driving him insane with her innocence. ''Tighter.''

She followed his instructions, pulling him into contact with her body. His arms slid around her and lifted her off the ladder. He knew her feet weren't touching the floor, but he couldn't release his hold. The feel of her against him was a heaven he'd never even known to dream of.

Suddenly, he could play the game no longer. Kissing

her was not a sport or a lesson, but a need so great he'd have died for the pleasure. He lowered his lips and claimed her mouth with a force that surprised them both.

A kiss meant to be chaste and light, turned warm and demanding. To his surprise, she responded in kind, learning from each move he made. There was a wonder about her that rocked his world at its foundation. This strong, self-sufficient female was all woman beneath her wrappings and more passion than most men could handle.

Finally, he broke the kiss and moved to her ear. "I don't think you need much practice. You seem to be a natural at this, lady."

"Again," she demanded, loving the way he made her feel. For the first time in her life, she was glad she was a woman. She loved the hard wall of his chest against her heart and the warm feel of his arms around her waist.

Zach couldn't keep his hand from shaking as he lowered her to the floor and cupped her face. "I'm afraid if I kiss you again, it will be more, and I don't relish being tied to the hitching post come morning."

Holly looked confused. "I thought you enjoyed the kiss?"

"I did. Don't press your luck on me being a gentleman if I taste those lips again and feel your soft breasts pressed against me with just enough pressure to drive a man mad."

Holly looked down at her breasts. "They've never been anything but in the way."

Zach suddenly understood why she bound them so tightly. "Oh, no." The firelight shadowed her shirt just enough to show the perfection of what she complained about. "How could you even think such a thing?"

"I'll think whatever I like!" she snapped, then couldn't hide a smile. "And I think I'd like to be kissed again."

"One more lesson?" he asked. "And I pray one of us will have enough sense to stop."

Closing her eyes, Holly waited for the next kiss. She'd never dreamed she'd like such a small touch so much. Most of the men she saw had brown teeth from chewing tobacco, and the thought of touching mouths with them had never been appealing. But this man was different. He was spotlessly clean and gentle when he held her. He'd also be gone tomorrow, and no one would ever know she'd learned a few lessons in life from him.

But his lips didn't touch hers. Instead, his arm encircled her and slid below her hips. In one sweep he lifted her in his embrace. Startled, she opened her eyes and started to complain, then saw the laughter in his gaze and knew this was part of the lesson.

He carried her to the chair by the fireplace and lowered himself with her atop him. "This isn't proper, but I can't leave without teaching you one more thing. Are you afraid?"

Holly could never remember being asked such a foolish question. She'd never been afraid of anything in her life. She was the best shot in the county and could outwrestle most men, including this Yankee. What could she possibly have to be afraid of? "Get on with the lesson."

This time he didn't lower his mouth to hers, but started at her neck and moved slowly upward. His soft lips felt wonderful as they moved over her skin, and she curled into his embrace. His fingers tenderly shoved her hair back allowing him to taste more of the flesh along her neck. She loved the way his hand twisted into her hair, applying just enough pull to move her head to his liking.

Carefully, he unbuttoned the first button of her shirt and slid the cotton from her shoulder so that he could taste more of her. She arched with pleasure, making the shirt slide dangerously low.

As though he could endure no more heaven, he leaned back and watched her curl contentedly in his lap. His hand touched her hair and drifted lightly down her cheek.

No one had ever stared at her with such eyes. In his gaze, she saw herself as a woman and for once she felt beautiful.

Leaning upward she opened her mouth slightly, silently asking for another kiss.

His lips played with her mouth for a few minutes driving her mad with waiting. While his kiss danced lightly against her, his hand moved to her waist. He knotted the shirt in his fist, pulling the material tightly over her chest. Slowly, as the kiss deepened, his fingers slid over the cotton of her shirt and lightly brushed her breasts. When she jerked as a bolt of pure pleasure shot through her body, his kiss turned loving and his hand lowered over the soft mound with passion's firmness.

His open mouth swallowed her surprise as the kiss deepened to match his touch. He knew he was holding someone whose loving was as wild and untamed as the land she came from.

Holly felt as if she were falling into deep water, far over her head. She'd always been in control. She'd always been the one to make all the decisions in her world. She'd always been the one to act, not react.

And now this stranger with his polite manners and loving lessons was changing all that. And she wasn't sure she liked it.

Pushing away from Zach, Holly climbed from the chair and his embrace. For a moment he looked as if he might pull her back, but he hesitated. Fire danced in his blue-gray eyes. His long fingers opened and closed into fists, as though he were trying to capture a dream. His longing to hold her was raw and warm in his gaze. A longing so deep, it must have taken more than one lifetime to cavern.

Turning away, she stared at the fire, for she couldn't stand seeing someone as lonely as herself. She'd thought she was the only one in the world who ached for another so dearly. But she couldn't turn to this man. Not this man who'd been willing to marry just anyone. She wanted a man who would have no other woman but her.

Zach stood and paced the room. "If you're waiting for me to say I'm sorry, you'll wait 'til hell freezes over."

"I don't want your apology. Neither of us seems very good at that sort of thing anyway. I asked you for the lesson." She could still feel her body tingling from his hand touching her. How could she tell him she loved his touch but was afraid of losing control?

He grabbed his coat. "I thought you wanted me to hold you."

She could hear the hurt in his voice. He hadn't tried to trick her. He'd been honest with her from the first, but she'd never hated a man more. He must know the power he had over her with his touch. A power she'd never allowed any other to capture.

"I want you gone tomorrow!" she said, and was answered by the slamming of the door.

Without trying to stop the tears traveling down her cheeks, Holly climbed the ladder to her bed. He had to be gone come morning, because if she ever stopped hating this man long enough, she might fall in love with him, and she'd never allow that.

She'd never love a man who'd marry any woman. She had to love a man who wanted to marry only her.

5

Zach walked out to the corral and back until his blood cooled to normal. He'd never met such a woman. He never knew a female like Holly existed. His mother had been soft and quiet and kind. He couldn't remember once in his childhood when she'd yelled at him. His former fiancé was cut from the same bolt. She hadn't even had the strength to wait for him to return from war, but married someone else who could take care of her. Other women he'd danced a few reels of love's melody with were so gentle, he'd been afraid of upsetting them if he allowed passion to surface.

He'd heard about the southern belles who could do nothing for themselves but weep for their men. Now he wondered how the South could have lost if the men were half as strong as the women. When he'd looked at Holly standing in front of the fire dressed only in her huge shirt, he'd thought he'd finally met a woman who could meet a man's passion with equal measure of her own.

But she'd shoved him away as though she'd only been using him to test her limits. The thought that she planned to use what he taught her to catch another angered him. Maybe he should be madder at himself than Holly for caring what happened to her. Any man foolish enough to marry such a bossy, demanding woman would surely be dancing with the devil's daughter as Sam had suggested.

When Zach stepped back into the house, Holly lay curled on a bench by the fire. For a moment all he could do was stare at her, for he'd thought she'd have locked herself away in the loft by now.

She raised to one elbow, her hair tumbling around her in a fiery golden mass. "It's gotten too cold to sleep in the loft," she said matter-of-factly. "I've divided the room. You'll not be counting your fingers and toes come morning if you stay on your side." She patted the gun belt lapped over the corner of the bench.

Zach looked at a rope strung across the room and tied to a chair at each corner. He took off his coat, trying to control his anger. His control had kept him alive more than once, but he couldn't take any more of being pinned in, not even if the jailer were as beautiful as Holly.

"No!" he said suddenly, as he walked to the rope and jerked it so violently both chairs tumbled. "Never again!"

Holly was too surprised to react. She hadn't thought the man capable of such an outburst. He marched to the fireplace and planted his hands on either side of the hearth as he breathed deeply, pulling raw nerves under control.

After a long pause, he said more to himself than her. "When I was in the prisoner-of-war camp at Andersonville, the guards put up a line ten feet from the wall. It was a stick pole a child could jump. Everyone called it the kill line. If a prisoner crossed it, he was shot before he could reach the wall. Every morning I would walk around the camp and count the bodies hanging over the kill line. After a while, I realized they were more suicides than attempts to escape. Being a fighting soldier was far easier than wasting away in the camp.''

Holly didn't know what to say. She'd heard the prisoners were treated badly on both sides. Somehow when she thought of the men going to war, she never thought of prisoners, only soldiers and the dead.

Zach turned to face her. "You're safe where you are without a gun. I've never touched a woman who didn't welcome me, and no line need be between us.''

He walked over and collapsed on the bed. All the fight gone from him.

Holly watched him lying there. He was a strange man, this Yankee. He didn't seem to care about the future, but he'd been willing to risk death rather than sleep with a rope between them. She'd only known him a few hours, yet she felt like she knew him better than she'd ever known anyone. Closing her eyes, Holly tried to forget about all that had happened tonight and think of only tomorrow and the Christmas Eve party. Tomorrow he'd be gone, and her life would return to normal.

She'd thought she'd just closed her eyes, when she smelled coffee. Sunshine danced in through the windows. Peering around the bench, Holly saw Zach in the kitchen.

He seemed to sense she watched him, for he turned and smiled. "Get dressed, sleepyhead. I'm cooking you breakfast before we leave.''

Holly stood and walked to the kitchen, unaware of how becoming she looked in her wrinkled shirt and wool socks. "I can cook breakfast," she offered as she stretched away her sleepiness.

Zach forced himself to concentrate on the stove. "No thanks. I had your eggs yesterday. Today, you try mine. Besides, tomorrow is both Christmas and your birthday. Consider it my farewell gift to you.''

He forked her a mouthful of the most delicious eggs she'd ever tasted.

''Now get dressed,'' he ordered.

Holly moved to the wardrobe. ''I never thought you'd be able to cook.''

''I can't, really,'' he answered, carrying the food from the kitchen to the table. ''Breakfast is about the beginning and end of my menu.''

Holly reached for the cotton binding she wrapped around her every morning.

''Don't bind yourself,'' he whispered from behind her.

''But everyone will know I'm a woman.''

''Everyone knows it already, except the blind.'' He didn't move, but he felt himself reaching out for her. ''This is the last day we'll be together. Allow yourself to be a woman today.''

''All right.'' She answered reluctantly, then picked up a change of clothes and went into the kitchen to dress.

''They have lacy things ladies wear that I think would be more comfortable than the binding.'' Zach was way out of his realm of expertise, but it seemed no one had told Holly about women's things. ''I suppose you can buy them at any ladies' dress shop.''

She had just finished tying her belt, when the door flew open with a bang. Sam and Luther stormed in as if prepared to see blood on the walls and a Yankee dead on the floor.

''Mornin', Captain.'' Sam looked at Zach, trying to see any bruises or stab wounds.

''Morning,'' Zach answered raising his mug. ''While you men pour yourselves a cup of coffee, I've something to say to you. First, I think as a common courtesy, you should knock before you enter a lady's home.''

"Knock?" Sam mumbled.

"Lady?" Luther echoed.

"And second, I don't want either of you getting any ideas about finding Holly a husband. She's got a mind of her own, and I'm sure she can rope her own man when the time is right for her.''

The two old men looked at one another. They didn't know whether to challenge this bossy stranger to a fight, or congratulate him for having survived the night in the same house with Holly.

Yesterday he'd been kind of quiet. When he passed out at the train station, they thought him the sickly type. But now, it was starting to sound like the Yankee was as demanding as Holly. A few good meals and a day without liquor had made major changes in Captain Hamilton.

Sam winked at Luther. Damned if he wouldn't give his uppers to know what went on in this house last night. It couldn't have been fighting. There was no blood. And it couldn't have been romance, 'cause the stranger was talking like he was leaving.

Holly sat down and filled her plate. "Sam, tell one of the men to saddle Cinnamon and another good mount. I'll ride with Zach into town, then bring the mount back.''

"But there ain't no train.''

"I know." Holly didn't look up from her plate. "But he can stay in one of the rooms above the saloon.''

"But it's a long ride," Sam added.

"I can make it in half the time you men did in the wagon. I'll be back by mid-afternoon. Have the men clear out the house and set up extra tables in the kitchen for the food.''

"But one of the men can go with Captain Hamilton," Sam rationalized.

"No." Holly glanced at Zach. "I've some shopping to do for a few things the cook can't pick up for me.''

Sam was out of "buts." He wanted to beg Holly to keep her Christmas present just one more day before she sent Zach back; but, as usual, she had made up her mind, and there was nothing short of a buffalo stampede that would change it.

Within an hour, Sam watched them disappear toward town. He'd warned Holly to take the main road, but he knew she'd take the shortcut like always. He set about hammering out tin holders for the Christmas tree candles with all the energy he could muster. It would be a sad Christmas with no present for Holly, but maybe he could make the party something to remember. Several of their neighbors said they were bringing sons and loved ones home from the war. For the first time in five years, there'd be a Christmas without war on everyone's mind.

Laughter boiled from Sam in sudden gulps. "Who knows?" he whispered to himself. "Maybe this year Holly will dance.''

6

Zach leaned against the peeling wallpaper of his room above the saloon and watched the street below. For five years in the army, he'd thought of someday going home for Christmas. But now there was no home to go to, and he'd be spending Christmas Eve alone in his room. He tried to block out the sound of the drunks below in the bar, acting as if they were happy.

Several Union officers strolled the boardwalk across the street. The bartender had told him that a company of soldiers were camped outside town. The day after Christmas, they'd be heading northwest toward the frontier line to fight Indians. Zach almost wished he were going with them. The army was a lonely life, but it was all he'd known for so long, the familiar would somehow be comforting. His leave would be up soon, and he'd have to decide whether to reenlist or retire.

A knock pounded on his door.

"Come in," he answered, knowing the bottle he'd ordered was finally being delivered.

Maybe he could drink the memory of Holly from his mind. They'd ridden into town without talking of anything important. When he'd offered to buy her lunch, she'd refused, saying the clouds looked like bad weather might be moving in and she'd best get back home. Maybe it was the weather, or maybe she didn't want to stand on a street visiting with a man in Union blue. He realized by the stares that if he stayed in the South another day, he'd be wise to buy himself a change of clothes.

Zach raked his fingers through his dark hair and moved toward the door as the knock sounded again. He wished he'd had the chance to kiss her good-bye. It had been tempting to pull her to him in the middle of the street and kiss her one last time just to prove to himself that she tasted as good as he remembered. But she hadn't wanted him. She'd made it crystal clear. Besides, she'd probably have shot him for embarrassing her in public with that old Patterson Colt she kept tied to her leg.

As Zach pulled the door open with swear words ready for the slow bartender, Holly fell into his arms.

"Zach!" She tried to catch her breath. "You have to help me."

He lifted her and carried her into the room. Her hair was wild with no hat in sight. Mud was smeared across her white shirt and cheeks. Her coat was ripped at the sleeve. For a moment he thought she must have been attacked, but her gun was still strapped and holstered at her side.

"What is it, Holly?" Worry lined his face. Only moments before all he'd thought of was how lonely he'd be on Christmas day. Now all he cared about was that she was unharmed. Holly might be headstrong and stubborn like Sam said she was, but there was a vulnerability about her that touched his heart. She'd given him a great gift without knowing it. The few hours he'd spent with her made him realize that he was still alive.

Huge tears bubbled in her evergreen eyes. "I took the back trail out of town. I thought it'd be faster."

Zach held her trembling shoulders tightly. "What happened?"

"It's Cinnamon. We fell." A single tear tumbled down her cheek.

Zach moved his hands slowly along her body. "Are you hurt?"

"No!" Holly pushed his hand away and stood. "You have to help Cinnamon. I remember you saying you were a vet, so I came here first. I rode the other horse and left Cinnamon."

Zach grabbed his hat and saddlebags, and was a step behind her as they ran down the stairs into the bar. Everyone in the room stopped to watch, but there was no time to explain.

When they reached the street, Zach tossed Holly onto the horse he'd ridden into town only an hour be-

fore, and climbed behind her. There was no need for
words. Zach knew if he didn't get to the injured horse,
the roan would be Christmas dinner for the wolves.

He held her tightly against him as they rode. She
molded so easily into his arms, as though a dream
finally found a place in reality. Wrapping his hands
tightly around her, he whispered, "It's going to be all
right," and wished he believed his own words.

She turned her head slightly, rubbing against his
chin. Holly wasn't the kind of woman to admit being
frightened or feeling helpless, but her action told him
she needed him if only for now. He kissed the side of
her forehead lightly, closing his eyes as he tried to
memorize the smell of her hair.

They climbed the bluff at full gallop where Cinnamon had fallen, but Zach didn't try to pull in the reins.
Concern outweighed their safety.

Holly's horse stood at the bottom of the uneven
ground. Though still saddled, the animal raised her
head in wild challenge. Pain had erased years of gen-
tling from the beautiful roan's gaze.

Zach jumped from the saddle and walked slowly
toward the horse. He hadn't practiced his profession
since the war started, but he knew animals. And this
one was as wild with fright as her owner.

"Easy, now." Zach moved closer. "I'm going to
make it better." He brushed the horse's mane and felt
blood oozing from a small cut on her neck. His hands
continued moving along the mare while he kept talking, trying to calm her. Her front right leg was cut
with an ugly gash, but no bones seemed to be broken.

He glanced at the strong woman who everyone
thought could spit fire. She was curled atop a rock,
looking like a child afraid to watch.

"I tried, but she won't put any weight on her leg," Holly whispered. "Will we have to shoot her?"

Zach pulled a shirt from his saddlebag and wrapped it around Cinnamon's leg. "How far are we from the ranch?"

"An hour's ride," Holly answered.

"How long if we walk?"

"Two, maybe three hours."

"Then we walk it." Zach pulled Holly to her feet. "If we can get there before she loses too much blood and before infection sets in, she might have a chance."

Cinnamon protested as he pulled her forward. "But you'll have to talk to her, Holly. She's your horse. She'll do things for you that she won't for me. She'll walk despite the pain."

Holly nodded and fell into step next to Cinnamon. She talked to the mare while Zach watched the bandage he'd made turn red and the sky darken.

They hadn't moved far before it started to snow. Light, huge flakes. A Christmas snow, his mother would have called it.

When Holly looked at him as if it were hopeless, Zach fought the urge to kiss her. "A little snow will make the ground softer." He couldn't help but smile. Here, walking in the snow with a lame horse and a beautiful woman was a hundred times better than anywhere else he'd ever been on Christmas Eve.

He wanted to put Holly on the other mount and tell her to ride home where it was warm, but he wasn't sure Cinnamon would follow him. They moved slowly across the open plains, step by step.

It was almost dark when they saw the light of the ranch. The snow had stopped, leaving the air clear and newborn. Lanterns sparkled against the blanket of white. Folks were already arriving for the party, for Zach could hear voices and music.

Only Sam ran out to greet them when they drew near. "I was worried half crazy about you," he scolded Holly. "If you hadn't been acting like you'd already eaten locoweed before you left, I would have saddled up and come looking for you."

The old man glanced at Zach without surprise. "Welcome back, Captain."

Zach touched the brim of his hat. "Evening," he said, as if it were nothing unusual for him to drop by. "Cinnamon's been hurt. I'm going to need boiling water, lots of wraps, a sewing needle, and a few bottles of whiskey."

Sam looked down at the horse's bloody leg. "There ain't nothing to be done," he forced out the words slowly. "I've seen horses cut up like that before. We'll have to shoot her. I'm real sorry, Holly."

"No!" Holly pulled the mare into the barn.

"But, Holly," Sam rubbed his wrinkled face with an equally wrinkled hand. "You don't want her to be in more pain. It ain't fair to the horse to let her suffer."

Zach didn't answer as he helped Holly pull the animal into a stall. Zach had been through more suffering than he thought he could have endured, yet he wouldn't give up one day of it, if it meant he had to give up the rest of his life. He figured Cinnamon might feel the same. Holly had taught him there was something worth living for.

"No!" Holly answered Sam. "We're going to let Zach try."

Sam shook his head and turned to Zach for orders. There was no arguing with her, so he might as well save his breath. "Do what you can, Captain, and I'll help."

"I'll want a cot set up beside the stall and as many lanterns as you can find lining the top. We'll blindfold the horse, so the light won't bother her eyes. Find some oats and mix them thick with whiskey. We've got to give her enough to take the edge off the pain, but not so much that she lies down on us."

Sam ran to issue Zach's orders. Holly brushed the mane of her horse, then slowly turned to Zach. "What can I do?"

"You can see to your guests. I'll call you if there is any change. I've got to get her calmed down and trusting me now, or she'll never let me do what I need to do."

Holly locked her arms around Zach's neck. "Thank you for helping. No matter what happens, I'm glad you're here."

"You're welcome." Zach wanted to pull her close and make her believe everything would be fine, but several men loaded down with supplies entered the barn. "Enjoy the party. You've done a great deal by getting her back here. We'll know little before morning."

"Promise you'll come get me if there's any change?" Holly shoved the tears from her cheeks.

"I promise." Zach brushed a strand of her hair off her face. He'd give all he owned if she cared half as much about him as she did the horse.

Suddenly she was gone, and Zach was surrounded by cowhands, each offering advice. Finally, Sam silenced them by telling them that Zach had gone all the way through Boston's vet school, so they might quit their "jawing" and learn a few things.

As he worked, his thoughts kept drifting back to

how beautiful Holly had looked the night before. He wasn't sure he could spend another night on this ranch without touching her again. That's why he'd had the cot delivered to the barn. He had to put as much distance between them as he could or risk making a fool of himself.

Her mind was on him also as she went through the ritual of welcoming the other ranchers. She'd much rather have been in the barn helping, but this one night a year, she was expected to host the Christmas Eve party.

The snow didn't seem to discourage a single guest, and by nine o'clock the room was filled with her neighbors. Several of the families had brought their children and planned on bedding them down in the bunkhouse, until all the grownups had their fill of talking and dancing.

To Holly's surprise, many of her friends brought with them young men for her to meet. They were welcomed as war heroes in a war where neither side won. Most of the men were still wearing all, or parts, of their uniform. Throwing away good clothing was not something a farmer or rancher did even if the war was over.

Two of the five Travis boys came home, and from what Holly could tell, they were as crude as they had been before they left. She never forgot how they'd teased her as a child, and how cruel they'd been because she didn't act like the other girls. Now both men had a woman on each arm, as though they were the most valued choice for a husband in the county.

Other single women were in new dresses to match the holiday season, but Holly's only change had been to wear one of the camisoles she'd bought at the dress shop in town. She could hardly show that to anyone, so she looked the same as she did the other three hundred and sixty-four days of the year. But the silk next to her skin made her smile to herself and feel pretty.

As before, no one asked Holly to dance. They probably heard she didn't do such things. As the night aged, the men drank more and the Travis boys began to tell stories of the war. The women formed small groups to chat. Once more Holly found herself apart, so she occupied her time with refilling cups and adding logs to the fire.

When Zach opened the door just after midnight, she jumped with concern for Cinnamon. His gaze scanned the room before coming to rest on her. She couldn't help reacting to his smile with one of her own.

He seemed unsure as he removed his hat and took only one step into the room. Everyone stopped talking at once and stared at the uniform he wore. Hatred chilled the air. Both Travis boys stood as though preparing for one last battle.

"I'm sorry to disturb the party," Zach said politely. "But I'm the vet Miss McCarter asked to treat her horse. I'd like to have a few words with her." He was thankful Sam and Luther hadn't told anyone of Holly's surprise Christmas present; maybe Holly's neighbors would believe his lie.

"Do your talking outside," Bret, the elder Travis, ordered. "We want none of the likes of you in here."

Several others mumbled oaths beneath their breaths.

Zach tipped his hat as if the bitter order had been only a suggestion, and stepped backward.

"Wait!" Holly hurried to the doorway. "Tell me about Cinnamon before you go."

Zach's gaze studied the room, looking for simmering trouble to boil over. "The bleeding has stopped," His words were low, yet all the room seemed to be listening. "and it looks like my stitches will hold. By morning we'll know if there's infection."

Holly's hand lightly brushed his arm. "Thank you," she whispered. "Can't you stay a moment and have some punch or a dance?"

Everyone in the room stood silently waiting for him to leave. He knew he was playing with fire staying any longer, but he couldn't turn down her request. "I'd be delighted to dance with you, Miss McCarter."

As he slowly removed his hat and coat, the musicians began to play a waltz. When he turned back to Holly, she was smiling even though everyone else in the room seemed to be frowning.

He lifted her gently into his embrace and danced across the floor. It didn't matter that everyone in the room was watching with either surprise or hatred for the Yankee. All that mattered was that she was in his arms once more. His need to hold her overruled his sense of danger.

Slowly, other couples took to the floor, as though unwilling to allow Zach and Holly center stage. When the room crowded with dancers, Zach knew it was time to get back to his work at the barn. If he didn't hold himself in very close check, he would hold her a little too tightly, and in this crowd that could only mean trouble.

Holly followed him to the porch. "Thank you for helping me in there." She wished she could explain how very alone she'd been feeling until he came. Maybe he understood.

Zach kissed the top of her head. "You're welcome."

She tried to hide the shakiness in her voice. "As soon as I can slip away, I'll be out to the barn to check on Cinnamon."

"I'll be waiting," he answered with a promise in his eyes that had nothing to do with the horse.

She'd hold him once more before he left, but not now when someone might step on the porch at any moment. "Later," she whispered, answering his promise with one of her own.

She watched Zach turn and walk toward the barn. He walked tall and proud, yet it was his gentleness that drew her to him. He hadn't even resented her neighbors for their rudeness, but understood them. For the most part they were good folks, but years of hating take a while to die.

Just before she turned to go back into the house, she saw several men run from the corner of her place to the back of the bunkhouse. A moment later, they crossed in the shadows between the bunkhouse and the barn. Holly felt icy fear coat her heart. Trouble, traveling in a pack, was headed straight for Zach.

7

Holly slipped back into the room and noticed several people watching her closely. She'd only been on the porch with Zach a few moments, but they looked at her as though she'd just committed a crime.

"So you're too good to dance with your neighbors." Bret Travis stepped in front of her. He hadn't more than glanced at her all evening, and now he was talking like they were engaged. Another glance around the room told Holly that Bret's brother, along with several other young men, were missing.

"None of my neighbors have asked me to dance," Holly pointed out. She needed to grab her gun and see if Zach was in trouble, but she had to get past this pile of rudeness first.

"Well, I'm asking!" Bret shouted loud enough for everyone in the room to hear.

Without waiting for an answer, he swept her into his arms and started stomping across the floor. His steps were uneven and unpolished, and his hold was too tight. Holly tried to pull away, but he held to her without noticing her discomfort. Dancing with him was nothing like dancing with Zach.

Finally the music ended, and he released her hand. "So you do dance, Holly McCarter. Most of the men were starting to wonder if you did anything but ranch." His arm still held her to him. "Shall we see if that Yankee taught you to kiss as well?"

He pulled her beneath the mistletoe and leaned over her. Before Holly could protest, his lips were on hers. The kiss was wet and sloppy with the taste of whiskey on his mouth. She heard several shouts for Bret to let her go, but no one came to her rescue as he continued to grind his mouth against hers, bruising her lips with the force of his kiss.

Holly reacted as violently as a volcano. She jammed her knee up between his legs as her fist slammed into his ribs. When he didn't let her go at once, her nails clawed into his face, taking layers of skin while her teeth bit down hard on his bottom lip.

Bret Travis jerked away from her, grabbing his bleeding face with one hand while he raised his other hand to slap her.

Before he could lower the blow, the sound of a rifle being cocked stopped all action. "I wouldn't do that if I were you, Bret." Sam's voice was calm, almost friendly. "If Holly doesn't want to kiss you, I'd suggest you find someone willing.'Cause if you ever touch her again, I'll shoot you myself after she finishes murdering you."

"Don't worry," Bret tried to gain back a little of his composure. "I wouldn't touch her again if she was the last woman west of the Mississippi. It'll take more than this ranch to talk a man into marrying her."

Sam didn't lower the rifle from Bret's gut. "I think we best be calling it a night, boys."

He glanced around to get Holly's approval, but she was gone. She'd vanished along with her gun belt that had been hanging on the peg by the back door. Sam didn't comment on her absence as he helped everyone gather up their things, but he had a feeling she was heading straight toward the barn.

Holly didn't care about the party. It was the farthest thing from her mind as she ran across the yard. She slipped in the side door of the barn and pulled her gun from its holster.

Five men were in the center of the barn. Two were holding Zach between them while a third jabbed one punch after another into his ribs. Judging from the cuts and bruises on all three attackers' faces, Zach had not been captured without a fight. The other two men were watching the main door, listening for the sound of anyone coming.

One of the watchers tossed the other a rope. "Tie him to the stall when he can't stand any longer," he ordered. Let's show this Yankee what we do to the likes of him."

While two men roped Zach's body to the top board of the stall, the third man stretched a whip across the hay with a pop. Zach didn't move as the whip snapped above his back, marking its target.

Holly moved closer as she heard the first slap of leather against flesh. The sound sickened her all the way to the core, for she knew the whip had just sliced across Zach's back. Another pop sounded as she stepped into the light and fired her gun.

The man with the whip grabbed his hand and yelled in pain while all the others turned to Holly.

"That's enough!" she ordered as she widened her stance. "Your fun's over."

"Now, Holly . . ."

Another shot struck the dirt an inch in front of the man who'd spoken.

"The war's over boys, and I aim to put an end to the fighting right now." She fired again.

The leader of the group ventured forward, his hands in the air. "But, you don't know how those Yankees treated us during the war. Then he had the nerve to walk right in and dance with one of our women."

Holly glanced at Zach. "I know this Yankee's got enough scars already, and I'd stake my life he never fought except in a fair fight." Not a man in the barn looked like he wanted to argue with a lady holding a gun. "As for dancing with me, he did so at my request."

Several other men reached the barn door as she continued, "If you can't leave the war behind, don't set foot on my property again."

Luther cradled his rifle in his arms. "You heard the lady!" he yelled as Sam joined him. Both men looked younger than they had in years.

The others moved to saddle their horses as Luther and Sam joined Holly. They stood like two aging pillars on either side of her as the attackers left the barn.

When the place was emptied, Holly rushed to Zach. His shirt was sliced open and a long thin line of blood dripped from his back. She lifted his head, but through the cuts and bruises his eyes remained closed.

"We've got a bunk set up near Cinnamon's stall."
Luther untied one of Zach's arms. "I'll see to him."

"No." Holly brushed the hair from his face. "Bring
him to the house. Sam, get a few men to run ahead
and move the bed close to the fire."

"He's been roughed up pretty bad, honey," Sam
said the obvious.

"I know." Holly tried to hide her tears. "But he's
my Christmas present, and I'm taking care of him."

Luther looked at Sam and shrugged. When the Yankee was in good shape, she'd sent him back. Now that
he looked like death warmed over in a dirty pot, she
wanted to keep him. There was no figuring Holly.

8

Holly tenderly spread the salve over the open cuts the
whip had made on Zach's back. She could feel other
scars and knew this was not the first time he'd felt the
sting of a whip. This man, so proper and proud in his
uniform, was so scarred beneath. She'd found what
looked like a gunshot wound in both his leg and the
left side of his chest. Besides the marks on his back,
she discovered several that could only have been made
with a blade. She wondered how Zachary Hamilton
was still alive. It was no surprise that all he wanted in
life was to watch the sun rise without people between
himself and the horizon. He'd probably seen enough
of people to last a lifetime.

She gently bandaged his wounds, then with Sam's
help, lay him on his side and covered him with layers
of quilts. Zach's face looked worse than she'd thought
possible. One of his eyes was completely closed from
swelling, while cuts and bruises seemed to fight for
space on the rest of his skin.

"He don't look so good." Sam pulled at his belt as Holly put a pillow beneath Zach's head.

"I've seen rabbits caught in a twister who looked better than he does," Luther added.

"He'll be fine in a few days," Holly corrected as she brushed strands of coal black hair from his forehead. "Now get out of here and let him rest. He'll be better come morning."

"If he ain't, we might as well bury him," Sam added as he moved toward the door. "I'll keep an eye on your horse. You keep an eye on your Yankee."

"He isn't my Yankee," Holly answered.

Sam and Luther glanced at one another, but neither of them would call her a liar even though they both knew their Holly was not being honest with them, or herself. He was her Yankee, whether she knew it or not.

She closed the door and returned to Zach's side. His bruises didn't matter. Somehow, a man had never been more handsome to her. He'd taken care of Cinnamon. He'd danced with her when everyone in the room stared at him with hate. From the minute they'd met, he'd treated her like a lady. Something no other man in the state had done. Even the little things he did, like standing when she walked into a room, were treasures she would tuck away in her heart.

Holly leaned over and very gently brushed the corner of his mouth with her own. After Zach's kisses, she should have never allowed someone like Bret Travis to kiss her.

"Trying to steal another 'Yankee dime,' pretty lady?" Zach mumbled.

Holly straightened in surprise. "How long have you been awake?"

"Long enough to feel your fingers brushing across

my back." Zach answered without opening his eyes. "Long enough to taste the sweetness of your lips against mine."

"I was only treating your wound," Holly tried to be calm, but she could feel her heart pounding as if she'd been running.

"And when you touched me other places?" Zach questioned remembering the soft brush of her fingers over his body.

"I was just making sure there were no broken bones."

Zach smiled knowing the truth. Her touch had been light, exploring, caressing. "And the kiss?" he asked.

Holly faced him directly. "Why didn't you tell me all kisses weren't wonderful?"

"I hoped you wouldn't find out," he answered.

"Well, I did and it was disgusting."

"What would you have me do?" Zach smiled. "Kill any man who kisses you poorly?"

"No," Holly laughed. "I can do my own killing." She leaned closer. "I'd have you kiss me again so that I don't forget what the good ones are like."

"With pleasure," he answered, and pulled her down to his mouth.

His touch was as gentle as it had been the night before, only now his lips lingered in a slow-stirring passion that swept across her as silently as spring air warms the land after winter.

She curled beside him, loving the way he cradled her against his side as though she were of great value.

Pulling back slightly, she whispered against his bruised cheek, "I don't want to hurt you. Be careful of your back."

"There is no pain in my world if you're by my side," he answered. "I thought I was all broken up inside. Nothing mattered to me anymore. I would have sold my soul for peace. But you've taught me differently.'' He leaned on one elbow and pulled her closer.

She felt the weight of his chest press against her side, and rolled into the warmth. His sudden intake of breath was from the pain of having pure pleasure resting beside him. His mouth covered hers as he erased Bret's kiss from her mind. All the longing was satisfied as she answered his need with her own.

When he finished the kiss, Holly stretched beside him in contentment and anticipation of the next touch.

Zach lifted his hand and noticed the bandage she'd tied to protect his bruised and bleeding knuckles. He bit at the cotton, but couldn't pull it away without taking his other arm from around her.

He lowered his hand to her. "Take it off," he ordered.

"But your knuckles are cut."

"Take it off," he insisted.

Holly unwrapped the bandage noting that the bleeding had stopped, but the skin was still raw along his knuckles. "It needs to be wrapped," she lifted her chin in challenge.

"I need to be able to feel without any hindrance." His voice was as insistent as her own.

When she opened her mouth to argue further, his lips claimed hers once more in a kiss. This time the kiss was hard and demanding, yet his hand gently stroked her side as his lips branded hers.

When he broke their kiss, she was breathless. Her heart was pounding, and her chest heaved up and down against his side. "Did you mean what you said about the war being over on this ranch?" he asked.

"Yes," she answered. "The hatred has to stop sometime, and it might as well stop here and now. A few of the folks may be angry, but they'll get over it by next Christmas.''

His fingers spread across her just above her belt and pressed gently before he suddenly knotted the material of her shirt into his fist. ''It'll be dawn in a few hours. Lie beside me 'til then. Let the war between us end.''

Holly started to answer, but he stopped her with his finger on her lips.

''Before you agree, I'll tell you that if you stay by my side, I plan to love you tonight.'' His voice was low with passion. ''I can't catch you if you run, so don't agree to stay if you're planning to bolt.''

''And if I stay and fight?''

Zach laughed. ''If you stay and fight, you'll probably kill me. No, pretty lady, if you stay it will be to love, not to fight.''

When she rolled suddenly from the bed, pain stronger than all the blows he'd taken earlier combined shot through Zach's heart. He leaned against the pillow and closed his eyes. Why had he even hoped to dream that she'd allow him to touch her? Hadn't she said often enough in the past two days that she'd never care for him? Why couldn't he have been happy with kissing her? Zach knew the answer. Kissing her was a sweet hell, when he wanted to love her every night for the rest of his life.

''Well?'' Holly's voice startled him. ''Are you going to lift the covers, or do I have to stay on top freezing 'til dawn?''

Zach looked up at her. She'd removed her trousers and shirt, and was standing before him in a camisole and white lace drawers that hung past her knees. If ever there was a woman who should have been dubbed an angel on earth, it was Holly—as long as she kept her mouth closed, of course. Her beauty put the sunset he'd seen to shame.

"Well, Yankee?" she snapped. "Do you want me to snuggle next to you for a few hours or not?"

Zach lifted the covers. He couldn't have gotten a word past his heart pounding in his throat if his life had depended on it. She slid in beside him and cuddled against his side as if she'd been doing it for a lifetime.

"I'll let you touch me," she said, as if to make sure he understood who was in charge, "if you continue to kiss me at the same time. I've grown to like your kisses more than a little."

Zach moved his hand lightly over the cotton of her camisole. The lace tickled his palm when he pulled the first ribbon.

She lay very still watching him moving to the second ribbon. When his fingers passed the valley between her breasts, he brushed her warm skin. "Before this night is over," he whispered as he pulled the ribbon and revealed more of her flesh, "you'll like my touch as dearly as you like my kisses."

"We'll see, Yankee," she smiled and stretched, loving the way her movements made him lose his breath.

His mouth lowered over her lips, and all the world but his arms disappeared.

9

Christmas morning dawned cold and clear as Holly slept. When the sun was high, she smiled in her sleep and rolled toward Zach's warmth. The night had been magic. He'd been right. She would never get enough of his kisses, just as she would never have her fill of his touch.

She reached again for his warmth, not wanting the night to end.

But he wasn't there. Holly sat up in bed like a shot and searched the room. Zach was nowhere in the room. The huge empty room decorated for Christmas was the saddest sight she'd ever seen.

She jumped and ran to the kitchen, expecting to see him cooking breakfast as he had the day before. But the stove was as cold as the muscles pushing around her heart.

She stomped into her clothes, trying to keep her anger down. There had to be a reason. Maybe he'd gone to check on Cinnamon? But he should have awakened her. Maybe he'd gone outside for water or wood. "Maybe, maybe," she shouted trying to ignore a small voice that whispered that maybe he'd left her.

Sam met her at the barn door. "The roan's going to make it!" he said. "She's even testing some weight on that right front foot this morning. Whatever that captain did, he did right. She may not still run like the wind, but she'll have many a foal for years to come."

Holly tried to act happy, but she doubted she fooled Sam. "Where's Zach?" she asked, looking past the old man for her Yankee.

The old man's face became a waterfall of wrinkles. "He rode out of here about three hours ago. It couldn't have been a minute past dawn."

Holly blinked hard and tried to swallow. "Did he say where he was going?"

"No," Sam tried to read her. "He knew you didn't want no part of a mail-order husband, not even as a Christmas present, so my guess is he'll be back on the train come tomorrow morning."

Holly fought the tears. "Well, he's wrong. I do want him."

"You want me and Luther to ride into town and get

him back for you?'' Sam asked. ''We'll hog-tie him in the wagon if we have to.''

''No!'' Holly had never wanted to cry so dearly in all her life. ''I want a husband who walks in of his own free will and asks me to marry him.'' She didn't add that she'd never want another man but Zach for as long as she lived. She'd give him the ranch if he'd just come back. It didn't matter to her anymore. Nothing mattered but the feel of his arms around her.

Sam scratched his balding head. ''Two days ago, you couldn't talk enough about sending him back. Now you've decided you want to keep him. Holly, you're a hard one to get a Christmas present for.''

She ignored his ramblings and stormed back into the house. The garlands and colorful ribbons only made her more lonely. Christmas was a time for rejoicing, yet all she wanted to do was curl up in a corner and cry. The most wonderful man in the world had been handed to her, and she'd been foolish enough to want more. What did it matter that he was willing to marry anyone? She only wanted him.

The sound of horses traveling fast drew her attention. She walked to the porch and wondered what sort of trouble was arriving now. If it were the pack of boys she'd run off last night returning, they were too late. Their beating hadn't run the Yankee off; her loving had.

Holly shielded her eyes as she spotted four men galloping across the land. All wore the same blue wool coats Zach had worn, and their hats were pinned as his, marking them as cavalry. She couldn't see their faces, but she knew trouble. Without any extra movement, she lowered her hand and unstrapped the gun's guard from her holster.

A cloud of dry snow surrounded them as they reined

to a stop in front of her cabin. With a sharp command, all four climbed down from their horses.

"Miss McCarter?" A nice-looking officer removed his hat as he took the first step up the porch.

"Yes," Holly answered.

He bowed slightly. "My name's Henry, Henry Anderson. I'm from Maine, but my mother was a McCarter before she married."

Holly tried to be polite, but her impatience was showing. "Nice to meet you, Mr. Anderson, but I'm sure we're no kin. To my knowledge, neither my mother nor father have any living relatives. May I ask why you've ridden onto my land?"

"I came to make proper introductions." The young officer looked nervous, but his smile was honest. "Even though we may not be kin, may I have the honor of introducing one of our most decorated officers to you."

Holly didn't answer, so the young man continued, "We met him in town this morning. We're on our way to the frontier to help with the Indian problem, but he asked us to take time to introduce him properly to you."

Zach stepped from between the horses as the man continued, "Miss Holly McCarter, I'd like you to meet Captain Zachary Hamilton."

Zach took her hand politely in his gloved hand and bowed as he kissed her fingers. "I'm honored, Miss McCarter." His bruised eye was barely open, but he'd never looked more handsome to her.

"If I may have the pleasure, I'd like to ask for your hand in marriage? I wish to marry only you and if you turn me down, I plan to ride with these men to the frontier, for I swear on my honor I'll marry no other."

An older man stepped to Zach's side. "Well, young lady, you'd best make up your mind. We ride out tomorrow at first light. I'm authorized to marry you now, if it's what you want.''

''It's what I want,'' Holly whispered.

Zach pulled her into his arms before she could say more.

Sam and Luther watched the wedding from the bunkhouse.

''I knew he was just what she wanted for Christmas.'' Luther grinned as he shifted tobacco from one side of his mouth to the other. '' 'Course, he might be safer in Indian territory than being married to Holly.''

Sam didn't laugh at Luther's joke. ''What are we going to do now with her birthday, Christmas, and their anniversary on the same day? We'll have to get her one whale of a gift next year.''

''Nope,'' Luther laughed. ''I think we got her just what she wants for a lifetime. We'd best stop while we're ahead.''

Sam shook his head. ''The way they looked at each other, there'll probably be a baby to get somethin' for next year. And another one the next year. And so on. Look what you started, Luther.''

Luther smiled as he watched Zach carry Holly into the house. ''I knew he was the perfect present for her the minute I laid eyes on him. Yep. There ain't a man in a million who can make Holly happy, but I could tell by the cut of him the first time I saw him, Captain Hamilton was our man.''

For the first time in fifty years, Sam was speechless as he followed Luther back into the bunkhouse. Just before Luther closed the door, Sam asked with a wink, ''By the way, ain't it your birthday next month?''

Luther swallowed when he should have spit.

Friends Are Forever

by Patricia Rice

Kentucky, 1881

LEAVING HIS wool coat open to the vagaries of the cold crisp breeze, Brian McGee breathed deeply of pure Kentucky mountain air for the first time in eight long years. Light snow flurried around him, blowing in a fine dust over the frozen, rutted mud of the track he climbed, but he admired its beauty rather than cursed its cold. Back in Cincinnati the snow would have looked like coal dust and the air would be tainted with the stench of thousands of fires. Out here he could breathe again, and he filled his lungs with the precious gift of air.

His companion climbed eagerly ahead, throwing shouted encouragements over his shoulder. ''We're almost there! See, there's the cherry tree!''

The old wild cherry hadn't changed much in eight years. Its branches spread in wild abandon across the road in one direction and over the dilapidated rail fence on the other side. The cherries weren't worth much more than food for birds, but Brian remembered climbing into the branches and hiding from his chores.

It had been a long hard road out of these hills. His feelings about returning were mixed. He had no relatives here any longer. The sight of run-down shacks and barren corn fields didn't stir anything but a fierce joy that he had made it out of them. But there were

memories here, too, memories that he clung to for
their warm familiarity in a world that he had discovered to be otherwise cold and uncertain.

As they reached the top of the ridge, Brian halted
and looked down into the hollow beyond. The house
was as he remembered it. The old stone chimney that
leaned slightly to the rear sent up a stream of wispy
smoke. The chinked split logs gleamed with silver in
the dying sunlight, and the glass windows that had
been the family's pride and joy bore the golden glow
of lamplight.

The wooden shingles over the old front porch were
loose in places now, and some were missing, but the
porch swing still swayed lightly in the wind. Brian
stared longingly at that swing, remembering sweet
summer nights when he had sat there with a young
girl, pouring out his dreams, feeding on her encouragement. They had been so dreadfully young back
then. In the foolishness of their youth they had
dreamed impossible dreams.

Gavin had said his sister was still unmarried, she
who had wanted babies and a home of her own—a
home in town, with shutters on the windows and running water and the school right down the road. Her
talented fingers could make ball gowns out of gunny
sacks and baby dolls out of corn husks, but they hadn't
carried her out of this hollow where she had been born
and would probably die.

Brian followed Gavin more slowly down the hill as
his companion raced on ahead to warn of their arrival.
He had said he would come back here one day a rich
man and take her away from all this. He wondered if
she still waited for him. It seemed unlikely. Their correspondence had been sporadic at best. He'd only been
eighteen when he left these hills, and they hadn't seen

each other much over the few years before he left. He'd been living in town by then, coming back only for a visit once in a while after the school term was out. But the memory of their shared dreams still lingered clear in his mind.

He was a man now. He wasn't rich in terms of the city where he lived and worked, but he was wealthy well beyond the means of the people in these hills. He wasn't even certain why he was here now, except that Gavin had been homesick and had pleaded with him to come back just for a visit, just for Christmas. And he hadn't been able to think of any other plans that would keep him in the city.

Cries of welcome echoed through the cold winter evening as Gavin reached the front door of the cabin and threw it open. Light poured through the open doorway, transforming the drifting snowflakes into something magical. Brian increased his pace, feeling the familiar welcome of this home reaching out to him.

This had been his second home in those lonely years after his mother had run away. His grandmother had been alive then, but she had lived in a bitter world that was impossible for a young boy to enter. When he had wanted love and understanding, he had come here.

Mrs. Allister had died the year before Brian had run off to town. Perhaps her death had been the instigator of his rebellion. It was too long ago to matter anymore. He just remembered the pall that had fallen over this happy household and compared it to the times that had been before. He had wanted the happiness to return, but by then he had been old enough to understand that it would never be the same again, that life brought changes, and that if he wanted to find happiness, he'd have to find it for himself.

And that was what he had set out to do. Brian wasn't

at all certain that he had succeeded, but he was content with himself as he stepped up on the old wooden porch and felt the warmth pouring from the cabin. He had the education he had wanted. He had a career that paid him well and regularly, which was more than a life scratching a living from the rocky soil or the mines would have given him. He had done everything he had set out to do. And now he was back here.

And one of the main reasons for his return was standing near the fireplace, turning around in surprise as Gavin spoke his name and Brian entered.

She had changed. He remembered her as a lanky filly, all legs and arms and wild strands of hair flying down her back as she ran. She would never be beautiful in the way city women were beautiful. She had never heard of cosmetics. She had never worn silk. Her hair had never been worn in elaborate coiffures, and her natural shape had never known the confinement of corsets or the sway of bustles. But in his eyes, she was more beautiful now than any woman he had ever known.

Eyes of a wide velvet gray that captured the mystery of a mountain fog watched him as he took off his hat and shook off the snow. Hair the rich mahogany of polished furniture gleamed in the firelight, drawn back into a thick chignon at the nape of her neck. Her gown was a simple cotton, layered over several petticoats with just a hint of lace at the throat and sleeves. She had always loved to sew, and he had never seen her look less than elegant, even in calico.

Brian returned her stare for a brief moment before politely turning to acknowledge the man sitting at the table, sipping his evening coffee. "Mick" Allister had never been an exceedingly large man—miners seldom were–but he seemed to have shrunk to a fraction of himself over the years. Perhaps it was just that Brian had grown from a gangling adolescent to a full-grown man in the years since he had last seen him. He felt uncomfortable looking down on the man who had been the closest thing to a father that he had ever known. He had long since become accustomed to the empty sleeve that was the reason Mick could no longer work in the mines, and he took no notice of that handicap now.

"Sir, I hope I'm not imposing. I could have stayed in town, but Gavin insisted that I come out here."

Mick grunted and gestured toward a chair at the table. It was Clare who answered for him.

"Of course you're not imposing. There's always room for one more. Have a seat and let me pour you some coffee. I hope you two didn't have to walk all the way from the station. That wind will carry you off after a while."

"Gary gave us a ride in his wagon as far as the bend. It's only five miles or so from there. Felt good after being cooped up in that train." Gavin answered his sister as he drew up a chair for himself while managing to perch two toddlers on his knees.

Brian hadn't paid much attention to the children littering this spacious front room when he entered. The Allister household had always been full of children. But as he began to count back the years and add them to the ages of the ones he had known, he couldn't find any explanation for the two bouncing on Gavin's knee.

Bobby had been the baby he remembered. He would have to be nine by now. Brian found the dark-haired child whittling at a block of wood in the corner, throwing him wary gazes. He counted around and found Missy and Katrina and George, all grown to the gangly adolescent stage that he and Clare had been in when they had last seen each other. The only one missing was Letty. She would have to be eighteen or nineteen by now, the next oldest after Clare and Gavin. Perhaps she had set out on her own. Girls married young in these hills.

Brian's gaze returned to the two toddlers who were now scrambling down from Gavin's lap and squabbling over a piece of toast. Gavin had never said anything about having a wife, and there was no woman here who acted that part. The boy had been footloose and fancy-free when he had shown up in the city asking Brian if he knew of any work. He had never mentioned children, and he was steadily dating a girl who lived near the law offices where Gavin worked. He was treating the toddlers in the same manner as his younger brothers and sisters.

Brian tried to concentrate on the conversation galloping all around him, but he couldn't pull his thoughts from the two children Clare was now picking up and carrying off to bed. Perhaps Mick had married again, but Gavin hadn't mentioned it, and there was no sign of a wife.

Brian felt an aching hollow open up on the inside as the only possible conclusion came to him and he pushed it away. Clare had to be nearly twenty-four now, more than enough time to have married and had half a dozen children. Life out here wasn't easy. She could have been married and lost her husband. It would only be natural to return to her home in that case. Or she could never have married at all. It happened more often than anyone acknowledged. Brian felt the hollow in his stomach become an aching crevasse.

Clare was a young, healthy woman. He couldn't have expected her to wait for him. That had been foolishness on his part if that was what he had thought all these years. Grimacing over his stupidity, Brian sipped his coffee and joined the discussion of the weather.

Although his back was turned to the doorway, he knew at once when Clare returned to the room. She wouldn't own perfume, so it must be the scent of her soap that he noticed—or perhaps the swish of her skirt. A chill went up the back of his neck as she lingered behind him, returning the memory of how they had once teased each other, sneaking up behind and placing fingers icy from the stream on each other's necks. She had been very good at sneaking, but he had been even better at pretending to be caught. He had loved having her hands on his nape.

She came into his field of vision then, but Brian kept his gaze on his coffee, seeing only the clasping of her hands over her waist from the corner of his eye.

"I hope you won't mind sleeping in the loft with the boys, Brian. I could make up a pallet down here, but I'm afraid I'd wake you when I got up to fix breakfast in the morning."

Her voice was soft and low and almost shy. He couldn't remember her ever speaking to him like that. Clare's voice had been laughter and anger and joy. Whatever had happened to her over these last years, it had robbed her of her youthful passions.

"The loft will be just fine, Clare." Brian forced himself to look at her again. Thrown back to the world of his childhood, he had to force himself to remember he was an adult, and so was she. Her lips wore no paint; that hadn't changed. But they seemed pale against her creamy skin right now. He didn't quite meet her eyes. He remembered her eyes too well. They could make him do things he had never dreamed of doing. He gave her a curt nod of reassurance and returned to the male discussion around the table.

Clare wondered what would happen if she dumped
a pail of icy well water over this stranger's perfectly
barbered hair. She felt a rage building inside her that
she hadn't known in years. She wanted to grab Brian's
hair and jerk his head up until he really looked at her.
She wanted to kick his shins and pummel his stomach
and wrestle him to the ground as she had when they
were children. And then she wanted to beat some sense
into his arrogant head.

Instead, she went to her rocking chair and picked
up her mending.

If shattered dreams could be sewn back together with
needles and thread, she would have them repaired by
now. She listened to the masculine voices around the
table and tried not to single out Brian's. It was good
to have Gavin home again. He had matured in the two
years since he had left. He had been the closest to her
in age, and she had relied on him more than she realized. Letty had never been a help, and George was
only fifteen, an age where he could be more hindrance
than help. It was good to have Gavin for Christmas.
She just wished he hadn't brought Brian with him.

Her childhood dream had grown into a handsome
man. At least she thought him handsome. His hair was
a brown so dark that it was almost black, and he wore
it thick and smooth and cropped short in back. She
didn't like the bristly mustache, but she had to admit
it made him look more a man of the world. She had
never seen him in a cravat and collar before, and the
waistcoat that molded neatly to his wide chest and flat
belly held her fascination. She knew some of the men
in town dressed like that, but to see Brian dressed like
a gentleman and sitting at their old kitchen table kept
her attention distracted. He wasn't the same Brian she
remembered, and she mourned the loss.

That was selfish of her. Brian had wanted to be more than a miner, and that had been the only opportunity open to him here. He had obviously accomplished what he had set out to do, and she should be proud of the changes in him. But she couldn't help missing the boy who had held her hand in the porch swing and promised to take her away to see beaches and cities and sights neither of them could imagine.

Bobby sidled up to the chair beside her and tugged on her sleeve. When Clare looked down at him, he whispered, "Is he going to stay for Christmas? Are we going to have to give him presents, too?"

Clare brushed a strand of unruly hair back from her youngest brother's face. "Brian doesn't have any family, Bobby. Just welcoming him into ours is gift enough. Christmas isn't about giving things, but giving of ourselves."

Bobby scowled. "I made wooden ponies for Jed and Judy and whistles for everyone else. There ain't time to make none for him."

Teaching a nine-year-old that there was more to Christmas than presents wasn't an easy task, and her patience was worn thin by the emotions of these last hours since Brian's arrival. It would be nice if she could revert to the child she had once been and give Bobby the sharp answer he deserved, but she bit her tongue and replied calmly, "You don't have to make him anything. Just be nice. Now it's almost bedtime. You'd better go wash."

Brian watched Bobby leave rather than look to the woman on the other end of the room. He couldn't hear their conversation, but the child's unhappy scowl was easily read. Strangers were seldom seen in these parts, and certainly not at Christmas when people should be home with their families. Bobby had been only a baby when Brian was last here. He didn't recognize him at all, and to him Brian was an intruder.

He thought of the carefully wrapped presents he had carried all the way here in his spare valise. He had tried consulting with Gavin about the needs of the various children, but with the selfish zeal of a twenty-one-year old, Gavin had dismissed Brian's concerns. He had wandered the stores for days, looking for just the right presents for children who had grown into young adults in his absence. He hoped he had guessed right.

But his thoughts drifted to the two toddlers sleeping in the room beyond. He hadn't known about those two. He had brought nothing for them. They were still young enough to believe in the existence of Santa Claus. How would Clare have provided for their Christmas? Brian knew from experience that there was never enough money at this time of year to provide the gleaming visions that children imagined. The others were old enough to know better by now, but not those two young ones.

He couldn't hand out the other presents if there weren't any for the babies. Angry at Gavin for not telling him the situation and feeling guilty at his anger, Brian resolved to set the problem aside for another day when his head wasn't clouded with Clare's presence.

"Clare can't sew gloves," a young voice hissed surreptitiously from behind the wood stove. "I don't know why you want gloves anyway. They're perfectly useless. Mittens work just fine."

"I want real gloves, like ladies wear."

Brian identified the second voice as thirteen-year-old Katrina's. The first had to belong to Missy, two years her younger. The two had been as inseparable as

twins from an early age, but it appeared as if the onset
of adolescence was about to make its mark. Missy was
still a child, while Katrina yearned to be a young
woman.

A young woman who ought to know better than to
expect what she couldn't have. Kid gloves were an expensive impracticality out here. Katrina knew better
than to expect such a gift.

His irritation was growing instead of receding with
the coming of a new day. Brian tried to be complacent
as he shouldered his share of wood for the stove and
lugged it in to add to the stack. The work didn't bother
him; it never had. But the constant necessity of working the hands to the bone just to stay alive was a reminder of a life he didn't need. After constant struggle,
there ought to be something a little extra to show for
it at the end of the year. Katrina ought to be allowed
her gloves if that was what she wanted.

But Missy was right. Clare couldn't sew kid gloves
out of moonbeams. Mittens would be the best Katrina
could hope for. He wished he had thought of something as impractical as gloves for a young girl. The
book he had bought her wouldn't be the same thing at
all.

"All right, crew, who's going to hunt the perfect
tree with me?" Gavin's voice carried over the bickering between Bobby and George about who was to
slop the hogs that day and the cries of the two toddlers,
Jed and Judy, energetically chasing make-believe
horses over the hearth. All heads turned instantly toward Gavin.

Cries of "Me! Me!" echoed through the front room
as all within hearing scrambled for coats and scarves.

"Can't imagine what you want with a damned old
tree in the house." Mick grumbled from his place at

the table. "You'll catch the place on fire with your fancy notions."

"Twee! Twee!" Jed called, holding his arms up so Clare could better fit his coat over them.

"If we didn't have a tree, where would we put the cookies and popcorn?" Clare asked calmly as she tugged small arms into heavy wool before reaching for Judy and performing the same operation on her.

Having already been outside chopping wood, Brian was dressed for the occasion, but Mick's argument caused him to hesitate. He was a guest here, and Mick was his host. Should he stay behind out of respect?

Clare threw him a scarf. "Make sure Bobby wraps up good. He has a tendency to get sore throats."

With this incentive and no further protest from Mick, Brian joined in the family outing. He'd gone on similar tree hunts when he had been younger than George was now and he and Clare had been the eldest of the expedition. The trees they had chosen had been pitiful specimens suitable to their abilities as wood-choppers, but they had always been objects of awe when set up in the front room. But that had been back in the days of the impossible. Those days were gone now, and Brian felt like an impostor as he tramped out in the midst of all the childish enthusiasm around him.

Somehow, Clare had managed to keep the children believing in the impossible, even at their ages. They spread out across the countryside now, looking for a tree that would hold all the presents that would certainly appear on Christmas Eve. The light snow of yesterday had continued throughout the night until the ground was covered with a layer of dry fluff they scraped their feet through, leaving tracks visible all the way back to the house.

"Why won't Dad ever come with us?" Bobby demanded, as he slid down the hill toward Clare. "Every year he tells us we don't need a tree. Don't he like Christmas?"

"Doesn't," Clare corrected him. "And of course he likes Christmas. It's just that he can't use an ax any more, and he used to always be the one to cut down the tree. If he says he doesn't want a tree, then he can stay home and let Gavin do the cutting."

"Oh." Accepting that explanation, Bobby slid off in another direction.

Finding himself walking beside Clare, Brian looked down at the cherry red glow of her cheeks and caught a fleeting smile there.

"Mick never really recovered from that accident, did he? You'd think after all these years he would be used to it. I've seen men use one arm to chop wood."

"He never really recovered from my mother's death. For her he might have chopped wood. I used to think something died in him when she did, and he only stayed alive because of us. Now we're all getting old enough to take care of ourselves, and he feels useless. I worry about him sometimes."

"I found a tree! I found a tree! Clare, hurry, over here!" Nine-year-old Bobby screamed at the top of his lungs from a rocky ledge just up the snow-covered hill.

The others had already gathered by the time Clare and Brian caught up with them. Gavin was looking at the massive cedar dubiously, bending his head back to measure the height and muttering words of disparagement. Beside him Bobby bounced up and down excitedly, assuring him it was perfect, looking eagerly to Clare for confirmation.

The twins danced between the sprinkle of trees along the ledge, happy just to be included. Missy, Katrina, and George still held out for an even more perfect specimen. But next to the twins, Bobby was the youngest, the one who was just discovering that Santa Claus didn't visit these hills, and his choice of the tallest tree in the vicinity meant more to him than to the others.

"Bobby, don't you think it's just a little too tall?" Clare asked carefully. "What will we do if it doesn't fit?"

"It will fit. I know it will. It will reach all the way to the ceiling and then we can cover it with popcorn and cookies. And peppermint sticks?" he asked hopefully.

Brian remembered the gleam in the boy's eyes all too well. He must have been about that age when his mother had gone to town and not come back. He had wanted a Christmas tree that winter, but his grandmother had told him that Santa Claus was sick and there wouldn't be any presents, so there wasn't any point in it. Selfishly, for that nine-year-old boy, Brian stepped forward to measure his own height against the tree's.

The top of the tree came easily three feet above his head. He grinned and hefted his ax. "Stand back, boy, you've found us a Christmas tree."

Bobby's whoops of joys brought everyone running. The girls raced around searching for holes in the perfect tree. George eyed it with the arrogance of his fifteen years, and the twins clamored to be taken into Clare's arms, from which viewpoint they watched as Gavin and Brian took turns chopping at the tree.

Cheeks and noses red with cold, eyes streaming in the wind, they still screamed and laughed with joy as the tree shivered, listed slightly to one side, then crashed to the ground in a graceful dive. A bright cardinal shot up from a nearby bush, chirping a protest as breaths freezing into mist, everyone gathered around to grab some part of the tree to haul it home.

The twins scrambled to the ground to grab branches and were more tugged along than tugging as the tree wended its way down the hill. Gavin led the group in a song that had more to do with swinging swords and killing armies than Christmas, but the children joined in with great gusto. Brian fell back to walk with Clare.

"What if it won't fit?"

He heard the anger in her voice and looked down at her in surprise. The Clare he had known had always searched out the biggest tree and assured everybody it was going to be just fine, even when they had to cut two feet off the bottom when they got it back to the house.

"We'll make it fit, just like always."

Just like always. Clare sent him a fulminating look. Last year she'd had to cut the tree herself, and it had been a miserable specimen, indeed. The year before Gavin had cut the first tree he came to so he could hurry off and join his friends in some more adult activity. In the last eight years the number of Christmas trees they had cut anywhere near this size could be counted on one thumb.

"There isn't any 'always', Brian McGee. You, of all people, ought to know that." With that rejoinder Clare slid off to catch Judy from toppling over an outcropping of rocks, leaving Brian to catch up as he could.

He didn't need Clare's cynical reminder. In the eight years since he'd left, the only Christmas tree he had known had been in the home of a professor who had befriended him at college and invited him to spend the holiday every year. "Always" meant their childhood, but whatever Clare had suffered since then had obviously put that innocent time out of her mind. He had

thought he was the one who had lost the spirit of
Christmas. It looked as though Clare could use a little
reminding, too.

So they weren't children anymore. That didn't mean
they had to spoil it for the young ones. He'd learned
to live without Christmas. Hell, he'd learned to live
without a family. He was too old for jingle bells and
fa-la-las. It had been much simpler not to have to rack
his brain and his pockets for just the right gifts for
everybody. But damn it, the children still thought
Christmas was special, and they deserved this little
dab of brightness. And in spite of Clare, he was going
to do what he could to let them have it.

Marching past her, Brian grabbed the heavy trunk
of the tree that was moving progressively slower down
the hill. Setting into a slightly off-key rendition of
"Deck the Halls", he lifted the trunk on his shoulder,
and moments later the hills were echoing with fa-la-
las.

Clare watched this dark-haired stranger incredulously. He wasn't the Brian McGee she had known and
loved so many years ago. He wasn't a shirt-tailed boy
who pelted her with cherries from the tree or who
wrapped up frogs in boxes for her birthday. Even out
here in the woods he was dressed in boots that gleamed
black against the snow, and wore a long wool coat that
was more suitable to city carriages than muddy hill-
sides. He looked at her with the eyes of a stranger,
spoke to her in the cold tones of a stranger, and now
he was usurping her family from her. Even Bobby was
clinging to his coattail and sliding through the snow
behind him.

Well, that wouldn't last for long. Men didn't know
how to handle a houseful of children. He would be
hiding in the barn before the day ended.

Triumphant with that knowledge, Clare sailed ahead of them to prepare the hot chocolate they would all demand when they got back to the house.

Chaos ensued the instant the tree hit the front porch. It was too wide at the base to go through the door. The hounds that had been busy tracking rabbits through the snow came to investigate now and left their marks upon the branches to the screams of the girls and the shouts of the boys. Mick added his bull-like bellows to the cacophony as he ordered instructions for wrapping the branches so the tree could be hauled through. And the twins began to cry from the cold.

Clare serenely moved through the chaos, bringing the twins in the back door and unwrapping their soaked scarves and mittens before sitting the children before the fire to dry out. She had the milk heated and the cups ready and supervised the handing out of hot chocolate into grateful hands as the men wrestled with the problem of wrapping twine around the tree.

When the tree finally popped into the house and Mick held it upright so the top brushed against the ceiling, bending over almost a foot, a sudden silence fell. All eyes swung to Brian, who measured the overflow, shrugged, and went back outside for the ax. Giggles of relief immediately filled the air.

While Brian cut off the bottom foot of the tree, Clare set the children to popping corn. While Mick and Gavin and Brian labored to set the tree upright, Clare started the girls on the cookie dough. The scent of cedar intertwined with the smells of popped corn and baking cookies, until everyone's mouth was watering and more popcorn was eaten than strung.

Clare took down a cured ham and sliced it and started heating it over the stove, then mixed up biscuits and popped them in the stove after the first batch of

cookies were ready for decorating. By the time the tree
was up and the cookies iced, dinner was on the table.

Brian couldn't contain his amazement as Clare managed to get all the children into their seats, set out
plates and food, fed the twins—who tended to fling as
much food to the dogs as went into their stomachs—
and still managed to get a bite to eat for herself. He
vaguely remembered her mother keeping rein on this
circus through many memorable meals, but Clare had
always been the one who had to be called to come to
eat. He had forgotten the riotous anarchy of family life
in these past years, but Clare had learned to cope with
it all on her own.

While he had been learning higher mathematics, she
had been learning to cook and bake while keeping
track of half a dozen children. While he had been
carving a career out of law, she had been schooling
children in manners and behavior. Their lives had di-
verged so widely it seemed impossible that they could
have ever come from the same roots.

But he still remembered those roots, and his gaze
swung to the twins, who were now sleepily pushing
the remains of their mashed potatoes into puddles. He
felt something very much like a jealous constriction of
his lungs as he watched Clare lift them from their
chairs and carry them off. He wanted to know who the
damned man was who had given her those children
and not stayed around long enough to help raise them.

But he couldn't make himself raise the topic, not
with Gavin, not with her father, and certainly not with
Clare. The twins were there, and something had to be
done about it.

They were gabbling excited questions about the tree
and Santa Claus as Clare carried them off for a nap.
Brian lingered over his coffee while Missy and Katrina

cleared the table and the boys went out to water the animals. A plan was formulating in the back of his mind, and he needed some quiet with which to consider it.

He could remember Christmases without presents. He could remember one Christmas in particular when he was certain that if he asked for nothing more than a baseball and bat, he would be granted his wish. But the sport had obviously been too new for these hills, and he'd received a red rubber ball instead. The immense disappointment even for a boy who no longer believed in Santa Claus had been the end of Christmas for him. But somehow Clare had kept these children believing. He would do the same.

He had bought a ball and mitt for Bobby, but the boy seemed to be more interested in carving with an old rusted knife that barely peeled bark off wood. Katrina wanted real gloves, and Missy spent her time scribbling on planks of wood with a piece of charcoal. He had noticed George eyeing his boots with envy, and Brian could remember being that age and wishing for clothes that would make him stand out in the eyes of the girls at school. He had not only no gifts for the twins, but the wrong ones for the others. He needed to rectify that mistake.

There were still a few days before Christmas. He could make it to town and back in one. He needed permission to borrow a horse, but most of all, he needed to talk to Clare. She would be the one to know for certain what the children wanted and needed, and she was the one whose cooperation would make it easier to carry off the surprise. All he had to do was get around her damned arrogant mountain pride. He knew all about that pride. She would insist that they needed nothing, but he knew better.

There wasn't any opportunity that afternoon. Delighted to be back on familiar turf and in the arms of his family for the first time in two years, Gavin was determined to do everything he had missed the Christmas before. Straight after dinner he announced it was time for a turkey hunt, and even Mick was right on his heels as the men and boys scrambled for guns and cartridges and swept out into the snowy afternoon, Brian right along with them.

They didn't return until well after dark. Clare heard them coming, and she hurried to the frost-covered window to look out. Her father had learned the technique of firing a shotgun with one arm, but Bobby was still too young to know caution around firearms, and George tended to be reckless. It shouldn't have taken them this long on a turkey shoot, especially since the snow had increased and the wind grown stronger. They could have had ham for Christmas. They usually did.

But it was Brian's hand that was wrapped in handkerchiefs and scarves as they came in, proudly swinging two feathered birds in upheld fists. Clare's glance went from Brian's white face to his wrapped hand, and all the blood in her body seemed to flow to her feet and stay there.

"That old pea-shooter near took Brian's thumb off when it exploded, Clare. Better take a look at it." Cheerfully Mick flung his shotgun on the table and began shrugging out of his coat.

Clare sent her father a scathing glance, and remaining close to the fire, she held out her hand. Reluctantly Brian came forward and offered up his injured limb.

"He brought down the biggest bird out there. Took the head clear off." Equally cheerful, George flung his prize down on the table beside his father's shotgun. "But mine's almost as big."

"You can take the boy out of the country, but you can't take the country out of the boy." Gavin spouted this ridiculous cliché as he dropped Brian's bird beside the other and went to pour coffee. "It wasn't Brian's fault that old gun has seen its last days."

"Someone should have thought of that before you used it," Clare murmured furiously in an undertone as she unwrapped Brian's hand. The next to the last layer of bandages came away encrusted with blood, and she felt him jerk with pain. She was tempted to rip off the last layer and make him know the extent of his foolishness, but instead she reached for a basin and poured in warm water from the stove. "Put your hand in it and let it soak a minute," she commanded.

Brian eased his burning palm into the soothing water and bit his lip to keep from crying out. He'd heard Clare's anger, but he didn't have any response for it. The gun he had used wasn't any older than the others they had taken out this day. Her father and brothers hunted with those things all year around. It was a wonder they hadn't blown themselves to bits by now. Life came and went cheaply out here. He'd forgotten how that was, and he didn't remember it fondly now.

"I'm fine. It's just a scratch and a powder burn. Just give me something clean to wrap around it." For some reason he didn't want Clare touching him. She had long, talented fingers, fingers that could send a chill down a man's spine even when they weren't icy. He would feel much better if she kept them to herself.

But he was to receive no such reprieve. With quick, gentle movements, she had the last handkerchief unwrapped and his hand resting in hers as she examined it. Brian wasn't certain how much was the burn and how much was Clare's touch as warmth seeped up his arm and into his body while she twisted his fingers to examine the extent of the damage. She did it in a wholly professional manner, but he was thoroughly aware of how close he was to her for the first time since he had arrived. He could even smell the scent of vanilla on her, and a light powdery fragrance that he inhaled with pleasure. He forgot about his palm while he admired the play of firelight against mahogany hair. He had forgotten what magnificent hair she had. It was thicker than he remembered.

Closing his eyes, he pictured those women he had paid for with their false curls and dyed locks spread against scented pillows, but he couldn't put Clare's face on those bodies. The gray eyes beneath those dark upcurved brows were too uncompromising, too direct. He needed to see them misty with hope and desire as he had in long ago days, when Christmas had still been a time of joy and not an obligation.

"I didn't mean to hurt you. Hold still and let it dry a minute while I fetch some balm." Her voice was as gentle as her touch as she took his closed eyes for pain.

Perhaps it was pain, but not the kind she thought. The hand throbbed, but it wasn't the same kind of pain that was racking Brian's insides. Something clawed at his rib cage as Clare returned and rubbed a soothing balm into the burn. He nearly bent over with the agony of it, but he couldn't let anyone see the gaping wound where his heart should be. It should have healed over long ago, but just coming back had torn it open again.

He should never have come. Even if the city had been cold and hollow and empty, it had been better than this. He had rooms in a lovely old home, with stained glass over the transom and a roaring fire beneath a marble mantelpiece. He had a leather chair in front of that fire, and a secretary bookcase filled to overflowing with volumes he'd read and re-read when the pleasure took him. He had invitations to dine in similarly lovely homes. He didn't need to be here.

But Clare was bandaging the burn and Gavin was handing him coffee and Katrina was passing around biscuits slathered with ham and honey and he was back in his childhood again. Brian gratefully took the rocker someone offered and warmed himself while listening to the two girls chatter near the stove. Katrina was certain she was going to get her gloves, and even Missy mentioned the watercolors she'd need to paint the picture she had in mind. They were so certain that Clare could produce magic that they didn't even wonder at it.

His gaze followed Clare as her long skirts swept the floor between stove and table. Her back was straight, her hair neatly pinned, her apron white as the snow falling outside. This couldn't be the same Clare who had climbed trees and waded in the creek with him. Maybe that Clare had disappeared with the twins.

Brian's glance traveled uneasily to the frosted window panes. Snow didn't usually fall this early in the winter around here. He could remember winters when there had scarcely been any snow at all. Surely it would stop shortly. He'd asked Mick about the horse. He just needed a few minutes of Clare's time after the children went to bed. Maybe she had done miracles and already purchased the gifts they were obviously expecting.

Mick said grace over the bountiful supper that so easily appeared on the table where guns and turkeys had lain just shortly before. Brian was beginning to understand why the children thought of Clare as a miracle worker. Food had always been plentiful on the Allister table. They were hard-working people who grew a garden and canned and raised pigs and chickens and hunted with skill. But Clare made it seem as

if the food appeared by magic from pots always simmering on the stove and pans always baking in the
oven.

But despite the bounty, Brian knew money was
scarce. Mick's income came from the odd jobs he
could perform with one arm, and at this time of year,
the jobs would be few and far between. He knew Gavin
sent some money back home, but his job didn't pay
well enough to send much. He suspected Clare sewed
for those who couldn't sew for themselves, but she was
as likely to be paid in jars of honey as cash. Perhaps
George had managed a tobacco crop this year.

But that money would be needed for clothes and
staples like flour and sugar. There wouldn't be any
extra for watercolors and kid gloves and penknives.
Brian waited patiently as one by one in order of age,
the children washed and disappeared into their rooms
until only Mick, Gavin, Clare, and himself were left.

He couldn't bring up the topic of Christmas with
Mick around. The older man had too much pride to
admit that he couldn't afford to give his children everything they wanted. Gavin might understand, but he
wouldn't know what had already been done about gifts.
It was Clare he needed to speak with.

Gathering up his lost courage, Brian set his coffee
cup aside. "Clare, are there any evergreens around the
yard that need trimming? I've a mind to try my hand
at a wreath."

She looked startled that he had spoken directly to
her. Dark lashes flew upward to reveal deep wells of
gray, and a flush of pink tinted her creamy cheeks as
she met his gaze. "I'd appreciate that. I could show
you a holly that the birds dropped some years ago. It
could probably be trimmed up a little, too. And there's
some nice pine cones down by the creek."

"Would it be too much of an imposition to ask you to go out tonight? I've got some errands I want to do in the morning, and it might be dark again before I get back."

He could tell that puzzled her, but Clare had always been a good one to keep her mouth shut when the occasion called for it. She nodded and went to look for her heavy cloak.

"Don't keep her too long, the neighbors will talk," Gavin called jokingly as they let themselves out.

The snow had become more a wet rain that clung to the branches of the trees as they crunched through the yard. The clouds overhead prevented any wisp of moonlight, but the pale yellow lantern light danced along with them as they walked toward the barn. Brian needed clippers to cut the branches, and he didn't want to keep Clare out in this weather any longer than necessary. Once he got her to the barn, they could talk.

"I assume you had some other reason for dragging me out in this weather besides a wreath." she said breathlessly as they slid through the trampled path to the barn.

Always direct Clare. Brian caught her arm and held it firmly. His boots were sturdier than her thin shoes, and his steps more stable. She flinched at the touch, but didn't pull away.

"I want to go to town and pick up a few Christmas presents. I didn't know what to get anybody. What would the twins like?"

Their mother, that was the first thing that came to Clare's mind, but she didn't say it aloud. Brian only meant to go to the general store at the coal tipple half-way down the mountain, not all the way into the town where Loretta lived. Clare tried to make her mind work, but ever since Brian had taken her arm her head had stopped functioning. She didn't remember him as being so strong. He'd always been older and bigger than she, but the differences now were positively unnerving. He stood practically head and shoulders over her. Where did a lawyer who worked in an office all day get shoulders like that?

"I've made them both raggedy dolls. They don't need more than that. It's foolish to go out in this weather for a little candy or something extra. They don't expect it. Christmas is Christmas just because we're all together." There, she had got it out. She breathed a sigh of relief.

Brian opened the barn door and guided her in. The lantern scarcely made a dent in the pall of darkness in here. He could hear the horse whickering at the intrusion and a stir where some of the hens had got in, but he could scarcely see his hand in front of his face as he looked for something to cut with.

Not that he was much interested in a saw when he had Clare in here to himself at last. He had been trying to imagine her with her hair spread across his pillow earlier. Right now his imagination strayed no farther than tasting her kiss. It would be so simple to do. She stood right there, so close that all he had to do was lean over . . .

Clare darted away nervously, rattling in the bin of tools in desperate search for whatever it was they were looking for. "Why don't you stay here and help decorate the tree tomorrow? Popcorn chains take forever, and we need someone tall to put the star on top."

"Clare." Brian came up behind her and caught her elbow, pulling her around to face him. The scarf she had wrapped around her hair fell backward, and she looked up at him through a curtain of thick snow-coated lashes. "You used to kiss me. In the porch swing, remember? When it got dark and the fireflies came out, you'd let me put my arm around you and when I kissed you, you kissed me back. Why are you frightened to give me a little welcome-home kiss?''

"Because this isn't your home and you don't mean to stay. If that's all you brought me out here for, then I'm sorry to disappoint you, but I'm going back in.'' She tried to pull away from him, but he didn't release his grip.

"I brought you out here to talk about the children, but you won't do that. You keep dancing around me like I'm some kind of monster to be avoided. We used to be friends, Clare. What happened?''

"I haven't seen you in over eight years, Brian. And I'll be lucky to see you again in another eight. That's not a basis for friendship. You're Gavin's friend now. I'm happy to welcome you into the house. Don't ask for more than that.''

She was fighting him, and Brian reluctantly released her. "Don't run away, Clare. I'm sorry you feel that way. I thought friends were forever. But at least help me with the children. I've never had anyone to buy presents for. I want to get them the right things.''

"You can't walk in here and buy their friendship!'' Clare swung around in a swirl of cloak and scarf and started for the barn door.

"What in hell's the matter with you?'' Brian got there before her, blocking her retreat. "Are you the only one allowed to give presents around here? Did someone die and make you Santa Claus? Even if I only buy them sugarplums, I'm going to town tomorrow. You can't stop me.''

"You do that!'' Clare swung her hand out dramatically. "Show them what a rich man from the city can do. Show them how city kids live. Let them come to expect sugarplums and peppermints that I can never provide. And let them ask why they can't have them when you're gone. Let them long for things they'll never have. Then they can go off into the world like you when they're grown and I'll never see them again.''

There was a sob in her voice as she shoved him aside and raced out into the snow-clouded night, a blur of black against the white landscape. Brian wanted to run after her, but he was too stunned from the shock of emotion in her voice to do anything but watch her. Somehow he had contrived to hit some chord that she had kept hidden since his arrival. The Clare he knew was still there; she had just been wrapped in layers of motherly perfection.

The words she'd said echoed words he'd heard long before, and with anger, Brian grabbed the nearest saw and grimly set out after evergreen branches. He'd had to leave this mountain. Clare had understood that when she was a girl of sixteen. Why should it be any different now? And if he showed the children what could be had outside this tiny sphere they called home, why shouldn't they pursue their own dreams someday? Did Clare mean to turn into the spitting image of his grandmother and force them to stay here?

He wacked at evergreen branches until his fingers were numbed with cold and his burned palm ached with an intensity that throbbed. He returned the saw to the barn and found some baling twine and wire and returned to the house, cold, wet, and still furious. Maybe he ought to take Miss Clare Allister down the mountain with him tomorrow. It would do her a sight of good to get out of this house and see a little bit of the world for a change.

She had already disappeared from the front room by

the time Brian returned to the house. Gavin and Mick scarcely looked up when he entered, so she couldn't have said anything. Clare wouldn't. She had never been the type to cry on anyone's shoulders. As the eldest, she had always listened to the problems of her younger siblings, and they didn't seem to understand that she might have a few of her own. That had been where he had come in, but not any longer it seemed.

Brian let the branches thaw out before the fire while he dried out and sipped a cup of coffee. He wasn't going to get to sleep any time soon anyway. He might as well make himself useful. His entire body ached from the day's activities, but it was something less physical that ached when he thought of Clare's rejection. Perhaps she was sorrowing after the twins' father. He ought to ask, but he couldn't get up the courage. The Allisters had more pride than kings. They would tell him about the twins when the time came.

He wasn't at all sure he was ready to hear it.

The next day dawned in a blizzard of frozen white, and Brian cursed vividly when he walked outside and found himself crunching through thick layers of snow that had alternately drifted and frozen during the night. He couldn't selfishly drag the Allister's one dray horse out in snow like this. He could easily damage the animal. The presents for the children would go the way of all dreams in this place—crushed beneath the weight of reality.

He cursed at the ice freezing the cut logs together. He hacked at them with a fury that had nothing to do with the ice. And when he returned to the house with his arms full to see all the shining expectant faces admiring the undecorated tree, he dropped the logs by the stove, scowled, and stalked back outside again.

Startled by the angry crash of logs practically at her feet, Clare swung around in time to see Brian walk out with a cloud around his head so thick that even she could see it. Hurriedly pulling her biscuits out of the oven, she called to Gavin and Katrina to set them on the table and to get the children seated. She had no business worrying about a grown man who could take care of himself, but this was Brian. They had spent too many nights and days telling each other their innermost secrets for her to deny the need now.

Besides, it was broad daylight out, and they would be bundled up to their ears in cloaks and scarves. She wouldn't have to worry about a repeat of last night's performance. She had been dangerously near to accepting that kiss, but daylight made it easier to see her foolishness. She just couldn't have Brian's ill mood ruin the holiday.

Leaving breakfast preparations in good hands, Clare pulled on her outer garments and hurried out into the snow. The wind whipping tiny flakes across the landscape had already almost obliterated Brian's tracks, but she guessed their direction. Wishing she knew how to curse properly, she wrapped her cloak more tightly around her and set out after him. It wasn't snowing that hard that she could get lost on this familiar path.

Brian didn't hear her coming. Not until the shadow of dark wool fell into step beside him did he even know of her presence. She said nothing as they walked into the forest of spindly sassafras and dogwood that decorated the hillside between the Allister place and his grandmother's.

"You'll freeze out here. Get back inside," he said gruffly. She had rejected him last night. He didn't have any desire to repeat the performance again, not while he was in this foul mood.

"We buried your grandmother near that stand of hemlock she tried to grow." Clare wrapped her arms around her waist for warmth. Once out of the wind, it wasn't too bad out here.

"Did you find someone to put up a marker?" When he'd been notified of his grandmother's death, he'd borrowed the money to put up one. That had been back in the early days, when he'd first got started. There hadn't been so much as a penny to send his grandmother at the time. He had felt the guilt upon occasion, but it was always accompanied by anger at her betrayal. The two didn't mix well.

"It wasn't enough money to have a stone made and hauled up here. So Dad and Gavin took one of those old oak planks from the barn and cut out a nice marker and carved her name and everything on it. Then we used the money to buy a pretty rosebush and some flower bulbs and things so there's always flowers on her grave. The Easter flowers have spread so they're a glorious sight come spring."

Tears came to his eyes, but Brian refused to wipe at them. "She would have liked that. Thank you. Now get on back to the house. I'll be in shortly."

"Why didn't you ever write to her? I could have read the letters to her. She grieved something fierce after you left." Clare forced the words out. She had to know. She could accept the fact that he wouldn't write much to her, a young girl who had nothing to do with the life he meant to lead. But his own grandmother?

Brian snapped a nearby twig, the icy branch cracking with a loud "pop" in the still air of the valley they had entered. Guilt ate at him, but it didn't help to feel guilty so long after the fact. "I wrote my mother. They could have shared the letter."

Clare stared at him with curiosity. "They hadn't spoken in years."

"Whose fault was that?" he demanded. The anger hadn't entirely left him. He trudged through the snow, remembering the child who had run this path forty times a day. Or so it had seemed.

"Everybody's, I suppose. Your mother shouldn't have left you behind when she went looking for work. Your grandmother should have been more understanding. You know how people are out here when they get their backs up. There's no bringing them down again. All we've got is our pride. It's hard to surrender it."

"Dammit, Clare! Don't make excuses for them. It's over and done with and nobody comes out looking good. Did you know my mother sent for me when she found work? And my grandmother refused to let me go?"

Clare halted in her tracks, forcing him to turn around and look at her. The face of the man beneath the hat might be a stranger's, but the haunted look in his eyes was that of the boy she had known so well. Her heart cried out to him now as it had then, and she longed to stroke his cheek as she had once before. But this cheek bristled with rough beard stubble and had hardened into the square jaw of a man. She hadn't the courage to touch him again.

"Why would she do that?" she whispered when the silence between them grew too long.

Brian's jaw tightened. "Because she needed me to hoe the corn and tobacco and carry it to market. How would she have lived out here without me to help her?"

Not very well. Clare silently started back down the path. Her father and Gavin had often gone down the hill to help Mrs. McGee with her firewood and to fix her well or whatever else needed doing. But they couldn't raise her crops as well as raise their own. Clare had often cooked for her to be certain she never went hungry. She suspected after a while those were the only meals the old woman ate.

"Not very well," Clare answered eventually.

"I know." Brian set his jaw and continued walking. "She could have gone to my mother. She was too damned stubborn to accept."

"How's your mother doing?" Perhaps if she changed the subject, he would slow down and come back to the house. Clare kicked the snow off her boot and hurried after him.

"I got a Christmas card from California. Her new husband has just opened a saloon in San Francisco. She seems to be happy. She hated this place and was glad to leave it."

The bitterness in Brian's voice made her wince. Clare looked up at the intertwining branches overhead, saw the beauty of those ice-coated skeletons, and wondered how anyone could hate all this. She had always loved the isolation, but there had always been the element of frustration at not knowing what was beyond this that she could be missing. A person had to live with what they were given, she guessed.

"I'm happy for her. And I'm glad you got a chance to meet up with her again. I just can't understand your grandmother letting you think your mother didn't want you all these years."

"It wasn't just that." Brian caught another branch and snapped it in his hands. They were almost there. He could see the stand of hemlocks from here, and he slowed his pace. "You remember how I worked at Dick's place that summer? How he promised to take me into town before school started so I could get a diploma?"

Beside him Clare nodded her head. Brian sensed it
more than saw it. His gaze was on the stunted pines
ahead. "He couldn't make it on the day he said he
would, but he sent his boy over to tell me we'd leave
the day before. I was out when the message came. My
grandmother never gave me the message. Dick went
on into town without me, thinking I'd changed my
mind."

The awful words caught in the wind suddenly whis-
tling over the hill. Clare tried to pretend he hadn't said
them, but she couldn't pretend away the pain with
which they were uttered. It cut through her like a knife,
leaving the wound open to the freezing wind. What
she did next was automatic, a product of the long
lonely days they had spent in each other's company
over the years. She closed her arms around Brian's
waist and rested her head on his chest, and when his
arms came around her, she squeezed him closer.

Somehow the pain was easier when shared like this,
as if the two wounds bound together healed each other.
Brian held her tight, not daring to think or feel, just
holding her until the warmth of their bodies blended
and the wind swept away the outside world. This was
what he had sought when he had come here. He had
no right to it anymore, but just for this one brief moment, he cherished this feeling of being home.

"She loved you so much Brian." The words were
nearly torn from Clare's lips, but she knew he could
hear them. "She cried for weeks after you left. I used
to take her flowers and things, and she would just be
sitting in that rocker, holding some shirt of yours, and
we'd cry together. And then she'd clam all up and go
to cooking something and bustling around, but the next
time I came, it would be the same all over. She thought
she knew what was best for you, Brian. She wanted

you to stay here where it was safe, where you wouldn't get mixed up with women and drinking and smoking and all those evils down in town. She didn't understand, Brian. She thought town had taken your mother, and she didn't want it to take you. But it did. In the end it did, and she never saw you after you went off to college.''

Brian rubbed her back, feeling her shivering against him. So many times he had tried to understand his grandmother's reasoning, but he couldn't get past the long rows of corn and tobacco, the blazing heat as he picked worms and chopped suckers and despised every aching minute of it, despised it because it was all he would ever know of the world if he couldn't find a way out. Clare was handing him the gift of another side to his thinking. The gift hurt. It made his eyes water as he thought of his grandmother sitting there, crying, while he so selfishly ignored her and went his own way. But the pain of her bitterness and betrayal eased somewhat, and he could handle the guilt better than that pain.

''I'm sorry, Clare. I was just a kid and I was so mad at her, so hurt, I couldn't see past the nose on my face. When I found out what she'd done, I walked all the way down to the general store and hitched a ride into town and never looked back. Some say you should always look forward, but I'm beginning to think that's not as good an idea as it sounds at first.''

''Why don't you come back to the house now? You haven't eaten.'' Embarrassed by her forwardness, Clare backed from his arms. Brian let her go, but his expression was still stony as he looked down at her.

''I'm going into town, Clare. Come hell or high water, I'm going to get those kids what they want. I've been looking back ever since I got here, and what I see isn't a pretty sight.'' He gestured up at the snow that was still falling, at the frozen path they followed. ''All I see is impossibilities and hopelessness, barriers to everything a child dreams, disappointments to every wish.

''Just look at you. You wanted to see the world. You had grand dreams of selling your dolls and designs and sewing in town where people could appreciate them. And what are you doing now? Raising a house full of kids and grubbing over a stove all day and night. And that's what you'll be doing tomorrow and the next day for the rest of your life. Dammit, Clare, I want those kids to dream. I want them to think of what they could have if they left here. And I'm not going to let you be my grandmother and keep them here.''

He strode off down the hill at a faster pace than before.

Clare ran after him, slipping and sliding until— hands outstretched—she crashed into Brian's back and sent him flailing face forward into the mud and snow. She tumbled after him, but it had been worth it. She grabbed the back of his head and shoved his face in the snow, rubbing his nose in it.

''Take that you insufferable arrogant miserable rotten hateful despicable monster! You horrible beast! How dare you talk to me like that! I ought to pound you into a pulp. I ought to leave you here to die of cold. I ought to let you rot in your own personal hell. Damn you, Brian McGee, who in hell do you think you are?''

She had never used such language in her entire life, but it was fittingly used on the likes of him. He wouldn't understand any other. Still furious, Clare jumped to her feet and started on down the hill ahead of him. Fury gave her momentum. Fury made her aware of every step of the man behind her. But fury couldn't hear the snowball coming.

It hit her smack between her shoulder blades. Balls of ice shattered and flew down her neck. Screaming, she grabbed a handful of snow from a tree branch and in one fluid move, smashed it into a ball, turned, and flung it at him.

He was too close to miss. It splattered against his already snow-encrusted coat. Clare grabbed another handful and tried to rub it in his face, but Brian caught her arm and pulled it down, forcing her to drop her weapon. Snow clung to his hair and collar and perched on the tip of his nose. His cheeks were red with frost and his eyes glittered with deadly menace as he held her firmly.

"I don't pick on people smaller than me, so you're going to get off easy, midget."

With that warning Brian swept her up in his arms and while Clare kicked and screamed, covered her mouth with his. The screams became a startled gurgle, then silenced.

She didn't remember his kisses being like this. His mouth was hot fire against hers. She struggled for some control, but the heat was searing, demanding and needful at the same time. She clutched the wool of his coat with her mittened fingers and hung on, but he didn't stop. She gasped for air, and his tongue touched hers, and she nearly leaped from her skin. She clenched her eyes closed and surrendered to the devastating force sweeping through her, just letting it happen as it had never happened before.

More shaken by the encounter than he was prepared to admit, Brian finally set her down. They would both have pneumonia, standing out here with their feet soaked to the skin and their noses dripping icicles. Not that there were any icicles left to drip after that kiss. He stared down at Clare in wonderment. No woman had ever kissed him like that before.

"I'm still going to town," he informed her. "You can go with me if you like. Or I'll just buy whatever catches my fancy."

"That old sleigh's still in the barn," she answered warily, her gaze never leaving his. Reassured that he wasn't going to turn into a ravening beast again, she turned and started back down the hill.

"It's probably in bad shape. And I'd have to borrow Dick's mule team."

"I can't go. Tomorrow's Christmas Eve. I've got too much work to do. I haven't finished the raggedy dolls yet." Cautiously Clare gave him a sideways glance. "I still hate you."

"Because I told you the truth." Brian took her hand and held it tight. "You're trapped here, just like my grandmother tried to trap me. But no one looks for solutions. There's got to be solutions. You just have to want them bad enough to work at them."

"I'm not leaving those children," she informed him firmly, but she didn't pull her hand away. "The twins had real bad earaches back in the spring. And Dad came down sick this summer. We used the tobacco money to pay the doctor bills. I couldn't get to town to buy Bobby his penknife. I polished up an old knife of Dad's and he put a bone handle on it, but the blade's too old to sharpen right."

"He'll have his penknife. And Kat can have her gloves, and Missy her watercolors. What size boot does George wear?"

Clare didn't look at him. They were almost at the stand of hemlocks. She could see the wooden headstone from here. "Same size as Dad already. You'll have to ask him."

As he came to a halt at the foot of the grave, she swung around and glared at him. "I want them to have a Christmas, Brian. I want them to know the joy our mother gave us. But we never complained about made-over knives and never knew about fancy gloves and watercolors. It's happening, Brian. The world's coming here, just like your grandmother said it would. I'm frightened, Brian. I've seen it happen already. I don't want them hurt."

Still holding her hand, he kneeled at his grandmother's grave and began to brush away the snow with his other hand. Beneath the ice lay a thorny cane, and another, and still another. He tested their resiliency and found them green. Come spring, the grave would be covered with roses. He patted the snow back in place again and kneeled silently in prayer. He prayed for the strength to do what was best. The world was a cold and lonely place, and this hollow was a piece of Eden in comparison. The children would be safe here, but safe wasn't enough. He bowed his head, made his peace with the past, then jerked Clare back to her feet as he stood.

"We'll find the sleigh. Maybe Gavin will go in with me. You still haven't told me what to get the twins."

This time Clare said what she had wanted to say the night before. "They need their mother. And their mother needs to know them. There isn't anything you can buy them, Brian. They're too young. And you can't possibly give them what they need. Just buy them a peppermint stick at the general store, and that will have to do."

Brian dropped her hand and slowly turned to stare

down at her. His eyes glittered strangely as they met hers and searched them carefully. "Their mother?"

Clare felt the intensity of his gaze clear to the pit of her stomach. She blamed it on lack of breakfast as she stared back at him. "Loretta. Didn't Gavin tell you? Letty got married when she was sixteen, had the babies when she was seventeen, and lost her husband just last year. We couldn't keep her home. Tom had shown her town, talked about buying a house there, and there wasn't any turning her back. She did like your mother, Brian. She went to town and left the babies behind. It's not any way for any of them to grow up. She needs to be with them, but she can't get home. There just isn't enough money to send for her."

"And with this snow the train won't be coming through either, even if we wired the money. Damn this place to hell!" Brian spun on his heels and stalked toward the falling-down shack that was politely termed a barn.

The sleigh was still there, if sleigh it could be called. Buried under long forgotten bales of wire and old boards, it was little more than a few hunks of steel and rotten leather. Brian stared at it in dismay. It would take a month of Sundays to put it back together. He would be lucky to get it down to the general store. All the way to town and back . . .

He would do it. He was going to do it. He would show her that this mountain wasn't the end of the world. People could leave it and come back. He had come back. So would Letty.

With a single heave he shoved boards and wire and acres of dust to the back of the barn, leaving the skeleton of a sleigh open for inspection.

"Oh, my word, you can't go out in that," Clare whispered from beside him.

"Oh, but I will, if I have to work all day and night to do it." Brian gazed at the wreck with satisfaction. "The twins are going to have Letty for Christmas."

She threw him an incredulous look. "You're mad. You can't get halfway down the mountain in that. You'll be killed, for certain."

"Then I will die happy." Catching her shoulders, Brian shoved her from the barn. "We've got to get back to the house. I need to talk to Dick and your father. There's bound to be a few old boards and nails and whatnot around to fix this thing up. I'll be on the way in no time."

Brian's jubilation had much to do with the knowledge that the twins belonged to Letty, but he couldn't let it show. He was ecstatic. Clare had waited. Even if she hadn't waited, she was still here, and the ties that bound her weren't as formidable as they had first appeared. There was no husband, no lost lover. There was just a home and family that she loved deeply, as he did. He felt as if he could rule the world today. One miserable little sleigh wasn't going to stop him.

By the time they returned to the house, the others were ready to send out a search party. Gavin and Mick sent their snow-covered clothing suspicious glances, but even they couldn't imagine what wrongdoing could be accomplished while wrapped in layers of wool and rolling in a snowbank. Brian's cheerful disposition, however, drew blank stares. His announcement that he intended to take the sleigh all the way into town brought instant chaos.

Gavin and Mick protested the impossibility. The children all wanted to go with him. When told Brian might not make it back in time for Christmas, they instantly retreated from that position, but had a dozen different questions with which to bombard him. When it became clear that his amazing journey relied on obtaining mules and supplies to repair the sleigh, the room became a blur of motion as everyone ran for boots and scarves and hats and mittens.

Brian had never seen anything quite like it. Gavin set out on foot for the long hike to Dick's place to ask about the mules. Mick began rummaging in the barn for what tools and supplies he might have to get started with. George set out to a neighboring farm with a list of what was needed. Missy and Katrina volunteered to take the supply of carefully stored cooking grease to oil up the runners. Bobby filled his arms with the first batch of tools and started on down the hill ahead of everyone.

Clare remained in the doorway, the twins clinging to her skirts as they watched the activity. Brian read the fear in her eyes, but understood it for what it was. She was afraid to raise her hopes. Any number of things could go wrong: the sleigh might not work, he might not make it down safely, Lettie might refuse to come home, they might not come in time. And even if everything worked out for the best, what would happen then? Would Lettie stay? Would she take the twins away with her to town? Would George demand to go with her? Would anything ever be the same again?

Brian couldn't answer those questions for her. He had questions of his own, but now wasn't the time for them. He left her standing in the doorway as he followed Mick down to the old barn and the rotten sleigh that held all their hopes and fears.

Clare kept Kat and Missy busy icing cookies and stringing popcorn, but she couldn't stop their conjectures at the wonderful surprises Brian might bring back if he came back in time. Not understanding any of the activity around them, the twins merely toddled through

their usual mischief—attempting to climb the still undecorated tree, stealing from the growing mound of
cookies, and falling asleep in the stack of quilts Clare
had brought out for Brian's trip.

Dick and Gavin stopped by on the way down to deliver the mules, and Clare filled them with coffee and
cake. George came by with two more of the neighbors,
all bearing armfuls of wood and nails and wire and
talking excitedly of the sleigh as if it were the most
exciting toy they had ever seen. Clare smiled and
warmed them with coffee and kept her own terrifying
fears to herself. It was Christmas. Only good things
happened at Christmas. She repeated this phrase to
herself as morning slipped past noon and the sun
started its downward slide.

She allowed the girls to pack up the noon meal in a
basket and carry it down to the men working in the
barn. They came back talking excitedly of sleigh rides
for Christmas and hoping for more snow so there
would be time to go to town again before Brian and
Gavin left. Town to them meant the little cluster of
buildings ten miles down the road where the coal cars
were loaded and the general store was located. They
had no concept of the sprawling town at the foot of
the mountain where Letty had gone and Brian meant
to go. They would have even less of a notion of the
terrifying city where Brian and Gavin would go when
they left here.

Clare tried to hide her dread, but when the first
screams echoed up the hillside, she was grabbing for
her cloak before the last one bounced off the walls.
Soaking her high-top shoes and hem in the well-
trodden snow, she slipped and slid all the way down
the path, catching at trees to break her run. The

screams began again, and she recognized them at once. Bobby.

Brian met her on the path, catching her before she could catch herself, wrapping her briefly in his warm arms before releasing her.

"Bobby fell from the hay loft. We weren't watching him, and he came right through those rotten rafters. Gavin's carrying him up. I think he's broke his arm. Is there a doctor around here?"

He knew better than to ask that. Clare started back down the hill, calling after her, "Get the quilts from the house. And some laudanum. I'll take a look at Bobby. If he's broken his arm, you'd better hope that damned sleigh works."

She disappeared around the bend, leaving Brian to stare after her. The ladies he knew back in the city never cursed as Clare had taken to doing these last days, but then they seldom had her reasons for cursing. He dashed up the hill to carry out her instructions.

When he came back down, Clare had Bobby wrapped in her own cloak, cuddling him in her lap as if he were still a toddler, speaking comforting words while the others either stood around helplessly or tended the mules they had hitched to the sleigh. Brian looked at this preparation and felt his heart sink in his stomach.

Clare confirmed his suspicion. "The arm's broke in two places. I don't dare try to fix it. Give me the laudanum."

Her tone was calm and dry, but Brian read the hysteria in her eyes well enough. An arm broken in two places could be set wrong and never be right again. A man with a useless arm could starve out here. Brian's gaze went to Mick's white, pain-filled face as his son faced a future like his own, and he clenched his teeth against the wave of bitterness sweeping over him. Where was the God these people had been raised to believe in?

Clare got some of the laudanum down Bobby's throat. He was almost unconscious with the pain already. Brian watched as she carefully tried to straighten his torn and bloody arm to the best of her ability, then wrapped it tightly in a blanket she had him rip in half. When she looked up at him and announced she was ready, he knew all thoughts of Christmas were gone.

Silently the crowd of men and boys helped them into the sleigh, checked the harness, wrapped Clare and Bobby in the quilts, and watched them off.

"What did you say to Mick? He was meaning to take Bobby down himself." Brian couldn't bear the silence. The mules weren't a fast-paced team of horses. The sleigh moved cumbrously around the rocky ledges of the faint track made by years of people and animals moving up and down this path. It was going to be a long ride.

"I told him the kids needed him for Christmas and they didn't need you. He wanted me to stay instead, and I should have, but I couldn't. Dad wouldn't have gone to see Letty when we got there. He knows I will."

"What do you mean, he wouldn't have gone to see Letty? Doesn't he know where she is?" Brian glanced down at the boy sleeping in Clare's arms. Bobby was stirring restlessly but not awake. He didn't know why he was taking on more problems than he could handle at once.

"He doesn't want to know. He told her not to come back. Your grandmother didn't have the world's corner on pride." Clare stared stiffly over the untouched snow ahead. Anyone with any sense would stay in on a day like this. The crunching, jerking motion of the sleigh as it pulled in and out of drifts kept her stomach knotted.

"He didn't know I was going to town to get Letty?" Brian didn't think he could believe what he was hearing. Mick had even found a rusty old timber saw with two handles so he and Gavin could work together on this project. He'd done the work of two men this morning.

"He knew." Clare's voice came from a place far distant from the seat where they were riding. "But he wouldn't admit it. He couldn't keep you from doing what you wanted. That eased his pride."

Brian muttered a string of curses under his breath as he guided the mules down the path. It wasn't this damned mountain that stood in the way; it was this damned mountain pride. Clenching his jaw, he urged the beasts to go faster.

They stopped at the rail head and asked at the general store, but it was almost Christmas. The visiting doctor wasn't making rounds. A telegram to town would be senseless. They could get down the mountain faster than the doctor could get up. Bobby was in pain now, moaning and thrashing in his sleep. They got more laudanum in him, drank the hot chocolate the proprietor offered, took the sandwiches he made, and set off down the road again.

"It's going to be dark." Clare's voice was still carefully numb.

"I figure it will be near midnight before we get there. Will we be able to rouse anybody?"

"I don't know. We waited for the doctor to make his rounds when Dad and the twins got sick. One of Dick's boys broke his leg a couple of summers ago, but we just set it ourselves. He still limps a little, but he gets by.''

She was telling him more than he wanted to hear. Brian stared grimly at the road, as if their plight were the road's fault. He'd stayed in town with his mother long enough to get his diploma and win that scholarship the year he had left the mountain. It wasn't much of a town, but it had a school and a medical clinic of sorts. There were saloons, too, and probably other equally unsavory places, but it certainly wasn't the city of sin his grandmother had thought it. It was just too damned far from the people living on this mountain.

He wasn't an oil tycoon. He couldn't move a town. He couldn't even build one. He could do nothing to better this situation. They needed roads and money before anything could be done at all. And nothing could be done in time for Bobby.

The gray afternoon slid into night, and Brian felt Clare shivering beside him. He stopped the mules for a while to let them rest and wrapped her more snugly in the quilts, bringing her next to him so they could share their body heat.

"Is he getting heavy? There's room enough for him to lie down on the seat." He brushed hair back from the boy's pale face, testing it for fever.

"I'll hold him. Maybe he won't feel the jouncing as much." Clare held herself stiffly though every muscle in her body ached. If she allowed herself to relax, she would disintegrate into a thousand tiny pieces.

It should have been a happy journey, filled with the anticipation of buying the children presents and finding Letty and returning her home. Brian had hoped for Clare's company, had wanted to rekindle that flame he remembered so well, had wild dreams that he didn't share with her yet. They could have been singing carols and sharing kisses, but that no longer seemed appropriate. The boy struggling in a drug-induced sleep prevented anything but fear for his life, for life was too cruel in these hills for any but the strong to survive.

It was shortly before midnight when they reached town. A church bell was tolling the beginning of Christmas Eve when they reached the clinic. A few people still wandering the street stared in astonishment at the ancient sleigh and its occupants, but more because it came down out of the mountain than for any other reason. Brian turned their curiosity to good use, and soon someone was running to fetch the doctor.

As soon as his pocket watch told him it was a decent hour, Brian trudged down the nearly empty streets in the direction Clare had given him. He was familiar with this section of town. Dilapidated shotgun houses mixed with boarding houses that seemed to lean in the direction of the river, all of them weathered to the same depressing shade of gray. His mother had lived here when he had found her. All those who crept out of the mountains looking for a place to stay found their way here. It was the side of town that didn't require much money to live in.

He hadn't seen Letty since she was a girl of ten or eleven, and he wouldn't have recognized her when she answered the door except that her hair was the exact shade of mahogany as Clare's and Mick's. Her face was thin and sallow, but the overlarge eyes told of a beauty hidden by lack of food and care. She would be lovely again when rested and well fed.

Her wary look told Brian he couldn't look much better after sleeping on the clinic floor for half the night. He rubbed a rueful hand over his unshaven jaw and tried to rake his hair out of his face as he spoke.

"Letty Allister? I'm Brian McGee. Remember me?"

"It's Greene now." She was still cautious as she studied him. "Brian? What are you doing here?" And then her eyes went wide. "What's happened? Is it the twins? Oh, my God, tell me!" She pulled him inside and slammed the door, her terror vividly apparent.

"The twins were climbing the Christmas tree the last I saw of them. It's Bobby. He's been hurt. Clare's over at the clinic with him. I thought maybe you could sit with the boy while she got some rest. She's been up all night."

"Just give me a minute, I'll be right there." She whirled off in a swirl of faded calico skirts, a picture of brisk efficiency without further question or a single hint of reluctance. This was what Brian had forgotten about this place—the tight bonds of family and neighbors in times of trouble. Nothing in the city could compare with it.

There was no point in accompanying Letty to the clinic. She knew the way, and he had a list of errands that needed to be done. On a few hours sleep, he knew he looked like a tramp just crawled out of a cave, but there was a letter crackling in his pocket that had been burning a hole there for some time. He had thought it immensely funny when he had received it. His perspective had changed drastically since then. The gift he had bought for Clare had taken on new meaning.

A little while later Brian had settled the business of the letter successfully despite his grubby appearance. A few questions and a handshake had been all that was needed. He still knew a few people here. People knew him. For the first time since he'd arrived on the mountain, Brian allowed himself a sliver of hope. Bobby's arm was set. The doctor had said he could go home when he woke. They might even make it in time for Christmas. Maybe there really could be a Christmas.

He found sugarplums and peppermints easily enough, and two tin drums for the twins. He wasn't certain about the size of Kat's gloves, but they looked lovely enough to please her. He bought the last box of watercolors in the store for Missy and found a pair of sturdy black boots for George. The mercantile didn't have any penknives left, so he wandered down to the hardware store. Mick could use a better saw than that rusty thing he had now, and there ought to be an assortment of knives for Bobby.

The clerk shook his head when Brian made his request. "It's Christmas Eve. Everybody wanted penknives this year. We're plumb out of them, I'm sorry. Have you tried the mercantile?"

Brian felt an instant's panic as he paid for Mick's saw and shook his head in reply. "They're out. What else do you have? He wants something for whittling."

"Don't they all." The clerk drew out a tray of assorted knives. 'I've got a good hunting knife here. He can use it for cutting tree limbs if he wants."

The weapon looked hideously dangerous for a nine-year-old, and Brian shook his head. The others weren't any better. A boy needed a knife he could fold up and keep in his pocket. None of these fit the bill.

"The boy just broke his arm, and it's going to be a miserable Christmas if he can't get what he wants. Isn't there anywhere else I can look?"

"Well, you might talk to Old Pete. He collects knives. He might be persuaded to part with one of them."

Brian took the directions and hurried down the street, practicing arguments in his head. What good was it to be a lawyer if he couldn't persuade some old man out of a miserable little knife? He'd have the knife in his pocket and they'd be on their way as soon as Clare had a chance to rest and Bobby was awake. It wasn't noon yet. They would make it home before Christmas morning. The sun was even trying to come out.

Of course, that meant they couldn't linger long or they would be trying to sled on mud. He hastened his steps and walked up to the house indicated, knocking briskly on the wooden door.

No one answered.

He pounded again, louder. Perhaps the man was deaf.

Still, no one answered.

Brian stood back and searched the windows. He couldn't see any lights, but it wasn't likely in the day-time. He didn't see any movement. Maybe he ought to just find a way in, help himself to a knife, and leave some money and a note of apology. He didn't have time to wait on the front stoop until the man returned.

Before he added breaking and entering to his list of crimes, Brian ran to the house next door. The woman who answered was friendly and delighted to talk.

"Pete? Pete went to visit his boys for Christmas. Took the train out day before yesterday. If that wasn't a sight to see! I offered to help him pack, but he had more of those knives in his valises than he did clothes, said he meant to pass the collection on to his boys as a gift. I reckon he figures he ain't got much more time to live." She shook her head in dismay at the thinking of some people.

Brian managed to pull himself away from her talk-ativeness and start back down the street with a pile of stones where his stomach should be. Maybe he should go back and get the hunting knife. It had been wickedly expensive; that's why it had been left over when everything else was gone. But despite it's strength and beauty, it wasn't a boy's toy. He'd have to ask Clare about it.

He stopped in at the barber shop, but the usual gang of men discussing politics wasn't there today. It was Christmas Eve, after all. The lone barber shook his head when Brian inquired about any other sources of penknives, and he went out with his hands in his pockets, feeling the spirit of Christmas slowly seeping out of him again. If he couldn't find something as simple as a penknife for a boy, how could he ever learn to make the kind of Christmas children dreamed of?

He hated to tell Clare of his failure, but he had to stop and see how Bobby was doing. It was almost noon. They were going to have to leave soon.

They were all waiting for him, their eyes anxious as he walked in. Even Letty had her bag packed and sitting at her feet. She looked nervous, but Clare was clutching her hand as if she wouldn't let go. Brian read the defiance in Clare's eyes clearly enough. Letty was going back with them if they had to walk up the mountain.

As Brian walked in, Bobby managed a sleepy smile and held out the sling supporting his arm. "It's black. The doc says only men get to wear black slings. Do you think I'll still be wearing it when school starts again?"

"I don't doubt it in the least. Ready to go, slugger?" Brian avoided Clare's anxious glance as he wrapped the boy snugly in his coat and a blanket. "Bessie and Bertie are waiting at the livery. You can show the sling off to the whole town as we go by."

"The doctor gave him something for the pain. He's

supposed to sleep,'' Clare whispered behind him as she fastened her cloak.

So much for stopping somewhere to see if the boy could find something else he wanted more than a knife. Looking down at Bobby, Brian could see he was nearly asleep on his feet already. He didn't even protest when Brian picked him up in his arms and carried him out.

Clare didn't ask about the packages bulging in his overcoat pockets. Brian read the anxiety and the weariness in her eyes too well. The children were at home without her and Christmas Eve was almost gone. The tree wasn't decorated and dinner wasn't cooked. There were two fat turkeys that probably hadn't been plucked. How was she going to provide Christmas when she was hours away from home?

And the present for the one child who most needed a happy Christmas wouldn't be under the tree, but Brian didn't tell her that. The boy wouldn't even be able to throw the damned ball or wear the mitt he had brought for him until his arm came out of the sling. Maybe he could give a kind of promissory note promising payment of a knife when he returned to the city.

''Look, the general store isn't going to be open when we get up there. Will you take this and get some things to eat while I'm harnessing the mules? Bobby can sleep in the seat while you're shopping. I don't mean to spend a night on the mountain without any food. Maybe there's enough in there to get the kids some apples and oranges, just as a surprise in case we're late.''

Clare glanced at Brian's face before accepting the purse of coins he handed her. His thick dark hair was practically standing on end where he had obviously dragged his hand through it several times. The shadow

of his beard made his square jaw look almost dangerous, especially when he defiantly jammed his hat on
beneath her stare. She remembered that glitter of defiance in his eyes, and she smiled.

"We'll be right back. Don't go without us."

Don't go without us. Holding Bobby, Brian stared
after her, shaking his head. He could still hear that
cry—"Don't go without me!"—echoing down the hillside and through the years. She had hollered it after
him often enough when he had wanted to go hunting
or fishing and she wanted to tag along. She had said
it those nights in the porch swing when he had talked
of leaving the mountain. She would probably have
cried it after him when he walked down the mountain
that morning he'd left, only he hadn't told her he was
going.

Finding the sleigh where he'd left it, Brian swung
the sleeping child into the seat and went to fetch the
mules. He didn't want to go without her again.

That thought was strong inside him when he watched
Clare hurrying down the street as he finished harnessing the mules. Her cloak wasn't fastened snugly to her
waist, carving her figure for all to see like the fash-
ionable ladies in the city. It billowed out behind her,
revealing the worn brown wool of her old-fashioned
gown. He would dress her in satin and velvet, and then
people would notice the beauty of her smile instead of
the old cut of her clothes.

Brian didn't want anyone to notice the trim figure
he wrapped in his hands as he lifted Clare into the
seat. That was a secret that would be his alone to admire. He could feel the heat of her through the thick
wool, and he allowed his hands to linger a moment
longer than they should. She looked down at him and

blushed, and he felt a little better. She could still tell
what he was thinking.

That look warmed Brian's insides for a little while.
He had wanted to make a perfect Christmas, a Christmas to remember for the children, and he had failed.
He had failed at any number of things in his life, if he
wanted to look back at them. But a man had to keep
going forward, looking back maybe to remember the
failures and how to avoid them, but then turning ahead
again. And he was looking forward with growing ex-
pectations.

As he drove the mules out of town, Brian watched
Letty helping hold Bobby across her lap. She didn't
even look back as they left. His hopes grew a little
stronger. Maybe she wouldn't want to return to town.
Maybe she was older and wiser now, and with a little
incentive, she might stay with her children in her father's home. He had to be ready with the incentive.

He found himself humming as the sleigh slid up the
path they had come down so recklessly not twelve
hours earlier. He was exhausted, cold, and hungry,
and he was humming, Beside him he felt Clare giving
him an odd look, and he tucked it away inside him
with his other treasures. He hoped she was as aware
of him as he was of her.

She shivered and moved a little closer, and he pulled
a quilt tighter around their legs until he could feel the
pressure of her thigh against his. He liked that feeling.
In a little while her frail soprano began singing the
words to the carol he was humming, and the crystal-
line air sparkled with the sound of song.

Letty joined in with more enthusiasm than tune, and
the old mules seemed to pick up speed in cadence with
the music. As the afternoon waned, an occasional
snowflake fell, but the wind was still. The worst of the

storm was over, but the snow remained firm beneath
the runners. With any kind of luck at all, they would
be home by midnight, in time to get the gifts under
the tree for Christmas morning.

Bobby woke and complained of his arm, but he eagerly accepted the sandwiches Clare gave to him. Brian
ate as he drove, urging the mules to hurry. It was almost dark now, but the road was clear enough to see.
The trees on either side of it made a wall he couldn't
miss.

He smiled as Bobby exclaimed over the orange Clare
handed him for dessert. It was beginning to sound like
Christmas already. Maybe it wouldn't matter so much
if he didn't get the knife he wanted. The twins would
have their mother.

Letty was practically bouncing in the seat as they
reached the dark buildings of the general store and
train platform. The town was deserted at this hour
on Christmas Eve, but there were lights in the back
of a few buildings where others celebrated the occasion.

That almost made it real. They were riding in an
ancient sleigh that by any rights shouldn't even be
holding together, freezing on an icy night when they
all should be home in front of their fires drinking egg-
nog and keeping warm, and still they could feel the
air of Christmas.

The dark silhouettes of trees glided by ever faster as
Brian urged the animals on and they responded to the
familiarity of their surroundings. He could feel the anticipation build, an anticipation he had never thought
to feel again. It was Christmas, and they were coming
home.

He looked at Clare to see if she felt it, too, and she
was smiling up at him, grasping his arm, and a surge

of happiness washed through him. He hadn't done everything right. There were mountains of problems ahead. He was terrified he was hoping for too much. But he couldn't contain his eagerness. He was no better than a boy at Christmas.

When they came around the bend and saw the blaze of fire, they all gasped. For a moment Brian nearly panicked. Then Clare cried excitedly, "Dad!" and he realized what he was seeing.

Gavin and Mick were lighting dozens of candle stubs on the cedar by the front porch. They must have had the tree ready, and waited until they heard the sleigh coming to run out and light them in one final blaze of glory. Then they stood there proudly by their accomplishment as the sleigh glided up to meet them.

"Daddy," Letty whispered as Bobby woke and tried to right himself in the seat. Then she was out of the sleigh and running toward her father, burying her face in his chest and leaving him no choice but to hold her with his one arm, tears running down his face as he looked up to the couple still sitting in the sleigh.

"It's okay," Clare whispered, squeezing Brian's hand beneath the quilt. "It's going to be all right." She took a deep breath and steadied Bobby beside her. He was staring at the tree with wide eyes.

"Holy Hannah, I ain't ever seen anything like it," he murmured in complete awe. The candles twinkled and flashed and caught in the breeze, dancing to nature's tune, sending a glorious light to the sky.

"They don't have anything like it in the city," Brian assured him as he climbed down and helped Clare out. And he didn't lie. It didn't matter what fancy gimcracks they used on city trees; none could compare to the grandeur of this one blazing glory against a snowy mountain home. The warmth of those candles seared a place to his heart and opened his eyes wider than they'd ever been. With firm assurance he added, "I bet they don't have anything like it anywhere in the world."

"I bet they don't," Bobby breathed incredulously. He turned to Gavin in wonder. "How'd you do it?"

"Just some wire and all of Sis's saved-up candle stubs." Gavin shrugged modestly. "Just wanted to make sure Santa Claus found us this year."

"He'd better bring some tallow." Clare muttered beneath her breath, but she stared up at the glittering tree with the same wonder as her younger brother.

George and the girls came out from where they had been watching at the window. Brian could see Letty looking eagerly for the twins, but the little rascals would be sound asleep at this hour. She hid her disappointment well as everyone exclaimed over Bobby's black sling and listened to his tale of their mad sleigh ride down the mountain. Clare started to leave his side, but Brian caught her arm and held her, nodding at Mick. Their father was reaching to lift Bobby with his one arm, hugging him close. It wasn't a time for Clare to interfere.

"Merry Christmas, midget," Brian whispered, brushing a kiss over her upturned lips. He wanted to do much more, but not while her family stood by. As it was, Kat and Missy were giggling as they watched.

"You know I can't thank you enough." Clare wrapped her mittened fingers around his gloved ones as she stared up at him. "I don't even have a gift good enough to give you."

"It's not your gifts I want. Now come on, it's time I got you in beside the fire before you turn into an icicle. I don't think anyone is going to get much sleep tonight.''

Perhaps that was true. There weren't many hours before dawn. But when all their heads hit their pillows that night, they slept soundly for what hours of the night remained.

Brian alone stirred restlessly on the narrow pallet that had been made up for him. He had given up on anticipating Christmases long ago. He knew there weren't going to be any surprises under the tree for him. He hadn't even got the gifts for the kids right, and the thought of Bobby's disappointment nagged at him relentlessly. But he still couldn't rid himself of this feeling of anticipation. He knew what he wanted. He had known that when he came here, but the obstacles in his way had been too enormous to expect that he might actually get his heart's desire. But now . . .

Some of the obstacles were still there. Clare would never leave her family. She would never agree to live in the city as Brian had half hoped when he came back. The bond was too tight. She would die of loneliness anywhere else in the world. He might persuade her to leave for a while to see something else of the world, but she would always want to come right back here. And he would never make a farmer or miner or survive in these mountains as her father had, even if he knew that Clare would have him, which he didn't.

So as he lay there on his pallet clutching a box in his hand, he debated the wisdom of giving it to her. He had come prepared with an alternative. He hadn't really expected her to be waiting for him. But the foolishness of that little boy of long ago had gone ahead and hoped, and now Christmas was almost here, and he still didn't know.

Quietly Brian rose from the pallet and pulled on

trousers over his nightshirt. It was almost dawn, and from the sounds of the snores around him, everyone was still asleep. He pulled up his braces and slipped down the ladder from the loft, holding the box in his hand.

The tree had been decorated in haphazard fashion while they were gone. The children had hung the gifts to each other on the lower branches where they could reach easiest, and the lighter ones blew softly in a draft from the window behind it. Gavin had hung the peppermint sticks he had bought once the children had gone off to bed, while Brian laid out the gifts he was contributing. Clare had deposited her neatly wrapped packages under the tree, and even Letty had brought out small bundles wrapped in old newspapers and added them to the growing collection. It was an impressive sight for anyone to see.

Before he could lay his one remaining gift on the pile, Brian caught sight of a piece of flannel and bare feet over by the rocking chair. He walked around the tree to find Letty wrapped in a quilt, rocking and watching him quietly.

"I want to see them as soon as they get up," she whispered at the question in his face.

"I heard them stirring. Let me make up the fire." Setting his package on a lower branch, Brian picked up his boots and pulled them on. He had done it. He had put it there for Clare to find. He didn't know what she would think of it. He would have to talk fast, and that wouldn't be easy with an audience around. But he was a good lawyer. He would state his case convincingly. This was Christmas, after all. Just once, he wanted to celebrate a real Christmas. He tied his boot string so hard it broke.

Pulling on his coat and gloves, he went out to fetch

wood for the fire. There were still sticks by the stove. It wasn't necessary that he drag himself out in the cold. But it gave him an excuse to be up and about. There wasn't a chance that he could sleep any longer.

When he came back, his arms loaded with wood to set on the hearth, he heard the first chatter of small voices. Letty sat up straighter, her fingers clutching nervously in the quilt wrapped around her. Brian edged discreetly toward the door.

"Santa?" One voice whispered from the hallway.

"Go," another urged impatiently.

Someone stumbled and the other giggled. Both voices went "Shhh" at once.

And then they were tumbling into the front room, their brown eyes blinking in wonder at the sight of all the presents heaped in piles around the tree, their fair hair falling into their sleepy faces as they rubbed at their eyes. And their mother was drinking in every moment of it from her chair half-hidden by the tree.

They both saw her at the same time. Jed was the bravest. Pushing ahead of his sister he looked up at this strange adult in the rocker with curiosity. It had been over a year, almost half of his lifetime. Letty sat still, frozen with fear as he examined her in the early morning darkness. He couldn't possibly know her. He had just been a baby when she left. But this was the first Christmas he could remember. Picking up a brightly wrapped package with a tiny bell on the outside, Jed tugged at her skirt.

"Me?"

"Let me see, baby. What does it say on the outside?" Letty reached for the package, and the little boy scrambled up with it, refusing to let it go.

Not to be outdone, Judy grabbed a similarly

wrapped package and clung to it, watching her brother jealously as he rocked in the stranger's lap. "Mama!" she demanded, holding up her arms, the package clutched fiercely in one little fist.

Brian felt a hot drop of liquid on his cheek at the same time as he felt a soft hand grasp his. While Letty cried and pulled the second twin into her lap, he grabbed the first cloak he came to by the door, wrapped it around the warm figure beside him, and pulled her out into the dawn.

He took Clare into his arms and kissed her hard, lifting her from her feet so she couldn't escape. She didn't even try. She wrapped her arms around his shoulders and wriggled closer, until he could feel the pressure of her breasts against his chest and sweet desire shot through him faster than a slug of whiskey.

Brian lifted his head for air and stared down into gray eyes misty with sleep and something else, something that made his insides stir with hope and longing. This wasn't how he wanted to do it, in the cold dawn with neither of them half-dressed, the beard stubble still darkening his face. But he couldn't wait, no more than the twins could wait inside. He could hear their screams of joy as they ripped open their packages.

He wanted that same happiness, and she was so close, right here in his hands.

"I want those to be my babies in there," he whispered madly. "I want that to be you in the rocker. I want every Christmas to be like this Christmas. I want to wake up with you in my arms every day of my life. I don't ever want to leave you behind again, Clare. Please, tell me you don't hate me. Tell me you knew I'd come back for you. Tell me you waited. Lie to me

if you must, Clare. It's Christmas, and I need to hear
you say those words.''

''I waited, you coward,'' she murmured against his
mouth, branding him there as he had branded her long
ago. The pleasure of his words almost exceeded the
pleasure of what he was doing to her body. She tingled
all over, not just where his hands rested, and they were
resting in increasingly daring places. She squirmed a
little closer, and was rewarded by knowing the extent
of his desire. ''I knew you'd come back, you horrible
beast. I thought you'd come back with a fancy wife
and a dozen smart-mouthed kids, and I was going to
kill you. I waited, all right, Brian McGee. You stopped
writing. Not once did you let me know what was going
on. But I waited.''

Those weren't precisely the words of love he wanted
to hear, but they were Clare's words, the Clare he knew
of old, and Brian smiled. At least he could be assured
she felt more than nothing for him.

The front door swung open and Gavin grabbed Brian
by the back of his nightshirt, jerking him away from
his prize. ''I'll break your face later, brother. You'd
better get yourself in here before you both freeze.''

Clare blushed bright crimson, but she sedately
brushed past her brother to join the chaos erupting
inside.

''Watercolors! Oh, Clare, I've got watercolors!''
Missy came dashing across the plank floor, throwing
herself into her sister's arms, the prized paints clutched
triumphantly in her hand.

Clare hugged her, then turned her to face a bemused
Brian, whose eyes were as wide as a child's at the
confusion of rapture around him. ''I think you have
Brian to thank for that particular gift.''

Brian blinked as the child threw herself into his arms

and covered him with kisses when he knelt down to
her level.

"Bwian! Bwian!" A tow-headed twin came swinging a peppermint stick and a wooden pony, practically
knocking him over with his enthusiasm.

After that Brian sat on the floor with the rest of
them. When Clare tried to wander off, he pulled her
down beside him and dumped packages in her lap as
fast as he could find them. He kept the small one in
his hand as she tore into the others.

He watched anxiously as Bobby opened the box with
the ball and mitt. A smile of delight split the boy's
face, and he exclaimed over the sensation they would
make when he got back to school. But Brian could feel
the disappointment. Everyone else was getting what
they wanted. Kat was already wearing her gloves.
George was trying on his boots. Clare was wrapping
a beautiful navy shawl around her shoulders. But
Bobby didn't have his knife.

The knife Clare and Mick had made appeared out
of the next package unwrapped. Bobby's smile faltered a little, but bravely he offered to carve whatever anyone wanted with it. The trinkets that he had
made for everyone were already being unwrapped
and praised, and Brian demanded that he be given a
whistle just like Gavin's as soon as Bobby's arm felt
better. Bobby smiled a little broader over that, but
as the twins crowed over their raggedy dolls and the
girls exclaimed over their new dresses, he began to
withdraw.

"Bobby, you haven't opened everything yet," Letty
called to him, pointing at one last package lost in the
torn newspaper wrappings under the tree.

With a sullen set to his mouth, Bobby sat back down
and pushed the paper around until he found a still un-

wrapped package. He recognized Letty's wrapping, and his expression got a little tighter. Letty had sewed handkerchiefs with neat monograms for the boys and lace for the girls.

"Tom had that. I remembered how much you liked to carve," Letty was chattering nervously. "I know it's not new, and now you've got a grand big knife with a bone handle and everything, but I thought maybe you could use it once in a while."

Bobby's eyes widened as he opened the package and beheld the perfect penknife, one that fit his hand as if it were made for it, one with two blades and carving on the sides and everything else.

Brian felt his insides twisting at the sight of the boy's delight, but he couldn't identify the emotion tearing at him. This was what he had wanted Christmas to be. But he had wanted it for himself, too. He wanted to know the joy of receiving that one special gift, the one made just for him, the only one in the world just like it. And the material things in packages around him weren't what he had in mind.

Catching Clare's hand, Brian pulled her to her feet. Ignoring the stares and calls of their audience, he threw the cloak back around her and pulled her out into the cold sun of a brilliant Christmas day. Making sure she had on her shoes, he led her out into the yard, away from prying eyes and little ears and brothers with fat fists. He walked fast, clenching the package in his pocket with one hand, holding Clare's with the other.

"Brian, have you taken leave of your senses? Where are we going?"

"I'd sit on the porch swing, but we'd probably freeze to it. Let's go to the barn."

He pulled her down the snowy slope and flung open the

barn doors. They should have come in here last night to see if it was true the animals talked. They whinnied and lowed and cackled now. Catching Clare's hand again, Brian brought her out of the wind.

"I can get a job in town," he said hurriedly, before she could question again. "A friend of a professor of mine is looking for a law partner. He's willing to take me on. We would have to live in town. I'm sorry Clare, but I'd have to go to the courthouse or office each day, and I couldn't do it from up here. But we could come up here anytime you like. And the kids could come down. George is almost old enough for high school. He could stay with us. And when the girls are old enough, so could they. If Letty will stay up here, she can take care of them for a spell. Tell me you'll come, Clare. Say you'll be my wife and come live with me. I don't think I want to wait any longer."

Breathless, Clare stared up at him. She had thought him a stranger in his fancy city clothes and starched collars and ties. But he was standing here now in nightshirt and braces and three days' beard, and she knew he was no more a stranger like that than he had been before. He was Brian. She could see it in the pain and eagerness of his eyes, in the hair she had used to pull in anger and drench in laughter. She could feel it in the tremor of his hand as he touched her cheek. He had always wanted things so intensely that he almost shook with the need of it. He had wanted to be somebody. He had wanted to see the world. He had wanted more than he could possibly find in these hills. And he had found them.

And now he had come back for her. He wanted her. He wanted a skinny nobody from the hills who didn't know how to wear a corset or a bustle or any of those other things that ladies in the city wore. He wanted something that she wasn't anymore.

She held his gaze as she answered him slowly. "I'm

not a little girl anymore, Brian. I don't want to fly to the moon or sail the seven seas any longer. I'm a woman who wants a family. I've got one here. I'll admit the thought of living in town and helping the children get their education is tempting, but you'd better be certain that it's me you want to do it with. There are a lot of women out there who would be happy to share Christmas with you. Maybe you better go back to the city and look around a little longer, let Christmas wear off a little bit. If you still want me, I'll be here. I'm not going anywhere else.''

She hadn't said no. Brian clutched the box in his pocket and pulled it out, holding it so firmly in his fist that his knuckles turned white. "It took me years to pay for this, Clare. I picked it out the first Christmas I went to the city. I've been paying them a little bit every week until I got that promotion earlier in the summer. I paid it off then, but I was afraid to come back. I was afraid it was too late. Gavin is the one who persuaded me to come, and I had to see for myself, see if you could possibly still be waiting. He said you weren't married, and I hoped . . .''

He held out the tightly wrapped box and Clare took it, touching the string and the fancy paper that had come from so far away. She could tell just by the look of the paper that it came from somewhere special, a place like they didn't have even in town. She had images of lighted stores with fancy carpets and silent clerks in elegant suits waiting patiently on customers in silks and furs. Just knowing he had been in that kind of place and had still come home to her made her happy.

She pulled off the ribbon and carefully opened the pretty paper. The box she held in her hand was covered in velvet, and she smoothed it with her finger, loving the feel of it. She looked up at Brian in wonder.

"I'll buy you a dress made out of that one day. Now open it.''

Open it. There was more? Gently Clare pushed at the crack until the box snapped open. She stepped back in surprise, and a ray of sun coming through the door caught on the lovely gem inside. It threw out dancing sparkles of light, just like the Christmas tree last night. She gave a gasp of awe.

"Brian, it's beautiful! I've never seen anything like it."

Impatiently Brian pulled the ring from its satin trappings. Holding it up, he slid it on her finger. The fit was perfect, and he breathed a sigh of relief. "That's what I want my wife to wear. Say yes, Clare, and make this the best Christmas of my life."

A ring. He had given her a ring, one he had bought years ago just for her, one he had continued to pay for even though he never wrote. He hadn't forgotten her at all.

A smile more dazzling than the gem on her finger curved Clare's lips upward as she reached to touch Brian's bristly jaw. "Merry Christmas, Brian," she said loudly and clearly, before standing on her toes and touching her lips to his mouth. "But I'm still going to kill you for not writing," she murmured before repeating the trick he'd taught her and touching her tongue to his.

Utterly paralyzed by the innocence and wickedness of that kiss, Brian could only repeat the favor until Clare's warmth and closeness melted into his bones. "Proper gentlemen don't write to ladies until they are properly betrothed," he murmured back, pushing her toward a stall filled with hay. "Should I have directed letters to your father?"

"Not if they were going to say what you're doing right now," Clare gasped against his mouth.

"I'll show you those letters sometime. After I show you what they mean. I signed all of them with love, Clare. Do you think your father would have read that out loud?"

"That's eight years of love we've missed, Brian. How are we ever going to make it up?"

"I'll think of a way." Catching her head between his hands, he proceeded to take the first steps in that direction.

And if the animals could talk on Christmas Day, they would have had a lot to say about this one.

The Gift

by Emily Bradshaw

New Mexico, 1880

PROLOGUE

SHE DIDN'T KNOW that the world could be so cold. The icy wind cut through the thin wool of her dress and shawl, through numb skin and shivering muscle to the very marrow of her bones. The scraggly juniper above where she lay afforded little protection, and the slab of sandstone at her back felt like a block of ice. Pellets of snow whirled in the relentless wind. When she'd first awakened in her tiny niche between juniper and rock, the sleet had stung her face. Now her skin was too numb to feel the assault.

"Where?" Lips paralyzed with cold could scarcely form the whispered question. What was this white world in which she was trapped? She had no memory of cold, of suffocating whiteness that smothered the air and muffled the sound of the wind. The truth was that she had no memory of anything—who she was, where she was, how she had come to be in this hellish place of cold and eye-searing whiteness. Terror clawed her heart at the sensation of being adrift in an unknown universe; such fear was a new experience. Had she ever suffered that painful emotion before?

Unexpectedly, a new discomfort began in her abdomen. Discomfort grew into pain, spreading outward in brutal conquest and overwhelming every other perception. Her muscles tightened and her body convulsed. A gasp of outrage turned into a cry of agony. That such pain could exist was a shock, but her surprise was drowned in torment. Cold and suffocating snow were forgotten. She twisted and instinctively bore down with the horrific pressure. Tears welled in her eyes and froze as they overflowed onto her cheeks.

As pain faded, the world slowly returned to focus—the cold, the wind, the dim shadow of a sandstone bluff rising above her. Her heartbeat thundered in her ears. Above the whine of the wind rattled the sound of her own terrified panting. Her mind roiled in hurt confusion.

After only a few moments of surcease, the pain came again. This time it was worse. The wind snatched her screams and carried them away, but they echoed in her head. She writhed. She pushed. She cried. And finally the pain faded, but she knew instinctively that it would come again. She longed to sink into the nothingness from which she had so agonizingly awakened. Each breath carried a prayer for merciful oblivion, but a small voice from deep in her soul commanded her to stay.

All through the day she struggled with torment. The world seemed to cease spinning, for the cold white that swirled around her neither brightened nor dimmed. The snow fell with insidious persistence. Cold bit into her flesh. She scarcely noticed. All her attention turned inward toward her body's agonizing labor. Instinct knew what it was about. Memory wasn't required to give birth—only strength and patience. That day she discovered that she had both—the first thing she learned about herself.

The child made its appearance in a spatter of fluid

that turned the snow crimson. Another writhing con-
vulsion further defiled the snow with bloody after-
birth. The new mother collapsed back against the cold
sandstone. Nature was neither neat nor efficient. Still,
against all reason she felt a swell of pride and warmth.
She struggled to a sitting position and wrapped the
screaming female child in the woolen shawl that had
covered her own shoulders, then she lay back and cradled the infant to her breast. Poor baby. Such a harsh
introduction to the world. They had both just come to
life, only to find life being sucked from them by icy
wind and relentless snow.

She closed her eyes. Now, mercifully, the snow
seemed very peaceful. Her numb body no longer felt
the bite of the wind. Drowsiness slowed her breathing.
A conviction that the world could be a good and beautiful place settled on her mind. Everything was fine,
that small voice in her soul assured her. The adventure
had just begun. The wind itself seemed to whisper that
she had no need to fear.

She opened her eyes and through the curtain of snow
saw a shadow approaching.

1

December was a hell of a month. At least so far this
year it had been. November, too. The settlers along
the Pecos River in New Mexico Territory might boast
of the beautiful Indian summers of other years, but the
autumn of 1880 was cold enough to freeze a duck's
behind. December was scarcely a week old, and another storm was already howling around the bluffs by
the river and ripping across the Llano Estacado to the
east.

Lucas Stone pulled his bandanna over his nose and

mouth, and hunkered down farther into his saddle. The battered hat pulled down over his brow did little to keep the stinging snow from his eyes and cheeks. One gloved hand held the reins, and the other tried to keep warm in his jacket pocket.

"Stupid son of a bitch!" he muttered into his scarf. After living on these godforsaken plains for thirteen years, he ought to be able to recognize the signs of a storm coming on. This one had developed suddenly, but not so suddenly that he couldn't have seen the signs if he'd been using his fool head. He should have stayed in Santa Rosa. Ginny would have been happy to provide him with a bed and entertainment—for a price.

Luke smiled and felt his lips crack in the cold. Ginny. He could blame her for his lack of attention to the weather. When he should have been looking at the sky and thinking about the way the wind rattled the branches of the tree outside the cathouse window, he'd been working with other parts of his body far removed from his brain. Ginny was a good whore. No two ways about it. Her smile was seductive, the sounds of her passion convincing—carefully rehearsed to make a man feel he was more than just one of a throng of customers. A man couldn't complain about Ginny. The rousing roll she delivered was worth the two bits she charged.

Lately, though, a session with Ginny at the Golden Dove always made Luke feel as empty in some ways as he was sated in others. He would almost rather be struggling through the snow instead of lying on Ginny's cot. The wind was cold, but at least it was clean.

Luke tilted his head to look up at the sky. He couldn't see anything but snow. This storm was going to be a bad one, worse even than the blizzard that had cost him twenty head of cattle three weeks ago. The critters had blundered off a cliff and broken their fool necks—something he could do as well if he didn't get down into the river valley while he still could see where the flat plains dropped away in steep sandstone bluffs to the Pecos. Home was still a long haul, and the snow was going to get worse, not better. He'd be better off riding the river trail than trying to stay up high.

By the time he'd picked his way down to the flats along the river, the storm had worsened. Luke was grateful that his horse knew the trail so well, because Luke himself couldn't see a thing. At least twice a month during the last years, the dun cow pony had followed the trail to Santa Rosa and back. Now he set one foot in front of the other with a confidence that was reassuring. The cold, the singing wind, and the rhythmic rocking of the horse's gait almost lulled Luke to sleep—until a brittle crack followed by a crash made him almost jump from the saddle.

"Damnation! Hammerhead, where're you taking us?" Very dimly through the snow, Luke could see that a dead cottonwood had blown down across the path. If he and Hammerhead had been two seconds farther along, the tree would have smashed them flat. The horse whickered nervously and crow-hopped in objection when Luke kneed it forward and to one side.

"Detour, old friend. Let's go. It's not getting any warmer out here."

Away from the trail, the horse was not as confident. He balked as an outcropping of ice-slicked rock forced them even farther from the familiar track.

"Slow and easy, boy. I can't see where the hell I'm going either." Luke attempted to clear his watering eyes. "What in damnation is that?"

Ahead and to one side, a light wavered through the snow. Or at least it appeared to be a light. Luke told himself it was an illusion. No one with a chipmunk's share of common sense would be out in this weather, and certainly no one would be able to start a fire in this storm.

He urged Hammerhead back toward the river—or where he believed the river was. "Let's find the trail again, boy."

Hammerhead balked. Eyes fixed in the direction of the light, he tossed his head and snorted. Apparently the horse was suffering the same illusion as Luke.

"Let's go!" Luke put a bit more authority into the nudging of his spurs. Hammerhead hopped in the direction he was guided. The horse promptly slid down an icy declivity and almost went to his knees.

"Easy! Easy there! All right, you jug head, we'll go where you want to go."

The only footing that seemed stable led them straight toward the mysterious glow. It was a trick of the snow, just as Luke had thought, for the closer they got the dimmer it shone, finally disappearing altogether. Storms along the Pecos could sometimes make a man see things that weren't there. Then, just as Luke reassured himself that things were back to normal—cold, icy, and miserable, but still normal—the wind began to sound like a baby's thin wail.

Hammerhead snorted and backed away. Luke agreed with him. "I don't like this."

A vagary of the wind momentarily cleared the air. Luke could see that they stood at the foot of a sandstone bluff. Several scraggly junipers clung to the apron of loose rock at the bluff's base, and curled in the meager shelter of one of the junipers lay a woman clutching an infant to her breast.

"Shit and damnation!" were the only words Luke could find to fit the situation.

* * *

She woke to warmth, color, and silence. The world was no longer cold and white, but still it was uncomfortable. A dull ache in her abdomen and between her legs turned into piercing agony at the slightest move.

The pain had not awakened her, though. The silence had. Strident wind no longer whined in her ears or curled around her with icy fingers. All that remained of its howl was a muted whuffing around the sturdy walls that enclosed her, as if the wind were a wolf sniffing at her shelter, trying to gain entrance.

Cautiously she looked around her, grimacing at the agony of propping herself up on her elbows. She was in a room with white plaster walls. A window was tightly shuttered against the wind. Along one wall stood a wardrobe and chest of drawers, and against another was a washstand with a cracked bowl and pitcher and crumpled towels. A glowing lamp stood on the chest of drawers, and a second sat on the small table beside the bed where she lay. The only other item in the room was a beautifully carved cradle.

A cradle. Her child. She almost melted from the warmth that suddenly flooded her soul. Her daughter still lived. How they got to this place was unimportant. What was beyond the closed door that led out of the room was equally unimportant for the moment. Her baby lived.

She struggled from the bed. The icy plank floor made her bare toes curl, and the cool air raised goosebumps on her skin. She ignored the cold, however, and also the acute discomfort of moving. When the cradle was within reach, she stretched out her hand and gently placed a finger on the infant's tiny mouth. The baby grimaced and puckered her lips in an attempt to suck. Blue eyes stared up at her in unfocused confusion.

"Hello my little love."

She lifted the soft blanket that covered the child, and examined fingers and toes—each one perfectly formed and rosy with warmth. Little arms and legs waved in the air, and the mother laughed.

"Uh . . . harumph!"

The sound of masculine throat-clearing shattered the peace. She whirled and almost fell, clutching at the iron bedstead to steady herself. Her first impression was that the intruder was old. His face was weathered to a mahogany that almost matched the dark hair that curled over his brow and spilled over his collar in undisciplined waves. His shoulders filled the door, and she guessed he had to duck to get through the door frame.

A muscle in his cheek twitched. "Are you all right?" He advanced slowly, eyes narrowed in suspicion, as if she were some wild animal that might attack.

"Yes, I believe I'm quite all right."

The man was not old, she decided on closer examination. His hair showed no gray; the suppleness of his movement belonged to a man in his prime. His voice contained the rich, deep tones of maturity without the wavering of age. His eyes, though, seemed to hold the weariness of years.

"You're going to catch pneumonia, if you haven't already." His eyes surveyed her costume expressionlessly. "That shirt is all I had to put on you."

She glanced down at herself. The shirt she wore covered her from neck to mid-thigh. The rest of her was bare. For a moment she didn't comprehend the problem that inspired the man's rigid expression—until the impropriety of her bare legs and feet suddenly struck her like a bolt from Heaven.

She rushed to the bed, grimacing from the sudden movement. "I'm sorry. I wasn't thinking."

He hesitated a moment, his eyes never leaving her. "I shouldn't have come barging in without knocking. Thought you'd still be asleep."

For an awkward moment, they stared at each other while she clutched the bed quilt under her chin. Suddenly he lowered his gaze. Under the bronze of his skin, she detected a darkening flush.

"Where am I, please?"

He looked up again, the flush conquered. "You're on the Stone Ridge Ranch. I'm Lucas Stone. I found you in the storm when I was riding home from town."

"Yes, the storm." A chill gripped her at the memory.

"Did you have a lantern lit out there? Or a fire?"

"No. Why?"

"Nothing." He scowled and shook his head.

"Have I been asleep long?"

"Almost a full day. I tried to give the baby some goat's milk a couple of hours ago. She didn't seem too happy with it."

"I expect I should feed her, then." For the first time she noticed that her breasts were aching and heavy with milk. "If you could just bring her to me."

He moved to the cradle and carefully lifted the baby from the blankets. For such a big man, he seemed very deft at handling such a fragile bundle. The baby girl blew a bubble in his face, bringing a smile that erased the lines of his scowl. He really did have quite a nice face, she decided.

"She's right something." He laid the infant in her waiting arms.

"She is, isn't she?"

"Wouldn't expect such a mite to survive the storm." His glance past the babe to its mother shed doubt upon which of them he meant. "How did you happen to be out in that storm—especially with your time due?"

"I don't know."

He scowled again. It seemed to be his favorite expression.

"I'm sorry to sound so dense, but I don't remember anything. The first thing I recall is waking up with the storm blowing around me."

"What's your name?"

"I don't know that, either."

"Your husband's name? Where you come from?" His scowl grew with each question.

She shook her head regretfully.

"You don't know who you are, where you come from, or even what your name is. Do I have that right?"

She nodded, daunted at his tone. He ran a hand through his unruly hair.

"Well, that's just grand."

"I'm very grateful for your rescuing us, and I'm sorry we're a trouble to you."

He had the grace to look chagrined. "It's not your fault, missus. When this storm dies down, I'll ride into town and ask some questions. Somebody's got to know something about why a woman would be wandering through a blue norther and birthing a baby behind a juniper tree. Your husband's bound to be looking for you."

That hadn't occurred to her. "I don't remember having a husband."

He glanced meaningfully at the babe in her arms. "It appears you do."

"Yes. I suppose."

"Maybe you'll remember something once you get some rest."

She wasn't optimistic about that. Memories of anything other than waking in the storm not only eluded her, but seemed so remote as to have never existed.

The baby grunted and waved little arms in frustration. The man's face softened slightly.

"I should feed her."

His eyes moved from the child back to her, drifting to the fullness of her breasts that not even the quilt could hide. Once again his face grew red beneath its tan, and he jerked his gaze away. "Yeah. And I have chores. If you need anything, just yell. My boy Jacob is in the kitchen mending some harness. I'll tell him to get you something to eat. You look like you could use some feeding up." He turned toward the door.

"Thank you, Mr. Stone."

He glanced back. "Huh?"

"Thank you again for rescuing us from the storm. You're very kind."

"I'm not kind, missus, but I couldn't very well leave you there, could I?"

A smile spread slowly across her face as the door closed behind him. Waking in the storm had terrified her; finding herself in a strange room had been almost as frightening. Now, however, fear and uncertainty had evaporated, even though she remained adrift in an unknown universe. She didn't know who she was or where she'd come from; she didn't know if she had a husband, parents, sisters, or brothers; she didn't even know her name or how old she was, whether she could cook or sew, play the piano, or dance. She found comfort in Lucas Stone, however. Despite her rescuer's gruff manner, there was something about the man that told her she'd found good shelter from the dangers of an uncertain world.

She unbuttoned the top three buttons of the shirt that was made to fit shoulders much broader than hers, and put the babe to her breast. The infant attacked her first real meal with enthusiasm while the new mother leaned her head back and wondered who and what she was.

The day moved slowly by. She peeked out the window once to see the snow eddying around the house. The sound of the wind made her feel warm and secure under the quilts with her child snuggled close to her side. The baby ate, burped, slept, and ate again. Inevitably, the little one's hearty appetite resulted in an equally hearty issue from the nether end. The mother was at a loss what exactly to do, and concluded that this baby was undoubtedly her first. Even to the most inexperienced, however, it was clear that clean diapers were called for.

"Hello?" she called out. "Mr. Stone?" Lucas had said that his son was mending harness in the kitchen. Would he still be there? "Hello?"

The baby began to yowl. The little one didn't like a soiled behind and had set about letting the world know about it.

A knock on the door heralded the arrival of help. The door eased open to admit a boy who was all arms, legs, and jutting elbows. Freckles spilled over his nose and sprinkled his cheeks, and two cowlicks swirled dark brown hair that was as unruly as his father's. His smile revealed a missing front tooth.

"Can I get you something, missus?" At her curious look, he introduced himself. "I'm Jacob. Pa told me I should get you something to eat when you're ready, but you were so quiet in here, I thought you was sleeping. You and the baby.'' His curious gaze went to the infant, who all but drowned out his words with her shrieks. He grinned. ''Sounds like you're awake.''

''I'm afraid I must bother you for some clean swaddling.''

The boy inched closer and wrinkled his nose. ''Oh. Yeah.''

''Could you ask your mother if she has anything I could use?''

''Got no ma, but there's clean dishtowels in the kitchen. Looks like that's what she just messed in.''

''I'm sure that would be fine.''

No mother. She was hoping there would be a woman around.

''There's some stew left in the cookshack. I could build a fire in the stove and heat some for you.''

''That sounds wonderful. The dishcloths first, though. I'm afraid the baby doesn't take to being soiled.''

''Yeah. I can hear. Be right back.''

Jacob fetched the cloths and then helped the new mother pin one of them securely around the infant's little bottom. He gamely carried away the soiled towel—holding it at arm's length—and returned fifteen minutes later with a steaming bowl of greasy beef stew. She tried not to grimace when she took the first bite.

''We got plenty of that if you want more.''

''This is fine.'' She all but choked.

''Pa says Skillet's stew is u . . . unique.''

''Skillet?''

''He wrangles the grub around here.''

''Oh.'' She sought a subject other than the terrible food. ''And you mend harnesses?''

''Huh? Oh, yeah. Since it was so cold in the barn, I brought the rig into the kitchen. It's got a couple of places that are near worn through. My pa says putting off mending a harness is just inviting trouble to ride along with the wagon.''

''You're not in school?''

''We ain't got no school around here closer than Santa Rosa, an' that's a long haul. Pa needs me around here. He says I'm better than some of the cowboys at workin' the herd, even though I'm only nine. An' he gives me lessons at night sometimes. I know how to read and do sums, and I can recite the hundred and twenty-first and the twenty-third psalms by heart.''

''That's very impressive.''

Jacob seemed content to take a break from his harness work and sit beside the bed to watch the baby.

''Was it the dirty pants that made her squall?''

''I imagine so. She's quiet enough now.''

''Do you have any other kids?''

''I don't think so.''

''You don't know?'' his eyes widened.

''I'm afraid not. I can't seem to remember anything before waking up in the storm.''

''Gee.'' He was silent for a while, then observed. ''She's pretty ugly, in a cute kinda way. Look at her yawn. She's got bubbles comin' out of her mouth.''

''Do you have any little brothers or sisters?''

''Naw. My ma took off when I was a little kid. She went back to St. Louis to live with my grandma.''

''Doesn't she ever visit you?''

''She's dead. Got killed in a carriage accident a couple of years ago. Grandma wrote us a letter telling us.''

''I'm so sorry.''

''Pa says it wasn't Ma's fault that she left us. He says ladies don't take to life in New Mexico. It's either too cold or too hot, too dry or too wet. When the sun's

out, it burns your skin till it flakes right off, and when
the clouds roll in, it either rains till the river floods or
snows till the cows freeze to death. Pa says there ain't
no room out here for frills or anything soft. Pa says
the only women who survive out here are jezebels or
ladies who're tougher than old shoe leather.''

"Your pa seems to have some pretty set notions."

"He knows what he knows. That's what Pa says."

The baby uttered a tentative cry and flailed one arm.

"Do you think she's hungry? Maybe she smells the
stew."

"I don't think she wants the stew."

"Could I pick her up? I'd be real careful."

"Of course you may pick her up."

"I helped deliver a foal once. I tore off the sack and
everything. It was a real mess, but it grew up to be a
real dandy of a cutting horse." Gingerly, Jacob picked
up the squirming infant.

"Careful of her head, Jacob. She's not strong
enough to hold it up herself."

"Yeah." He carefully slipped his hand behind the
baby's head and cradled her in his arms. "I think she
likes me. See the way she stopped her fidgeting."

"I'm sure she likes you."

"What's her name?"

"To tell the truth, I haven't named her yet. I don't
even know my own name."

"Oh. That must feel real strange. Maybe you'll remember it soon."

She smiled at his earnest sympathy. "Maybe."

"We could think of a name for the baby." Jacob sat
down on the bed, still holding the infant, and spent
several thoughtful moments just looking at the child.
"You know," he finally said, "it wouldn't be too bad
to have another kid around here. There ain't no kids

closer than the Marshall place, an' the Marshall kids are mostly brats. At least that's what Pa says. He says they don't have no manners and can't do a solid day's worth of work without whinin' about it.

"Course this baby ain't rightly a kid yet. And she's a girl, too, which ain't good, I guess."

"Some people do think that girls have their uses in the world."

"I reckon you're right. Maybe you could name her Sarah. That's my grandma's name. Well, nope. I guess not. Look at her frown. We'll have to think of something else."

"Maybe we can think tonight and then talk about the names we've thought of tomorrow."

"Yeah. Sure."

"But right now I think the baby needs to eat."

"Yeah. I gotta go anyway. If I don't have that harness mended by the time Pa comes in from fixin' the stalls in the barn, Pa'll skin me."

"Thank you for helping with the baby."

"Sure." He carefully placed the infant in her mother's arms. "I hope you can stay around for awhile, missus. It's different havin' a lady here. And a baby, too."

"Thank you, Jacob."

"If you need anything else, just give a holler. Skillet's fixing hash for supper, and it's better'n his stew. I'll bring you some of that later. Bye."

She put the baby to her breast as Jacob softly closed the bedroom door. The little one sucked nosily and wasn't distracted in the least when her mother fondly touched a finger to her cheek.

"Perhaps Jacob will think of a name for you, my little love."

She only wished she could think of a name for herself. Her real name. Her family name. Her husband's name, if she had a husband. And how she had come to be lying frozen and giving birth under a juniper tree in the middle of a snowstorm.

Lucas Stone rarely had trouble sleeping. He had slept on the hard ground with only a saddle for a pillow and a saddle blanket to protect him from the snow. He had slept in a room above a saloon, oblivious to a fight in full swing in the barroom below. He had slept in barns undisturbed by the whuffing and stamping of horses and mules, under a wagon in a torrential rainstorm, and in beds that made the stony ground seem comfortable in comparison.

Tonight, though, in his own bed, on a comfortable straw-ticked mattress, he couldn't sleep for the life of him. He kept thinking of the woman who lay in a bedroom just on the other side of the kitchen.

She was a pathetic little waif—no name, no memory, no knowledge of family or home, a rag doll of a Madonna with only a bloodied wool dress and a day-old baby to call her own. Did she truly have no memory, or did she simply hide her past? If she had a husband, what kind of husband would let his wife get into such circumstances? If her husband was alive . . .

Luke turned over and pulled the blankets up around his shoulders. He rearranged his pillow and pounded it into place with unnecessary vigor. Unanswered questions made him restless, and the woman herself disturbed him. She wasn't the kind of woman who got a man's blood to running, but there was something about her that kindled a softer, deeper response. The eyes were what did it, Luke concluded as he mentally cataloged her appearance and manner. Bright green and too big for her elfin face, they looked right through a man as though she could see to the depths of the soul. Those eyes fit right in with her smile. The woman didn't have much to smile about, heaven knew, but when she did smile, her whole face took on a glow that was beyond physical beauty. A man forgot her pale face, drab hair, and rather ordinary features when he saw that smile.

"Damnation!" Luke cursed aloud into the cold darkness. He was acting like a green boy. He should know better than to let a female get under his skin. Women and all the frills that went with them were nothing but trouble at a place like Stone Ridge. He had no time for this nonsense. That woman and her baby had to go as soon as he could get them out of here. Why did it have to be him who found them?

Closing his eyes, determined to sleep, he had almost drifted off when a sound awakened him. A soft thump followed by a muffled "Oooof!" brought him fully awake. In a swift economy of motion, he swung out of bed and reached for the pistol that hung from a peg above the bed. What he found stumbling through the dark kitchen, however, didn't necessitate gunplay.

He lit a lamp, and the girl squinted against the sudden light. She clung to the pinewood railing of the stairs that led to the loft where Jacob slept.

"What do you think you're doing? You shouldn't be out of bed."

She looked at the pistol in some alarm. He put it on the kitchen table. "Sorry. We still get occasional visits from Apaches out here. When I hear someone creeping around the house in the middle of the night, I assume the worst."

"I didn't mean to wake you. I"—she flushed a bright pink—"I was looking for a way to the privy."

From the pained look on her face, she must have

been putting off this particular problem all day. Wasn't it just like a woman to be so silly about such a matter? He pointed to the pantry that led from the kitchen to the back door. "Go through there and down the porch steps to the left. The outhouse is about fifty feet from the house, against the bluff."

"Thank you."

The woman didn't look as though she could make it to the pantry, much less the outhouse.

"Go on back to your room. I should've given you a chamber pot. I'll get the one that's under my bed. I never use the thing, anyway."

She still clung to the rail, as if movement pained her. A tear dribbled down her cheek. Luke feared a flood was about to follow. "Now, missus, there's no need for that."

"I . . . I'm sorry. It's just that . . . that I'm so loathesomely dirty. I'm still caked with mud and . . . and"—she gestured despairingly to where her legs were streaked with dried blood.

"You must be feeling stronger if you're worried about a little thing like dirt." That was the wrong thing to say, Luke realized instantly, for tears began to fall in earnest now. Worse still, the woman appeared ready to collapse. "Don't turn into a water pump on me. Let's get you back to bed, then I'll fetch the slop jar and heat some water so you can clean up."

She didn't protest when he picked her up, bare legs and all, and carried her back into the room where her baby slept peacefully. He couldn't help but notice that her legs were long and slender, even though she herself scarcely came up to his chin. They were also firm and shaped just exactly as a woman's legs were supposed to be shaped.

Luke left her in privacy to use the chamber pot while

he heated water. Leave it to a woman to insist on being clean in the middle of the night; but he granted that after all the girl had been through, she had a right to be a bit strange for a few days.

When he returned with a basin of hot water and clean towels, the girl was bending anxiously over the cradle. Her expression of absolute adoration as she gazed down at the child sent an arrow straight to Luke's heart. That was how a woman was supposed to look at a child. An image of his own beautiful Maggie came into his mind—Maggie, who had hated New Mexico and finally hated the husband and baby who held her there so much that she had deserted them both.

He cleared his throat awkwardly. She looked up and smiled one of her heart-stopping smiles.

"Your water."

"Thank you so much. I'm sorry to be such a trouble."

"That's all right." For a moment Lucas thought of offering his help. Though she'd regained her composure, she looked almost too weak to wash herself. Still, women were skittish about such things, and he'd just as soon keep his distance from this female. "Holler when you're through, and I'll take the basin away."

"Thank you."

He beat a grateful retreat and went to warm himself by the stove. Ten minutes later, she called out in her soft voice. When he stepped into the room she was lying in bed, a clean, rosy glow to her face and a sheen to her wet hair, which wasn't drab at all, but an intriguing shade of gold that was almost silver. The room smelled sharply of the lye soap he'd given her.

The sight that made Luke stop in his tracks, though, was not the girl's fine features, or the luminous green

eyes, or her silvery hair. It was the way she held the
baby to her breast, which was modestly concealed by
a towel. He remembered Jacob at Maggie's breast, and
how Maggie had been so concerned that nursing would
make her breasts sag. From the radiance in this waif's
eyes as she looked down at her baby, Luke guessed
that she hadn't given sagging breasts a single thought.
Suddenly, absurdly, he wanted to tell her about the joy
he'd known when Jacob had been born. He bit back
the words before they were spoken. The girl was a
stranger without a name or a past, and in a few days
she would be out of his life forever.

"Are you through with the water?" he asked gruffly.

"Yes. Thank you." Her voice was warm and silky.
It was indecent for a woman nursing a baby to have
such sensual appeal. Damn her.

Without another word, he turned and left the room.

2

The baby's whimpering woke her early. Beyond the
window shutters, the world was still dark and silent.
The plank floor felt like ice on her feet as she got out
of bed, lit a lantern, and bent over the cradle.

"Hungry again, my love? And wet, too, I see. It's
a good thing Mr. Stone doesn't begrudge you his dishcloths. I can see I'll have to do a wash today, or you'll
have to lie here bare as God made you."

After nursing and snugging the baby back into a
warm quilt, she tied a blanket around her waist to serve
as a skirt and ventured through the bedroom door.
Cleaning herself had gone far toward making her feel
better. She was restless to be up and doing, to see for
herself what kind of world she'd been catapulted into.

The bedroom opened directly into a large kitchen.

Along one wall, stairs led up to a loft. Across from
the stairs was a wide bank of windows above a sink
and hand pump. The rest of the room's wall space was
utilized by a wood stove, cupboards, and shelves. Iron
pots, skillets, and a Dutch oven were stacked haphazardly on the shelves along with cutting knives, scattered tinware, and chipped china plates and bowls. A
rectangular pine table with attached benches sat in the
center of the room. On top of the table were spread
the leather straps of a harness—presumably the harness Jacob had been repairing.

"Oh my!" Hands on her hips, she looked for some
order in the mess. "This will never do!" The stove
was caked with soot. The plank floor, shelves, and
table boasted a layer of grime that would make the
devil himself shudder. No wonder that Mr. Stone had
so many clean dish towels lying around; he never used
any of them.

"Well, there's no time like the present!" She hung
her lantern on a hook attached to the rafters, rolled up
the sleeves of Lucas Stone's shirt, and set to work preparing breakfast. Cooking a good breakfast was the
least she could do after the kindness the Stones had
shown her. Serious cleaning could come after the meal,
she told herself. If Mr. Stone and his son had survived
this pigsty up until now, one more meal eaten in it
wouldn't kill them.

Kindling and split firewood were stacked by the
stove. She started a fire and put water on to boil for
coffee. A tin canister on one of the shelves contained
flour thick with weevils, so she searched the pantry for
fresh. The pantry did not have fresh flour; neither did
it have very much of anything else. A tin of unsavory
lard and a few canned goods—beans, soup, tomatoes,
corn, and condensed milk—had gathered a thick layer

of dust. A small slab of bacon hung next to a canister of salt that was almost empty, and the only sugar was a faint trail of white that showed the tracks of numerous insects.

Undaunted, she tried to make the best out of what little was on hand. A strainer served to separate weevils from flour, and with the addition of salt, lard, and water she was able to mix up a passable biscuit dough. With biscuits ready to go in the oven, she sliced the slab of bacon and set it to sizzling in a cast iron skillet. While the meat cooked, she put the biscuits in the oven, then took down another skillet to make a thick gravy from the bacon drippings, rescued flour, salt, and condensed milk. She hummed softly as she worked.

"What's this?"

Startled by Luke's voice, she ended the humming with a tuneless squeak. "Mr. Stone. I thought you were asleep."

As he surveyed her attire, his mouth twitched in something that was almost a smile. "I can see we're going to have to get you something to wear. Can you sew as well as cook? I think my wife left some bolts of material here."

"Sew? I don't know. I didn't realize I could cook." She smiled as she surveyed the bubbling gravy and sizzling bacon. "I see that I can, though. When I started, I didn't even think about it."

"We usually eat in the chow hall with the men." He peeked into the oven. Nose twitching from the aroma, his expression softened. "If those biscuits taste as good as they smell, I'd say that Skillet could learn a thing or two from you."

"Skillet. He's . . . Jacob called him your . . . your grub wrangler."

"He tries his best."

"Gee! What do I smell?" Also summoned by the aroma of bacon and coffee, a sleepy-eyed Jacob half stumbled down the stairs from the loft. "Breakfast?" he said hopefully.

"You'd think you never got fed around here."

Jacob grinned sheepishly at his father's halfhearted reproach.

"Put the harness where it belongs, son. It looks like we're going to use the table for something other than a workbench this morning."

The windows were just beginning to light with a rosy glow when she set platters of bacon and biscuits with gravy on the table along with a fresh pot of coffee. Luke and Jacob ate in silent concentration, a tribute to both the cooking and the hearty appetites engendered by the cold morning. Through the silence, however, she could feel the father's eyes bore into her when he thought she wasn't looking at him.

"I couldn't find any sugar for the coffee, Jacob. I'm sorry."

"That's all right, ma'am." The boy sat a bit taller. "I take mine straight, just like the rest of the men. You make decent coffee, ma'am."

She smiled at how seriously grown-up the boy sounded. "Thank you, Jacob. Mr. Stone, would you like more biscuits and gravy?"

"Don't mind if I do. I gotta admit, your cooking's an improvement over Skillet's."

"I'm glad you're enjoying the meal."

"You didn't have to get up and cook, you know. I expect you're still feeling poorly."

"I'm feeling much better, and cooking you a meal is little enough to repay your kindness. I am sorry about last night. I didn't mean to wake you. It's just that I woke up feeling so filthy. I find that I don't tolerate dirt very well.''

Luke grimaced. "That gives you a lot in common with just about every other decent lady of my acquaintance, so there's no need to be sorry about it. Most women come out to the territory and discover they can't tolerate the dirt or the Indians or the snow in winter or the sun in the summer.''

His voice was suddenly sharp with bitterness, and she was glad that Jacob chose that moment to interrupt.

"Pa, we gotta think of a name for the baby. The missus said we could.''

"A mother ought to have the right to name her own baby, Jacob.''

"But she told me I could, didn't you, ma'am?''

"Yes, I did.''

"We can't name her Melinda, because the Marshalls' girl is a Melinda, and she's a real pest.'' He looked thoughtful, as if giving Melinda the benefit of the doubt. " 'Course, maybe all girls are like that. She's the only real girl I know.''

Luke smiled ruefully. "Son, there's not a female in the world who isn't a pest at times.''

Jacob shrugged. "The baby needs a really pretty name. She's sorta ugly now, but I'll bet she grows up pretty. Look at her ma.''

Luke's eyes darted toward the baby's mother, clung there for a moment, then shied away.

"Carolina!'' Jacob said with sudden enthusiasm. "We could call her Lina for short. That's a pretty name.'' His face lit with a smile. "Do you like that name, missus?''

"It's very nice.''

"Can we name her that?''

"I think we should."

Jacob was on a roll and reluctant to quit. "How about a name for you, ma'am? You don't remember your name, and we can't keep calling you missus."

"Jacob," Lucas chided. "Don't be disrepectful."

"That's all right." She smiled. "You're quite correct, Jacob. Everyone should have a name."

"Delilah! Preacher Tolliver told me a story once about a lady named Delilah, and how she was really pretty and had this beau named Sam—"

"Jacob! That's enough! Delilah isn't a proper name for the missus, here."

"How 'bout Mary, then. It's almost Christmas, and Mary had her baby at Christmastime. She almost had to have hers outside just like the missus had Lina."

She laughed softly. "Likening myself to Mary would be a bit presumptuous, don't you think?"

"Eliza," Luke offered unexpectedly. He looked a bit startled himself by his contribution.

"Eliza's a beautiful name."

Luke buried his gaze in his plate of biscuits. "I once had a schoolteacher named Eliza. She was a good woman."

The name felt right, somehow. Not familiar exactly, but right. "I like it. Eliza will do very nicely. Thank you."

"No thanks needed. It's just a name."

"But a name is very important. Don't you agree? Already I feel less lost. I'm not a nameless nobody. I'm Eliza."

"You don't have a last name, though," Jacob complained. "I know! You can be Eliza Stone! We can give her our last name, can't we, Pa?"

For a moment Luke's face froze. He darted a glance at Eliza, then looked quickly away. "No, son. That wouldn't be right. A last name comes from family, and Eliza's family wouldn't like it if she took somebody else's last name.''

''But she doesn't have a family.''

''She has a family somewhere. Curly Simms is taking the wagon into Santa Rosa today. He'll ask around about Eliza's folks. Or her husband. She'll be back with her own people soon.''

''Oh.'' Jacob sounded disappointed. ''Well maybe her husband will let her and Lina visit us sometimes.''

''If Eliza's husband has the sense God gave a bluejay, he'll take his wife and baby to St. Louis or San Francisco where ladies can lead the lives they were meant to lead—where they don't get lost in snowstorms or fear getting scalped by Apaches.''

Jacob's face fell.

''Son, don't get too attached to that little baby. It's not a puppy that you can keep. And neither is Eliza. They need to go someplace where they can be safe and comfortable. This is a hard land, and making something of it requires us to work hard and be strong, and sometimes give up the nice things that other people have. But it's a land that's worth that price.''

''Yes, Pa. I know.''

''Would you like to go into Santa Rosa with Curly and help him pick up supplies?''

''Yeah. I guess.''

''Then you'd better run on. Curly won't be waiting for the sun to get much higher.''

''Okay.'' The boy turned to Eliza. ''Can I look in on Lina before I go?''

''Of course you may.''

Jacob bounced up.

''Where's your manners, son? We're not eating in the chow hall.''

"Uh . . . thank you for breakfast, Eliza. May I be excused?"

"Yes. Of course." She watched him stop abruptly before her bedroom door and tiptoe into the room.

"He's a fine boy, Mr. Stone."

"Call me Lucas. Or Luke."

"He worships you, you know."

Luke smiled crookedly, "I'm the only one he has to worship. His ma left before he was old enough to walk."

"I'm sorry. That must have been dreadful for both of you."

He shrugged. "I guess she had her reasons. Life out here's hard on a woman. She was from St. Louis and used to having nice things and being done for. I tried to fix the place up so it'd be a house a lady would be proud of, and she tried her best to like it here, but I think the very loneliness of the place drove her wild."

Eliza couldn't imagine how a woman could leave her own child behind. Neither could she understand any woman giving up Luke Stone. He was a hard man. Stern. Not given to flowery words. He felt deeply, however. Eliza could see in his eyes—when he allowed her to read them—how deeply he felt. Perhaps he felt so deeply about the things that mattered to him—things like his son and his ranch—that he held his feelings in check for fear they would rule him. But anyone who cared to look could see through his curt pretense.

"Jacob seems to have grown into a fine boy in your care."

Luke smiled, his pride in Jacob showing through his reserve. "He's got a good head on his shoulders."

"He's a very serious child."

"It's a world where a man has to be serious to survive." At her hesitant silence, he continued. "The kindest thing a father can do for his son is to teach him to recognize the world as it is, not as he wants it to be or thinks it should be.''

''A very sensible attitude. But it would be a shame—don't you agree?—to concentrate so hard on survival that one fails to enjoy the very things we survive for.''

''What things are those?''

''Things like a beautiful morning at the end of a storm, a friendship, a child that tugs at your heart, a special holiday with friends gathered around . . .''

His smile was cynically amused. ''You amaze me. Of all the people I know, it seems that you have the least reason for such cheerfulness. Right now you don't have a home or even a name. What are you finding to lighten the load of the world?''

''For one, I have a beautiful, healthy daughter sleeping in your spare bedroom. For another''—her mouth curved upward in gentle humor—''I have a beautiful new name. And if those weren't enough to convince me of kind fortune, when I was in very dire straits and near to freezing, I was found by a man good enough and generous enough to take me in.''

He looked away, and Eliza could see a muscle twitch along the strong line of his jaw. After a long silence, he grimaced. ''I'm sorry about the place being so dirty.'' He looked at the mess rather than her. ''Since Maggie left and Jacob grew big enough to walk on his own feet, we've been chowing down with the hands. We didn't expect a guest.''

Eliza was momentarily nonplussed by the abrupt change of subject, then yielded to the switch. Luke Stone obviously wasn't comfortable with his own kindness. ''Then that's why the pantry is so empty,'' she said lightly.

''I'm surprised you found enough to make a meal.''

"I suppose somewhere in my past I learned to make do. If you'll ask your Mr. Simms to pick up some food staples in town, I'd be glad to cook for you and Jacob while I'm here."

"There's no need. Like I said, we usually eat with the hands."

"I assure you, I needn't spend all day in bed. I'm well on the way to recovery. And I enjoy cooking." She laughed softly. "Only one of the many things I have to learn about myself."

He refused to meet her eyes. "If you enjoy it."

"I'll give you a list of what's needed. Do you have a paper and a pen?"

Eliza watched Luke get up and disappear through the living room door. She had no right to feel so protective and possessive about this man. He was not hers, and she certainly wasn't his. For all she knew, she might have a husband waiting for her, wondering what had happened to his wife. Or she might have no husband, and be a woman of such low character that she could never hope to be part of the life of a good man like Lucas Stone.

Against all reason, however, he did inspire imprudently strong feelings within her. His smile, rare though it was, stabbed clear through to her heart. A lock of mahogany hair hanging askew over his brow called to her to brush it back, and an occasional, quickly hidden gleam in his deepset eyes filled her with a quivery warmth that was most certainly improper for a new mother who might well be a married woman. Eliza wondered suddenly if she might indeed be a tart. For these unseemly feelings didn't feel wrong to her. To the contrary, they felt right. Very right.

Before Eliza could ponder this further, Luke returned to the kitchen with paper, pen, and an inkwell. "Can you read and write?" he asked.

She lifted one brow. "I don't know. Let's find out."

As if having a name of her own had revitalized her, Eliza felt full of energy for the rest of the day. She tackled the grime in the kitchen with a liberal application of elbow grease and a bottle of vinegar that she found in the pantry. After many hours of scrubbing, the kitchen shone, and she transferred her attention to the living room. The largest room of the house, it was brightened by banks of windows on three sides. The fourth wall was lined with cupboards and shelves on which were haphazardly stacked several editions of the Sears and Montgomery Ward catalogs, a large Bible inscribed with births, deaths, and marriages of three generations of Stones, a collection of books on animal husbandry, veterinary medicine, dryland farming, and, curiously enough, a dusty volume of Shakespeare's poetry. Eliza smiled when she came across this last treasure. It had probably belonged to the late Mrs. Stone, but perhaps not. She could imagine Luke Stone reading such a thing. Not recently, perhaps, but sometime before he had decided that the world was a serious place that had no room for such frills.

Eliza managed to clean the living room and also measure the windows for curtains she planned to make from the cloth Mrs. Stone had left behind years ago. Luke had showed her the bolts that morning, telling her to make herself some decent clothing from the material if she found that she could sew as well as she cooked. He had no use for the fancy muslins, wools, laces, broadcloths, and ginghams. Eliza did plan to fashion herself a dress or two to replace the britches and shirt Lucas had given her from Jacob's wardrobe, but she certainly didn't need all of the material. Curtains would go a long way toward making the Stone Ridge ranch house look more like a home, she decided. Even if she was here only a few days, she should have time to make some up—if she knew how to sew. Once the living room was clean and she sat down with needle and thread in hand, she discovered that she did.

In between sewing and cleaning, Eliza cared for Lina, boiled and washed the dish towels that served as her daughter's diapers, and fixed a supper of beans, bacon, and biscuits. As the sun approached the western horizon, Luke came into the house, his nose leading the way. "I thought I smelled something good." He made a beeline to the stove, where a large pot of beans simmered. Then he noticed the rest of the kitchen gleaming in the late afternoon sun. "Lord Almighty! Look what you've done! I thought you were resting."

"I don't feel at all like resting."

"Is that why you're the color of a sheet?"

She did feel a bit weary, Eliza admitted. And the soreness in her lower parts was starting to drag her down. Perhaps she had overestimated her stamina.

"I don't think you're human," Luke mumbled as he ladled himself a dishful of beans.

"What did you say?"

"I said you're not human. Ordinary women stay in bed two weeks after childbirth. Maggie did."

"I suppose that some women have less difficulty bearing children than others. Maybe I'm a natural-born mother."

"Maybe you are." The usual dark flintiness of his eyes softened as his mouth curved slowly into a smile. "You might wash those dirt smudges off your face before you eat."

She scrubbed self-consciously at her face, warm from the look he was giving her.

"You're just making it worse. Here." He took a basin from it's nail on the wall and filled it from the kettle on the gleaming stove. "Go have yourself a good warm wash. Look's like you've scrubbed everything in the house except yourself. I'll stick those biscuits in to cook while you're gone."

Warmed by his apparent concern, she took the basin with a smile. "I'll be right back."

"Take your time."

Eliza felt his eyes follow her to the bedroom door.

The next day foreman Curly Simms and Jacob returned from Santa Rosa with the food staples Eliza had listed. She set about the task of organizing the pantry and fixing a dinner whose aroma inspired Jacob to hang around the house like a hungry puppy. When supper was served and the three of them sat down to corned-beef hash, lima beans with bacon, and fresh-baked corn bread, Lucas fixed his son with a stern eye. "Jim was out by the barn digging the postholes for the new corral when I rode up. He was alone."

Jacob's gaze dropped to his plate. "Yes sir."

"What've you been doing all day?"

"I been helping Eliza hang the curtains she made. An' I watched Lina while Eliza made supper."

"That was kind of you to help Eliza, son. And it's mighty kind of Eliza to be doing for us like she is. But you told Jim you'd help him with that corral."

"Yes sir."

"After supper you go ask him what you can do, you hear?"

"Yes sir."

After Jacob was excused from the table, Eliza apologized. "I didn't mean to keep him from his chores. He meant well."

Luke smiled and shook his head. "He generally does."

"He seems very young to be carrying a man's burden."

"People grow up fast out here."

"But everyone has to be allowed to be a child sometimes. Especially children, but grown-ups as well. Don't you agree?"

"Is that part of your outlook on appreciating the good things in life?"

"They're put here to be appreciated."

Luke took a final swipe at the gravy on his plate, put down his fork, and reached for his hat—an accoutrement he seemed to doff only at the table. Eliza irreverently wondered if he wore his hat even to bed, and immediately chided herself for unseemly thoughts.

"Do you feel up to a tour of this place?" He was deft at changing subjects, it seemed, when their conversation threatened the wall of his reserve.

Eliza immediately brightened. "I've been looking forward to seeing what's outside these walls. Jacob has given me a glowing description of your ranch."

The Stone Ridge Ranch lived up to Jacob's description. Eliza had no comparison from which to judge, but the place seemed admirable in both its self-contained efficiency and its rustic beauty. The house, built of sandstone blocks mortared with native clay, looked as much a part of the Pecos River valley as the bluffs that rose from the river to the plains. Cottonwood trees stretched bare gray branches over the tile roof. Eliza pictured it as shady and cool in the summer. With an unexpected pang of longing, she wished she could be here to see the trees sprout spring buds that would unfold to summer green.

With Lina sleeping contentedly in her arms, Eliza followed Luke to the corrals, barn, smithy, smoke-house, and the cellar where the smoked meats and vegetables were stored. (She made a note of this last for future meals.) She surveyed the cookshack, which was every bit as grime-coated as the kitchen used to be, and peeked into the empty bunkhouse and chow hall, where the ranch hands slept and ate. Twelve men, including cowboys, a blacksmith, two horse wran-glers, and a cook worked on the ranch. Each cowboy had a remuda of thirteen or fourteen horses, Lucas explained to her, which accounted for the sizable herd of horses grazing through the crusty snow in the pas-tures.

"But where are your cattle?" she finally asked.

"On the open range for miles around. Out here in this dry land each animal requires a big piece of land to graze on."

They had stopped in the barn, where Eliza sat down to catch her breath. Lucas had been trying to say something to her during the whole tour and had not quite gotten it out; it lay waiting beneath his casual explanations of the working of the ranch. Eliza could guess what was bothering him.

"What did Mr. Simms discover about me?"

Luke was leaning on a stall door, stroking the nose of a white-faced mare. Her words seemed to startle him out of deep thought.

"I knew you would have said something if the news was good, Lucas, so I hesitated to ask. But I must know. What did he find out?"

"Nothing." Luke sighed, pushed away from the stall, and gave her his customary scowl. "Nobody remembers seeing a woman of your description in town. Nobody's been asking for a lost wife or daughter or mother. Nothing.''

Somehow, she'd known what the answer would be. ''Maybe I don't really exist,'' she said, almost to herself.

''Don't be foolish.'' He grabbed her hand, his face intense with feeling. ''You are real. You have a history, a family, probably a husband. Somewhere, someone will know who you are.'' For a moment his gaze seemed to bore through her, as if the scrutiny could tell him who and what she was. Eliza had almost lost herself in his eyes when he abruptly and self-consciously dropped her hand.

''It's getting dark,'' he said brusquely. ''Time to go in.''

Night had fallen when the parade began. Jim Cruz was the first cowboy to come to the house. His excuse was a question about the new corrals. The men sat in the living room discussing the details of painting the corral posts with creosote when Eliza brought them coffee and biscuits. ''Ma'am, Jacob's been singing praises of your new little one,'' Jim said to Eliza. Sitting on the window seat with his lesson in grammar, Jacob gave them a quick grin and returned to his studying. ''I suppose she's sleeping, is she?'' Jim said diffidently.

''You'd be welcome to peek in at her if you like, Mr. Cruz.''

''Thank'ee, ma'am. It's been awhile since I seen a sight as purty as a freshly minted baby.''

After he'd looked his fill, the cowboy turned to Eliza, hemmed and hawed for a few seconds, then reached into his jacket and took out a rough-carved little rocking horse. "I made this when I heard we had a little one in the house."

"Why, Mr. Cruz. How kind of you!"

"T'ain't nuthin', really. I carve all the time jest to have something to do with my hands."

"You're quite talented."

He flushed fiery red.

Lucas watched with a crooked smile as the cowboy said his good-byes and left. "That man once spent two years in the hoosegow for shooting another man in a poker game. He was eating out of your hand like a puppy dog."

"Don't be silly. He was just being polite."

"Jim Cruz doesn't know the meaning of polite. Believe me."

Eliza gave him an imp's grin. "Women and children are known to have a very civilizing influence on wild men."

He eyed her quizzically, then they both laughed. Eliza decided Luke's laugh was as nice as his smile.

The rest of the evening saw a parade of five cowboys, the blacksmith, and one horse wrangler call on Luke for one reason or another. Each visitor looked longingly toward the kitchen until Eliza offered one of breakfast's leftover biscuits, and each viewed Lina with varying amounts of wonder. One would think they'd never seen an infant before. Last in the line was Skillet Mackenzie, a grizzled fellow who'd lost most of his teeth—probably to his own cooking. He was more interested in Eliza's recipe for biscuits than the baby.

"I cook up the best beans and sowbelly in the territory. Next time I whip up a batch, I'll let you watch," he offered magnanimously. "These are mighty good biscuits, missus. I'll admit you've got me topped on that."

Finally the procession ended. Jacob had trundled off to bed before the last of the visitors left. Lina slept peacefully in her cradle, which Luke had placed by the fireplace when it became apparent that she was the evening's main attraction—along with her mother's biscuits.

"We have disrupted your ranch," Eliza said to Luke once they were alone.

Luke shrugged noncommittally. "As long as they don't come sashaying through here when they're supposed to be tending to work." A spark of humor in his eyes reflected in his slight smile. "I haven't seen that crew so clean and shaven since the last Fourth of July picnic in Santa Rosa. Just don't get 'em too civilized, missus, or they won't be any good to me." He stood up. "Time to turn in. It's been a hard day."

Eliza took the empty coffee mug from his hand and, scarcely considering what she did, raised on tiptoe and gave him a kiss on the cheek. For a moment he froze in place, then cleared his throat awkwardly. His face pinkened, and a muscle twitched along his jaw.

Eliza, also, turned red. What had she been thinking?

"Well, uh, good night, Eliza."

"Good night, Lucas."

Eliza listened to his footsteps clunk through the kitchen and into his bedroom. One by one she heard his boots drop. The springs on his bed creaked with his weight. She closed her eyes and raised a hand to her lips. His warmth still lingered there, mingling with a heat in her face that was all out of proportion for a simple peck on the cheek.

3

Even in the barn, Lucas's breath froze in front of his face. Inside thick leather gloves, his fingers were almost too numb to thread the latigo strap of his saddle through the ring on the cinch. Hammerhead's muzzle sported an icicle from almost every whisker.

In typical New Mexican fashion, clear skies brought plummeting temperatures. Lucas reminded himself to make sure Eliza had plenty of split wood for the stove and fireplace before he and Jacob left. They were off to check the windmill water tanks on the north range and were likely to be gone most of the day. It wouldn't do for Eliza to split wood herself to keep the house warm—though she'd no doubt do the chore without a thought to her own delicate condition. The woman just didn't seem to realize that the human body had certain limitations—especially a female body which had just given birth. Maggie had kept to her bed for three weeks after delivering Jacob, and had pleaded delicacy for two months after that.

"Jacob. You saddled and ready, son?"

"Yes sir."

"Then check the firewood in the house. Make sure there's enough for all day. We wouldn't want Eliza and Lina to be shivering when we get back."

"Yes sir!"

Luke smiled as his son eagerly ran off to the house. The boy was glad to get a chance to see Lina before they left. The baby hadn't been awake when they ate breakfast. In just a week, Jacob had become mighty attached to the little girl—to her mother, too. If Luke admitted the truth, the pair had grown on him as well. Especially the mother. He was getting downright spoiled by Eliza's cooking, and her smiles—which were never the empty smiles that some women wore on their faces like paint. Eliza's smile could light up a dark room, or a dark day. Her optimism and faith in the essential goodness of the world and those who lived on it seemed unshakable. Life seemed lighter with Eliza around.

Still, Luke wasn't sure that was a good thing. Idealism and hope didn't help a man when the chips were down—only strength, determination, and hard work could do that.

He was about to go after Jacob and scold him for dawdling when the rattle of a wagon rolling under the Stone Ridge arch distracted him. The wagon was a sight—a canvas-covered rig in the style of the emigrant wagons that had crossed the continent before the railroads spanned the country. On the side of the canvas covering, boldly painted letters proclaimed "Salvation Today!"—the words written in the upper-left and lower-right quadrants delineated by a huge cross. Preacher John Peter Tolliver had arrived on his annual visit.

Luke looped Hammerhead's reins through an iron hitching ring and went to the barn door. He stood with legs spread and hands on hips as the preacher pulled his two-horse team to a stop. "Mornin', John Peter."

"And a good morning to you, Lucas! You were expecting me, weren't you?"

"We always expect you this time of year," Luke said somewhat ruefully. "Right on time."

"Punctuality is next to godliness, my friend." Tolliver swung down from the wagon and clasped Lucas's hand in a bear-like grip. He was one of the few who could look Lucas Stone in the eye without looking up, and his bulk matched his height. Where Lucas's breadth was in his shoulders, however, Tolliver's was around his waist. "How has the year treated you, my boy?"

"Can't complain. Been chased out of many towns since last I saw you?"

"Yes, indeed! I'd not be doing my job if I failed to prick the tempers of the self-righteous Pharisees of the world."

"Well, I can see that you escaped with your skin intact for another year." He saw his son run from the house. "Here's Jacob. He'll want to say hello."

"Jacob!" Tolliver took the boy by the shoulders and surveyed him at arm's length. "You've grown three inches at least since last Christmastide! Straight and tall as can be. 'As the twig is bent, the tree's inclined,' isn't that right, boy?"

"Uh . . . Yes sir. I guess."

Unhitch John Peter's team and take them into the barn, Jacob." Luke clapped their guest on the shoulder as they walked toward the chow hall. "You're a bit late for breakfast, but Skillet probably has some beans and sowbelly left if your stomach's empty."

"My stomach's almost always empty, my friend. Hunger brings a man closer to God. In moderation, of course." He grinned, creasing his leathered face with deep lines. "And only when my pockets are empty, as they are now."

The preacher looked up, and a gleam came into his eyes. Luke turned to see Eliza coming toward them. The blue wool dress she'd made herself revealed curves and valleys that Jacob's old trousers and shirt had hidden. Her hair, pulled back to the crown and let fall simply like a young girl's, caught the fire of the morning sun and tossed it back in sparks of silver-gold. "What is this, Lucas? You've roped yourself a filly and didn't tell me first thing?"

"Don't jump to conclusions, John Peter."

"Lucas!" Eliza scarcely seemed to notice the stranger when she reached them. "I wanted to ask you before you left—oh! I'm sorry. I thought you were with one of the hands. I've interrupted."

"Lovely lady!" Tolliver intoned. He snatched his hat from his head, allowing shaggy brown hair to fall to his shoulders in disarray. " 'Tis sweet interruptions such as this that lightens a man's burdens on this world." He bowed over Eliza's hand while sliding a glance upward toward Luke.

Eliza's eyes widened, then they warmed to a smile, as if she'd instantly taken the man's measure and found it to her liking.

Luke scowled. "This isn't what you think, Tolliver."

"How disappointing." He smiled widely, revealing a full mouth of crooked teeth. "Are you going to stand there like an ill-mannered jackass and make me introduce myself?"

"Eliza," Luke said with a resigned sigh, "this well-oiled fellow is Preacher John Peter Tolliver. He drops by each Christmas to conduct a service for the ranchers hereabouts. Tolliver, this lady is Eliza. She and her baby are at Stone Ridge temporarily, until I can find her family."

Tolliver cocked a brow in Luke's direction, making clear his opinion of just how Luke should go about providing the lady with a family. His smile for Eliza, however, never wavered. "Perhaps I've run across your people in my travels, fair lady. What name?"

"I'm afraid I don't know."

Tolliver's brows lifted.

"Eliza had her baby up by Indian Head Wash during the last blue norther that ripped through here. I found her and brought her home. She doesn't remember anything about herself.''

''How unusual.'' Tolliver surveyed Eliza with an appreciative eye that made Luke bristle. ''My dear girl, we must pray together for the restoration of your memories. I see the Almighty's hand in this. You must have faith that all that has been taken from you will be restored and then some.''

''Don't waste your preaching on Eliza, Tolliver. She can match you word for word on talking about what's right and good. Why don't you go over to the chow hall and see if Skillet can rustle you up some food. I'll have Jacob dump your bedroll in the bunkhouse.''

''But surely Mr. Tolliver will be staying in the house,'' Eliza said.

''Your concern warms my heart, good lady, but I prefer to park my boots in the bunkhouse. There I can touch the souls of these hard-bitten sinners that Lucas has in his employ. But we will talk later, you and I. I look forward to it.''

Eliza clasped her hands together in delight as Tolliver ambled away toward the bunkhouse. ''A service for all the neighbors! What a wonderful idea, Lucas!''

''It wasn't my idea,'' Luke denied with a growl. ''Tolliver just announced my barn was the place for his service about five years ago. He's been here every year since.''

''You should have told me! What do you want to serve at the gathering?''

''What—''

''Oh, don't bother yourself. I'll handle it. And we should decorate, since all your neighbors will be coming.''

''But—''

''Could you bring a tree back with you today or

tomorrow? A juniper would do, though it's not exactly traditional. And perhaps someone could drive into town for the extra food and decorations we'll need. Did I see some smoked hams in the cellar the other day? Yes, I believe I did. And yams as well.''

She impulsively grabbed Luke's hands, and a jolt of undisciplined desire shot through him with heart-stopping power. He opened his mouth to deny that he'd ever intended any celebration to go along with Tolliver's preaching, but he couldn't speak.

''This will be such fun, Lucas! What a lovely surprise!''

Luke felt as though a whirlwind had twisted him around and spit him out dizzy and dumb as Eliza jauntily walked back toward the house. Walked? Hell! The woman almost skipped like a child. What could he do? He'd just been roped and hog-tied into wasting time on a party. He'd known from the first that having her around was going to be trouble.

Four days remained before Tolliver's Christmas service, and Eliza spent those days inventorying food-stuffs and materials for decorations, finishing the curtains for the living room, and sewing curtains for the kitchen and two bedrooms. Lucas made her a cradle board so that Lina could ride on her back while she bustled around the house. The device was an Indian idea, he told her, and she found that it was very convenient indeed, and kept Lina content and quiet.

Luke rode into the ranch yard with a juniper tree the evening after Tolliver's arrival. Tolliver, Jacob, and Eliza held weighty discussions on where the tree should be set up. They finally decided to move the horsehair settee that sat beneath the eastern bank of living room windows, then stood the tree where it would bask in the rays of the morning sun. Eliza and Jacob strung popcorn and cranberries, and criss-crossed them down the length of the tree. Jim Cruz, Curly Simms, and several other cowboys carved ornaments for the branches, and all the hands leapt into the spirit of Christmas, with Eliza's encouragement, by tying juniper trimmings together in wreaths to hang in the house and the bunkhouse.

"You'd think we had this much time to waste," Luke commented with a shake of his head. He didn't stop the ranch hands from helping, however, and once or twice Eliza saw him smile when he thought no one was looking.

After the tree was up and the wreaths hung, Baldy Garcia taught Eliza, Jacob, and the other Stone Ridge hands how to make the traditional New Mexican Christmas luminarias. All around the perimeter of the house, the smithy, the bunkhouse, the smokehouse, and the corrals, they placed paper bags weighted down with two or three inches of sand. In the sand was set a votive candle. The night after the Christmas service and every night thereafter until Christmas, the candles would be lit. Baldy, whose family had lived in New Mexico since before it became American territory, assured them that the glowing display would be the most spectacular thing they'd ever seen.

One evening after supper, as Eliza and Jacob put the finishing touches on the Christmas tree, Luke and Tolliver sat with their feet propped in front of the fireplace and watched them work.

"I don't think I've ever seen this house so cozy before," Tolliver commented with a mighty yawn. "Surely does make a difference having a woman around. Left to themselves, menfolk tend to get a touch ornery." The preacher slanted a meaningful look at

Luke, whose head rested against the back of his chair, eyes closed wearily. "Women are a level or two closer to Heaven, far's I can figure. They remind a man that food for the belly and hard work for the hands don't necessarily keep a man's mind from the Devil."

Luke slitted his eyes open and regarded Tolliver without moving his head. "Is that so?"

"That's God's own truth. Now, I'll admit that some women aren't as close to Heaven as others, mind you. In fact, some females are the Devil's own tools designed to beckon man to his downfall. I figure you're well acquainted with that kind, Lucas, and it's not our poor fallen sisters whereof I speak. No, I speak of females who catch a man with their outer beauty and then destroy him when he discovers their inner soul is as empty as a rain barrel in June."

"Are you getting to a point?"

Tolliver blithely continued. " 'Course there are some women who are so close to Heaven they might be angels in disguise. In fact, my sainted daddy once told me that every once in a while an angel up in Heaven might come down to earth in the form of an ordinary person. Come down on missions of mercy, most likely." He glanced at Lucas. "God knows there are plenty of men walking this earth who could use an angel in their lives. Or maybe angels sometimes get tired of all that flitting around Heaven and get a hankering to see what us creatures on earth are up to. But I tell you true—" He stabbed an intense look toward Eliza. "Miz Eliza, if there ever was an angel who decided to walk the earth in the form of mortal woman, I expect she'd be just like you."

Eliza dropped the tin snowflake she was hanging upon a juniper branch. Ignoring the ornament, she turned and looked at Tolliver, her eyes green pools of surprise. "Preacher Tolliver, I think you're full of Christmas foolishness."

"Dear lady, I never indulge in foolishness. My calling is a very serious one—and it's a calling that qualifies me to recognize an angel when I meet one."

"Fiddle." Eliza retrieved the snowflake, averting her face in a vain attempt to hide the flush that stained her cheeks. "I don't know precisely who I am, but I can assure you that I'm very far from being an angel."

Tolliver merely smiled.

"If you gentlemen will excuse me, I think I'll retire. I'm quite tired, suddenly. Good night Lucas, Jacob. Good night, Preacher Tolliver."

"Good night, Eliza," Tolliver said softly as she left the room.

Luke shook his head. Poor girl. Tomorrow he'd have to tell her what a crazy old reprobate Tolliver was. He should have stopped the man's foolishness before it upset her.

"That's one fine woman," Tolliver commented when Eliza had disappeared. "Interesting to talk to. Can't say that about a lot of women, but she and me have had some interesting discussions in the past few days."

"Yeah," Luke agreed laconically. "I noticed you hanging around the house a lot more than you usually do. Give up trying to save the souls of my cowboys?"

"That's an ongoing project, my friend. They're every bit as stubborn as you are. But Eliza—she's a mystery that lures a man from the ordinary work of the day."

"Tell me about it. The hands have been finding excuses to come by to see her and that baby ever since she got here."

"She has a peculiar innocence about her and an ignorance of things that anyone—even a person who's lost her memory—should know. Yet when she needs a skill or a piece of knowledge, it comes to her. Almost like she was born the day you found her, complete with a brain full of knowledge but no notion of how to use it."

Luke shook his head and sighed. "This is Lucas Stone you're talking to, friend, not one of your flock. Eliza's not an angel come down to earth any more than I'm Saint Peter. She's a girl who's had a bad experience that affected her mind. Sooner or later she'll remember who she is."

"You're a closed-minded, stubborn man, Lucas."

Luke chuckled cynically. "John Peter, if there were such a thing as angels, and if one of them decided to pay New Mexico a visit, I doubt she'd be stupid enough to land in the middle of a snowstorm nine months pregnant."

"The Almighty isn't dumb, my friend. I wonder how long it would've taken you to pack her off to somewhere else if it hadn't been for that fragile little baby."

"You've been listening to your own preaching too long. You're beginning to believe yourself."

Jacob had been listening solemnly while he strung cranberries onto a thread as Eliza had shown him. Now he contributed his sage opinion. "I think Eliza's the nicest lady I ever met. She even looks like an angel. Except she doesn't have wings."

Luke groaned. "Son, believe me. Any angel worth her halo would have better things to do than drop in on the Stone Ridge Ranch. Go to bed. It's late, and tomorrow's going to come early."

"Yes sir." Jacob wrinkled his nose as he headed for the loft. "I think Eliza would make a nice angel."

"To bed!" Lucas shook his head and watched his son reluctantly climb the stairs. "John Peter, I don't know why I still let you use my barn for your damned service every year. You're nothing but trouble."

Tolliver took a pull on his pipe and smiled. "Because some small part of you still wants to believe the world is more than dirt and stone and cows' asses, Lucas."

"The world is what the world is. You can preach from here till Sunday and not change it."

"There's where you're wrong, my friend. There's more in this world than you or I will ever know. If you don't believe in miracles, you don't recognize one when it jumps up and slaps you in the face."

Lucas merely grunted. For some moments, both men gazed silently into the crackling fire that warmed their feet.

"You know, Lucas. You really ought to find that girl a more suitable situation. You being unattached, people might begin to talk."

"Chrissakes, John Peter! The woman's just had a baby! You think I'd carry on with a female who's just up from childbirth?"

" 'Course not. I know you're a upstanding man, Lucas. Mule-headed at times, but upstanding. Some folks might not realize you're such a rock when it comes to the ladies, though. And after all, the woman's got curves in all the right places. That hair of hers looks like it might slip through a man's fingers like silk, and her eyes—have you ever seen such a shade of green?"

Luke folded his arms across his chest and snorted.

"Now, I've seen you look at that woman, Lucas, and if you're not working up a furnace full of sinful heat, then I don't know sin when I see it. And I've seen her look at you a time or two as well."

"Don't be casting stones at Eliza. She's a decent woman. One minute you say she's an angel, and the next you're accusing her of being a slut."

'I'm not accusing her, Lucas, and I don't rightly know what or who she is. But she's young and susceptible—and mighty pretty, especially when she smiles. And she smiles a lot, in spite of having to put up with a horse's ass like you. People are going to talk. If you've got any respect for her, you'd best find a good Christian family to take care of her until she can care for herself."

With that pronouncement, Tolliver tapped his pipe against the fireplace grate, stretched, and marched out the door as if to strains of "Onward Christian Soldiers." Alone with his own thoughts, Luke grimaced.

"Damnation." He tilted his head wearily against the back of the chair. Eliza's gentle smile danced before his closed eyes, along with green eyes, silver-gold hair, and several more intimate attributes that the preacher had called to mind. "There isn't a woman born that isn't trouble," he muttered, then shook his head. "And that includes female angels."

Eliza kept her eyes firmly closed, but she was wide-awake. The bed quilt was warm and cozy. Lina's steady, peaceful breathing was a lullaby floating through the darkness. But still Eliza couldn't sleep.

Over the past days, she had tried not to fret about her lack of identity. In time, she assured herself, she would remember her name, her family, how she came to the desperate straits of giving birth in the teeth of a blizzard. Time would reveal all. She simply had to be patient. Among the many things she didn't know about herself, she didn't know if she was a patient person. But up until this night, she'd been very unruffled in the face of difficult circumstances.

John Peter Tolliver had disturbed her with his speculations, however. Even with her memory gone, she should have an inkling of her life before the storm. She didn't. Though her brain seemed to contain all the knowledge and skills that she needed, everything in the world seemed new to her—weariness was a shocking discovery, hunger a novel experience. And love . . . She reined her thoughts to a halt.

She couldn't allow herself to fix her affections on Lucas Stone. Somewhere in the world she had a husband—probably. Sometime before this she had made a vow to love and cherish. She closed her eyes more tightly. Surely if she had been so intimate with a man, he couldn't be completely wiped from her mind. But the only image that arose was Luke's face. Her feelings for him, for his son, his home, felt so right. How could she not belong here?

Eliza sighed and threw back the bedclothes. Perhaps a drink of water would help her sleep. She pulled on wool socks against the icy cold of the floor and wrapped a blanket around her shoulders. Thus clad, she padded into the kitchen.

The kitchen was not dark, as she had expected. A solitary lantern hung from the hook in the rafters and cast long shadows across the room. Mingling with the shadows was Lucas Stone. He sat at the table, chin propped on one hand, and looked disgusted with the whole world.

Suddenly uneasy, Eliza tried to back into her room, but Luke looked up before she could retreat.

"Eliza? Is anything wrong?"

"No. I . . . I'm sorry I disturbed you. I was merely wakeful and thought to get some water."

"That's easy enough." He rose and pumped water into a tin cup. When he handed it to her, their fingers touched. It was a mere brush of flesh against flesh, but Eliza felt it all the way to her toes.

"Sit down," he said.

"I should go."

"Sit down."

She sat. He cut them both a piece of bread and sat down beside her.

"You shouldn't let Tolliver's ramblings disturb you. John Peter's a good man, all in all, but he sees angels, demons, and miracles around every bend."

Eliza smiled. "He does have rather imaginative ideas, doesn't he? Heaven is really nothing like he describes it."

Luke's eyes narrowed suspiciously.

Eliza bit her lip. What had made her say that? "I mean, John Peter might not know quite as much about the spiritual world as he thinks he does, though he seems to be a very good-hearted man."

"He is." Luke studied her for a moment, then shook his head as if ridding his brain of cobwebs. "Though some of the things he says make him sound loco as a moonstruck coyote. Don't let him bother you."

"What he said didn't bother me, precisely. He merely pointed out the uncertainties of my situation. Usually I'm not broody like this." She smiled ironically. "Or at least I don't think I am. But it is difficult to go on with a new life when I don't know the obligations of the old one. I could be anything. In fact, I might not even like myself if I knew who I was."

Luke sighed. He took Eliza's hand in his much larger, calloused one. "I know what you are, Eliza.

You're a good person. Losing your memory doesn't change who you are. You're one of those rare people who change the world around you instead of letting the world change you. Your husband, whoever he is, is a very lucky man.''

Eliza glanced at his hand covering hers on the table. She should take her hand from his, but couldn't quite do it. The small caress seemed so natural.

''It's strange,'' she said softly. ''I have a newborn baby, and even if I didn't know who she was, I would feel that she's a part of me. But I don't feel as though I have a husband. I feel as if I've lived here at Stone Ridge my whole life, and you and Jacob are my family.''

Lucas looked down at where their hands were joined. His face and eyes were hidden from her, but Eliza felt the heaviness of spirit that weighed him, as if it were a stone on her own soul. When he looked up again, his face was carefully expressionless.

''Don't let it fret you, Eliza.''

He leaned forward and pressed his lips to her cheek in a brotherly kiss of comfort. The light pressure of his lips on her cheek aroused a vibration deep inside her that made her shiver.

''Eliza.'' His voice was suddenly heavy with need. She clutched at his arm as his mouth brushed across her face and fastened on her mouth in a kiss that was far from chaste. Eliza was immediately lost in a warm wave of sweet passion. She opened her lips to his caress and felt him groan into her mouth. He devoured her as a starving man might fall upon a succulent feast. His arms enfolded her like warm steel. The solid wall of his broad chest flattened her breasts with delicious pressure as his whisker-roughened face scraped sensuously across her cheeks.

"Eliza. Eliza."

When he whispered her name, it seemed truly to be hers. Once again his mouth—his wonderful mouth—sucked and caressed and warred with hers, as though he were trying to steal the very breath from her body to make it his own.

Eliza willingly surrendered. More than surrendered—she urged him on while the joyful certainty of rightness thundered in her heart and spiraled in warm coils through every nerve in her body. How long they kissed she didn't know, for the moment seemed to stretch into a delicious eternity. Yet when Luke abruptly pulled back, the cold air that rushed into the space between them made the warmth of that moment disappear like a fragile puff of steam.

For a moment he stared at her as if he didn't know her. Then his mouth drew into the all-too-familiar harsh line. "I'm sorry, Eliza. I had no right."

She took a deep breath. She wasn't sorry. And yet she'd been wicked. They both had. .

"I didn't mean to—"

"Of course you didn't. It was more my fault than yours, Lucas. Don't be sorry." She saw the agony in his eyes and felt it weigh on her own spirit. What a coil they had woven for themselves.

The world was as white as an angel's soul, and cold with a wintry bite that gnawed through sheepskin jacket and denim and flannel straight through to the marrow of Luke's bones, or so it seemed. Or perhaps it was the morning's errand that made the world seem so cold.

Luke reined in Hammerhead atop a bluff overlooking the river. He'd been riding since before sunrise so he could get to Widow Calhan's and back before the day was well begun. If he'd waited, he would have thought of a reason not to go. If he'd spent his morning eating Eliza's breakfast, watching her chat so easily with Jacob and care so lovingly for Lina, he would have given in to his own weakness and found an excuse for her to stay. His weakness would have brought heartache for them both. Once already it had led to his breaking his honor and hers, and Luke knew that the next time he gave in and kissed Eliza, he wouldn't be able to pull back.

"Hell and damnation!" He turned the horse toward the wash that provided a path down to the river. The brilliant blue sky was almost as blinding as the virgin snow. In the piñon and juniper trees, birds fluffed themselves into feathery balls against the cold and chirped about their business. This kind of bright morning was no doubt one of the things Eliza would pause to appreciate, one of the good things that made survival worthwhile.

She would be better off at Widow Calhan's Juniper Springs Ranch, Luke told himself. Mary Calhan had welcomed his suggestion that she give Eliza and Lina a home until their family could be found. The widow was lonely, and she had more work than she could handle since her husband had died two years ago. If an angel was going to light on the earth on a mission of mercy, she should have lit at Mary's place, not his. Luke and Jacob were doing just fine the way they were. They didn't need a woman cluttering up their lives. He'd learned years ago that a good woman was a luxury that left heartache in her wake.

At the bottom of the bluff where the wash opened out into the river valley, Hammerhead pranced to a halt without signal from his rider.

"What is it?"

Hammerhead tossed his head, snorted, and backed a few paces.

Luke's hand went to his pistol as he surveyed the valley in front of them, prepared to find a snake, coyote, bobcat, porcupine, or some other creature likely to spook a horse. What he found was a bushy juniper growing beside a boulder at the base of the bluff. He recognized the spot instantly; it was the little niche where he'd found Eliza. Sunlight struck the snow and created an odd glow where she and Lina had lain.

Lucas stared at the spot for a long while, then wheeled Hammerhead and spurred him forward, refusing to look back. He was becoming as balmy as John Peter Tolliver.

4

The Sunday before Christmas, Preacher John Peter Tolliver conducted the Christmas service that had become a tradition along the stretch of the Pecos River between Santa Rosa and Fort Sumner. Ranchers and ranch hands alike crowded into the Stone Ridge barn to visit and celebrate the season, paying little mind to the cold that was only partially alleviated by fires set around the barn in cans that once held axle grease. The service was Eliza's first chance to meet Widow Calhan, who had offered her a home until her family was found or her memory somehow returned. The widow was a brick of a woman who at fifty had outlived a husband and two sons. She ran her ranch and bossed her cowboys herself. Eliza's help would be a boon, she assured the girl heartily. Mother and babe could ride back to the Juniper Springs Ranch in her wagon the morning after the Christmas service.

Eliza made the vague excuse that she needed a few

days to set things aright at Stone Ridge before she could leave. The widow gave her a canny look and patted her hand. The next day or the next week—whenever she came to Juniper Springs, Eliza would be more than welcome.

The people who gathered in the Stone Ridge barn to hear John Peter Tolliver preach were an assortment that rather surprised Eliza. They were weathered and tough; their manner and conversation displayed strength and self-reliance. But most seemed unashamed to show their softer side. They gossiped, laughed at jokes, complained about the price of beef, wished each other a happy holiday, and speculated on Lucas Stone's invitation to eats and merry-making after the service. It was a grand idea, all within Eliza's hearing seemed to agree, but who would've thought that Luke Stone cared anything about holiday festivities.

Eliza, with Lina content in a cradle board at her feet, sat with Jacob and Lucas during the service observing the crowd of neighbors ranged on haystacks in the barn. Gus and Sarah Marshall and their four children crowded close to battle the cold. The seven- and nine-year-old boys slanted looks at each other that promised mischief after the service. A ten-year-old girl—the Melinda that Jacob had pronounced a pest—sat beside her mother, prim and tidy, and the eldest son, a lanky thirteen-year-old, somehow kept his head erect while he dozed behind closed eyes. Beside the Marshall family sat John and Anita Severn with their three-year-old girl. Young and intense, they paid strict attention to Tolliver's long-winded sermon while the toddler squirmed.

On the second row of haystacks, Mary Calhan sat beside Eliza. On Eliza's other side Jacob fidgeted, his fidgets interrupted every few minutes by Luke squeezing his arm. Beyond Luke sat brothers Will and James

Sutherland, bachelors who had eyed Eliza with interest ever since they were introduced, and beside the brothers were José and Marguerita Apodaca. José was a middle-aged man of serious mien who had engaged Luke in earnest conversation before the service. Luke's face had settled into a stony mask as he nodded at the man. Eliza wondered what troubled him, but the service had begun before she could ask.

"You tell me miracles don't exist!" Tolliver's voice rose in what Eliza hoped was a concluding climax. John Peter did enjoy the sound of his own voice. If he talked much longer, the ranch hands wouldn't have time to light the luminarias before dark. "I say to you, good people, that anyone who denies that miracles exist will never see one, but anyone who will look at the world with unshuttered eyes will see the miracles that are with us every day! And in this wonderful Christmas season, the season of miracles, our eyes should be joyfully open to see Heaven's mark on everything and everyone around us."

He paused weightily, then fixed his eyes on Luke. "Be grateful, my friends, for the gifts Heaven has given us this season."

Out of the corner of her eye, Eliza saw Luke grow red.

"Shall we pray?" Tolliver intoned solemnly.

After the service, everyone took great pleasure in lighting the luminarias. By the time dark fell, Stone Ridge glowed with the warm, welcoming light of hundreds of candles. The serious mien everyone had maintained during the preaching melted into smiles and laughter as the Stone Ridge cowboys attempted to enact one of Los Pastores—folk plays brought long ago from Spain to Mexico, and thus to New Mexico, by Franciscan monks. Hay bales were pushed back to

serve as makeshift benches around the central aisle of
the barn. The Marshall children giggled with delight
when they were drafted to portray the *diablitos*—little
devils who whirled and danced angrily as Skillet Mackenzie portrayed Lucifer raging at Isaiah's prophecy
of a savior. The barn rang with laughter as Stone
Ridge's blacksmith Butch Carey acted the part of Bartolo, a drunken shepherd who sank into inebriated
sleep while three cowboy-shepherds—blankets tied
around their heads as costumes—offered gifts to Mary
and Joseph and their baby in the stable. But all is well
when Bartolo awakes, sees the Nativity scene, and re-
pents his life of laziness and drinking. Eliza laughed
with the others when one of the little Marshall *diablitos* relieved Bartolo of the bottle sticking out of a
pocket of his jacket and rushed with it to Tolliver, who
refused to return it to the red-faced cowboy-shepherd.

Eliza's heart was only partly in the celebration,
though. Most of her mind was on the coming move to
Widow Calhan's. She tried very hard to hide her disappointment at the prospect of leaving Stone Ridge. It
was much more proper, after all, that she live with the
widow. Lucas was an unattached man in the prime of
his life. Stone Ridge was a male domain. None of the
cowboys had wives. There wasn't a woman in sight
who could offer Eliza the protection of her compan-
ionship. People would talk. No matter how kind the
good neighbors were who celebrated here this night,
they were bound to wonder at a decent woman accepting hospitality in such a place.

But Stone Ridge had become her home, and Lucas
. . . Lucas had become one of those things that made
survival worth battling for. From the first she had been
defenseless against his appeal, and though her mind
knew her affection was unseemly, her heart felt that it

was right. Against all logic, to the depths of her soul she felt that Lucas Stone was the only man who would ever hold her heart.

Since their kiss, Lucas had avoided her as much as possible. For that small blessing Eliza was grateful. The more she was with him, the more painful became the knowledge that they could not be together in the way they both needed. Their intimacy had shaken her loose from the hope that what she felt for him stemmed from gratitude. Gratitude did not give birth to passion or the intense desire to lie in a man's arms and watch together as night rolled into morning. Gratitude did not make her love the curve of his lips, the warmth of his rare smile, the way his hair insisted on curling over his brow no matter how many times he brushed it back. Eliza prayed that Heaven would give her enough strength and wisdom to rule her confused heart.

After the play was over, everyone crowded into the house for the holiday meal that Eliza and Skillet had collaborated to prepare. They both had spent much of the last two days cooking, and the guests were appropriately impressed by a table laden with beef, pork, chili soup, sweet potato pudding with brandy, plain and sweet bread, potatoes baked with tiny onions, vinegar pies, pumpkin pies, apple pies, and honey cookies.

After eating only a small amount, Eliza sought the privacy of her bedroom to feed Lina. Eliza's appetite was not its normal healthy self, but Lina's was. Babies were not subject to foolish fantasies about men they couldn't have. Babies didn't wake from sleep to remember that they'd dreamed a love scene that would never come true. Eliza sternly reminded herself of her own belief that one must concentrate on the good things of life, not the bad. All would resolve itself the way Heaven had intended.

Just as she put Lina in the cradle to sleep, a knock sounded on the bedroom door.

"Eliza?"

Luke's voice. Eliza's heart raced in spite of herself. "Yes?"

"Can I talk to you a moment?"

Eliza opened the door. There stood Lucas—not alone, as her unruly heart had secretly hoped, but with José Apodaca. "Of course you can, Lucas. Can we go into the living room? I just put the baby down."

They had the living room to themselves. Eliza's stomach clenched with apprehension as she sat on the window seat. She didn't like the look on Luke's face.

"What is it, Lucas?"

"Eliza, I think we've located your family."

Eliza felt her whole body go numb. Luke looked as though he wanted to take her hand in comfort, but of course he didn't. Eliza wished that he would.

"I'll let José tell you about it."

José nervously twirled his hat in his hands. "I was down at Fort Sumner yesterday, missus. This sergeant told me that a patrol found a family of travelers about twenty miles north of here—all huddled in their wagon and frozen stiff."

Eliza felt as though she couldn't breathe. José cleared his throat.

"These people started out west from Brownhorn, and the army figures they got off the trail in the storm. They found a middle-aged man and woman and a younger fellow. According to what the army found out from Brownhorn, it was the Crosby family—George and Charity and their son Stephen. When they left Brownhorn, Stephen's wife Amanda was with them, but the army didn't find her with the others. They figure she wandered off and got lost. The folks in Brownhorn say she was . . . uh . . . in the family way.''

Eliza glanced quickly at Luke. For once he didn't avoid her eyes. ''This is who I am?'' she asked softly.

''Looks that way.''

''From Brownhorn?''

''No, ma'am,'' José said. ''They didn't live there. Just passed through to pick up some supplies and talk with some of the locals about farming hereabouts. Where they came from or why they were dumb enough to travel in the winter—well, nobody seems to know.''

''Amanda.'' She said the name slowly and softly. It didn't feel right on her tongue. She didn't feel like an Amanda with a husband named Stephen. The news jogged no memories of a journey west through Brownhorn.

''Where's Brownhorn?''

''Near the Texas border,'' Lucas answered. ''Eliza . . . Amanda . . . ? Are you all right?''

''Please don't call me Amanda. Eliza feels more like my name.''

''Eliza.'' Lucas finally took her hand. His long fingers curled around hers in a cocoon of comfort. ''You can keep any name that you want.''

She fought back a sudden feeling of panic. ''Will . . . will you excuse me please. I think I'd like to retire.''

''Sure,'' both men were quick to say.

She got up and walked off, feeling as though she was in a trance. At the last moment she turned and looked at José. ''Thank you, Mr. Apodaca. I'm much obliged to you for inquiring into the matter.''

''Yes, ma'am. Hope I've been of help.''

Eliza managed to give him a smile. Now she knew who she was. Why did she feel more alone than ever?

"I'm almost ready," Eliza said. She folded the little quilt that Sarah Marshall had sent over for Lina and laid it in an old satchel on top of the two dresses she'd made herself, the three flannel baby gowns that Anita Severn had sent, and a pile of clean diapers. She turned to Luke, who leaned casually against the bedroom door frame. "Are you sure you don't mind me taking these dish towels for Lina?"

"Do you think I'm going to use them to wipe dishes after what she's used them for?"

Luke was glad to see Eliza smile. Her usual sunny smile had been absent for the last two days. He supposed that was natural. After all, the girl had just discovered that her whole family had frozen to death. But Luke thought it was more than the Crosbys' tragedy that had upset her. She didn't allow anyone to call her Amanda, saying the name didn't feel right.

Luke had ridden to Fort Sumner himself the day after the Christmas service. The sergeant whose patrol had found the Crosbys had a description of the family from several shopkeepers in Brownhorn. The description of the young wife was vague—just an average girl. No one had noticed much about her except the pregnancy.

That no one had much noticed Eliza—or Amanda— was puzzling. How could anyone see those bright green eyes and silver-gold hair and not remember them? How could anyone not remember her smile? Were those things noticeable only to a man in . . . in what? In love? No. Luke Stone had too much sense to fall in love again—and Eliza was still going to Juniper Springs. The wagon was hitched to the team and ready to roll as soon as she had finished packing her few belongings into the old satchel he'd given her.

The girl would be better off with Mary Calhan, Luke assured himself. If she wanted a man, she could have her choice of any bachelor in the territory. There weren't many decent women fool enough to want to settle in New Mexico, and women were at a premium. Luke would be damned if he'd go soft on the woman and let her upset the fragile equilibrium he'd forged since Maggie had left. He hadn't the courage to turn his life upside down and walk back into the fire that had once burned him so badly.

Yet the thought of another man claiming Eliza's gentle smiles, running his fingers through her silver-gold hair, feeling the sweet warmth of her lips made Luke's fists clench, the better to break the nose of any man who would dare do such a thing. He was well down the road to being bedeviled by the woman, he told himself, and the sooner she was out of his sight, the better off he would be.

Eliza closed the satchel and handed it to Luke. "I just have to wrap Lina a little more securely, and we can go. It's very generous of you to let me take the cradle."

"No reason for me to keep it."

"It's still generous of you. You're a good man, Lucas."

Eliza read Luke's uncertainty in the slight pucker of his brows. She loved the way those brows arched over his eyes. She loved the jut of his strong jaw, the curve of his mouth, the sun lines that fanned out from his eyes. But she wouldn't beg for him to let her stay. He knew she loved him—how could he not know after the kiss they had shared? Lucas loved her also; she could sense his feelings in the surreptitious looks he gave her and the strangely wistful smiles he sent her way. And his kiss. She would never forget that kiss. Lucas loved her. But apparently he didn't love her enough.

"I'll get Lina," Eliza said as evenly as she could. "She was coughing a bit earlier. I've got her wrapped in so many blankets, she won't fit into her cradle board."

Luke followed her to the cradle. "I'll take her."

A shock of golden baby hair was just visible in the swath of blankets. Lucas picked up the infant with a gentleness that no one would expect of such a big man. "She's not catching cold, is she?"

"I'm sure she's fine."

When they turned, Jacob was in the doorway. "You'll come back to visit, won't you, Eliza?"

"Of course I will. You don't think I'd abandon you completely to your father, do you?"

Eliza's heart squeezed as Jacob's face lit in a smile. He was the only one on the ranch beside John Peter who hadn't tried to convince her that she was Amanda Crosby. "I know you're an angel just like Preacher Tolliver says," he had whispered to her the night before.

Eliza herself hadn't quite decided what or who she was. Perhaps her memory would never return, and she would have to accept a life that began in a snowstorm at the base of a bluff on the Pecos River. Such a life would be easier to fill with good memories if Lucas Stone were part of it.

"You'll come often?" Jacob pumped her.

"As often as I can." She bent down and kissed the boy on the cheek. "Take care of your father, Jacob."

"You bet!"

The moment Eliza stepped from the house, the wind attacked her with a bite that cut to the bone.

"Where did this come from?" Luke clamped his hat more firmly onto his head.

"A storm's coming up, Pa. You'd better not go."

Luke frowned. Fifteen minutes ago the sky had been bright and clear. The minute Eliza had stepped out the door, the wind had kicked up and tattered gray clouds had obscured the sun—almost as if someone didn't want her to leave. "Get back inside," he told Eliza. "We'll wait to see what this crazy weather does."

Two hours later the sky was once again clear, but the four-hour wagon ride to Widow Calhan's was out of the question. Lina's cough had become a croup, and the baby was hot with fever. Luke watched helplessly for the rest of the day as Eliza bathed the baby in cool water to bring the fever down—to no avail. When he touched one of the little hands that flailed restlessly in the air, the smooth baby flesh felt as though it had been held over a hot stove. Tiny fingers closed around his as though the infant expected somehow that Luke could make her well.

He gently unwrapped the little fingers and stuffed the dimpled arm under the blanket. "How could she be this sick?" he demanded with a frustrated scowl. "She was fine last night."

"I don't know." Eliza looked as though she was about to become ill herself. Her usually radiant skin was pale and almost translucent, and shadows under her eyes made her look as ethereal as a wisp of smoke. For hours she had sat holding Lina, bathing her, rocking and crooning, trying to get the infant to nurse. Jacob had long since been sent off to bed, and the pile of wood by the fireplace was reduced to a few scraps.

Suddenly, Luke couldn't bear to be in the room. He wasn't used to feeling helpless. When he had a problem, he solved it by the strength of his arm or the determination of his will. But neither strength nor determination could rid Lina of an illness that could well cost the baby her life. He shot up abruptly from where he sat, hands clenched at his sides. "I'll get more wood for the fire."

Eliza scarcely stirred as he walked out. Her head was bowed over the child, her eyes closed. Sorrow had robbed her of the vitality that usually made her seem so much stronger than her slight frame would allow. She looked more fragile even than when he'd found her, and Luke wondered if he were about to lose not just the child, but the mother as well.

The rest of the night passed without change, and the next day as well. By nightfall Eliza looked as ill as her child. That she was near exhaustion was certain, for under no other circumstances would she have so readily handed Lina over to Luke when he asked. The child seemed as frail as a paper doll in his arms. Her wispy blond hair was damp with fever, her round cheeks red and hot.

"She won't eat." Eliza's voice filled with tears. "She won't sleep, and she's not getting any better. I don't know what to do."

Luke didn't know what to do, either. Eliza was the one who had faith in happy endings. Eliza was the one who believed fate was kind and everything worked to the good of those who trusted themselves and the world's goodness. Yet she was losing to tragedy.

Placing the baby back in her mother's arms, he helped Eliza to her feet. "The window seat is more comfortable than that chair. Come sit with me. We'll watch out for her together."

Eliza willingly leaned back into his arms as they sat together. Even exhausted and frazzled, she smelled like a fresh wind. Her hair was soft beneath his chin. Luke could feel her heartbeat against his chest.

He'd had all this within his grasp and had wanted to send it away. Staring loss in the face, Luke cursed himself for a fool. Stone Ridge would be empty without Eliza and Lina. He'd been so reluctant to change his life—as if it was such an enviable existence. But he'd changed in spite of himself. Eliza had swept in like a blue norther and made him see how joyless his life was. His future would be bleak without her.

Eliza's head tilted back onto his shoulder as she slipped into sleep. Luke tightened his grasp, his arms circling both her and the infant. He would not let them go. Eliza was part of him. Lina was also. And it was going to take the power of Heaven itself to take them from him.

He sat still and silent for a long while, listening to Eliza's breathing and feeling his resolve harden to stone. Finally he lifted both mother and child in his arms, and carried them into Eliza's bedroom. Eliza didn't wake as he laid her on the bed, and as Luke snugged Lina into the blankets of her cradle, he wondered if it was his imagination that made the child seem to breathe easier. He pulled off his boots, stretched out on the bed beside Eliza, and prepared to watch over both mother and child through the long night.

Luke woke with a start to bright sunlight streaming through the bedroom window. He didn't remember falling asleep, so the morning took him by surprise.

Today was Christmas Eve, he remembered. Closing his eyes, he recalled the words of a song they had sung at Tolliver's service. "Silent night, holy night. All is calm, all is bright." The day was bright, for sure, and all too calm. A few inches away he could hear Eliza's quiet breathing. Nothing from the baby. No coughing, wheezing, or whining. His heart clenched. He didn't want to open his eyes to face what he feared—feared both for himself and Eliza.

A gurgle from the cradle derailed the somber train of thought. Luke opened his eyes in disbelief. Carefully, as if sudden movement might break the fragile bubble of hope that swelled in his heart, he leaned across the slumbering Eliza to look in the cradle. Lina burbled up at him, blue eyes wide open, a glow of health on her skin that had been ashy pale the night before.

Those who don't believe in miracles never see them. Luke could hear John Peter Tolliver's words in his mind.

Looking up at him, Lina puckered tiny brows and let forth a hungry yowl. Beneath Luke, Eliza jerked awake. "Lina?"

Luke stared down into Eliza's face, suddenly very aware of the impropriety of their juxtaposition, but he couldn't force himself to pull away. "Your daughter's awake and hungry."

Uncomprehending green eyes gazed up into his. "Hungry?"

"She sounds hungry to me."

Luke watched Eliza draw in a deep, hopeful breath. He wanted to kiss her, to touch the shadows under her eyes, to smooth the lines of strain from her brow and tell her that Lina would be fine. He knew a miracle when he saw one; Eliza and Lina were his own personal miracle.

Dawning awareness touched Eliza's eyes, as if she had just noticed that she was caged by Luke's arms and pinned to the mattress by his chest. He pulled back self consciously. "I . . . uh. . . . ."

His face heated, but she only smiled one of her special smiles that turned him inside out, then raised herself on an elbow and peered into the cradle. The look on her face as she touched the baby's cheek struck through to Luke's heart like an arrow tipped with warmth that spread through his whole body. His own personal miracle.

The baby slept and ate her way through the day as if she'd never been ill. A rosy bloom returned to Eliza's cheeks, but a touch of melancholy still darkened her eyes until Luke suggested she unpack the belongings she'd stuffed into his satchel two days ago. When she threw him a questioning, wary look, his throat closed on the words he longed to say, the words he'd intended to say. Instead, he managed only a lame "It's Christmas Eve. Besides, you and Lina both need to rest up a bit."

As evening fell, the luminarias were lit once again. Stone Ridge Ranch glowed with a warmth that defied the wintry bite of December. The ranch hands joined the family for a dinner that was as festive as Eliza could manage, given her sapped energy and the short time she had to prepare. Baked ham, biscuits, brandied sweet potatoes, white potatoes cooked with red chili, cranberry tarts, and mince pie inspired Curly Simms to declare that he'd work a year without pay for another Christmas Eve dinner like the one setting on his stomach.

"Done!" Lucas accepted quickly.

Curly grinned. "Jest jokin', boss." The foreman's expression grew almost reverent as he turned to Eliza.

"If you don't mind, ma'am, could I peek in at the baby afore I leave?"

"Of course you may."

A line of cowboys formed behind Curly. Every man wanted to look at the baby before heading back to the bunkhouse. Lina lay peacefully in her cradle and accepted their homage as if it was her due. Only Skillet Mackenzie stayed behind.

"You jest set yourself down in front of the fireplace," he told Eliza. "I been washin' up the messes that these hogs make for so long I can do it in ma sleep. No sense in you havin' to cook and clean up, too."

The hour was late before Luke, Jacob, and Eliza were left alone. Eliza surprised Lucas by presenting both him and Jacob with shirts she had made from the cloth Maggie had left behind so many years before. Luke self-consciously produced a shawl he had bought for Eliza, and Jacob proudly gave Eliza a box carved from juniper wood.

"Jim Cruz helped me carve it," Jacob told her. "It's for . . . you know . . . hairpins and ribbons and stuff." He blushed at the mention of such intimate feminine items.

"It's beautiful, Jacob. It's the most beautiful thing I own. Thank you very much."

He blushed again and studied the toes of his boots. "Tweren't nuthin'."

Then the moment Lucas had been anticipating came to pass. Jacob went to bed. He and Eliza were alone.

"You're lucky to have Jacob," Eliza said. "He's such a good boy."

"Yeah." His hands broke out in a sweat. In his chest his heart hammered fiercely. All day he had been looking forward to this moment, but old fears died hard.

"I . . . uh . . . I've been pretty much of a . . . a jackass since you got here." Damn! That wasn't what he wanted to say. He wanted to be eloquent with gentle words that would impress her with how much he'd changed.

One corner of her mouth twitched upward. "Yes?"

She wasn't going to politely deny that he'd been an ass. Okay. He deserved that. "Eliza." He drew a deep breath. "We've only known each other a short time, but in this country, things happen fast, or they don't happen at all. I'll own that I'm a jackass and a fool at times. Heaven knows I'm not the easiest man to get along with or any woman's idea of a perfect husband, but I need a wife and Jacob needs a mother . . . and I'd be honored if you'd stay here at Stone Ridge and marry me. I'll be the best husband I can to you, and the best father I can to little Lina."

For a heart-stopping moment, she just looked at him with those bright green eyes. His proposal sounded dry and lame even to his own ears. No wonder she wasn't jumping into his arms.

"Eliza"—he took her hand as if he would hold onto her by brute force. "What I'm trying to say, and saying very badly, is that I love you. You can call yourself Eliza, or Amanda, or whatever you please. For my part, I think John Peter was right. I think you're an angel sent straight down from Heaven to teach me what a damned fool I really am. I don't know what I did to deserve you, but you're the best Christmas gift I ever had. Say yes, Eliza."

She cocked her head inquiringly, looking as though she listened to something Luke couldn't hear. Then her eyes came to rest on him, and she smiled. "Yes."

"Yes?"

"Yes, Lucas. I love you."

A grin split his face as he pulled her into his arms. "You'll put up with me the rest of your life?"

"I'll manage."

She seemed to melt into his embrace as he kissed her. Her lips were as sweet as he remembered, her skin as soft. The feel of her breasts pressed against his chest filled him with a heat that rivaled the fire on the hearth. While he still could, he set her from him.

"How does a Christmas wedding sound to you? John Peter's still in Santa Rosa. He could drive down and marry us. But maybe it's too soon," he said, remembering she was only two weeks up from childbed. "It's too soon. I shouldn't have—"

Eliza shushed him with a finger on his lips. "It's not too soon, Lucas."

"You're sure?"

"I'm sure."

He kissed her again and tasted the sweet promise of passion on her lips. Suddenly tomorrow seemed very far away. He forced himself to let her go.

"Tomorrow," he said in a husky voice.

"Tomorrow."

Abruptly he stood up. "If I stay here much longer, it's going to be a good deal sooner than tomorrow." He reached out and touched her cheek. "Good night, Eliza."

Rather than take offense at his brusqueness, she seemed to understand. "Good night, Lucas."

Eliza watched Lucas leave. Inside her bloomed a comforting feeling of completion. Her life would start right now, with no past, but a beautiful future. The darkness beyond the window seemed to beckon. Leaving the warmth of the fire, she lifted the window sash and leaned out into the icy night. The sky was crystal clear and spangled with stars. For a brief moment one of those stars gleamed with an odd brilliance, then settled back to its normal twinkle. A wink from Heaven?

Eliza smiled and winked back.

A Time for Giving
by Raine Cantrell

Stone Ridge, New York, 1864

JACOB DEWITT let the chilled winter's silence seep into
him as he stood at the bottom of the drive on Lilac
Hill. In the woods behind the two-story farmhouse,
the faint snap of a dead branch cracking beneath the
weight of ice made him start. But it wasn't sniper fire.
There were no moans of the wounded and dying. No
ear-deafening roar of continuous cannon. Blessed
peace surrounded this last farm on the road outside of
the New York village where he had been born.

The air he inhaled was spiked with a clean innocence. The smoke rising from the house chimneys held
only a welcome of the warmth he would find inside,
and not the terror of finding a barn burning with soldiers trapped inside. His gaze swept the shadows cast
by the bare-limbed apple trees on the snow-crusted
sloping lawn. No enemies hiding there intent on killing him. There was no blood. There was none of the
stench that the devastation of war had brought to the
southern lands far from his home.

He could leave the war behind, would force himself
to do so, and think only of how to convince Miss Ellie
Wintifred to marry him. The precious two-week
Christmas leave granted him as the war between the
states dragged into its fourth year was little enough
time for him to renew his bond with his children, much

less get married. In the letters exchanged over the past eight months, Ellie's obstinate refusal to consider his proposal was all that stood in his way.

He had recently been promoted to quartermaster captain for his sharp assessment of farmlands and their possible yield. He had met his quotas, but without leaving families stripped of all foodstuffs. Nor had he ruthlessly set fire to barns and fields so that it would take years before the land could once again be planted. His skills to coax, negotiate, and threaten when all else failed had been sharply honed by war. By the same means, he would use those skills to obtain security and a home for those he loved.

Marriage to spinster Ellie Wintifred was not a sacrifice; it was expedient for his peace of mind.

This small village of Stone Ridge was about to see another revolutionary battle fought near the old New York state capitol of Kingston. The weapons would be words, not sabers or guns, but it was a battle he intended to win. War had taken two of his brothers' lives, and his grief had nearly destroyed his marriage that ended in his wife's death. But he no longer mourned Lucy's passing. He had come to terms with death and grief. War left little time for sentiment when a man struggled to stay alive.

Despite the cold seeping into army boots from the ice-encrusted ruts of the drive and the weariness of his body after traveling for three days to come home, Jacob remained where he stood.

He desperately needed to clear his mind and keep the taint of war from his children and younger brother.

He had discovered what a powerful weapon memories could be. He never allowed himself to dwell on them while he was on duty; he couldn't afford to let his memories surface and distract him, but after each skirmish, each battle, he called them forth to help him cope with the destruction of war.

The Wintifred homestead was prime farmland. His own adjoining farm was larger in acreage but barely matched its yield. With so many of the young men gone to fight, his land lay fallow, but he would survive to see it green from seeds he had sown.

He loved the stillness, the clear sky, and remembered the times he and Ellie stood on the knoll behind the house, trying to reach for the brilliant stars. He had fallen from the tallest pine and broken his leg after promising Ellie he would get a star for her. She had picked buckets of blackberries for him while his leg healed, swearing she would never ask him for another thing if he promised to hurry and get well.

They had played hide-and-seek in the cedar trees that stood like sentinels along either side of the road, their thick green branches acting like a windbreak.

Up near the house, on the same side as Ellie's bedroom, the man-high lilac bushes were stripped bare, with snowdrifts piled against their thick root branches. But in the spring, the tiny blooms were heavy clusters releasing their perfume to fill the air. Ellie loved lilacs almost as much as she loved maple syrup.

He eyed the tall stately maples scattered up the slope of the front lawn. Jacob could almost hear his grandfather's deep raspy voice declare the trees were ready to be tapped. It seemed to take forever in those days before the sugar buckets were at last filled with the sap dripping from wooden spigots tapped into the maples' trunks. Then came the waiting for the yield to be boiled down for a few days before it was cooled and stored in jugs. He licked his lips at the thought of tasting sweet maple syrup dripping off the edges of a towering stack of hotcakes.

From the long, low milk barn behind the house came the lowing of a cow. Jacob knew evening milking chores were long over. Ellie was likely in the kitchen almost ready to serve supper. He fought the guilt that wormed its way up, guilt caused by his thought that hunger wouldn't prowl like another hidden enemy while he was home. There'd be soft, sweet roasted chestnuts and sweetmeats from the hard-shelled hickory trees that Ellie loved.

The two of them dared each other one autumn to see who could eat more chestnuts. They both became sick, and neither one of them won, but it was the last time he had shared anything with Ellie.

Lucy had come to live with her cousin Ellie that winter. And Jacob had had no time for the painfully shy Ellie. Childhood memories swamped him, tangled with images of soft-spoken Ellie, always standing apart, never joining in the parties and church socials that began the pairing of Jacob and Lucy, resulting in their marriage. He couldn't remember who had first called her the little winter mouse, but the name remained with her.

When had Ellie developed the thick streak of stubborness she revealed in her letters? He felt somehow cheated that he didn't know.

His little winter mouse presented an obstacle, but not an insurmountable one. Despite all of the reasonable advantages he had pointed out in his correspondence with her, Ellie refused him. Jacob knew how deep his own stubborn streak ran, and he intended to find out why she said no.

He was aware there were no suitors beating a path to her door. No one had ever courted Ellie. Now that she had taken in his younger brother and two children after a fire had destroyed his house and his elderly aunt

had died, no one would. He didn't like calling Ellie a
spinster, but she was twenty-eight years old. She had
used her age and the fact that she was two years older
than him as one of the reasons for refusal. But despite
saying no to marriage, she insisted on keeping the
children with her.

It made no sense to him. And he was foolish to
stand there freezing while attempting to work out the
contradictory female mind. Light spilled from the
lower windows and the two post lanterns near the front
door. Green garland festooned with ribbon reminded
him of Christmases past. Jacob slung his haversack
over his shoulder and lifted the heavy carpetbag filled
with Christmas presents. With every step he took up
the long drive, he couldn't ignore the feeling he was
coming home.

Ellie twitched the edge of the worn velvet drape back
in place. Jacob was home at last. She grew worried as
she stood watching him remain out in the cold staring
up at the house, and had to fight the need to run down
to him and see for herself that he wasn't wounded. His
letters mentioned little about the war, or the depriva-
tions he had suffered. But she read as many of the
newspapers as she could find, and knew the sufferings
for soldiers on both sides.

Smoothing her apron, she tried to still the excitement inside her. They had been waiting every night
for the past week for Jacob to come. Tonight, when
his younger brother Thomas had wanted to light the
post lanterns, Ellie found she had to be the one to do
it. Some inner sense warned her just as she was about
to close the door, and minutes later the creak and groan
of wheels alerted her to the farm wagon stopping at
the end of the drive. Dusk cloaked the lower end of

the hill, and she couldn't see, but knew Jacob was home. The very air was charged with the same tension she had begun to feel that last summer before Lucy came to live with them.

She rushed from her sentry post in the front parlor and went into the kitchen, blaming the flush heating her cheeks on the warmth of the cedar-paneled room. Each room in the farmhouse had tongue-and-groove wood planks cut and fitted from the trees in their woods. Cherry, pine, oak, and hickory gleamed on the walls. Ellie tried to distract herself from thinking about Jacob's arrival.

From the dining room came Thomas's instructions to his little niece Krista on the proper placement of napkins. He then sent Caleb upstairs to wash his hands again. A smile teased her lips when the thirteen-year-old's voice pitched from low to high, then broke somewhere between. He loudly cleared his throat before repeating his instructions.

Ellie knew how hard he tried to fill the man of the family role, and when opportunity presented itself, she allowed him. She knew the DeWitt pride. Until she had been fifteen, she had gleefully challenged Jacob's at every chance.

But that was before Lucy. This wasn't her real family no matter how she pretended it was. Thomas was the last of Jacob's brothers alive. Caleb and Krista were Jacob's children. They were the ones with claims on him. She was only his deceased wife's distant cousin, and she warned herself not to forget it.

Lifting the lid on the simmering pot of chicken and dumplings, she pressed each steamed dough top and saw that they were cooked. Sliding the heavy pot to a cold burner, Ellie gave up and thought how easy it would be to accept Jacob's proposal. He had set forth the practical advantages for her, even one that made her laugh. Jacob thought the farm was too big for her to manage it on her own. This, despite the fact that she had done quite well these past three years. Of course, Jacob had been gentleman enough not to mention that her father's will left him the farm if she never married. She did love the children, longed to have her own, but there were no suitors.

All perfectly sensible reasons for her to marry him. But Ellie couldn't forget that she was the lone child of a loveless marriage. She would never marry without being loved.

"Will he come tonight, Ellie?" Thomas asked, impatience in his voice.

"I know it's been hard, but maybe the wait will be over sooner than you think." Ellie couldn't look at him. She was afraid he would sense the excitement she felt. Excitement that melded a bit with fear.

Taking the biscuits from the warming oven over the stove, she placed them in the linen-lined basket. "Will you take these inside to the table? And see what's keeping Caleb. He's been gone long enough to take a bath."

Thomas laughed, and Ellie with him. Caleb was almost nine, and it was a game to get him near bathwater. She had turned to give Thomas the basket, and her smile deepened, for the gangly boy so resembled Jacob at the same age.

"Ellie," Thomas began, taking the basket from her, "you will let Jacob stay here with us, won't you?"

"Silly question." She couldn't help herself and reached out to ruffle his thick dark brown hair so like Jacob's. He had already begun to shave, and there was a hint of dark shadow on his cheeks. "Where else would your brother stay? There's no house left on the farm, and the barn roof needs repair. I'm sure Aunt Faye would put him up, but then he would spend time traveling to and fro to see you and the children.''

It was the way he shuffled his feet and stared down at his boots that made Ellie hesitate. ''There's something more to you asking me about this.''

''I just—'' Thomas cleared his throat. ''You don't go down to the village much, and there was some talk. Folks were saying how it isn't right for him to stay here with you.''

''With me? Oh, Thomas, we do not listen to gossip. Idle tongues make mischief. And your brother is not staying here with me, he is going to be with you and his children.''

''Well, I said as much. But I didn't like hearing them say that you're a maiden spinster lady.''

''Oh, Thomas,'' she said with a sigh, cupping his cheek. ''Pay that talk no mind at all. I tend to go along my own way, and make folks uncomfortable doing it. Go on now, take the biscuits in.''

She turned away, hiding the hurt she felt. She should have thought about the gossip that would spread. Krista tugged on her apron, and Ellie gave her a quick hug. The children had filled such a void in her life, she didn't know what she would do if Jacob tried to take them away from her.

''Lambkin, I need one of your smiles,'' Ellie whispered, smoothing the neat crown of braided hair that was as soft and fine as her own deep auburn braids. Krista gave her one, clinging as she sometimes did when something bothered her. Ellie thought she had heard what Thomas said, and anger rose inside that gossip should hurt these children. At least no one suspected that she. . . .

The sharp knock on the mudroom door off the

kitchen interrupted her thought. Her breath seemed to lock itself inside her for a moment, but before she could move, Thomas ran in front of her and Krista to yank open the door.

"Jacob!" The rest of Thomas's greeting was muffled, and Krista took off in a flurry of short skirt and petticoats.

Ellie had a glimpse of Jacob through the doorway, but Krista's cry of "Papa!" brought Caleb running, and Jacob was lost as he knelt to be engulfed in their hugs and kisses. He gathered his brother and children close, and Ellie longed to be able to fling herself into his arms, too.

She had never felt so alone. Not when Jacob married Lucy, not when she stood by her parents' graves and realized she would live alone.

For a brief moment, she felt the start of tears and fought to hold them back. She glanced up and saw that Jacob's dark piercing gaze was on her. "Welcome, Jacob. Welcome home," she managed to whisper, unsure if he heard her over the children's cries. Moved by the glimpse of tears in his eyes, Ellie turned away and took the forgotten basket of biscuits into the dining room.

What did you expect? Jacob isn't yours. He never was.

She closed her eyes and prayed for strength to get through his visit. His face was thinner, lines bracketed his light brown eyes and mouth. She wondered how much of a toll the war had taken on him.

Ellie didn't even realize she had crossed to the mantle in the dining room. The fire blazed, and she stared at the flames knowing she had to give them time alone. Reaching for the wooden matches in the china holder, she was surprised to see that her hand trembled when she lit it. Jacob was really here. For a little while she could pretend he . . . no, no, that would never do. Pretending would only make his leaving harder to bear.

Cupping her hand around the match flame, she moved to light each of the candles gracing the round dining table's centerpiece of fragrant pine and cedar cuttings in her best silver bowl. The candlelight set a glow to the good china and soft patina of the silverware. These, like the handmade lace tablecloth, had been part of her mother's dowry. There were five places set as there had been each night this past week in expectation of Jacob's homecoming. She had no intention of keeping the room for Sunday meals and holidays.

Ellie glanced around at the gleaming cherry-wood panels, the high-polished glow of the sideboard with its silver tray and pewter bowls arrayed with silky soft green and pinecones. She felt chilled as the wind picked up and rattled the small-paned windows. The same worn velvet draperies that hung in the front parlor covered the windows here, for her mother had insisted on bringing some of the elegance she had left behind in her home in Albany when she married her father's choice.

She understood where the chill had come from. Inside herself. Now that Jacob was here, now that she had seen him again, she wasn't at all sure she could continue to hold out against his practical proposal of marriage.

Jacob had charmed his way out of trouble and into the affections of any young woman that caught his eye. He had become the leader of boys at school, a role he continued when they all reached manhood. No matter how she tried to stem them, memories came, one after the other. Lucy in the dry-goods store in Kingston one day, claiming to her friends that Jacob could coax the skin off a bear if he set his mind to it. The giggles that followed when Lucy was asked what he had coaxed from her. Gay, lovely, flirtatious, and daring Lucy had wanted Jacob for her own. She was everything that Ellie was not. It came as no surprise when Jacob courted, then married her. When she died, everyone knew Jacob's grief had sent him off to war.

"Ellie, why did you leave us?"

Jacob's low male voice sent a shiver of awareness along her skin. She squeezed her apron, then released her grip on the cloth before turning to face him. He leaned one broad shoulder against the door frame, his hip canted to the side. His body was lean, and she sensed a tension in him, but when she looked up, amusement warmed his eyes and a smile curved his lips.

"Jacob."

"Is that all you can say? Why did you run off, Ellie?"

She couldn't seem to look away from his gaze. "Welcome home," she managed from a suddenly too dry mouth.

"No hug or kiss for the returning soldier?"

"Jacob!"

"Oh yes, Ellie," Krista piped in, snuggling next to her father. "You must give Papa a kiss and a hug, too. He said he needs lots of them for all the days he didn't have any. I gave him a whole bunch of mine, and Caleb and Thomas did, too. Now it's your turn." Beaming a bright smile that seemed to add sparkle to her eyes, seven-year-old Krista tugged her father forward until he stood towering over Ellie. "Go on, Papa. Kiss Ellie hello."

She heard the thundering footsteps of the boys racing up the stairs, but Ellie wondered if the sudden pounding of her heart didn't add to what she heard. "It isn't proper, Jacob." But the words didn't make him stop from leaning forward and brushing his lips against hers. His lips were warm, and feather light. The touch hardly lasted a moment, but Ellie felt her toes curl tight in her high-buttoned shoes.

"Later, you and I will talk," he murmured.

"Y-yes, Jacob."

"Have you changed your mind?"

"I—"

"Now a hug, Ellie. Papa kissed you, now you give him a hug."

Ellie raised her arms uncertain where she should place them. Jacob was most helpful. He stepped closer, lifting her arms around his shoulders, forcing her to stand on tiptoe while his own arms encircled her lower back.

"A hug, Ellie. Just a small hug."

But it was so much more for her. The wool of his uniform jacket wasn't as soft as she remembered, yet it held the familiar scents that were his. He was more than a head taller than she, and his arms felt like a homecoming to her as he pressed her closer still. Jacob here and safe. Tears welled in her eyes, and she tried to blink them away, tried to keep aware that his daughter watched them. But Jacob rocked her gently, whispering words she could make no sense of, and Ellie allowed herself to have this stolen moment of being held by him.

The boys' excited voices came from far away, but it was warning enough for Ellie to pull back. She felt Jacob's reluctance to let her go. A flush brightened her cheeks when he slid his hands over her hips before he stepped back and swung Krista high in his arms.

And not a moment too soon, Ellie thought as Caleb and Thomas rushed in.

"We put his bags in the big front bedroom, Ellie," Thomas announced, coming along with Caleb to stand on either side of Jacob.

"The front room? But that was your parents' bedroom, Ellie. I can't chase you out of your bed."

"Oh, Ellie doesn't sleep there. She gave her room to me and Caleb, Krista has mama's old room, and Ellie sleeps down here."

Krista held her father's cheeks, so he had to look at her. "Ellie has the smallest bed, but she lets me curl up with her when I cry at night, Papa, 'cause I miss you."

"You've been happy here with Ellie."

It wasn't a question, and Ellie took it as a good time for her to escape. She couldn't sort out the strange feelings that were unfolding inside her.

"Ellie?" Jacob called, just as she reached the doorway.

"You must be hungry. I'll set supper on the table."

"Chicken and dumplings, Papa," Caleb said, licking his lips. "Our favorite."

"And biscuits, honey, and butter," Thomas added, grinning, and looking at Krista to continue their game.

"Carrots and apple cider that I helped press. Now you, Papa."

"No fair. I didn't get a chance to peek at the kitchen."

"Favorites, Papa. Think of all the things you said you missed the most." Krista added a hug for good measure.

Ellie couldn't help softly laughing as she ladled the chicken and dumplings into the big soup tureen. If Jacob continued with the list he was giving his children, he would sit and eat for the entire time of his visit. From the pie safe in the pantry, she took both a dried apple pie and a cherry one. The pan was already filled with nuts for roasting later by the fire in the parlor. She quickly grated nutmeg and a bit of the sugarloaf over the buttered carrots before taking the dish inside.

Suppertime was filled with the children's stories, and Ellie knew Jacob encouraged them to go on, feeding on Krista's hushed voice telling him about the barn swallows building their nest outside the barn eaves, as much as he did the food. The children seemed to sense the need for laughter, and Caleb told of the day the horses got loose and they all chased them through pouring rain in fields knee-high with water.

"There was Ellie in her papa's big boots making a grab for Sugar's halter, when the mare bolted and Ellie went facedown in the mud. She was madder than a wet hen, Papa, but she kicked off those boots and went after Sugar until she led her back to the barn."

"Ellie lets me help feed the little chipmunks that live by the boulder near the creek, Papa. I got to name them, too," Krista said, then turned to Thomas. "You tell Papa about the rabbits."

Thomas glared at his niece's smug smile and swallowed. He could do nothing about the blush stealing across his cheeks.

"What's wrong?" Jacob asked, glancing around the table, his gaze fixed on Ellie, expecting an answer.

"It's best—" Ellie began, coughing and hiding her smile in her napkin.

"I'll tell," Thomas said. "I went down to Cripple-bush—"

"That comes from the Dutch, Papa," Caleb cut in. "It's a *creupel bosch*. A place of—of—"

"Stunted trees," Ellie finished for him.

"Yes, that's what it is and—"

"Caleb," Thomas interrupted. "It's all right, I don't mind it so much now. Let me tell him what I did." With a shrug, Caleb nodded. "The Van Dorns had an auction of their farm animals when they decided to sell out. All three of their sons died fighting, and they wanted to go home. I bought Krista two rabbits and told her they were her pets. The others were for me to breed and sell. Mr. Van Dorn made a nice profit selling rabbits to women who had no men to hunt for them, and I wanted to help Ellie."

"And?" Jacob prompted, leaning back in his chair, unable to understand his brother's hesitation.

"Oh, he doesn't want to tell you, Papa, I will," Krista said. "I named one Lady and the other Miss Oliver, only I thought Lady got sick. She was pulling out her fur and wouldn't let me pet her, but I didn't tell anyone 'cause I was afraid Thomas would get mad."

Ellie rescued them. "Jacob, we discovered that Miss Oliver isn't a "miss" she is a "mister." Lady won't eat if they are apart, and the baby rabbits haven't stopped multiplying."

"Haven't stopped—just how many do you—"

"Oh, Papa, wait till you see them. They're ever so tiny, like little kittens and so soft. They follow me, too."

Jacob looked around at each one trying to stifle their laughter. "Ellie? How many?"

"She doesn't want Thomas to sell them, and his breeding pairs are not producing. It was too late to demand his money back from Mr. Van Dorn. So at last count, for you do appreciate how difficult it is to keep track of constant litters, we think there are about two hundred.''

"My Lord, do you know how many men they would feed!''

Ellie saw the horrified look in Jacob's eyes before he closed them. Thomas stared at his plate, then pushed it away. Caleb too, understood what his father meant and hung his head. Only Krista glanced around, puzzled.

"Papa, I won't let—''

"Krista, help me clear the table,'' Ellie said in a firm voice she rarely used. She could see that Jacob was at a loss to say something to his daughter, and she hurt for him. But the war could not be kept outside these walls, and he wasn't going to spend his visit denying it was real. "There are men who go hungry and your papa's job is to feed them, Krista. When farms are destroyed, there is no food from the fields, no animals left to hunt. Now, you know what your papa meant. It wasn't meant to hurt you, lambkin.''

Krista set the bowl she had taken back on the table, and went around to her father's side. Sliding her small arms as far as she could around him, she rested her head against his chest.

"I'm sorry, lamb,'' Jacob whispered, stroking her back. "I didn't want to bring the war home with me. I—''

"Have you been hungry, Papa?'' she asked.

His gaze met Ellie's in an agony of indecision. His need to protect warred with the fact that he had never lied to his children. When his brothers died, he had explained to them his own desire to enlist and help end the war no matter how small a role he played. As a soldier, his courage was measured time and again, but faced with his child's question, Jacob didn't know if he could answer her. The warmth and encouragement in Ellie's eyes gave him a quiet strength. Her nod confirmed his decision.

"Yes, little one, I've been hungry."

Knowing Jacob's pride, Ellie understood what the admission had cost him. Krista's whispering that he would not be hungry here, Caleb and Thomas joining her to simply hold him close as if they, too, wished to protect him, made a lump form in Ellie's throat at the unified family picture they made.

Hunger rose inside her to be a part of it. A hunger so deep, it was painful. She barely managed to take the soup tureen into the kitchen. Her resolve not to marry without love weakened in a dangerous manner. She loved Jacob, more for his simple courage.

It was close to midnight when Ellie once more climbed the stairs. Earlier, she had come up to hear the children's prayers and help them get ready for bed. She left to finish cleaning the kitchen when Jacob gave in to their demands for stories.

The strong protective urge to hush them and let Jacob rest took her by surprise. She knew he was exhausted, but would not thank her for interfering. It had been some time since she had heard him moving around, and she felt hurt he had not come down to say good night.

A single candle lit her way, its carved wooden holder one she would not part with, for it had been a gift from Jacob long ago when he first learned how to whittle. The drafts chilled her in the upstairs narrow hall as the winds picked up and found the small gaps in the blue stone's chinking. Another repair that needed tending.

Setting the candle down on the chest just inside the

doorway to the boys' room, Ellie shook her head and smiled. Caleb, as usual, hogged more than half of the double bed that had once been her grandmother's, then Lucy's. He slept sprawled on his stomach, one bare foot dangling off the edge of the bed. She tucked his leg beneath the thick down quilt, and with a light touch, smoothed back the unruly lock of his hair before she pressed a kiss to his head. Silently wishing him the sweetest dreams, she saw that he was clutching the small wooden horse Jacob made for his last birthday.

With a sigh, she moved around the bed to Thomas, wishing she could get Caleb the pony he wanted for Christmas. Thomas had set his hope on getting a new rifle for hunting, but that too was a gift beyond her means.

Jacob sent almost all his pay to her, but the money went to pay the men hired to work the fields. This year, the corn was high, near ready to harvest when a hailstorm destroyed most of it. There wasn't enough left for such expensive gifts.

Thomas lay on his side, hugging the edge of the bed. The quilt was pulled nearly to his ears. He no longer gave or received kisses without a great deal of embarrassment, but Ellie could kiss him now while he slept.

Across the hall was the closed door to her parents' bedroom. She fought the temptation to knock and see if Jacob had everything he needed, or if he, too, was asleep with a quilt half off him. If they were married, she would have the right to enter that room. She could set her candle on the dressing table and unpin her braids, then brush her hair while Jacob waited within the four poster—No! She shook her head, forcing herself to stop envisioning such intimacy with Jacob.

Krista's door was ajar, and Ellie tiptoed inside, then stopped. Jacob was asleep in her rocking chair with his child cradled within his arms. The faint glow of the candle revealed the smiling peaceful look on Krista's face, her rag doll tucked between her body and Jacob's chest. Ellie saw his uniform's jacket had fallen to the floor, and hesitated before she went closer and picked it up. She rubbed her cheek against its wool, glancing at Jacob. Ellie knew he would have a crick in his neck from sleeping with his head tilted to one side, but she didn't have the heart to wake him. Placing the candle on the floor, she set his jacket on the bedpost and took a wool comforter to cover them. Staring down at the sleeping child's face, she had no doubt that Krista's dream would be sweet this night, for she had her father home.

But once in her own room downstairs, Ellie found she was suddenly restless. The fires had been banked for the night, and she bundled her shawl tight over her night rail and robe as she went into the parlor.

Jacob remained where he was on the stairs, sure Ellie had not noticed him. He went to the doorway, watching her, aware of how much he owed her for not only taking his children into her home so they could remain together, but for the love she had showered on them and his brother.

She stood facing the fire, looking into the flames, and he wondered what thoughts brought a dreamy look to her face. Her hair in its single braid nearly reached her slender hips. His hands curled at his sides as he remembered the brief hold he'd had on her. Jacob couldn't forget the sweet touch of her lips, or the way she fit perfectly in his arms. It had been a long time since he had been with a woman, but from all he had learned in the talks with his brother and children, Ellie was still an innocent.

He was bound by honor that she remain so. Unless she consented to marry him.

The contrast between Lucy and Ellie came to his mind, and for a few moments he allowed it. Lucy lusted for laughter, for gaiety, and for him. Her passion for living touched anyone who knew her. Ellie was her opposite, soft and quiet, sober in dress and manner . . . The thought suddenly came that Ellie was passionate, too, in her own way. She had fought his family to keep the children and Thomas together, fought to hold onto both farms, was still fighting him about marriage.

Sap popped, and a shower of sparks had Ellie jump back. Jacob moved to catch her, afraid she would trip on the trailing hem of her robe.

"You're awake!"

"It would appear so, Ellie." His hands tightened to hold her upper arms and kept her against his chest. Jacob rested his chin on the top of her head, unconsciously rocking her body with his. "There's snow falling. I've missed the peace to be found in nights like this. The children safe and asleep, the house warm, and the sweet smell of apple wood burning. All that's missing," he said softly, stilling her small move to be free, "is—"

"It's late, Jacob. The boys and I do all the milking now, so I must go to sleep." Warmth that had nothing to do with the fire heated Ellie's body. Warmth that came from Jacob's hands holding her against him, warmth from his deep, soft voice that seemed to stroke her from the inside out. All she wanted to do was to turn and have him hold her. *Liar,* a little voice whispered. *You would love to have Jacob kiss you again.*

As aware as she was of his height and masculine presence, Ellie couldn't help but notice that Jacob's male scent melded with spicy pine. It was wrong to be here with him this late, alone, and allowing him to continue to hold her. But Ellie couldn't summon the will to move. It felt right to be here.

"There's so much I want to say, Ellie. So much I need to thank you for. And I find that I'm at a loss for words. Just holding you is a contentment—"

"Jacob, please, don't say more."

"All right. I won't." He spun her around in his arms. Ellie didn't pull away as he expected. She offered no resistance at all. Her gaze was searching and curious. Jacob couldn't help smiling. "Not frightened?" He waited, but all he heard was the small catch in her breath.

He gave in to the overwhelming need to kiss her. She was woman warm, woman soft, and he had been alone too long. Her sigh when their lips met, sent a shaft of pleasure through him. He kept the kiss chaste, rocking his mouth over hers, and felt the softening of her body. The sweet taste of her played havoc with his good intentions. He forgot this was Ellie, and that she was not his wife, pressing her closer, deepening his kiss until her lips parted. Moments or minutes—Jacob didn't know. He was hard and aching, and wanted to lose himself in loving her.

Loving her? Ellie? The questions disappeared the second she made a small sound of need.

Ellie found her dreams were pale imaginings compared to the intense pleasure of kissing Jacob. She knew this was wrong. Jacob was tired, lonely, and didn't love her. She fought with herself, and found the strength to press her hands against his chest to be free.

Jacob reluctantly relinquished his hold on her, and

let her step back. It was let her go or pull her down to the carpet before the fire. If he had ever been aroused so quickly or wanted a woman so badly as he wanted Ellie, he couldn't remember it. More passionate than he believed, he could only look down at her face, his breath coming hard and fast in an effort to restrain himself.

He shouldn't have kissed her. A fool's thought. He couldn't call the kisses back. Didn't want to. But he had to fight the need to have her back in his arms.

"Ellie, I—"

"Don't. Not a word," she whispered, backing away, then turning to run from the parlor.

Jacob followed her into the kitchen. She struck a match, and he saw the tremble of her hand as she lit the lamp. From the top shelf of the corner cupboard, she took down a small jug.

"Ellie, did you find my kisses so unpleasant you need a drink of applejack?"

"No."

"No? No, what? You don't need a drink? You liked my kisses? You found them unpleasant?"

"Yes, I want to taste the applejack, Jacob. Yes, I want it because of your kisses." She managed to pull the swollen cork out, keeping her eyes on the jug. Jacob stood on the other side of the table, but even that was too close. "Go to sleep, Jacob. You're tired. You're not yourself. You've been lonely. You . . . you—"

"I *wanted* to kiss you, Ellie. Don't make excuses."

She didn't answer him. She lifted the jug and brought it to her lips. Her eyes met Jacob's disbelieving gaze, and Ellie smiled before she took a small sip. His gaze remained on her until she set the jug down. Ellie shuddered as the liquor burned a path down her throat, leaving a heated glow behind. She licked her lips, saw that he was reaching for the jug, and pushed it over to him.

Jacob took a healthy swallow, needing the drink as much as he wanted to make sure it was applejack. The homemade brew still kicked harder than a mule, and beat anything the southern boys had to trade over the picket line.

"Well," he asked, setting the jug down between them, "are you going to tell me what this is about?"

"Ah, Jacob, it's a truth I've been hoping to discover."

Her voice was soft and teasing, just like her gaze, which only blended an unreasonable anger for being the object of some secret riddle with the desire tightening his body. He looked again at the moist sheen of her lips, and almost went around the table to take hold of her.

"Did you ever hear the whispers about your kisses, Jacob?"

"Whispers? What whispers?"

He was suddenly all indignant male with his fur ruffled the wrong way at the mere thought of a possible affront to his pride. Ellie covered her mouth to hold back her laughter.

"Ellie," he warned, "if I get my hands on you, you'll—"

"No! I'll tell. They said your kisses were as potent as Mr. Moser's applejack. I think they were wrong."

"Wrong? Why? And who were they?"

"Every girl in the county that you kissed."

"But you."

The hard edge of his voice stopped her teasing. With a stricken look, she whispered, "Yes, all but me."

Jacob came around the table, but did not attempt to

touch her. "And tell me why they were wrong, Ellie." When she shook her head, Jacob leaned closer and smiled. "Should I kiss you again to make sure you know?"

Temptation loomed before her. The sort of temptation she knew the minister warned about in his weekly sermons. But this was Jacob, and she couldn't heed her own warnings about him.

"Good night, Jacob."

"You disappoint me, Ellie," he murmured, giving in to the need he had to touch her again. Her hair was soft and fine, and he stroked her braid, then lifted it over her shoulder. "Ellie, tell me the truth." Satisfaction filled him that he had stopped her from leaving. But her spine curved as she wrapped her arms around her waist protectively, and his satisfaction disappeared.

"I never meant to hurt you, Ellie. I can't, with any honesty, apologize for kissing you. We've been friends for a long time, and you never held back from having your say."

"Yes, we've been friends," she said after a moment, then turned without looking at him. "They were wrong about your kisses, Jacob. Your kisses are more potent than Mr. Moser's homebrew."

Relief swept him. "Then why did you stop me?" Since she refused to look at him, he didn't think she would answer him.

But her voice, while soft, had the same impact as the tear-filled eyes she revealed. "Lucy."

"Lucy? She's dead, Ellie. I'll never forget that she was my wife, but my time for grief and mourning are over. I wouldn't have asked you to marry me if it wasn't." Jacob disliked the thought that formed, but he voiced it. "You brought her up deliberately, didn't you?"

Ellie fled to her room. Jacob had honed in on the truth too quickly. She *had* mentioned Lucy deliberately. It was the only way to stop herself from running back into his arms.

"Ellie?" Jacob heard the closing of her door as final as any words. He absently lifted the jug and took another drink before he recorked it and put it back in the cupboard. Why had Ellie mentioned Lucy? Ellie didn't have a vengeful bone in her body. But she used Lucy's name to erect a wall.

Only Ellie had waited until after their kisses, he had to remind himself. And she was right. He was too tired to explore her contrary female mind.

Morning ended the night's snowfall, leaving behind a frozen landscape that glistened as the sun rose. Chores were dispatched quickly with Jacob lending a hand to feed the animals while Ellie and Thomas first washed, then milked the cows. Caleb, with Krista's help, mucked out the stalls and pitched fresh bedding hay.

Ellie had given Jacob the trunk of her father's old clothes, since all his had been lost in the fire. Jacob shed his role of soldier with his uniform. It was easy for him, with the games and laughter they shared collecting the eggs from the chicken's nests in the barn loft, avoiding rabbits of all sizes and color scampering to get out of the way.

Jacob was declared the undisputed winner of being the fastest milker, and for having the best aim. The barn cats and kittens sat patiently waiting for their share of the warm milk squirted from the cow's teats,

and Jacob gathered the biggest group around his milk
stool.

His prize bull was housed in a small, separate pen,
and Jacob added yet another thank-you he owed Ellie.
The animal's hide gleamed with the good care he had
received. His farm team were in stalls along with Ellie's, and he enjoyed the simple pleasure of currying
their coats, tails, and manes. Pigs squealed and scrambled when he fed them their corn. Ellie helped him
give the two sows their morning back scratches, and
together they brought the full milk pails to the springhouse.

Thomas had cleared the paths and joined them for
breakfast. Bowls of thick porridge topped with cream,
sweet butter, and maple syrup made a special treat.
Jacob guiltily caught himself taking a third helping of
hickory-smoked bacon and eggs, but Ellie merely
pushed the plates closer to him. He swore Ellie's muffins were the lightest and most delicious he had ever
tasted, and left not one crumb on the plate.

Jacob sipped his coffee as Ellie and Krista cleaned
up the kitchen. He felt a contentment that was bone
deep. This is what he missed; the sense of rightness,
the glow of nurturing his own, the smiling faces of his
children and their unexpected hugs, as if they were
afraid he would disappear.

"Jacob," Ellie said once the last cup had been hung
in the cupboard and the last plate dried, "you'll be
expected at your aunt's this morning. Word will spread
that you're home and—"

"No, Ellie. Aunt Faye and my cousins can wait.
There are only five days to Christmas. Time we got
our tree. Thomas said you had one picked out up on
the ridge. You'll come with us to make sure we cut
down the right one."

234 *Raine Cantrell*

"But I need to—"

"It can wait, Ellie. The children and I want you to come with us." Her quick nod made him rise. "I'll get the ax and the sleds." Ellie was shy with him this morning, but Jacob had no intention of allowing her to retreat from him. Not after those unforgettable kisses . . .

When they reached the long sloping hill that led down to snow-covered fields, it was too inviting. Ellie and Jacob gave in to the children's pleas to go sledding. The longest wooden sled barely held Jacob's tall body. He lay down first on his stomach, holding the long wooden slat to steer, and Krista laid flat on top of him.

After a brief scuffle, Caleb gave in and let Thomas steer their sled. Ellie rooted for both teams to win, which earned her scowls and dire threats when the four of them climbed back up the hill.

She ignored them, and continued her cheering, enjoying the children's delight in having Jacob play with them. The day was crisp and chill, but the sun was bright, and there was no wind. Ellie paid no attention to Jacob gathering the children and his brother around him before they once more dragged their sleds back to where she waited.

"Oh, Ellie," Caleb announced, "it's your turn now."

"Oh no. I couldn't."

"Yes, Ellie. We've all had turns, and now it's yours," Thomas said, circling behind her. "And you'll ride down with Jacob. He can make his sled go the fastest."

"Jacob?" Ellie flashed him a surprised look. "Did you put them up to this?"

"Go with him, Ellie," Krista insisted, taking hold of her mittened hand. "It's such fun. If you win, Papa will kiss you like he did me. He said I was good . . . good—"

"Ballast." Caleb shot Krista a smug look.

"I don't believe I would make good ballast." But as Ellie protested, she backed away from Jacob only to come up against Thomas. He caught her and relinquished her to his brother.

"You wouldn't dare spoil their fun, would you, Ellie?"

The wicked slant of his mouth and the laughter gleaming in his eyes brought on her rueful smile. She was outnumbered. "One ride, Jacob. That's all."

He took hold of her hand and drew her near the sled. Ellie stilled the panicked feeling inside when Jacob was facedown on the sled. She gathered her heavy woolen cloak, grateful that both Thomas and Caleb lent their aid to help her lie down on top of Jacob.

"Hold my shoulders," he ordered, stifling a groan when she wiggled this way and that to get comfortable. He spread his legs so hers fit between them. The boys were ready. Jacob used the toes of his boots to shove off. He squeezed Ellie's legs between his.

Ellie's small cry was lost as wind rushed past. She clung to Jacob's broad shoulders, pressing her cheek to his back, and wondered how the heat of his body could climb inside her. The intimate press of her body to his instantly brought the picture to her mind of him holding her against him last night.

Ellie thought Jacob yelled something, but the wind rushing by whipped the words away before she understood him. She gripped his shoulders and shifted her body forward, shouting at him to repeat it. Her move upset the balance, sending the sled into a rocking slide before tumbling them off. Jacob grabbed her, and she held him tight as they rolled over and over down the hill.

Stunned by the rapid tumble, Ellie couldn't catch her breath. She lay beneath Jacob, and the cold, wet snow chilled her back. But where his body covered hers, there was a blazing warmth that made her think she was too close to fire. He stirred, and his smallest moves brought her an awareness of the strange tension taking hold of her.

She gazed up at him when he crouched over her, tearing off one glove with his teeth, his warm hand gently brushing the snow from her face and hair. The tender concern of his touch, repeated in his gaze, sent a painful yearning through her. Even his low, deep voice was concerned as he murmured questions.

"I'm all right, Jacob," she managed to say. He had lost his hat in their tumble, and his hair fell down his forehead. Ellie clenched her hands around the snow to stop herself from reaching up to brush the snow from his hair. "I guess," she said, offering him a crooked little smile, "that I wasn't good ballast."

"Oh, Ellie," Jacob said, rocking back to rest on his heels, "only you would think of that." He couldn't seem to resist her smile and leaned close again, drawing her up and against him. This was the Ellie he remembered. The one that could bring a smile despite his real concern that she had been hurt. He leaned his head back to see her and found himself staring into her eyes. There was glazed desire there, but he was sure Ellie wasn't aware of it. It was a look he would be pleased to see again, and again. And that smile beckoned him. He kissed her briefly then pulled back.

"Jacob? We didn't win. You shouldn't have kissed me."

"I needed to, Ellie." He shook his head, wondering what was happening to him. He was fighting with himself not to have another taste of her mouth. He had never even noticed that her eyes were wide, and the color of rich brown sugar. Jacob wasn't conscious of rubbing her arms with his hands, drawing her closer to him, until Ellie put up her hands to stop him.

"Why, Ellie? You feel it, too."

She closed her eyes in defense of what she might reveal to him. The day had been perfect until now. Her secret pretense that this was her family, her love, disappeared. Jacob didn't love her.

"Why didn't you answer us?" Thomas demanded as he neared. "Were you hurt, Ellie?"

"Ellie's fine. Go on up," Jacob answered, then added, "we'll be along in a moment."

Jacob stood up and lifted Ellie to her feet. He began to brush the snow from her cloak, startled that it took some effort to keep his touch impersonal.

"Something is happening Ellie that we need to talk about." Jacob snatched up the sled's rope and held out his other hand.

Ellie hesitated. She sensed that Jacob wanted her to accept his hand, and demand that they talk.

"Ellie?"

The soft, questioning note in his voice, made her decision. She placed her hand in his. His smile was all the reward she could have hoped to have.

"Can you walk up or would you like me to carry you?"

"I'll walk, Jacob. My legs are quite steady now."

"Pity," he murmured, "I'm not sure mine are."

Ellie followed in his footsteps, for his weight tamped the snow and made it easier for her to walk. She stopped suddenly, and Jacob did, too. "Are you flirting with me, Jacob?"

Her serious voice, the earnest expression on her face made his heart skip a beat. He thought about teasing her and then swallowed the words. Just as serious as she, he answered, "Why, yes, Ellie. I am."

"Oh. I see."

"The thought troubles you?"

"I'm not sure," she replied, starting to walk again behind him. "Would we still be friends?"

"Friends and more, Ellie. Much more." An unexpected tenderness welled up inside him. "Don't worry about it, Ellie. I'll see to everything."

"That's what I'm afraid of," she whispered to herself.

"Push harder, Jacob. It won't fit."

"I am pushing, Ellie! You and Thomas aren't pulling hard enough."

"Testy, contrary male," Ellie muttered.

"What was that?" Jacob shot back, having heard her clearly.

"Nothing. Let's try again, Jacob."

"Thomas, come 'round to the front and help Caleb. I'll pull from the inside with Ellie."

The switch took a few minutes. Jacob made sure the wide, thick bottom boughs of their tree were squeezed as tight as could be to the trunk. He scowled at his son's suggestion that he should have cut the smaller tree Ellie had picked out. Krista told him Ellie wished for a big tree, and a big tree is what she was getting.

Rather than taking the opposite side from Ellie, Jacob stood behind her. His hands fit between the position of hers on the top branches. Keeping Ellie in a state of heightened awareness of him wasn't fair, but he couldn't help himself. He felt the slight tremor of her body as he curved his body to the bend of hers.

"Ready," he called out. Jacob pulled. The boys shoved. The tree suddenly came free like a battering ram through a gate. Jacob crashed backward with Ellie under the force, landing half on and half off the settee. The fragrant pine branches smothered them.

"You're gracious not to say I told you so, Ellie."

Ellie lifted the tips of pine away from her face. She knew Jacob had always had the largest Christmas tree he could find. She shifted and managed to face him.

"I wanted you to have a special Christmas, Jacob. You and the children that is. Just like when you were home."

"I could always have that if this was my home, Ellie. All you have to do is say yes and marry me."

"Oh, you did it!" Krista yelled.

"Thanks to cousin Will's help," Thomas added, then realized that his brother and Ellie had disappeared. "Jacob! Cousin Will's here." He shared a look with his older cousin and nephew. "The tree!" he shouted, scrambling to get around the spreading branches to the other side.

Jacob pushed aside branches to reveal himself. Ellie did the same on the other side. Assuring everyone that they were fine, they pushed as Will helped the boys to lift the tree away.

"A cheer for Ellie," Krista insisted. "She's going to make this the best Christmas ever."

"Yes, by all means," Jacob said, lifting Ellie's hand to his lips. "A cheer for the lovely and most gracious, Ellie." But his eyes met hers with a wicked gleam as he pressed his lips to her hand, and softly, so no one but Ellie heard him, said, "A home, Ellie, just say yes."

With Will's help, Jacob and the boys made short work of getting the tree in place. Chairs and tables had to be moved to make room for the tree in front of the windows.

Ellie busied herself in the kitchen getting supper ready, while the children sat with Jacob and Will in the parlor. Thomas came in to see if the wash water was heated. He filled a bucket to carry it upstairs, taking the children with him. Ellie heard the soft murmur of the men's voices as she sliced and fried rounds of potatoes, just like the elegant Moon Lake Lodge in Saratoga Springs served to their guests. An article in the newspaper said an American Indian chef working there had once sliced the potatoes so thin to please a disatisfied guest, that the potatoes couldn't be eaten with a fork. But the crisp fries were featured on the menu as Saratoga chips ever since then.

The children loved them, and she hoped they would be a surprise for Jacob to enjoy. Since the stock pot was always simmering on the back burner, a rich broth would be warming. Thick slices of bread, cold smoked ham and pickled corn and another pie would complete their supper.

Ellie didn't even realize she was listening hard for Jacob's voice. In the short time he had been here, she found herself wanting to know its every nuance. Her own warning to herself about weakening once he was here, was dangerously close to coming true. *"A home, Ellie, just say yes."* Over and over she repeated Jacob's words, then came to with a start. Jacob's raised voice to his cousin, drew her nearer the doorway to hear him.

"I don't care what anyone believes. My children are here, as is my brother. I won't miss a moment of time with them."

"But Jacob, there's talk. It's not right for her to let you stay here."

"You dare to talk to me about what is right, Will? My home was destroyed, and the best my family could do was to suggest separating my children and brother. Ellie is the only one who offered to keep them together."

"That's true. And we are all grateful to her. But Jacob, you will be leaving and Ellie will be left to face the gossip."

"I've asked her to marry me, Will."

"We didn't know," Will said, coming to his cousin's side near the fireplace. "She never said a word, Jacob. This puts a different—"

"She hasn't said yes. Don't be making any plans, Will. And I would appreciate your keeping this to yourself."

"But the family—"

"Have their own troubles. I know them all well enough."

"Why hasn't she agreed to marry you, Jacob? With the farms adjoining boundaries, you'd be the largest landowner in the area. And it isn't as if there is anyone else to offer for her. She's got a sharp tongue, for one thing, and she's too old for any but a widower to want to marry her."

Jacob swallowed the words that would have revealed his growing feelings for Ellie. His cousin did not deserve to hear them first. He wouldn't believe him anyway. Will was as close as a brother to him, and knew how much he had loved Lucy. He would be the last one to believe that Jacob could think of loving another woman.

For Ellie, Jacob's silence was damning. She knew he was grateful to her, but it wasn't a strong reason to marry. She returned to her cooking, vowing to put the conversation out of her thoughts. Just as she vowed to put Jacob out of her heart.

At the top of the stairs, Krista, with her face pressed against the rails of the banister, turned to her brother. "You heard? We've got to help Papa. He wants to marry her. I love Ellie a lot, Caleb. She's good to us and makes me feel better when I cry about missing Papa. And I want a mama of my own."

Caleb, sitting on the top step, rested his chin on his fists. He wouldn't admit it to Krista, but he loved Ellie, too. "I kinda like her a special lot, too. It's been nice living with her. She don't yell. Well, not much. And she doesn't get mad like Luther's ma if you forget to wipe your feet or if you're late for chores. But I don't know how to make her marry Papa."

"I think she loves us, Caleb. You're just a boy and don't know about love, yet. But I'm a girl and do. Aunt Faye said Ellie must love us to take us in to live with her and be so nice."

"We need Thomas. He's bigger. And even if he's a boy, he'll know more about than you do."

They ran into the boys' room and hurried to tell Thomas. His solution met with Krista's approval. "A special gift!" she cried, clapping her hands. "It's perfect. But it has to be something that only grown-up men give to ladies."

"I guess," Caleb said. "If you and Thomas think it's right, I suppose it is. Sure wish we had some money. I used all of mine to buy Christmas gifts. Ain't no one hiring on for extra work now. Still makes no sense to me how a gift is gonna make Ellie love Papa and marry him."

" 'Cause ladies love pretty things, Caleb."

"Stop it, both of you," Thomas warned. "Ellie

needs a new shawl. I heard Mrs. Ackerley tell her it was high time she had one, and Ellie agreed with her. She's been wearing that same one to church for almost three years.''

''That's not special enough or pretty enough,'' Krista informed him. ''It has to be a . . . a romantic gift.''

''Romantic? Where did you learn about that, little sister?''

''From cousin Matilda. She said the flowers she got for her birthday from Spencer were romantic.''

''Well, he's gonna marry her.''

''What about a new bonnet,'' Thomas suggested, hoping to stop their bickering. ''The ladies were all talking about Mrs. Van Tyek's new hat. Said it looked like she squashed it flat and then plucked her rooster clean for the all feathers it had. Ellie'd look real pretty in a new hat.''

''Ellie could use a sewing box.''

''No, Caleb. Ellie would love a fan. A fancy one that's painted and has lace.'' Wide-eyed, Krista waited for approval.

''Never saw one like that in the mercantile. We'd need to go to Kingston, and not tell anyone why. 'Sides, what would she do with it? Fans are for ladies who dress up all the time. Ellie doesn't. And those flowers sound better, but there ain't any in winter.''

''We can't pay for it,'' Caleb added.

''Stop it! You're both being . . . being boys! It's a perfect gift. Ladies don't want things they can use. Sometimes it's nice to have a pretty just to look at.''

''That's so silly only a girl would say it,'' Caleb countered. ''Tell her, Thomas. Tell my silly sister I'm right.''

Ellie called them to supper. The three of them

rushed off the bed and headed for the stairs. Just be-
fore they reached the bottom, Thomas whispered,
"Listen. I know how we can get the money and buy
Ellie a fan."

Will didn't stay for supper with them, but he did
remind them of the skating party planned for the next
night down at Aunt Faye's pond with a covered-dish
supper afterward at the schoolhouse.

"You come with Jacob and the children, Ellie.
Folks'll be expecting you."

"She'll be there," Jacob answered before Ellie said
a word. "And, Will, tell Aunt Faye I'll be over to visit
once our supper is done."

Ellie waited until Jacob was ready to leave before
she said anything about the skating party. "I haven't
been skating in years. I can't go. But I will make
something for you to take to the supper."

"You don't forget how to skate, Ellie." He buttoned
up his greatcoat and leaned close to plant a light, quick
kiss on her mouth. "I'll be there to hold you so you
won't fall."

It was futile to argue with him. Ellie nodded, then
had to admit to herself that Jacob's words did not re-
assure her. His proposal to hold her to prevent a fall
came too late. She was already falling. Falling deeper
in love with him.

Caleb grabbed his skates and ran off the moment
Jacob drew the horse-drawn sleigh to a stop. Ellie
called out a warning to be careful and cautioned him
to keep his hat on. She stopped herself when Jacob
started laughing. She had taken over his role as parent
and a flush stained her cheeks, but he merely whispered, "It's the place I want you to have, Ellie."

Thomas secured the horse, then he, too, took off down the path leading to the pond. Krista shrieked when Jacob lifted her high to swing her down from the sleigh. Another family arrived, and she ran over to greet a friend.

Jacob ignored Ellie's hand, and lifted her down with his hands on her waist. He kept her between himself and the sleigh. "Are you warm enough?" he asked, cupping his hands over the scarf around her neck.

"If I become any warmer, Jacob, I'll melt the snow beneath my feet."

"That's good, Ellie. That's real good. Just what I wanted to hear." He raised his hand and tucked the lap robe inside the sleigh just as Krista came back to them.

Krista took hold of Ellie's hand and rubbed her cheek against her sleeve. "We'll have the best time, Ellie. I'm so happy you came with us. Papa is, too. Tell her, Papa."

"Very happy, lamb." Jacob slung three pairs of borrowed skates over his shoulder. "We need to thank Aunt Faye for not giving away anything, or we wouldn't have these. And we'll make sure that Ellie has fun."

His gaze met Ellie's. He knew she wasn't happy being here. The talk he had with his aunt revealed the whispers that spread over his staying with Ellie without benefit of a chaperon. When he pointed out that his children were there as well as his brother, his aunt said most neighbors didn't count them as being proper adult chaperons. Jacob had been forced to confess his intent to marry Ellie to enlist his aunt's aid in quelling the talk. He wanted this time with Ellie to be a happy one.

Other sleighs arrived, the greetings called out to the

three of them. He merely smiled at Ellie's questioning
look, and with Krista between them set off down the
path.

Bonfires dotted the banks to allow light for the skaters to see and warm those who were not skating. Jacob
led them to an upended empty wooden keg where
Krista promptly sat for him to put on her skates. She
called out to other children, urging him to hurry with
the straps.

Ellie knew the greetings and smiles were for Jacob.
At first that is, she began hearing her own name mentioned with shouts to hurry and join them.

"Your turn, Ellie."

She started, lost in her thoughts, and saw that Jacob
held his hand out to her. Krista was already a part of
a laughing group of children forming a ragged line to
race up the center of the pond. She gripped his hand
tightly, and even through their gloves could feel his
warmth as he helped her to sit.

Lifting her foot, Jacob carefully brushed the snow
from her shoe. "While I'm away, I dream about winter
nights like this," he murmured. "Nights when the sky
is clear and the moon full. More than the quiet, I
longed for the sense of the stars being close. Remember when I tried to take one down for you, Ellie?"

"Yes, I remember. Bold and brash, that was you,
Jacob." She loved sharing his thoughts, and warmth
unfurled inside her. "You swore you would get one for
me."

"And never did." He checked the straps to make
sure they were secure on her skates, then sat in the
snow to put his on. "But I discovered something tonight, Ellie. If you looked in a mirror right now, you'd
see the star's sparkle in your eyes."

"Hush, Jacob. Someone might hear you."

"Let them. You look lovely."

His smile was all male and a delicious shiver added itself to the warmth inside her. Anticipation laced her voice. "Are you flirting again?"

"I've only begun, Ellie." Coming to his feet, he held his hands out to her. "Take hold, Ellie, and trust me. I won't let anything or anyone hurt you."

Trust him. Jacob never asked for small things. She had to take hold of his hands not to hurt him. He walked backward toward the edge of the frozen pond. Ellie knew she was weakening. Sharing times like this, hearing Jacob reveal his thoughts, might be enough. She had loved him for so long, and loneliness stretched before her. Greed was a sin. One she was guilty of if she held fast to wanting his love before she consented to marry him.

The center of the pond belonged to the children. Jacob slid an arm around her waist, keeping her close to his body, the other arm extended with Ellie's hand firm in his. "Ready?" Her smile was answer enough. He began to skate slowly, joining the others keeping to the edge. He guided them over the rough spots in the ice, humming softly. Ellie was tense, but as neighbors skated near, welcoming him home and talking of Christmas plans, he felt the tension ease from her. Children shrieked and tumbled, daring each other to spin around.

Ellie thought Jacob had told his aunt that he had asked her to marry him. If he didn't, his cousin Will told her, for there was warmth in the greetings given them, as well as the looks cast their way. Suddenly she didn't care that they were being linked together. She was a part of the skating party because of Jacob. She wasn't alone. She wasn't left out. All the invitations for him to visit included her.

Thomas raced toward them, stopping so fast, ice chips flew up from his skates. Caleb joined them, but when he tried to stop, his skates went one way, his body another, and the boy ended in a spraddle-legged pose. Thomas lifted him up in seconds, but they had to laugh at Caleb's exaggerated dignity as he brushed himself off.

Krista, with a smug smile for her brother, came up beside them with a graceful turn. "It's time! They're going to make the whip."

"Have fun," Ellie said, looking at each one in turn.

"Oh, we will," Jacob added, his gaze a warning to his brother and children not to say more. Skaters were already taking their positions around the edge of the pond. There was a whispered excitement in every voice.

Will and a few other young men urged Jacob to join them near one of the fires. Ellie watched him go, and saw the flask they passed around. It puzzled her to see Jacob vehemently shake his head when Will spoke to him.

"What's going on, Thomas? What are they asking your brother to do?"

"Wait and see, Ellie."

Krista tugged her hand for attention. "Ellie, did you hear Marybeth showing off about her new muff? She bragged it costs lots more than mine. Said it was better, too."

"It is lovely. But lamb, Thomas worked hard to tan the pelts for yours. You look every bit as pretty." Ellie hugged her tight. "Krista, we've talked about this before. Marybeth shows off her possessions to have attention. She wants people to like her."

"Yes, I know, Ellie," the child answered with a long sigh. "It's not nice to envy someone. Even like

Marybeth, who can be hateful. I get picked first in the games, and Timmy Whitegate likes me better than her. Emmaline is the only one who's her real friend, and that's because Emmaline is a little mouse.''

Krista didn't know the memories she raked up for Ellie. But it was her own guilt for envying her cousin Lucy that made Ellie add, ''Emmaline is shy. If you were nicer to her, she wouldn't need to depend on Marybeth alone. You're a bright ray of sunshine, lamb. Try making someone else feel good, and it will come back double to you.''

''Oh, Ellie, I love you so much. You always make me feel better. I wish you were my mama. Who cares about Marybeth and her silly old muff. I have a better present.''

''What's that?''

''Can't tell her, Krista,'' Jacob warned, coming up behind Ellie and sliding his hands around her waist.

''They're starting!'' Caleb yelled, drawing their attention to the center of the pond where Will stood holding out his hands as he began to slowly turn.

Ellie saw his sons sprint free to catch hold of him. Then they began circling, calling out names as they passed people. Arms linked, the circling group grew larger. Thomas and Krista joined them, and Ellie looked up at Jacob. ''Is that what they wanted you to do?''

''Will's a better center post than I could be. I'm— oh, Caleb will have to skate fast to catch hold.''

They yelled encouragement to the boy, but Ellie wondered what Jacob had been about to say. Faster and faster the circle went, making it harder and harder for each one called to catch up.

Jacob looked down at her glowing face. ''You're enjoying it, aren't you?''

"Oh yes! I didn't know—"

"You never came with us. I would look for you, Ellie, but you were never there."

Ellie lost herself in the heated gaze he bestowed on her. She wanted nothing so much as to have him kiss her, right there, regardless of the others. She had a feeling Jacob wanted to do it. But he was tugging her hand.

"It's our turn, Ellie. Trust me." He pulled her onto the ice, sweeping her before him with his hands firm on her waist. Wind rushed by, Ellie's breath faltered, but the shouts of encouragement added to Jacob's made her feel as if she could do anything. They had to skate around the pond, Ellie kept missing the hand held out to her.

"Faster, Ellie, or we'll never make it."

"Either that," she yelled back to Jacob, "or we end in the snowbank!"

"Then I'd have the fun of warming you up!" Jacob gave her a push and saw that she was held fast. She instantly turned to look at him, holding out her hand and yelling.

He showed off, deliberately missing her. To see the joy on her face made it worth his effort to skate harder and faster each turn. It was a small gift to give Ellie, a time she could be as happy and carefree as any young girl being courted. She teased, then laughed at him. Jacob wanted more, and with a burst of speed, he caught hold of her hand to deafening cheers.

The moment they slowed, he pulled her free and kissed her. "My prize, Ellie," he whispered.

She blushed, thankful no one but Jacob could see. But he was wrong. The prize was hers. Another kiss. She could have more. All she had to do was say yes. Temptation loomed again. Did she really have to have his love, too?

Ellie carried both the burden of her indecision and the glow of the evening into the next day. Jacob brought down the small trunk of Christmas decorations for the tree, teasing her that she could be the angel gracing the top since her eyes sparkled so much. She held his words in her mind all day. Krista helped to turn the fruitcakes they had made weeks before, shooing her father and brother off with a broom when they wanted to steal one. But by early afternoon, the snow flurries began, and Ellie fretted that Thomas wasn't home yet from his mysterious errand that required him using the sleigh.

Jacob found her once again at the front door, looking for his brother. "Ellie, Thomas is nearly a man grown." He closed the door, but kept her caged between his warm body and the wood. "Boys his age are fighting in the south. It sickens me to see them, young and scared, dying before they've had a chance to live. I can understand why men on both sides desert the armies. It doesn't make a man feel like one to beat those weaker than himself."

The roil of emotion in his confession made Ellie turn. She allowed instinct to guide her, and slid her arms around Jacob to hold him close. "You are brave and strong, Jacob. To stay in the army, fighting this war, takes more courage than running away."

"You've always made it easy to talk to you, Ellie." He buried his lips against her braided hair, loving the faint scent of lilacs. "I'm so tired of death and war. I want to come home and plant my fields, watch my children grow, and see life around me. I long for an end to this senseless rage that builds inside me with every week that the war drags on. And I admit to you, Ellie, I'm weary of it. If it wasn't for your letters that I read over and over, I think I would lose my hope.''

''No. Don't say that, Jacob. There is so much waiting for you.'' She rocked her body with his, longing to say more, afraid she would whisper her love. She knew why the words couldn't be said. Jacob believed he needed her now, but once he was home for good, he would think clearly. She never wanted him to regret asking her to marry him. She was certain he would find someone to love. Letting him remain free would ensure his chance for happiness.

''You're so good to me, Ellie. You listen without judging, and make me feel more a man, for having confessed my weak—''

''Don't, Jacob,'' she pleaded, pulling back to look up at him. His eyes were closed, but the lines bracketing his mouth had softened and tempted her fingertips to touch.

As if he had sensed her thought, Jacob brought her hand to his lips. ''You are a special Christmas present,'' he murmured, pressing kisses to her fingertips, ''who goes on giving long after the day is over.'' He kissed her palm, drawing her hand around his neck. His lips touched her temple, and he smiled against her hair to feel the tremor of her body. ''Shy, little, Ellie, what will tempt you to marry me?''

He had to tease her to banish the dark mood, angry that time was against him. ''Have I told you how pretty you are, or that you have the loveliest neck? Or that I've come to crave more of your kisses?''

''Jacob? This isn't flirting, is it?''

''No, little mouse . . .'' *Just a desperate man's gamble*.

Ellie covered his mouth with her hand. ''You

mustn't. The children . . ." She faltered, for Jacob opened his eyes and the desire she saw there left her breathless.

Dark and low, he whispered, "How like a wife you sound, Ellie. The children are upstairs, conspiring some mischief, I vow, for I was politely shown the door and warned not to enter." He laced a string of kisses across her cheek and down the arch of her throat, nuzzling the warmth of her skin despite her irritating starched linen collar. "You like that," he said, hearing the small catch of her breath. "Ellie, do you know what would happen now if we were married?"

"No. And we're not. You mustn't say improper things." It was a halfhearted protest at best. Ellie grew dizzy from the heavy scent of pine from the tree that blended with the clean, woodsy, masculine scent of Jacob. She had the strange thought that this was the cause of her blood appearing to heat. The room was certainly too warm, Jacob's lips against her skin too hot, but rather than pull away, she angled her head to one side.

"Now, who's flirting, Ellie?" But he gave her no chance to answer. He brought his lips to hers, whispering of need. She loved his children and brother, enjoyed his company and kisses, but did not love him. The thought of seducing her entered his mind and left as quickly. He couldn't do that to Ellie. But he could speak honestly about his feelings. "I need you to let me forget for a little while what is waiting for me. Let me show you how good it could be with us."

Need, but not love. Ellie understood. She needed, too. No one could be hurt by these stolen moments. The tender way his mouth cherished hers was a present that would last longer than any Christmas memory.

But tenderness gave way as passion awakened, and its power was more than she could fight.

Jacob drew her small cry inside himself. He made no concession to her innocence, kissing her with a need as strong as the storm that was beginning outside. The way she held him tighter, the softening fit of her body to his, granted a sensual pleasure he had not imagined, and gave him the forgetfulness he desperately needed.

By the time he lifted his head, Ellie was overwhelmed with the powerful sensations he created deep inside her. She was breathing as heavily as he, and it was an effort to lower her arms.

"Ellie, you can't ignore the passion between us. Just as you can't keep running from talking to me about marriage. Why won't you accept my proposal? You love my children, I've seen that for myself, read it in their letters. They care a great deal for you, as does Thomas."

She didn't attempt to push him away. Jacob wasn't going to move, and it was time just as he said. "I know you think these are good reasons, but they are not enough."

"What then? I don't have time to court you properly. I can't go back to the war and wonder what will happen to my children if I die."

"Don't say that, Jacob! You won't die!"

"Men die everyday. I want the security of a home and someone to love and raise my children, Ellie. You can give that to me, to them." When she lowered her head without answering him, he pressed his demand. "You know I'll be a faithful husband. If I survive the coming months and return home, I'll do all I can to make you happy. With our adjoining farms—"

Ellie heard enough. With a wrenching cry she shoved him and ran from the room.

Bewildered, Jacob stood there, wondering what he had said to make her cry.

Ellie knew time was against her, in all ways. She could not indulge herself by hiding in her room, the farm chores would not wait. She called up to the children to remind them of the time, dressing quickly, then taking the clean milk buckets to the barn. It was steamy warm, and she shed her cloak before lighting the lanterns against the early dark.

Her hands shook as she measured out grain for the cows. Jacob had started a flame inside her, and she couldn't put it out. She wanted him. Her hope for love was that of a foolish young girl. Time was long past to stop dreaming. She loved Thomas and the children. Jacob's mentioning the possibility of his dying brought home a shattering truth. Without marriage, the children could be taken from her. It was only Jacob's agreement that allowed her offer to be accepted by his family. He didn't want them separated.

Why then, couldn't she give him the answer he wanted?

She heard the barn door open, and with it, came Jacob's voice calling her. Ellie stepped around the feed bin so he could see her.

"I told the children to stay in, Ellie. The snow is coming down harder, and they need to replenish the wood boxes." He could still see a glint of tears in her eyes. "I'm sorry for whatever I said that upset you."

"It wasn't you, Jacob." She couldn't quite meet his gaze. "Is there any sign of Thomas?"

"No. Please stop worrying about him. Thomas has sense enough to take shelter if the storm continues." Jacob rolled up his sleeves, then lifted the two buckets

near the door. "You rushed out without the wash water." He came toward her, stopping before he was
close enough to touch her and set one bucket down.
"I won't touch you again, Ellie, if that's what has you
watching me so intently."

"I didn't—I mean—" She silently pleaded with him
to understand what she couldn't say. But Jacob stood,
patiently waiting. "I need time, Jacob."

"I don't have time to give you." He turned then,
and pulled out the milking stools. "I see you've fed
them, I'll wash and you can begin milking." Jacob set
to work, hating the tension between them. Old Betsy
turned her head, large brown eyes on him in reproach
that he had forgotten to scratch her ears before he began milking her. To make her displeasure known, she
swished her tail in Jacob's face. Jacob kept milking.
Her tail hit him again, this time with a forceful impatience.

"Jacob, pet her nicely or she'll kick over the pail,"
Ellie warned as she went to set her stool down.

"One ornery female is all a man can stand," he
muttered.

"I'm not being ornery, Jacob. I'm being careful.
For both of us," she amended, knowing she had to
voice her reservations. "Your losses and the war have
given you a need for security as you said. I think marrying me for those reasons is a mistake."

"There are others, as you well know." The cats
purred, entwining themselves around his legs and the
stool. Betsy moved away as far as the stanchion allowed. Jacob grabbed her tail to urge her back in place.
Rabbits scampered above, making the chickens
squawk, and bits of hay drifted down from between
the wood planks.

"Give Betsy what she wants, Jacob, and she'll be-
have for you.''

Jacob ignored her. Betsy kicked the pail and nearly
upset it as if to add her own warning to Ellie's. Two
of the larger cats, anxious for the milk, rose with their
paws on the pail's edge, and Jacob barely snatched it
up in time to save it. With a bellow, he came up off
the milking stool, holding the pail high.

Ellie's laughter erupted behind him. He spun
around, his gaze warning her, but it only stopped her
for a moment. "Poor Jacob. You look like an outraged
goodwife who was pinched at the market. Or are you
protecting your worldly possessions?''

Betsy's moo and the chorus from the other cows was
the last straw. Jacob fought the smile that twitched his
lips. His mock growl only made Ellie laugh harder.

"Laugh at me, will you?" He set down the pail and
went after Ellie. Her shriek of alarm satisfied him to
no end. He let her dodge him, and think she escaped,
but he herded her toward the barn doors. The animals;
restless stampings came with neighs and squawks,
moos and meows, Ellie's fake screams of fright and
Jacob's dire threats.

Ellie escaped outside. Thick flakes of snow fell in a
soft, blinding swirl. Her shoes slid, and she tried to
hold her balance. Jacob scooped her up into his arms
before she took a headlong spill.

"Thought you could get away, did you?''

"No, Jacob. Not I." She wrapped her arms around
him as he turned slowly, then faster, barely keeping
his own balance. "You are utterly mad!"

"Likely! And it's all your fault, Miss Ellie Wintifred.'' He drank her laughter like a man thirsting for
drink, sharing his own with her.

"Now that I have you, I'll need to think of a fitting

punishment. But are you cold, my dear?'' he asked
with a leer.

"Dreadfully so, you villain."

Jacob began to walk back into the barn, cradling her
against him. "I know how to warm you, Ellie," he
whispered, lowering his lips to hers. A snowball splattered against his back, soaking his shirt. "We're under
attack. Make use of your position, wench, and tell me
where the enemy is."

Ellie peered over his shoulder just as Jacob reached
the barn doors. "It's Caleb by the woodpile."

Two more hits found their mark. "The boy wants
war." Jacob set her down and bent quickly to mold
the snow into ammunition. Krista joined her brother
and Ellie set about supplying Jacob, for his aim was
better. Ellie had to leave Jacob to defend himself as
the cows bellowed in pain from too full udders.

The snowball fight ended with a great deal of teasing
and laughter over who would be declared the winner,
as they trooped back inside the house. Ellie shooed
the children off to get changed, admonishing Jacob to
do the same. His wet shirt clung to him, revealing the
dark hair that made her fingers curl with the urge to
touch his chest.

Ellie rushed to her room, changing into a soft blue
wool gown, but leaving off her corset. She felt bold
and daring for doing so, but it was the only one she
had, and it was damp. She was flushed with excitement when she returned to the kitchen, stopping still
when she saw Jacob at the stove.

"Don't be alarmed, Ellie. I can stir the stew you
made without ruining it."

She watched him absently brush back a lock of his
hair that had fallen over his forehead. She felt a new,
strange, heated awareness of him. When Jacob turned

to look at her and his eyes darkened, she lifted her hand to her hair. Still damp, she had merely pinned the sides back and left it loose.

"I know it's not proper, but I . . . I—"

"It's lovely, Ellie. I like it down and no, I suppose it's not proper for anyone but your husband to see your hair loose." He heard the thickening passion in his own voice and turned back to stirring the pot of stew. He was not going to seduce Ellie into agreeing to marry him. And he was well aware how easy it would be to do. Jacob knew time was slipping away from him, but he realized he wanted Ellie to come to him because she wanted him, wanted to carry his name and his children. His children? The thought settled comfortably in his mind, as if it had always been there. With a studying look, he turned to Ellie. It was far too easy to envision her slender waist rounded with his child.

His gaze darkened and narrowed. Ellie grew alarmed. "What are you thinking about?" she asked softly, afraid some memory of the war had taken hold of him.

"I'm multiplying, Ellie. I've just learned that one plus one can equal three or four or perhaps more."

The amusement in his voice that was slowly reflected in his eyes bewildered her. "You're not making any sense."

"Not to you. I know that. But it makes perfect sense to me. You see, Ellie, I've just discovered the answer to a question I didn't even know I had."

With a brisk move, Ellie waved her hand in dismissal. "Did Caleb hit you in the head? Go into the parlor, Jacob, and I'll call you when supper is ready." She took her apron down from its hook and tied it around her waist.

Jacob came up behind her and planted a kiss on her shoulder. "You, my dear, have been ordering children about for too long. A man, Ellie," he informed her as he turned her within his arms, "would like a woman to coax him, to ask prettily, to take him most seriously . . . ah, Ellie," he murmured, planting a kiss on her upturned nose. "I'll help set the table. I've too little time to spend with you as it is."

The sound of sleigh bells announced Thomas's return just as they sat down to eat. Jacob went out to tend to the horses and sent Thomas inside to change. Seated around the table later, Jacob shared a smile with Ellie as Thomas embroidered his twenty-mile trip home through the storm. Never had such danger lurked beyond every turn on the narrow mountain road. Pride gleamed in the boy's eyes when Jacob brought him a glass of blackberry brandy and proposed a toast for his surviving a harrowing journey home.

Krista and Caleb hurried everyone through supper, anxious to decorate the tree. Ellie wrapped up the crumbs and end of the bread, reminding Krista to put it out for the birds in the morning.

While Ellie heated apple cider with a few cinnamon sticks, Jacob sliced up a fruitcake. Ellie added a plate of gingerbread, then set them on the big silver tray that Jacob carried into the parlor.

Ellie had never shared the decorating with anyone. It was her pride and pleasure ever since she had been old enough to climb a footstool and reach the top branches to decorate the tree. Of course, she reminded herself, she had never had so large a tree. Caleb filled the metal corn popper with dried corn, and promised to help sew the strings of popcorn they needed. Krista wanted to help him, but Thomas opened the trunk.

"How pretty, Ellie," the child said, staring at the

wooden tray filled with star-shaped tin candle holders. She took one and brought it to Ellie. "You should put the first one on top. Papa can lift you up."

Ellie fitted one of the small bayberry candles she had made in the fall into the holder, then shyly turned to Jacob.

"Papa wait," Caleb called out. "Have you forgotten? We always light a candle to remember someone special." He got up and went to Ellie. "Would it be all right with you? I want to light a candle for my mother."

"Caleb—"

"No, it's all right, Jacob," Ellie said, handing over the first candle to him. "Light it, Caleb."

"You don't mind?"

Ellie blinked back the tears in her eyes. "I think it is a beautiful tradition, Caleb. I'm happy that you want to share it with me."

Caleb glanced at his father, and at Jacob's nod, took the candle to the fireplace to light it. He held the candle steady as Jacob lifted him high where he stretched to fasten the holder to the highest branch. "Now you, Ellie."

She lit her candle in rememberance of her parents, wishing they could have shared the joy that Jacob and his children had brought to her. Her gaze met Jacob's and she was sure he lit his for his brothers and Lucy, but Ellie no longer felt any envy.

She watched Thomas and Krista, saw their lips move, and knew Jacob understood what she was feeling when he whispered, "It's good to keep the happy memories of the past, Ellie, but we can make our own new ones."

Aunt Celia had a candle and prayer, for she had risked her life to save them from the fire and her heart gave out. Ellie basked in the glow of their warmth and memories shared. She watched Jacob's hands, admiring their strength and the gentle way he handled the small wooden dolls as he looped their frayed ribbons over the higher branches. Her body reacted to the heated memory of his touching her, and her gaze met his. Ellie couldn't look away, not even when Jacob glanced at his hands, then back at her eyes as if he, too, remembered holding her.

She no longer heard the sounds of Caleb's furious shaking of the pan as corn popped. Krista's excited voice exclaiming over the small wooden dolls Ellie's grandfather had made for her faded as did Thomas's off-key singing. The wild beating of her heart filled her ears, and she was overcome with a breathless feeling. Surely, she was dreaming. There was desire in Jacob's eyes. Desire for her.

Jacob reached over to cover her hand with his. He was lost in the bright sparkle of her eyes. She gazed at him like a woman in love, a woman who saw all she ever wanted in one man. Now he knew what Ellie wanted, what had kept her from accepting his proposal. Ellie loved him. It was there all the time, and he was too blind to realize it. But it was the stunning force of his own powerful feeling to have and claim that love as his own that left him shaken. He wanted her and her love for his own.

They were so lost in each other, that they didn't see Thomas exchange a look with the children, then motion them to leave the room.

Krista didn't understand, and she objected loudly. "We can't leave. We haven't put the gingerbread men on the tree."

"Krista!" Thomas yelled.

"No. It's all right," Ellie whispered, breaking the

spell that had held her. "I left the tin in the kitchen."
She wanted to run, but did not, knowing it was too
late. She had revealed too much to Jacob in those special few moments.

Alone in the pantry, she confronted her own feelings. Did hearing the words of love from him matter
so much? He wanted her. He would care for her and
be a good husband. If he survived the war.

What if Jacob didn't survive? What if this was the
only chance she would have to give her love to him?
Jacob had asked for nothing for himself. He asked for
the love and security of a home for his young children
and his brother. She could—

"Ellie!" Jacob called, coming into the kitchen.
"Where are you?"

The alarm in his voice made her rush out of the
pantry. One look at his worried expression, and she
knew something was wrong. "What is it, Jacob?"

"It's my fault. Not once have I looked out to see
what the storm was doing. Wind has blown high drifts
across the drive."

"The animals!"

"If I don't start clearing the path to the barn, we
won't be able to get there come morning." He turned
to go into the mudroom, telling her, "A pot of coffee
would be nice, Ellie. It's going to be a long night if
the snow keeps up."

"I'll be right there to help, Jacob."

Jacob stilled and dropped his greatcoat. He hurried
to her side. "Ellie," he said, cupping her cheek, "I
know how often you've done this with only Thomas
and Caleb to help you. I'm aware of your very special
woman's strength. But please, let me do this. Let me
know you're here, warm and waiting for me."

She looked up at him, forcing down the protest she longed to voice. "Will that make you happy, Jacob?"

"Very, very happy."

"All right. The rope is on the top shelf above the door. Please tie it tight to your waist. I don't want to lose you in this storm."

"You won't lose me, Ellie. I promise you that."

But before he went out into the blinding storm, she checked the knot he tied, then let him go. There hadn't been a winter past where some farmer or child hadn't been lost and froze to death close to home.

Ellie lost track of the coffee she made laced with applejack. The stock pot offered them all another liquid warmth as the night slowly passed and the storm intensified. Krista brought her quilt and pillow down to the parlor where Ellie fixed a bed before the fire. She was with the child until she finally fell asleep, then went back to keep her vigil near the kitchen window.

Caleb and Thomas came in, exhaustion in their faces and the sag of their shoulders. Hot soup and her firm order sent them up to bed.

Ellie replenished the fireplaces, and fed the wood stove in the kitchen the last of the kindling in the wood box. She couldn't stand the waiting and dressed warmly, worried about Jacob.

The rope was strung tight from the back porch post to the barn. Ellie stepped into ankle-deep snow, despite the many times the path had been shoveled clear. The wind howled, sending snow in a blinding swirl around her. Even with her father's old work gloves over her own, her fingers were stiff with the cold. She could feel the wet wool of her muffler freeze to her nose and mouth. Her eyes teared from the cold air she inhaled that seemed to chill her from the inside out.

She fumbled with the heavy barn door. Cussing to herself when she couldn't get it opened. She silently cried out Jacob's name, afraid as she had never been. A blast of wind sent her to her knees. Ellie knew real fear that moment. She couldn't see the door. The numbing cold took away the ability to think. She felt her tears freeze on her lashes. And all she could do was call Jacob to help her.

A strange shiver slid down Jacob's spine as he gave up trying to use the pitchfork to spread another layer of bedding hay for the horses. He tossed the fork aside and shoved the last pile into the stall. Every muscle in his body screamed with pain from the constant shoveling he had done not only to the barn, but the springhouse for water as well. His eyes burned, and he swiped at them before stumbling back to take down the lantern. He had done all he could.

The wind howled a challenge as he opened the door just enough to slip out and bend his head while grasping the rope. He took a few steps and stilled. Something drew him to turn around and for a moment, he resisted, so weary that he longed for rest. Jacob swore to himself that he heard his name, but knew it was impossible. Yet he couldn't move forward. Sagging against the rope, his grip slipped from the anchor line and his only thought was to get back into the warmth of the barn.

The swirling whiteness lifted, and he saw the dark shape off to one side. He knew, even as he called Ellie's name, he knew it was her.

Minutes before he had no strength left, but he found there were still deep reserves as he lifted her into his arms. She made a weak sound like a kitten's mewl. He staggered and prayed that the brief respite of the storm would last until he got her into the house.

It wasn't until later, as he replaced the cool bricks wrapped in flannel with hot ones around Ellie, that he knew the Lord had heard his prayers. There was a flush on her cheeks, but her breathing was deep and even.

Jacob knelt by her single bed and slid his hand beneath the thick blankets and quilt to hold hers. She was warm and he bowed his head, finally giving in to the sleep his body craved.

Ellie awakened to the sound of Thomas hushing the children. She opened her eyes to a room shadowed like dusk. Snuggling deeper beneath the blankets, her toes touched the flannel-wrapped bricks and she discovered Jacob's hand at the same time. A tiny cry escaped her as the memory rushed back.

"Don't cry, Ellie," Jacob mumbled, stirring from his awkward position. "Cold's almost gone. You'll soon be warm."

"Oh, Jacob, my poor darling, Jacob," she whispered, reaching out to stroke his head. A fierce tenderness filled her, as did the knowledge they were both safe. But when he lifted his head and she saw his shadowed eyes, Ellie was overwhelmed with the need to care for him. "You belong in bed, Jacob."

"Is that an invitation, little winter mouse?"

She didn't understand why his whimsical smile made tears start. But it did. His hand shook as he brushed them away, and Ellie caught his hand and brought it to her lips. *I love you, Jacob DeWitt.* But her heart was too full, and she couldn't say the words to him.

A slight movement at the doorway drew her gaze. "We're awake."

Three heads peered around the door frame, worried expressions in triplicate revealed themselves to Ellie

and Jacob. He beckoned Thomas and his children inside, managing to right himself.

The three children started talking at once. Ellie
looked at Jacob's bemused expression and shouted for
quiet. "One at a time. But first, Thomas, heat water
for your brother and take him upstairs. Help him to
bed." When the boy came forward to take Jacob's arm,
she added, "And use the broom if you must to keep
him there. Caleb and Krista, wait in the kitchen for
me. I'll get dressed and—" Ellie stopped herself. She
just realized she was wearing her nightgown.

Jacob's avid gaze found hers. "Red as a cherry in a
bowl of cream and twice as tempting."

"Jacob? Come back here and . . . and . . ." He was
gone, and Caleb had closed her door.

If Ellie had any lingering chill from the exposure of
the night, she lost it with a heated flush that began at
her toes and burned the tips of her ears.

Tired as he was, Jacob stopped on the top step and
smiled when he heard the merry peal of her laughter.

Jacob claimed that Thomas was nearly a man grown.
When Ellie heard all that he had done, despite the storm
continuing while they slept, she knew Jacob had been
right. He had kept the path cleared and with the children's
help done the chores. He even made a trip to the smoke-
house to get a ham for their Christmas Eve supper.

"There's no way we could get to the church service
and social tonight, Ellie. I doubt we'll make it up to
Aunt Faye's for Christmas dinner tomorrow."

"Then I must ask your help, Thomas. Yours and the
children's to make this holiday extra special with whatever we have. I want your brother to carry a happy
memory with him when he leaves us."

"Well, he's still sleeping. What can I do?"

* * *

Tired but happy to be together, they all joined hands to say grace over their supper. Ellie began with thanks for the bounty yielded from their garden, which filled the best china bowls covering the table. Baby carrots were glazed with honey, peas and small onions swam in a cream and herb sauce. Buttered beans, pickled corn and acorn squash baked with maple syrup tempted by sight and smell. The ham had a thick brandy-glazed crust dotted with cloves. There hadn't been time to make yeast rolls, but biscuits and muffins, the ones Jacob loved, filled a basket.

Jacob thanked the Lord for this time he had with them. He glanced at Ellie sitting across from him and knew she had never looked lovelier to him. There was such peaceful contentment in her eyes as she caught and held his look. With every candle in the dining room lit, the light brought glints of gold to her hair. He inhaled sharply, the air fragrant with the drying pine garlands, but there was a faint scent of the lilac water she used. He was in a fever of impatience to be alone with her. And the flirtatious way she lowered her lashes told him she was aware of it.

And Jacob wanted her very aware of him.

Caleb squirmed in his chair. A loud rumble of hunger sent everyone looking at him. "I'm sorry. But we worked so hard today, and I'm awfully hungry. Can't we eat?"

"Yes, please, Ellie," Krista seconded. "Papa and Thomas stole muffins before we sat down. That's why they can wait."

"Such lessons to teach the children, Jacob. But then, we didn't cook all this just to look at. Jacob, will you slice the ham?"

It took no more than that from Ellie, and bowls were passed with dizzying speed back and forth, until the plates were filled to overflowing.

Ellie enjoyed their praise as much as she enjoyed their hearty appetites. This was the first Christmas eve she had not been alone in four years. She knew the children had looked forward to the special Christmas service and the social that followed. They had talked about the delicious treats of candy, cookies, and cakes, even puddings that everyone brought for samplings. They would miss being given a bag of nuts and an apple, but she had those for them.

". . . and won't that be nice, Ellie."

"What, Krista?"

"Papa asked Thomas to read to us from the Bible later. And we mustn't forget to hang our stockings. I can't wait for morning."

"You never can," Jacob reminded his daughter. "Will you be impatient, too, Ellie?"

"Oh, I think this year I will be." Four days was all that Jacob had left of his leave. She thought of the decision she had made.

Far from annoying him, her secret smile made Jacob grin. He had come to a decision while he worried and cared for her last night. The thought prompted him to ask her why she had been out.

"I was worried about you, Jacob."

"And nearly got yourself lost and frozen," he returned.

"But you found me, didn't you?" Ellie tried hard not to think about what had followed. No matter how she tried to forget waking up in her nightgown, it haunted her all day. And what's more, the way Jacob grinned at her, she had a feeling he knew it, too.

"Krista found another litter of kittens. She thinks

we might have more rabbits, too,'' Caleb said. ''Babies sure make a lot of work.''

It was such an innocent remark, Ellie told herself. Why then had Jacob's gaze locked with hers? Why had her hand moved of its own volition to cover her belly? Baby? Jacob's baby?

She saw the meal was finished, and rose to clear the table. With every dish she brought out to the kitchen, she returned with one to replace it. Roasted nuts, dried apple tarts, fruitcake, and pudding with brandy sauce had everyone groaning they couldn't eat another bite. The dozen apple tarts disappeared with a pitcher of sweet, heavy cream. Jacob cracked nuts for everyone, managing enough for himself.

With them all helping, the cleaning up went quickly and they retired to the parlor. Ellie finished stringing the forgotten popcorn while listening to Thomas read aloud. She was somewhat surprised that Jacob urged the children to bed once his brother was done.

There was a race and scramble up the stairs to change and bring their stockings down. Krista needed one more hug, one more kiss until Thomas took her by the hand, then carried her to bed.

''I hope,'' Jacob began, ''that you have no intention to run off to bed. I want to talk to you, Ellie.'' The soft smile on her lips, the even softer look in her eyes as she agreed, pleased him immensely.

She finished the last string and draped it over the wide lower branches. Sometime during the day the children had hung the gingerbread men with their thread loops. Stepping back, she admired the tree. ''Jacob, it is the loveliest tree I've ever had.''

He glanced up at the tin star before his gaze swept over Ellie. ''I still think you'd make a beautiful angel to grace the top.''

"You're just flirting again, Jacob."

He heard the underlying question in her voice and moved to stand behind her. With his hands on her shoulders, he drew her back against his chest. "Not this time, Ellie. I meant every word. You are beautiful to my eyes. You can't see yourself as I do. You are all that makes a woman that a man wants to cherish."

Jacob kissed her hair, then turned her around to face him. Now that he had her alone, he was hit with the realization that he had very little to offer her in the way of a future. He used his thumb to trace the rounded curve of her chin.

Ellie, nervous as a long-tailed cat in a roomful of rocking chairs, caught his hand with hers. "I want you to know that I've come to a decision, Jacob."

"Wait. Hear me out first. I've handled this all wrong. I never took your needs and wants into consideration, Ellie." He looked at her face bathed in firelight, his gaze warm at the hope that flared to life in her eyes. "Come and sit with me."

Ellie went to the settee and sat down. Jacob was so serious that her hope died a little. Had she made a mistake in thinking he cared a little for her? What if he changed his mind? Jacob took up most of the small sofa with his large frame. He had to touch her, and knowing what he had to say, merely held her hands. "I've set out all the practical reasons for us to marry, Ellie. We both know marriages take place for far less, but I didn't know it wouldn't be enough for me."

"But your letters—"

"I'm aware of what I wrote in my letters. I know what I've said since I've come home. But I need more, Ellie. You deserve more than I offered."

The chill of her hands made him raise them to his

lips where he pressed kisses upon them. "When I married your cousin Lucy—"

"Don't!" Ellie tried to pull her hands free. He held her tightly. "Please, Jacob," she pleaded, trying to rise.

Jacob lifted her up and set her on his lap. "Don't move." His arms locked around her reinforced the order. "I'll not be responsible for the consequences, Ellie," he added when she squirmed. "I want to tell you about Lucy so you will understand why it has taken me so long to come to my senses."

Having set her on his lap was another mistake Jacob added to the many he had already made. She was tense. His body was fully aroused by the sweet, feminine scent of her, and the warm weight of her body. Gritting his teeth, he determined he would get through this.

"Lucy was passionate about life, Ellie. She caught everyone with it, hoping for a share. I loved Lucy. We created two very special children that will always hold a place in my heart and my life. I can't forget the time I had with her. But a man has a need for a deeper, more abiding love. The love of a woman who doesn't judge him, whose strength enhances his, and one who gives a man hope for tomorrow."

He caressed her cheek, wanting to see the guarded look in her eyes gone, and knowing he had to finish.

"You're a strong woman, Ellie. I made the mistake of believing that your stubborness was female foolishness. But you were wiser than I. The friendship we shared as children has been renewed in these few days. But it deepened, Ellie, without my knowing." He drew her closer, tilting her chin up so she had to look at him.

"I want to marry you, Ellie. I want you so badly.

You can feel me shake with the desire I have for you. But I need you for myself. I want the honor of declaring to the world that you are my bride, my woman. Grant me the honor of being my wife and the mother of my children. Not just Krista and Caleb, but those we could have together. Oh, Ellie, don't cry,'' he whispered, kissing the tears that slid down her cheeks.

"Don't, love,'' he repeated, threading his hands into the thick wealth of her hair and scattering kisses over her face. "I never wanted your tears. I only want to make you happy.''

He cherished the softness of her mouth, while a new, fierce possession swept over him. "Say you'll take my name, Ellie. Say you'll share your life with mine. I love you, Ellie. Love you and never knew. More the fool I. Say yes . . .''

He kissed her with all the hunger inside him. Jacob gave her his heart, knowing with a certainty he didn't question, that Ellie would take his precious gift and keep it safe. He longed to make love to her, to claim her as his. His body demanded he do so. Jacob fought to control his passion. She came to him with a shy, sweetly heated flowering that revealed her vulnerability. Her total trust was generously given with her kiss, and he tempered his desire.

With the greatest reluctance, he parted his lips from hers. "Say you will marry me, Ellie. Just say yes, Jacob.''

Ellie kept her eyes closed, and a dreamy smile curved her mouth. She leaned her head against his shoulder. Here was strength and gentleness. Here was Jacob, her love.

"Teasing minx. Will you keep me in agony waiting for your answer?''

Her fingertips rose and silenced him. "Yes, Jacob.''

"And you'll be my strength, my hope, and my love?"

The heavy beat of his heart matched her own. Ellie looked up at him and saw the world of love reflected in his eyes. She thought of all the years she had secretly loved him. And it was time to give that love, freely, as he had asked, as she had dreamed.

"Ellie, please."

She kissed him lightly. "Yes, Jacob. I will be all that you've asked me."

"And will you love me, Ellie? Will you give me the promise of your love?"

Ellie's tear-bright eyes searched his. A storm of emotions made her tremble. "Jacob, I have loved you forever," she murmured against his lips. "You make me feel whole. I want—"

"Show me, Ellie. Share your love with me."

Hidden in the shadows at the top of the stairs, Thomas waited until he heard the door to Ellie's room close. He thought of Ellie, and the way she had praised him for taking over as man of the family today, and other times, too. The secret he carried brought an understanding that there were other ways a man became one like his brother. Courage, as Jacob said, came in many forms. Honesty always won in the end, and families were built on the love they shared.

He knew where Ellie hid the Christmas presents, and Jacob's were still in the carpetbag in his room. Thomas didn't think they would mind if he took their place, and set them out beneath the tree.

Ellie told him that this was a time for giving, not only gifts that could be seen, but those that couldn't.

* * *

"Oh, Jacob, look. The sun's out and made jewels of the ice and snow."

"I have my own jewel. A Christmas bride." He cradled Ellie, and knew he had all his gifts within her. She had showed him how deep the sharing of two hearts could be, and he cherished it. But her small cry about the sun sent alarm through him. "Ellie, the children! The presents!

"Oh, sweet Lord. This is not how I wanted to wake you."

"I can't think of a better way, Jacob. You made me feel like a bride last night. I love the thought of being a wife this morning." She hid the wince climbing out of bed caused, and began to gather her clothes. Jacob was already buttoning up his shirt, tucking it into his pants.

He caught her admiring look. "Love, if you don't want to see how impatient children expecting their gifts to be under the tree, treat their mother, hurry." But he blew her a kiss, not daring to do more.

Ellie hurried.

They both stopped short at the parlor door. Thomas, Caleb, and Krista sat waiting for them. "Merry Christmas," they chorused.

"Merry Christmas," Ellie and Jacob said together, then shared a bewildered look. The presents were all under the tree. The stockings were filled with the bulge of nuts and apples.

"We've been waiting and waiting for you to wake up."

"Well, they're here now, Krista, so you don't have to wait," Caleb and Thomas said in unison.

"Make them sit down, and I'll get the present," Krista told her brother and uncle. She found it quickly, and returned to hand the small brown paper package

to Ellie. "It's very, very special. I know you'll love
it, Ellie. Ladies—"

"Krista!" the boys warned, avoiding the questioning look that Jacob gave them.

"Well, she needs to know that it's from Papa."
Krista squeezed herself next to Ellie on the settee. "Do
hurry. I haven't seen it yet."

Caught by her excitement, Ellie loosened the string
and spread open the paper. "A fan! And oh, what a
beautiful one," she added, touching the lace-trimmed
edge.

"Open it, Ellie. I want to see the picture painted
there."

She did as Krista asked, exclaiming and thanking
them over and over. Beneath the boughs of a flowering
tree, sat a lady in her court dress. On his knees beside
her, a swain appeared to pledge his love with his hands
crossed over his heart. "The painting is lovely. I don't
know what . . . more . . . to—" Ellie turned her face
to Jacob's shoulder, taking refuge there as she had during the night.

"Isn't it romantic, Papa? Doesn't she like it? We
thought and thought so hard to get a gift that would
make Ellie love you."

Holding one love, and looking at his son, his
brother, and his daughter, Jacob knew he was blessed.
"Ellie," he whispered, "shall I tell them?"

She shook her head and sat up. "I do love him. And
I will marry him."

Whoops and yells, hugs and kisses greeted her news.
Ellie was hard put to contain the joy in her heart. It
was sometime later when they got around to opening
the other presents. They all sat on the floor in front of
the tree and listened to Jacob praise the scarf Krista
made for him. The boys gifted him with a new whit-

tling knife. And more than the shirts Ellie had made for him along with new knitted socks, he treasured her grandfather's Bible that had seen him safe through earlier wars.

Krista loved the new dress Ellie had sewed with its matching ribbons for her hair. The doll from her brother and uncle wasn't the bisque one she longed for, but Ellie had made a matching dress to hers. But best of all, she loved the miniature Noah's ark with the pairs of animals from her father.

She nearly knocked him over with the hug she gave him, and was content to sit on his lap while the boys opened their gifts. Like Jacob, Ellie made them shirts and socks, but there were new pocketknives, too. It was the gifts that Jacob made for them that drew a strange silence.

Thomas stroked the new rifle stock, engraved with his name and carved with a flight of geese. Caleb stared at the fancy wooden stirrups and a leather bridle.

"Don't you like them?" Jacob was forced to ask when the silence grew uncomfortable. "I know you wanted a new rifle, Thomas, but we can put the stock I made for you on your rifle."

"Yes, we could."

Jacob tried to swallow his anger. "Son, I know you wanted a pony, but I couldn't get one this year. I traded another pair of those stirrups for that handworked bridle, since Ellie lets you ride her mare."

"Oh, they're fine gifts, Papa." Caleb glanced at his uncle. "You better tell him."

"Tell me what!"

"Jacob, we didn't have any money to buy a present for Ellie. So Caleb and I traded my rifle and his saddle to buy the fan."

"That's where you went—"

"The day of the storm," Thomas finished for him.
"We didn't want to ever leave Ellie, and if you couldn't
get her to marry you, we had to do something."

Before Jacob could move his daughter from his lap,
Ellie was up and hugging the boys. "I love you both.
You're a fine man, Thomas. As generous and unselfish
as your brother. And you, my Caleb, I'm so proud to
know you'll be my son." Krista wormed her way between them while Ellie cried.

Jacob gathered them all close in his arms. "No one
has had a better Christmas. But please, let me get Ellie
to stop crying long enough to open my gift to her."

But she couldn't stop, and in the end, Jacob had to
unwrap it for her. The walnut box was satin smooth,
and he watched Ellie trace the flowers and vines he
had spent hours carving in the wood. She whispered
her love when she saw the heart in its center, and the
initials entwined. Theirs. At his urging, she opened
the box, and the soft strains of a waltz played. As
much as she knew she would treasure this gift from
his hands, the plain gold band that Jacob lifted from
its cotton nest and placed on her finger was every
Christmas wish and dream come true.

They married on the last day of his leave. Ellie had
to say good-bye at the church. Krista, not to be outdone by her brother or uncle, had a last-minute gift
for her father.

Ellie waited her turn to kiss Jacob one last time as
he made his way through family and friends who came
to offer good wishes. She loved the way he took the
good-natured teasing over his young daughter's gift.

Krista loved being held up high in his arms. But she
had a wifely tone when she issued her last-minute in-

structions. "Now take good care, Papa. Be very careful." With a smothered giggle, she looked at the loaded wagon, then kissed his cheek. "Now I know you'll never be hungry again, Papa."

"No, little one, I certainly won't."

Ellie had been as surprised as her husband, for Krista had caged all her grown rabbits with the help of the boys.

"She's your daughter—" Ellie and Jacob said at the same time. He was laughing when he finally held his wife.

"She's ours, Jacob. Like the tomorrows that will come. Keep safe and come home to us, love. Our time for giving has just begun."

O Christmas Tree

by Karen Harper

Chicago, 1897

1

IT WAS BARELY light this Friday morning, December 17. Bent against the biting wind, the two young women linked arms for stability and warmth. Zigzagging block by block toward their goal, they hugged the next line of buildings, which gave them a momentary windbreak. Their mackintosh capes, ankle-length skirts, and wool headscarves flew back as if to detain them, but they had no intention of being late for work.

Other seasons of the year they might have taken the streetcar; the last three months they had been scrimping to save every penny for Christmas. The Sears and Roebuck Building was only twelve blocks from their rooming house on Hubbard Street, but today, bundled and burdened as they were, it seemed as far away as the steamy month of September in the city.

Still, Charlotte Miller told herself, there were other good reasons to walk to work, whatever the weather. Not only was it good for one's constitution and character, but her boss, Mr. James, had once let it slip that Chicago's wind polished her lily white cheeks to roses—before he looked most annoyed with himself for that blurted compliment and hurried back to his duties.

"I swear, if this turns to snow, Char, I'm taking the streetcar home even if I can't buy my mother that swell fringed tablecloth," Charlotte's friend, Agnes Leigh, muttered.

"Not me. Not with all the gifts I want to buy!" Charlotte declared. "You've only got your parents and one brother, you lucky duck. Try shopping for a family as big as mine."

"Mm," Agnes managed through stiff lips, "but you've got the job with higher pay."

That silenced Charlotte for the next block. Besides, it was one that ran directly into town from Lake Michigan and not parallel to it to cut the cold. Yes, she had some salary benefits as well as more variety in the position she'd held the last nine months. Agnes, like their friend Mabel back at the rooming house with a wretched cold today, was still in the confining typing pool of the correspondence department, where Charlotte had begun.

Although Charlotte valued her job for several reasons, having the handsome and illustrious Mr. Donald James, fourth floor overseer, as a supervisor was the real wonder of it. Mr. James—the man of her dreams, however distant he, and therefore the dreams were—made her job heaven. But knowing she would never be more to him than Miss Miller, chief shelver of the book and stationery department of the Sears and Roebuck Catalogue and Supply House, was a bit of hell, too.

She silently scolded herself for such ungrateful thinking. Her parents would have a conniption if they knew she was mooning over a man in terms of holy heaven and hideous hell. Maybe the big city had made her a fast woman, just as mother had warned. But if she thought about all that now, she'd be woebegone about home and Christmas all day. She'd just concentrate on gifts for the family and not the fearsome possibility of their being refused again this year.

Three years ago at age twenty-one, Charlotte Miller had left home as Charlotta Schwartzmiller. She used to hate the sound of her first name, all harsh and accusing the way her mother shouted it to summon her in to household duties when she was reading out in the yard: *"Car-lot-ta!"* Never had mother softened it to her nickname, Lottie, which the others, even Father, fondly called her at home.

Charlotta had first gone to live with her older brother George and his wife here in Chicago. When George left home, it bothered her parents only a little as the two oldest boys were working the farm and helping in the smithy, but it was a major battle when she wanted to work in the city.

And now that she had chosen to live in a rooming house with "other lonely, unchaperoned spinsters," as Mother had put it, she was not welcome home at all. Her mother had never forgiven her for going out on her own—nor for turning down Andreas Kurtz's proposal of marriage back home. The first Christmas Charlotte was away, she had tried to give her family a holiday gift of money, as George always did. Her parents sent it back, so, in a flare of pique and protest, she refused to return for the holidays and made herself utterly miserable in the process.

The second year she sent gifts early to test the icy waters; they kept the ones for her younger siblings and returned the rest with George, so she dare not go home again. At least, she had thought in her sadness last year, she was making progress with them.

This Christmas, the third away, she was longing to dare to deliver the gifts herself, but she was afraid.

"Third time's a charm," Agnes had tried to encourage her. "But remember, three strikes and you're out," Mabel had warned to make Charlotte dread Christmas even more this year. Now, each day, she bent against the wind of her own fears of failure with her family, just as she did against the blow off the lake right now.

At last the six-story Sears and Roebuck building loomed before, then above them. They hurried in the employee entrance on Wayman Street, had their time-cards marked, and darted into the women's cloakroom to leave their capes and tidy their hair. Charlotte always took an extra peek in the full-length mirror. Mr. James was so well-organized and orderly in his own life that she knew he appreciated the same in others. She saw her cheeks were pink, but, unfortunately, her nose was, too. A good German nose, her father had always said, but she thought it a bit too broad. She smoothed her hair back into a semblance of an upswept topknot, waved to Agnes until lunch, and ran up the steps to the fourth floor.

She opened the door to the world she loved, her refuge, the place where she felt purposeful and needed. Here she could sometimes ignore that she was estranged from her family at this family time of year. She would try to forget that there were no marital prospects on the horizon so she could have her own family to share Christmases someday.

Her gaze caught the small, bare Christmas tree the staff would decorate soon. It had been Mr. Wembly, the head packer's, idea; he had claimed decorating a tree inside was an English custom begun by Prince Albert, the long-gone husband of old Queen Victoria, and that it was becoming the thing among those of British heritage here. Charlotte had not corrected him by saying it was a custom as German as Prince Albert had been. But now, staring at that tree, she stopped and remembered.

The cutting and decorating of the tree had always been the most special time of the holiday season at home in the country. The tradition of fetching the tree and singing "O Tannenbaum" had been brought to the little farming village of Bromberg, Illinois, twenty miles outside the city by her parents and other immigrants. She could almost see the tall fir tree reaching to the parlor ceiling with candles glowing among its spiked branches to make the blown-glass ornaments sparkle. The crisp forest smell when they brought the tree home, the crunch of snow, and Mother's voice telling them to wipe their feet. The family jests and teasing about getting it nailed straight to its wooden cross pieces, and the heated arguments about which side of the tree was the fullest to face the room—she could hear their voices now. All those familiar, cherished sights and sounds and smells swamped her senses as she stood among them again . . .

"You're letting in a draft, Miss Miller," Joseph Wembly called to her, squinting up from crating a set of *Chambers Encyclopedia.*

"Oh, sorry," she said and let the door swing shut behind her. With that the sights and sounds and smells of reality—leather and paper and ink, chalk, even dust, however hard they tried to keep clean this vast expanse of shelves and boxes and books—assailed her to obliterate dreams of a country Christmas.

Donald James stepped off the crowded streetcar and held on to his hat as he hurried into the S & R Building. He immediately took the steps up to his small fourth-floor office, nodding to associates or workers, tipping his hat to the only woman he saw, one Agnes

Leigh, who was obviously nearly late. Her face was red from the wind, but she seemed to blush right through that. Drat, but he'd hardly passed the time of day with her, so why must she look at him like that, as if he'd asked her something embarrassing? Why couldn't she be more diligent and serious, like her friend Charlotte Miller?

Now, there was a woman to be admired for her good sense and dedication to her work. The young lady had risen quickly from typist to shelver of the myriad titles and stationery supplies the company sent out in this fourth year of their mail order business. She had read many of the books they sold, too, just as he did; he'd spoken with her about what she thought of some of them, when he supposed he should have kept things all business. But perhaps Miss Miller was the one to watch how the sales of those new popular women's novels were faring in this big book-buying season.

Don James frowned as he hung his coat and hat on the coat rack and promptly tore yesterday's page off the wall calendar. Christmas was a week from tomorrow. It was a season he detested, but for the special services at church and the opportunity to give a bit more to the needy and hope they, at least, had a warm and pleasant Christmas. Hard to believe that the happiest holidays of his twenty-eight years were those early ones in the orphanage; he supposed he ought to go back there to visit someday, but he always sent money instead. He would keep busy Christmas Day— perhaps go skating, then briefly stop by with a rum fruitcake for his neighbors—and it would pass like every other. After all, December 25th was not one minute longer than other days; it only seemed more interminable each year.

He wadded up the page from the calendar and sailed

it into his wastebasket. Then, through the single, clear window in his door, set amid the smoked glass of his office walls, he noted Charlotte Miller bustling by, cradling a stack of books in her arms. Quickly he went to his desk and skimmed his appointment calendar, jotting comments in his notebook. He was soon annoyed that this task and his busy schedule did not clear Miss Miller from his mind. Far too often she intruded there to walk its aisles and fill its shelves with remembered glimpses of her and their brief conversations.

For, unfortunately, Charlotte appealed to him personally as well as professionally. She was tall and slender, fair with caramel-colored hair and wide-set, clear sky blue eyes that seemed to ask personal questions and a full mouth that, sadly, did not. She dressed prettily but properly; usually her hair was neatly pinned, but today he had noted, the wind had winnowed it to a halo around her comely face.

She was a fine figure of a woman, but his employers' strictures were firm about socializing too familiarly. Rules were rules. Mr. Sears had been almost a father to him, despite his businesslike demeanor and having his own family. Donald James felt he'd struggled too hard and long to get where he was—and planned to go further—to tempt fate. He supposed, if he hoped to found his own family someday, he should be more attentive to the lovelies who smiled at him in church. But now, to the morning's business, for that, unlike his thoughts, he could control.

He took his pencil and notebook with him and began to make his rounds.

In her kingdom of books Charlotte was usually very happy. And lately it kept her off in the canyons of volumes where she wouldn't have to listen to people share what they were planning for the holidays, although it did keep her from catching a glimpse of Mr. James through his office door. Often using her sliding ladder to reach the heights, she shelved the volumes as well as school and business supplies; two other employees pulled them to be shipped. But in the holiday rush she unshelved as well as shelved, and appreciated the extra duties.

Each title seemed an old friend; when she stacked one on the wheeled cart to be shipped, she wished the reader well and wondered if he or she would like, or dislike, the book as heartily as she had. She lifted down three *Payne's Business Encyclopedias,* two *Lorna Doone*s, a *Tennyson's Poems,* and twelve copies of *Parlor Games for the most Staid and Sedate Adult.* Well, those numbers showed what entertainment families had in mind for the holidays, she noted, before she thrust from her mind again holidays and parlors and families.

She added four Hyatt Noiseless Slates, so-called because chalk supposedly did not squeak across them. Just the thought of that from her days in the one-room Lutheran church schoolhouse in Bromberg made a shiver run up her spine. Students had learned English there, for German was mostly spoken at home. Actually it was the Schwartzmiller children who had taught their parents more English than just a few phrases. Both languages were spoken in the village, especially among the younger generation. She sighed at the memories as she consulted the next title on the list and took down two copies of the *Science of Life or Creative and Sexual Science* by Professor Fowler.

"Includes manhood, womanhood, and their mutual interrelations," she said, reciting the subtitle from the mail order catalogue they all knew by heart. She had taken this book home as she did something every night and ended up reading most of it aloud to the rapt Agnes and Mabel. "Love, its laws and powers. Pure and Elevated in Tone and Eloquent in Denunciation of Vice."

The words were still on her lips when she rolled the laden cart around the corner of the shelves—and directly into Mr. James. He huffed as the rail bumped his stomach and the end hit his shins. The wheels just missed his polished shoes. She squealed and grabbed for the top slate, which slid off and shattered noisily between them.

"Oh, I'm so sorry, sir!"

"It isn't really a noiseless slate, is it, Miss Miller?"

She wasn't certain whether to laugh or cry. Mr. James making a joke? He looked deadly serious, despite that strange twinkle in his brown eyes. As ever, especially when she came upon him suddenly, his disarming good looks—and direct way of examining her with those intense brown eyes under dark brows—made her go ridiculously weak-kneed. Each time it was as if she had somehow summoned a chivalrous hero from *Ivanhoe* or an exotic Roman emperor from that new book *Ben-Hur*. But it was only Mr. James, and that was jangling enough.

"I'm afraid I overloaded the cart. Things are usually in boxes to be shelved when I deal with them, and I wasn't thinking."

"Ah," he said, and he bent to help her pick up the biggest pieces of slate, "I was hoping you *were* thinking today. I wanted to get a general overview from you about how the new women's novels are selling. I mean, I can look at the numbers, but I had a feeling . . . a feeling," he repeated as their fingers brushed before they both stood to put the fragments on the cart, "that you might spot trends. You know, be able to give me an idea what to buy after the New Year so we don't just restock but can meet needs—if there . . . are any needs, you see.''

His voice trailed off in a hesitant manner that was most unlike him. She was so nonplussed he stood this close in this private valley of high shelves and regarded her so steadily, and had really asked her opinion that she almost answered him in German.

"Ja, ich . . ." she began before she quickly amended it by a quick cough. ''Just one moment until I get these orders back to Mr. Wembly, and I'd be pleased to help with that.''

She shoved the cart down the aisle toward packing, and he put a hand to it to push it along, too. She remembered too late she would have go back to replace the broken slate, but perhaps Mr. Wembly was enough in the holiday mood to do it without complaining. Wiping her hands on the canvas apron she always wore over her skirt and shirtwaist, she followed Mr. James into his glassed-in office and sat across his orderly desk from him. He poised his pencil over paper, but still studied her intently.

''I would say,'' she began, ''that anything by Bertha M. Clay is very popular. Why, her titles alone help sell her books, but the stories are wonderful, heart-warming ones.''

''Titles such as?''

''She wrote *Love Story, A Golden Heart,* and *Mad Love.*''

''I do discern a pattern. Love stories, romances.''

''Oh, yes. But ones that are uplifting and pure and elevated in tone!''

''Of course. So, how do these golden hearts of mad love meet and get to know each other?''

That brought her up short. He wanted her to repeat how the lovers met and courted? Was he mocking these books? Sometimes she thought she wouldn't read another one because they reminded her of what she did not have, but somehow they comforted her, too. They made her feel the vibrant emotions of falling for a man and warned her against the snares of loving the wrong person. But now, as she sat here a mere five feet from the object of her own golden heart's mad love story, she could not find the words to explain.

She began to worry he would think her a dunce. The books she had reshelved from his personal reading had all been self-betterment titles or the Horatio Alger series. Mostly those were for younger readers, so she had fretted at first he was wed and had a son. But then, when he left for his week's vacation in August, he had mentioned that, since he had no immediate family, he was going by himself to Cincinnati simply to see another city.

Now she got to her feet, appalled she was blushing. She could only hope her skin was still red from the wind today to hide her feminine foolishness over a man who was all business and ambition.

"I'll . . . I'll keep an eye out for other authors or trends," she said and backed to the door as if he were royalty in the King Arthur tales. But she didn't curtsy; she fled. Ordinarily a private talk with him could make her day, but now she'd ruined things. She gave the bare office Christmas tree a good bounce with her elbow when she hurried past it and scolded herself all the way back to the shelves.

After work Charlotte was almost glad that Agnes had said she was taking the streetcar home. She felt inordinately low, a combination of dreading the season and the disastrous interview with Mr. James this morning. He had been busy the rest of the day, thank heavens, for she wasn't certain whether to try to pick up the conversation or not, apologize or not—for what she had no idea. But she tried to buck herself up, if she could forgo the streetcar fare home today, she'd have the rest of the $1.78 for her sister Edna's vase lamp on sale—with the ten-percent employee discount.

Edna was but a year younger; they had been reared almost as twins. But since Charlotte had been courted by Andreas, Edna, who had been secretly sweet on him, had hardly spoken to her, except of necessity in their parents' presence. Why couldn't Edna realize, Charlotte fumed, that she had turned him down for good? True, at first she had let their old childhood friend come calling because his avid attentions were so flattering. She was curious to be kissed and wondered how it would be to fall in love. But the kiss seemed a disappointment, and she put an end to his social visits even when Mother urged she would come to care for him "that way" in due time.

Perhaps, Charlotte thought, she should include a note with the lamp, imploring her once fond sister to see the light and forgive her. Could she help it that she'd left Bromberg, Illinois, and Andreas behind and he still had not turned his attentions to Edna?

She would not even know that, if her youngest sister, Anna, hadn't been kind enough to correspond with her to keep her abreast of family events. Without that single ally at home, she would have to pump poor George all the time or guess what gifts people needed or longed for, and things longed for always made the very best Christmas gifts.

Besides Edna's lamp, she still needed to buy Anna's washbasin, pitcher, and chamber pot painted with English roses. She bought her family's gifts in order from eldest—Father first, of course, then Mother—to youngest in the family of ten children, although this year she had bought young Claus and John's waterproof schoolbags when they were on sale in September. She had longed to get them whist cards, but Mother would not approve. Good old euchre was the only card game allowed at home.

She set a quicker pace. The wind was softer and at her back; snowflakes fluttered through the dusk like summer moths. She clicked off in her mind the gifts she had waiting at home to be wrapped: a thermometer for Father's blacksmith shop; for mother—a choice she always agonized over—sterling-backed hand mirror and hairbrush; for Albert and Fred, who kept the small farm going, husking gloves; for dear George an enamel and iron inkstand and automatic pencil; for Louisa an engraved fern dish for her new parlor, for she, lucky duck, had been wed this summer; for Elenora silver sugar spoons for her hope chest—

She thought the heard her name and turned. "Miss Miller! I hope I might have a word with you!"

Mr. James! She stood still in the swirl of snowflakes, staring. Had he followed her? They were a good three blocks from the building.

"Sorry if I startled you," he said as he caught up. He looked like an S & R fashion plate in his gray wool overcoat with a camel wool scarf about his neck. "Wherever do you catch the streetcar?"

"I decided to walk home today."

"Alone? Might I walk a bit with you? I regret that our discussion today seemed to end in the middle. I want to apologize for putting you on the spot about personal reading preferences. I didn't mean to make you uncomfortable."

She had to smile at that. The man made her uncomfortable in the most thrilling ways. But he evidently thought her smile was a gracious acceptance of his apology and smiled back at her with a taut tilt of his mouth and flash of teeth. The effect on her knees, heart, even her cartwheeling stomach—all of her—was devastating.

"You don't live far then?" he was asking as they began to walk.

"A ways. I like physical exercise as well as mental, you see. And, the truth is, I walk to save fare to put toward Christmas gifts for my large family."

Strangely he frowned at that. Now that she thought of it, he seemed more of a Scrooge about Christmas than she, for he had been brusque toward others when asked about his holiday plans. He had told them they shouldn't lollygag about to decorate the office tree until closer to the holiday. Perhaps he had lost a loved one at Christmas or his relations lived far away. She realized she knew so little about the man. Yet how strange it was she felt so attuned to him right now, deeply calm and caring instead of flustered and rattled.

"Look, there's an oyster parlor," he said and pointed with a leather-gloved hand. "A good public neighborhood one. I've been there with Mr. Sears himself once," he added hastily. "Let's stop by for a cup of coffee to warm up a bit."

She hesitated but her mind raced. A dream come true that he had sought her out, that he broke fraternization rules for her and would dare to go into a place Mr. Sears perhaps frequented. But she must not tarry here with him. She would have to walk home in the dark, and wouldn't he think her fast if she accepted? But she could not manage a no, and her traitorous

Karen Harper

head nodded acquiescence as he gestured she should enter before him. The narrow shop with its stand-up wire tables, sawdust-strewn floor, kegs of open oysters, and steaming coffee urn smelled wonderful. It was quite busy and she was relieved to see several ladies with gentlemen.

When he removed his hat, she noted his hair was so dark it almost gleamed blue in the close overhead lights. It was immaculately trimmed, as was his mustache. He ordered coffee and two bowls of oyster stew for them.

"I too believe in good physical exercise, even in the elements," he said, to jolt her back to what she had said earlier. "I skate at Grant Park on weekends. You should come by tomorrow about ten to watch, or do you skate? I thought you might be Dutch, and they skate like the wind."

Suddenly she wondered if he had somehow found out she had changed—actually lied—about her long *Deutsch* name when she had applied for a job. She had done it not because she was ashamed of it or her family, but because she was angry at them then. It was a tiny act of rebellion or retribution she now regretted. But she realized he must mean she was really Dutch, from Holland, and not German. Still, his interrogation about that touched some tender spot in her.

"Dutch?" she retorted more tartly than she intended. "I was born in a small town nearby, and I'm as American as . . . as you are!"

"I didn't mean to imply otherwise. It's just you have a hint of some accent—you know, the way you say your r's."

"Oh. I'm from Bromberg to the east. There are a lot of Germans there."

They spoke of work, the weather, of Chicago, of

oysters—she was determined she would pay her share, but he would not hear of it. Something vital and luring leaped back and forth between them, whatever they discussed, as if they actually talked of intimate and not only polite things. Later she realized that neither of them had spoken of their families nor of Christmas, as if by unspoken, mutual consent.

Over her protests, he hired a hackney cab to take her home. When Agnes saw it pull up to the house, she flew out into the cold to hear what had happened to her, and Charlotte swore her to secrecy. Her landlady, Mrs. Ramsey—soon to be Mabel's mother-in-law—scolded her for being out after dark but it was worth it.

In bed that night while the wind howled outside, Charlotte felt so warm. She played everything she and Donald James had said back in her mind as if on a new-fangled graphophone. And she pictured him again, too: his square-jawed face; the tiny cleft in the very middle of his chin; the thick, dark lashes framing those warm, brown eyes; his straight black eyebrows that lifted now and then at something she said. She had looked only at him, but right behind his head on the wall someone had nailed a keg cover, which had read, "Atlantic Oysters, Aphrodisiac to the World!" She had been rather glad Mr. James had not seen that.

But what moved her most about this day was that, if all went wrong again with her family, Mr. James's attention—the admiring way he had regarded her—was perhaps the only real holiday gift she would receive this year.

2

The next day Don James left early for the skating pond in case *she* should actually take him up on his invitation. It was a dazzling day of promise with bright sun on last night's snow. He always took along several extra pairs of Sears skates and let the ragged, wide-eyed boys who sledded on trash-can lids or stood about smelling the rich aromas from the sausage stands borrow them.

He had given them impromptu skating lessons several weekend mornings and bought lunch for the little urchins, too. In warm weather he organized games of baseball, though fewer of them came each weekend as the necessity of jobs to help feed their families loomed. He had often lectured them on attending school and working hard to make their way in life, too. Whenever they would sit still long enough, he read to them from the Horatio Alger books that had so inspired him. He supposed they had only listened because he provided fun and food. He never asked about their families though; he couldn't bear to. If he had heard any of them were from St. Mary's Orphanage, he would probably have adopted them on the spot, and then what would his bride say of that someday when he found her?

Just after he sat down on a bench to clamp the skates on his boot soles, his favorite little chum, Mickey, ran down to join him. Don didn't see him until the boy was ready to barrel into him; he had been looking across the pond the way *she* would come, if she did.

"Hey, Mr. James, got a swell pair a sliders I can borrow today?" the boy shouted and flopped down beside him.

He playfully tugged the boy's tattered cap down over

his eyes. "Who else would these be for but my friend Mickey Finnegan?" he asked, though he wished they could be for a certain lady. He imagined her feet were about the size of these boy's skates. In case she'd let him instruct her, he would save a pair this size. When he handed Mickey the skates, Don noted with relief the leather mittens he had given him last week were still intact.

"Gonna be round here till lunch, Mr. James?" Mickey asked.

"It depends on how things go, my boy. Have you had breakfast yet?"

"Naw, waiting for lunch with you," Mickey said with a sheepish look that made Don's next breath painful. The freckled face was dirty. What Sister Theresa had always called sleep clustered in the corner of each blue eye. The lad was lean-cheeked and obviously hungry, but too proud to plead.

"In case I'm dining with someone else today, take this two bits for a sausage and a hot chocolate now, and don't forget to give the skates back next week if I leave before you do."

The boy stared at the silver quarter, his eyes as wide and bright as the coin itself before he snatched it. "Can't thank you 'nough, Mr. James, and I'm paying real good 'tention in school like you said," he shouted back over his shoulder as he skated across the pond directly toward the sausage stands.

Drat, Don thought, Mickey was more than hungry; he was ravenous. Though he tried to forget it all these years, he remembered that hollow-bellied, light-headed, desperate feeling when he'd first gone out on his own, before he met Mr. Sears. He'd give Mickey another coin for lunch before he left with *her* for lunch. Funny, he mused, as he scanned the ladies on the outskirts of the pond again, but even well-fed adults were ravenous for something, and they sometimes didn't even know what until it was dangled before them. And then they sometimes lost control to snatch and bolt like little boys.

Charlotte had been arguing with herself all morning, but her feet had made the final decision. She had gone out on an errand for Mabel, whose cold was finally mending, but now she'd marched clear to Grant Park, blocks out of her way. What could be wrong with merely stopping by the park pond to watch a few skaters? As much as she adored the city, there was something so countrified about this big park. Besides, *he* had invited her.

Everything was aboveboard and out in the open, she pleaded before her stern inner judge again. She beat down the evidence that her mother would call her fast or loose for meeting a man on her own without a chaperon. But, golly, this was modern Chicago, and it was nearly the twentieth century!

She stood back a ways, just watching when the pond came in sight with the expanse of glittering snow, shore, then lake behind it. How she had loved this city the first time she had seen it during the World's Columbian Exposition four years ago when Father had brought three of them to visit George and tour the fair. That celebration of the fourth centenary of the discovery of America by Columbus had been her discovery of Chicago and freedom.

Chicago had heated her blood like nothing since— except, of course, Mr. James. She had loved all that purposeful, bustling activity so different from quiet, stolid Bromberg: sleek private yachts the well-to-do owned and sailing ships from all over the world heading up the river; long iron ore vessels in Calumet Harbor near the great grain elevators and glowing steel mills; carts and carriages thick in streets of shiny windows stacked up buildings several stories high. She could hear the thousands of cattle in the vast Union Stockyards miles away on the night breeze from George's house instead of the single family milk cow out by the small barn in Bromberg.

But now the sounds were of skaters' shrill shouts and men hawking food and drink. The sights were of a busy scene with only one thing that held her eye: Mr. James waving at her from the edge of the pond.

Her feet took her quickly to him. She felt foolish waving and grinning back, but she did it anyway, like an excited little girl.

"Just in time for your first skating lesson!" he called to her.

She had intentionally dressed for this weather and the challenge of the new sport—and his approval—in her best burgundy walking suit and high-laced bicycle boots. Now she giggled and protested as he knelt before the stone bench to strap the skates on her boots, resting each first on his knee!

"I'm afraid I'll be the ruination of your day on these."

He smiled up at her in crisp sunlight. She could actually see her own reflection in each dark eye. "You have made my day by even stopping by," he vowed. "I'll not let you fall."

And he didn't, though she felt like a rag doll flopping about out there while others skimmed by like birds. He held her elbow firmly, and his other strong arm often encompassed her shoulders or waist, leaving a firm feeling there as if he held her still. Despite her trepidation of sprawling and finding herself, posterior

down, on the hard, slick ice, she loved every moment
of it. Even the redheaded boy named Mickey, who
kept cutting so close around them until Mr. James gave
him a quarter and sent him away for lunch, did not
make her falter.

"Whew, how can you do this for hours?" she asked
as they finally glided toward the bench to remove their
skates. "I'm sapped."

"It gets easier, believe me, but perhaps not so much
fun."

Another joke or a trifling remark? She dared not
look into those eyes. She only knew in most of Bertha
Clay's books, frivolous banter often led to something
far more serious. But today she didn't care about
warnings; everything seemed bright and brisk and
beautiful.

They ate sausages on thick buns smothered in mustard and Kosher dill slices and washed that down with
mugs of hot chocolate. They put coins in the Salvation
Army kettle, then bought popcorn for themselves and
the squirrels, which came up to eat out of their gloved
hands. Despite the biting breeze, the park was crowded
now with skaters and strollers who had been shopping.
But to Charlotte it seemed they were alone, the only
two in the entire, vast city.

"How can these squirrels be so hungry," she asked,
"when all they did this autumn was store nuts?"

"But they like what they see now, even if they had
other plans all laid," he said, his eyes suddenly narrowed against the wind. "You know," he added
quickly, as if to change the subject, "popcorn and
cranberries strung on thread was all I had to decorate
one Christmas I remember. But another boy and I had
to spend the whole afternoon on our knees in penance

for draping the statue of the Holy Mother and the crucifix with strings of it when we were altar boys."

Oh, dear, she thought, in that little voice in her head that sounded painfully like her mother's: *he's Catholic and no good Lutheran can abide that.*

He cleared his throat as if he would say more, but his head jerked around. Now she heard it, too, the familiar and unwelcome real world intruding.

Joseph Wembly and his wife were walking by, chatting, and unfortunately, saw them. Mr. James stood and doffed his cap, but he did not look so jaunty now. Seen breaking company rules, Charlotte had no choice but to nod, though she could not force a smile. The portly Mrs. Wembly gawked and lanky Joseph stopped talking and squinted to be certain what he saw was real.

"Lovely day, isn't it?" Mr. James brazened to them, but any such thing seemed ruined. After they plodded on, he slumped back down on the bench beside her. Silence descended; they felt awkward with each other again.

"Oh, dear," she said, staring solemnly down at her hands in her lap. "It might as well have been Richard Sears or Alvah Roebuck themselves."

"My fault. I don't like the policy, at least off company grounds. Yet I know why they have it."

"Well, you were only teaching me to skate, and I must be heading home. I'm ever so late on my errands. I . . . I'm sorry we were . . . were noticed, Mr. James."

Her voice began to tremble as she thought of all the possible repercussions: a calling on the carpet, a demotion, a dismissal from all she—both of them—had strived for. She could not look at him as she stood and shook her skirts out. He stood too. "I cannot thank you enough for your kindness,'' she said. ''Obviously we must not do this again.''

''Just bad luck we ran into Wembly. But with so many employed at S & R, it had to happen. I regret being careless with your reputation. But, just once before we part, may I ask something of you?''

She stared up at him, nodding as if mesmerized. She supposed if he had requested that she walk out onto partially frozen Lake Michigan and swim clear to Canada, she would have blithely done so. She tried to memorize his face, to remember always the intensity of his personality that warmed her, even this day that suddenly felt so chill again.

''Just once, call me Don,'' he said, ''and I will call you Charlotte.''

Her lower lip dropped, trembled, then pressed closed. ''Thank you for this lovely day, Don.''

She thought for one moment his eyes watered from the sting of wind. ''I shall not forget it ever, Charlotte.''

She bit her lip, nodded, and turned away, buffeted farther from him by the wind as if she were a sailing vessel. She sniffed hard once, twice, but did not look back. After all, she had found a treasure of memories to hoard for the rest of her days, even if she, like the books she loved, ended up on the shelf.

That evening as she wrapped her family's Christmas gifts, her mood bounded between ecstasy and despair. How would she ever face Mr. James—Don—if Mr. Wembly reported them or spread the word? And how would she live with herself if her parents would not accept her gifts again? Would they even want her there for the holidays if she dared to go? If she were actually dressed down or dismissed at S & R, should she return home, admit she was wrong when she didn't believe that, and ask for their forgiveness? But no, though Bromberg was her hometown, it was not really home anymore, not the place she wanted to live. Nor was Andreas Kurtz, whom Anna had written appeared to be waiting faithfully for her to fail and return, the man with whom she wanted to spend her life.

Charlotte jumped at Mabel's familiar flutter of raps on her door. Since her promotion she had taken this small, third-floor room on her own, while Agnes and Mabel shared the larger one across the hall. But next month Mabel was marrying Tom Ramsey, their land-lady's son who worked at the stock exchange, so Charlotte would be moving back in with Agnes.

"Listen, Char, just everyone—Mrs. Ramsey, Agnes, Tom—they all want to know if you'll help decorate the parlor," red-haired Mabel reported, dabbing at her cold-roughened nose with her lace handkerchief. She still sounded as if she were talking from inside a barrel. "I see you're not reading tonight. In the mood for a little bit of Christmas?"

She wasn't, but she nodded. Downstairs she could tell they were glad she had joined them, and that moved her deeply. She hoped they wouldn't think her a stick-in-the-mud, but their good-natured bantering as they decked hearth, window sills, and banister with pine boughs and red ribbons, and—you might know— with popcorn and cranberry strings, made her feel quiet and alone. But it also made her very determined that she would visit George and ask what he thought of taking her home with him when he went for Christmas Day.

While they sang carols, she strung a few extra long necklaces of popcorn and cranberries for that bare tree at work. It could be a secret message to Don—no doubt now Mr. James to her forever after—that she shared with him the memory of his escapade one boyhood Christmas. She only hoped they would both still be working at S & R when it came time to decorate the office tree with Joseph Wembly and the others. She had found, then been forced to forfeit, a friendship with Don James; how would she ever bear it if the additional price for those precious, stolen moments was her career?

And the thought he too might lose his position churned her stomach so that she turned down a delicious-smelling cinnamon hot toddy. Would Mr. Wembly keep quiet since Mr. James was his immediate supervisor, or would he think he could try for the overseer's job if his boss were disciplined or dismissed? If only she could buy Mr. James something for Christmas to cheer him, what would it be? One of those graceful wire lawn settees for two she had been mooning over in the catalogue? A silk bow tie? A gold-filled pocket watch for $7.95 like the one she had wanted to buy Father but didn't have the money? Monogrammed stationery so Mr. James could send her passionate trysting notes so Mr. Wembly would never catch on how they adored each other . . .

"Ouch!" she cried when she stuck her finger with the needle and bled a big Christmasy crimson drop on the next piece of popcorn. And that pricked the bubble of her foolish dreaming, too.

At work on Monday she was even more on edge. She had no idea if Joseph Wembly had reported them. He seemed as obsessed with his work as Mr. James did each time she dared to glance their way, but she didn't blame either of them for avoiding her after imminent disaster.

The morning seemed endless to Charlotte, waiting for the other shoe to fall, as Agnes always said. At eleven o'clock her stomach cartwheeled when Mr. Wembly appeared in the aisle where she was pulling books and said only, "You're wanted in Mr. James's office. Someone there to see you."

She stood staring after his departure, wiping her palms repeatedly on her canvas apron. He hadn't gloated or given her any further hint. But surely he had told someone, and she was being summoned for that. All she'd worked for and hoped for seemed as smashed as that slate she had broken here last Friday. Was it only four days ago her brief time with Mr. James had begun? And now it was all, of sad necessity, ended.

The packers and Mr. Wembly were staring at her without trying to look as if they were. Her stomach twisted tighter. Inside she saw a man sitting, facing the desk, while Mr. James was in his chair on the other side. The man was blond, so it wasn't Mr. Sears or Mr. Roebuck at least, but no doubt some underling here to pronounce the penalty. Back straight, chin up, she knocked on the office door as she entered, although it stood ajar. And then, as Mr. James's eyes lifted to her, the visitor turned and stood.

"Oh, Andreas!" she blurted. "Whatever are you doing here?"

But he was already calling her *Charlotte, Fraulein Schwartzmiller* and rattling off German so fast she could not keep up. Mr. James rose and walked around the desk to her as if he had to prop her up on her feet.

"I wasn't certain what he wanted at first, Miss *Schwartzmiller,* but he said he was a *very* close friend who has come to take you home."

"Home? Why?"

And then Andreas's German spiel sank in. "Your mother is ill and wants to see you," he was saying. "I was bringing the last load of potatoes to town and came to fetch you in my wagon. This man has given you permission to leave now."

"It's all right if I leave to see my mother?" she asked Mr. James. She could not read his eyes beneath that stony frown. Concern of course lurked there, but anger, too, perhaps at hearing her real name or at Andreas's intrusion and his claiming close familiarity. Or was it even relief she read that she would be away from here not to get in his way or be interviewed if worse came to worse with the company reprimand they were expecting?

"Of course, it's all right—necessity, Miss Schwartzmiller," Mr. James assured her, his tone taut. "And since everyone's out in three days, don't feel you must rush back before Christmas."

"I see. So . . . I can't thank you enough."

"My best wishes to your mother."

She stood there, so appalled she wanted to cry, actually to hurl herself into his arms for comfort and understanding. That was not like her. But everything was ruined between them now, not only by company rules, but by her being *Fraulein* Schwartzmiller and not Miss Miller.

Andreas stood near them, as if to leap in to stop them from touching. But they didn't touch; she wasn't sure they ever really had. She bid Mr. James farewell—Andreas did too, in perfectly good English—and hurried out the door, her thoughts on her mother. If Mother were really ill—Andreas strode behind her saying Mother was having trouble breathing—she must rush to her, but there was so much to keep her and Mother from touching, too.

"Andreas, thank you for coming here to fetch me home," she said as they hurried out onto the windy street where he had paid a newsboy to watch his horse and wagon. He gave her a hand up the high single step onto the board seat.

"I have been wanting to do it for three years, but not for this reason," he told her as he unwrapped the reins from the brake.

As they jerked away from the curb, Charlotte looked back and up to the fourth-floor windows. Don James stood there, looking down. She was sure he was frowning, though the distance was great and the reflection washed out his face. He, let alone Mr. Wembly, now had grounds for her reprimand or dismissal: she had given a false name on the initial employment application and she had misrepresented herself for three years.

The big S & R building disappeared around the corner as they headed toward the rooming house to get her things. The mere twenty-mile journey ahead loomed endless. She feared finding her mother ill and facing everyone at home; she regretted Andreas still seemed intent on having her. But she was sickeningly certain now that she had seen the last of Mr. James and her exciting days at S & R.

3

How strange it seemed to be going home for Christmas but for all the wrong reasons. At least Andreas did not speak of their past, only of things they saw along the way or recent events in Bromberg. Yet the occasional stiff silences between them were even worse than what she and Mr. James had come to after being seen by Mr. Wembly.

Bundled under a lap rug, jolting along on the hard seat with her satchel and wrapped gifts bouncing behind in the wagon bed, she studied the familiar road into town. The single street of Bromberg's brick and wooden facade businesses and shops, including her father's smithy with its painted sign SCHWARTZMILLER AND SONS, BLACKSMITH AND FARRIERS, looked nearly unchanged from her girlhood days. Next to the smithy stood the two-story, L-shaped brick house in which she had grown up. Out back the rooster weather vane on the roof of the small barn creaked to turn in the sporadic shift of wind. The family's fields were beyond the town; most of them abutted Andreas's family's bigger farmlands.

The old homestead looked like a Currier and Ives lithograph with the recent snow and wind etching its stone sills and dull red bricks. As dusk descended, from the parlor and her parents' bedroom window lamps glowed, casting thin paths of gold onto the blue-shadowed snow. The evergreen Advent wreath still hung on the door. At the sight of this house where she had been born, tears stung her eyes. Home, but not a welcome home.

Yet she was only partly right. Anna and Elenora came running out, John and Claus, too, all babbling about Mother taking a turn for the worse yesterday. Charlotte jumped down before Andreas could help her; she quickly hugged her four youngest siblings, though all but Anna stood in her embrace like stiff, cold tin soldiers. She hurried across the wooden front porch, her heart thudding as hollow as her steps.

Inside the achingly familiar smells of homemade *kuchen* and *sauerkraut* hung heavy in the air. She was sure someone had been making the traditional Christmas *lepkuchen* cookies with the heady mingled scent of cardamom seed and molasses. And then her father came downstairs. He hesitated but one moment, then held his arms out to her.

Though perhaps he meant only to grasp her shoulders in greeting as was his custom, she hugged him hard, her single word muffled against his broad shoulder. *"Vater!"*

"Mein Charlotta," was all he managed in a deep voice before he released her and stepped quickly back. He was looking almost guiltily up the stairs at her sister Edna, standing on the landing with her arms crossed over her chest.

"The late, great Charlotta," Edna said, sounding and looking so much like their mother that Charlotte hesitated on the first step up. "I see Andreas brought you back as he said he would."

Edna's expression was hardly one of welcome, so Charlotte approached her with, "How is she?"

"Doctor Keppler says it's acute pleurisy."

"Her life's not in danger?"

"Mother thinks so, and the doctor won't say. It started with a bad cold."

Charlotte hurried up the stairs. Edna and Anna followed her into the dim bedroom, which smelled of mingled medicines. Lying swathed in bedclothes, Olga Braun Schwartzmiller looked much smaller than she had standing and scolding the last time Charlotte was home three years ago.

"She's probably sleeping, Lottie," Anna whispered, tiptoeing forward to touch Charlotte's elbow. "She needs to rest and not talk much and move very little or it pains her something awful. She's got her ribs all wrapped and taped."

But her mother's eyes slitted open; her voice came low and breathless. "It hurts like a knife to the heart," she wheezed, glaring at Charlotte. "Like I've felt before."

Charlotte got the point, but she bent over the bed and took her hand. It was cold and waxy; the feel of it scared her more than anything since she had first heard she was ill. "Mother, thank you for sending for me." She also spoke in German.

"*This* is where you belong," came the old argument, only quietly this time.

"At any rate, this is where I am now, and for Christmas as well as to help tend you. Wait until you see what I brought you."

"Nothing this year either, if it is not yourself home to stay," Olga pronounced and turned her head stiffly away on the mound of pillows. Even in the wan lamplight, Charlotte noticed her long brown hair was heavily threaded with many more silver strands. Though she seemed to sleep, Charlotte sat down to wait.

The next afternoon was the first time Charlotte ventured out of the house. Mother seemed to be sleeping soundly, despite the fact her shallow, raspy breathing and occasional wrenching spells of coughing unnerved all of them. The doctor had come and gone again, leaving syrups and mustard packs and warning them to keep her propped up on pillows and to turn her position so the pleurisy would not become dreaded pneumonia.

Other than a few hours of sleep while Anna watched her, Charlotte had stayed by her mother's side, though it was evident—now that she had summoned her home—her mother had not really forgiven her for choosing to be a city girl. And it was painfully evident that Edna had not excused her one bit for being the erstwhile object of Andreas Kurtz's attentions.

Now, hugging her mother's knitted shawl close about her shoulders, Charlotte went out to speak with her father in the blacksmith shop. He had never really done the farming; except at harvest time, he left the tending of the fields he owned to his eldest sons, Albert and Fred, especially after George moved to town. Her eldest brothers had their own families to support, so they helped in the smithy during the winter, too. But today, she knew from watching out the window, Father was temporarily alone. If she could just win him over, perhaps he would help her with Mother and even Edna.

She had always loved the smithy, perhaps because as a child it was forbidden to her. The roaring forge, flying sparks like fireworks, the hot pincers, anvil, and skittish horses made it no place for a curious child, let alone a girl who was not expected to learn the trade. Today she still felt like a bit of an intruder in this man's world, but she did not let that daunt her anymore.

When she opened the door, Otto Schwartzmiller looked up and nodded his permission for her to enter. Then he went back to hammering something small against the anvil. She closed the door behind her and, still hugging herself for warmth, edged closer to the heat of the forge.

Her father had always been a stoic man of action and not of emotions or words—that was mother's realm. He was a big-boned, strapping man of girth and muscle, a man for handling horses, fire, and iron rather than women and fragile feelings. He had controlled his children with a stern look or single swipe of his big hand if the boys got too unruly or disobeyed. Since he was a man of few words, just one from him could make the girls quake. But now she was an adult and must speak with him about adult concerns.

She peered at his work, not recognizing what he was making. It appeared to be a rectangle of thin hammered iron with a frame of soldered shoeing nails.

"What are you making, Father?" she asked when he put his tools in a bucket of water and rinsed and wiped his huge hands.

He gestured her over to the wooden work bench under the window. A foot-square piece of paper lay there in the thin winter sun. "I still cannot read all of it, but I am framing it anyway," he said.

She leaned closer. Her eyes fell first on the big gold seal, then the many lines of printing and hand-written calligraphy that covered the faded page, divided by stiff folds as if it had been pressed somewhere for years. Now she recognized his Certificate of Citizenship that had been kept in the family Bible. It stated in part that Otto Frederick Schwartzmiller, a native of Wittenberg, Germany, declared ended all former allegiance to the emperor of Germany, and herewith became a citizen of the United States of America. It was dated December 21, 1864, thirty-three years ago today.

"Do you want me to read it to you?" she asked.

He shook his head. "I know what it says. Best Christmas gift ever."

So he was making a frame for it to hang proudly somewhere, she surmised. And, without meaning to, he had given her her chance to speak to him about needing his help.

"But this doesn't mean that you have no good feelings for, respect for, or love for your old homeland," she said. "You have always been proud of Germany and German tradition, even though you have been an American all these years."

He nodded, his broad face suddenly both curious

and wary. She noted that his jowls had softened and sunk a bit and that his crisp brown hair had thinned and silvered.

"That's how I feel about things here at home, Father," she went on, choosing her words carefully until her feelings took over and she talked faster and faster. "I love this place, I love you all dearly, but I choose now to live in Chicago. I enjoy the benefits of my life there, but it does not change how dearly I love all of you here. I just wish Mother could understand!"

His big hands smoothed his certificate flat on the workbench as she talked, but his eyes now gazed out the frost-framed window toward the house.

"I know, my girl. But with your mother it *is* different, difficult, not like it was when George left. There are things about her you don't know."

"Things like what, Father?"

He shrugged as if he had already said too much. "Things that cannot matter if she will not tell you herself. Things maybe when she sees this paper hanging in our bedroom she will tell you when she feels better."

That had to be enough for now. The two youngest Kurtz boys who helped Andreas farm came in with a plow horse to be reshod, so she made a quick retreat.

Two days before Christmas—the day that S & R let everyone off one hour early for the holidays back in Chicago—Anna and Edna ran out of almonds for their holiday baking, and Anna asked Charlotte if she would go uptown to the Reidelbach's General Store for them.

"Besides," Anna added, looking so stern for her eighteen years, "you need a breath of good country air. You're looking pale as wallpaper paste."

"Thank you very much for the charming compliment, chum," Charlotte teased with a poke.

Only with Anna had she felt she could be herself since she'd been home. Edna had made it abundantly clear Charlotte should tend Mother to free her sisters to keep house, cook, and prepare for Christmas. As for Mother, as much as Charlotte had hoped for a reconciliation, things were almost worse than last time. Then Mother had ranted and raved; lately, she whispered orders and refused to discuss anything. Yes, even if for a little respite, she would welcome a walk uptown.

She knew almost everyone she met on Main Street; some chatted briefly, some simply called out *Guten Tag;* a few nodded and avoided her as if she were an escaped felon from the Illinois State Penitentiary. But as she headed home with her bag of almonds and a small sack of citron she knew Edna liked, Andreas appeared at her side and snatched off his wool cap. His blond hair was slicked down, and his cheeks looked like two polished apples in his earnest, round face. He seemed dressed far too fine to be doing farmwork of any sort today.

"How is *Frau* Schwartzmiller, Charlotta?" he asked, effectively pinning her into the doorway of Stahl's Furniture Store and Funeral Parlor.

"Better, thank you, Andreas, though it pains her greatly to breathe, let alone talk or laugh."

"She hasn't laughed since you went to live in Chicago and won't again until you come home to stay."

At that accusation she ducked around him and began to walk toward home again. But his long legs made it easy for him to keep up.

"You can understand how she's missed you," he

amended, his voice less strident now. "How we all have."

"Mother has three daughters still at home and another living within a mile she sees several times a week, not to mention her sons all in easy reach but one."

"But her life would be perfect if you lived here too. Charlotta, I must tell you that, despite the life you've led, I still regard you highly, and wish I might call upon you again."

She turned to face him on the board sidewalk before they neared the smithy. Best to have this out now, though after that final, furious talk they had before she left home three years ago, she thought any independent man would have gone on with his life by now. And yet part of her sympathized with him. She could grasp setting one's sights on only one person and desperately hanging on when all seemed lost.

"Andreas, I do not like your implications about the life I've led. Living on my own in Chicago does not make me some . . . some fallen woman, you know! And my feelings about us have not changed since I left. You and I were good friends once, but my feelings did not grow as yours did. I thought at first they might, but . . . they just didn't. And do not fancy I left because of you or even because of the disagreements I have had with my mother. I left for myself, because of what I had to discover and to offer—"

"Offer city slickers who don't really care about you as I . . . as we all do! Like that man who looks at you with hungry eyes!"

"Hungry eyes? I do not want to discuss Mr. James any more than you evidently wish to discuss Edna. She cares deeply for you and always has, you know that. She would be the perfect wife for you!"

"So, I am a *dumkopf* to want the sour fruit hanging far above me and ignore that which is sweet and ripe for the taking," he muttered, half to himself. "But, really, I only came to tell you that your mother, through Claus, has asked me to go with your family to cut their Christmas tree tomorrow afternoon. I assume you do not want me there."

"You may do as you wish because I will be staying with Mother while the rest of them get the tree. Sour fruit that I am," she added, fighting to keep her temper in check, "I hope you will join the family and realize how much Edna cares for you. And thank you for your concern about Mother. *She* is obviously concerned with *your* welfare, too, though evidently not enough to speak to you on Edna's behalf. Good day."

He followed her no farther. If only he would forgo his need for her. "But absence makes the heart grow fonder," Agnes had said when she'd confided once in her Chicago friends, though Mabel's "I don't know why it's not out of sight, out of mind," was more what she wished for. She wished for so much this Christmas, and none of it material gifts. Peace on Earth with her own family would be grand. Edna and Andreas happy together; and for herself . . .

She sighed as she caught a glimpse of the Meinhart boys skidding across the pond beside the barn. They had no skates on their feet but pretended they did. She thought of Don James, of their lovely day in the park, a little bit of country in the city. Now, here she was, really in the country, and it didn't seem right without him.

Instead of going in, she walked around the side of the house to watch the boys. Their shrill cries of "Whee! Whee-eee!" as they sailed across the small pond made her smile.

"Whee, indeed," she said. She leaned against the thick old walnut tree under which she had once loved to sit and read. How exhilarating her brief moments with Donald James had been, like a glorious, reckless skid across the pond. All those months she had studied him, thought about him, treasured brief words with him—yes, yearned for him—seemed to have slipped away so fast after their two private times together.

And now, much too late, she realized she loved him. As little as she knew of him, she loved him, for the things that really mattered in a man. His kindness and helpfulness; his strong but gentle nature; his stern demeanor tempered by a sense of humor; his deep inner aloneness, however good he was with people. She felt his kindred spirit in some of those things. How strange, how ironic, how wrong to know she loved him when she had lost him, if indeed, she had ever had him at all. And how different from her feelings for Andreas, like comparing lightning bugs to lightning.

The snow crunched hard under her feet, and branches of the bare walnut tree groaned overhead as she trudged toward the house.

Friday afternoon, Charlotte told her father she would stay behind to tend Mother while the others went to the woods to get the Christmas tree. He said Claus and John were old enough to cut one down and he would stay with his wife, but Charlotte finally convinced him to go along. She felt proud of herself that he had listened and been swayed by her wishes. If only things could be that way with Mother! Olga Schwartzmiller was a strong woman, but the most stubborn one Charlotte had ever known.

All bundled up on her way out the door, Edna shot Charlotte a squinty look when Charlotte urged her to

keep an eye on everyone, including Andreas. At least
Edna accepted that challenge as easily as the bag of
citron yesterday. And she did not seem vexed about
obviously being set up with Andreas, for Mother had
said he would be there no matter what. But Charlotte
knew Edna would kill her if she discovered she had
spoken to him yesterday about Edna's still being sweet
on him.

"If I'm asleep when they come back," her mother
said when Charlotte returned to the bedroom, "be sure
they all wipe their feet before traipsing in on the parlor
carpet."

At least she seemed to be speaking to her today,
Charlotte thought—of necessity to save the carpet if
not their relationship. "I'm sure everyone knows that
by now, Mother."

"Just because they're grown doesn't mean they have
a bit of good German sense."

Charlotte saw her frown at the newly hung citizenship certificate on the wall facing the bed. She wished
she had the backbone to speak to her about it as she
had to Father, but when it came to Mother, her pluck
suddenly failed her. She sat perched on the edge of
the ladder-back chair by the bed, hoping inspiration
would strike. She had always had trouble talking to
her mother; perhaps they were just too different.

"So," Olga whispered, "no marriage prospects for
you and this Agnes in the city? If this Mabel friend of
yours can find someone nice, you know you can, too—
here in Bromberg."

"It's not Andreas I love, Mother."

Olga managed the derisive snort she had perfected
lately since it didn't take as much breath as scolding.
"But you mean there *is* someone there you love,

then?'' she asked, her sharp blue eyes boring into Charlotte's.

"Not someone I can ever have. Just someone who was very kind to me, that's all.''

"That's not all, I can tell. What's his name?''

"It's not German, Mother. I said it's nothing.''

"Nothing, ha. I didn't think that for one moment when I met your father,'' she whispered and glared at the evidently offending certificate on the wall again. "I knew it was *something* from the first. Ah, curse these sore ribs.''

Charlotte jumped up to plump the pillows. "Tell me, if it doesn't hurt you to talk about it,'' she urged, resuming her perch.

"Hurts me in more ways than you know. I left my family for that man, your father. Left my country, my home. I swore when I said good-bye to my beloved mother and three sisters the day we sailed from Bremen I would keep my own family together. That's what good times in America should mean, so I promised her that—I promised myself!''

Charlotte sat tense, her hands gripped in her lap so hard her fingers went numb. But the outbreak of words and emotion was too much for Olga, and she began to suffer an attack. The wrinkles on her brow furrowed deeper. Charlotte clasped her hands to steady her until the pain subsided this time.

"Charlotta, my Charlotta.''

"Mother, don't talk now. Rest, just rest.''

"You come back home. You're my firstborn daughter. Marry Andreas or don't marry him, it does not matter then, but come home. Ach!'' she groaned and began to cough and heave in wracking spasms.

Later Charlotte blotted tears from her mother's cheeks, then held her head up while she sipped water.

But she did not promise what her mother wanted most. She could not. She berated herself for it, but she could not let this battle go. She had to make her mother see that whatever vow she had made to her own mother years ago, this mother and daughter bond would only be broken by forging tighter chains.

Her forehead pressed to the cold windowpane while her mother slept at last, Charlotte heard voices before everyone came into view. They spilled out of the wagon and dragged the six-foot tree through the snow toward the house. The boys propped it against the gate and pounded its trunk on the brick walkway to make the snow shower from its thick branches. Charlotte glanced back at Mother; surely they would remember to wipe their feet if they tried to get the branches clean.

But a chill swept her when she realized Andreas was not with them. Perhaps he had left the wagon sooner, but the Kurtz farm was out the other side of town. Had he not gone with them at all? Mother had told Edna he was going, and Charlotte had banked on that when she exhorted Edna to take good care of him. But she had hurried up to Mother's room so quickly when they left, she had not thought to look for him. No, she guessed he had not gone at all, for even from here she could see Edna's shoulders slumped, her head down as if she were not part of this happy scene at all.

Claus and John were making snowballs and pelting each other. Anna, Elenora, even Father all responded with missiles of their own. Evidently, though, they knew not to pull Edna into the fray; her mood showed she would massacre anyone who did. Didn't they know that ruckus could waken Mother?

Charlotte was just about ready to run downstairs to hush them when a man in a topcoat and top hat on a black horse turned in at the house. It could not be Andreas, not dressed like that, nor the stout village doctor. This was a tall, leaner man who carried a large basket out to the side. From her high vantage point, Charlotte could not see his face.

Then a snowball caught his hat and sent it spinning. She gasped and pressed her clasped hands to her mouth and nose. Mr. James—here in Bromberg—being blitzed by snowballs by her family—and Mother like this—and Father shouting at the boys to stop.

She skidded across the rag rug on the polished floor as she charged downstairs. She passed a fuming Edna halfway but did not stop. At the moment she could not even grieve that Edna was sadly, sullenly alone. For, with good news or ill, Donald James had come to Bromberg.

4

Don James's hat went flying in the storm of snowballs. He had the urge to jump to the ground and join the fray. But, careful not to dump his basket, he dismounted, using the big horse for a shield, even as the man bellowed at the boys.

The barrage stopped. For one moment he feared he had overstepped—not that they meant to attack him, but that everyone evidently spoke German. If Charlotte was not here to translate, whatever would he do?

And then he saw her. Without a coat or cape, she ran out onto the wide wooden porch, then navigated the slippery steps. He moved around the horse, realizing how stiff and sore he was, for he seldom rode. He had leased this mare from a Chicago livery stable this morning and set out on what he considered the adventure of his life. Actually he supposed it was a fool's errand, but there had been a compelling force—and here it came now.

"I cannot believe you're here. Come in . . . welcome," Charlotte said and gestured toward the house. She looked as wide-eyed as a child.

But neither of them moved farther; they seemed to hang suspended. The wind lifted her shoulder-length hair she wore fetchingly loose, caught up in a blue ribbon; he felt the falling snow wet his hair and nose, but he could not look nor move away to retrieve his hat.

Good color flushed her lovely face. Her dark blue shirtwaist had huge puffed shoulders, but fitted close in the arms and bodice to emphasize her fine womanly figure. Below her narrow waist gentle swags of cloth draped her hips and fell to a graceful skirt, its hems darkened by the snow. He just drank in the sight and sound of her before he found his voice.

"I wanted to assure myself that your mother—you too—were well. I wanted to tell you I spoke with Joseph Wembly on your behalf, and he said he decided to let the incident pass, as we could just have stumbled upon each other in the park, even as he stumbled on us."

"Oh. Good."

"I told him I considered it a great kindness, and I would not forget it, but I suppose we should not be seen together in public in town again. Charlotte—Charlotta, if you prefer—I was hoping there would be a hotel or rooming house in Bromberg so I might stay here until tomorrow to pay a proper Christmas visit on you and your family."

He had hoped so much more than that, but he didn't really know whether to trust anything she had told him now or not. He had been agonizing all the way out here. Why she had changed her name and tried to cover up this big, boisterous family was beyond him. He could not help but hold it against her. People's names and families were important. Was she ashamed of their Germanness? Did she have something else to hide?

Worse, that man Andreas Kurtz had implied he was something special to her, so why had she met another man to go skating? A nice woman in love with or promised to someone else would never have done such a thing. He could tell from the way she had looked at him—drat it, just like she looked at him now—that she felt something of the magnetism that arced between them, too.

That he was her superior at work worried him for more than one reason. Was she the sort who would cozy up to him, hoping for advancement, even at the risk of dismissal? How quickly she had said they must not meet again when Wembly spotted them. Still, as bad as it looked—and basically as forbidden as she was to him—he had skipped one of his favorite church services of the year tonight and turned down friends for Christmas dinner tomorrow and come clear out to the snow-swept country on a wintry day for exactly this.

Only a fraction of a moment passed, but everything seemed slowed. They stood staring at each other while voices swirled by like falling flakes. The two boys, curious about this stranger who knew their sister, came up, snow-speckled, to gawk. He was used to boys hanging about and wished Mickey were here to be part of this snowball fight and this noisy family fun his arrival had hushed. He did not turn to the other girl, no doubt a sister, when she came close and spoke.

"Lottie, you'll catch cold like Mother if you don't go in."

"I'm fine, really, Anna."

"Then ask your caller in, and he can help Father get the tree up straight."

"I asked him in," Charlotte said to him and not to Anna.

"Then your mother is mending?" he asked as he descended to solid earth once again. Time seemed to trip along at its regular pace now.

"Slowly. Yes, please come in. Claus, put Mr. James's horse in the smithy stall, won't you?" she said, finally turning away.

"Here, I brought a smoked ham, and a few presents for your family, though I don't know how many of them there are. All of these?"

"And more. But you didn't need to do that. Only yourself would do just fine," she said, then blushed even deeper pink.

At that, whatever lies she had told or whatever she meant to hide, he forgave her temporarily. He noticed the boys were elbowing each other and snickering and the big, brawny man was staring. That evidently registered on Charlotte, too.

"It is an honor to meet you, Mr. Schwartzmiller," he said when she introduced her father. The man's girth made two of him. Don ran his finger between his neck and the scratchy wool neckscarf. Chill or not, he was suddenly sweating as if he'd skated all the way here. Nodding, trying to keep straight all the names, he felt immensely relieved that everyone had switched to English. And then they escorted him into the best-smelling house he had ever entered, with the Christmas tree carried shoulder-high before them.

Charlotte sat across from Don James while he ate a knockwurst sandwich and a huge piece of breakfast stollen she had brought into the parlor on a tray for him. She had been helping her sisters more in the kitchen, so she knew where everything was again after these years away. What a strange joy it gave her to prepare and serve this man food with her own hands. She tried not to stare at him as he ate.

She hoped he liked the parlor despite its old-fashioned, rural character. The sofa was slippery horsehair with two worn spots on the seat, though the chairs were tufted velvet. Mother's maroon patterned tapestry carpet was the only modern thing in the room. The white walls looked blank not covered with the floral print wallpaper in vogue in the city; sitting before the old hearth, the stove was a big-bellied, iron, wood-burning one instead of nickel-plated to handle coal. The mantel was not decked with clusters of lovely, stylish bric-a-brac, but was nearly bare. The carved creche nestled there among a few pine boughs from the big tree in the yard. The thick, worn family Bible lay on the marble tabletop under the front window instead of a display of novels as in several Chicago homes she'd seen. At least things did not look so plain in here with the creche and the tree.

"We decorate the tree after Christmas Eve supper tonight," Charlotte explained to her surprise guest. He was her *surprised* guest, too, because they had finally convinced him there were no hotels in Bromberg, but he must sleep in the extra bed in the boys' room tonight. He was obviously quite moved by their offer of hospitality.

Fortunately he seemed very tolerant of Claus and John's fidgeting and festering, as Mother used to call it. He had even gotten in the spirit of family fun—though some of it had fallen back into German—tossing in his opinion about whether the tree stood straight on its crosspieces and where the boughs were the fullest to turn to the room. But Father was going to carry Mother downstairs tonight, and they all knew they would hear then how they had really done. And, Charlotte thought, they would all hear what Mother thought of this non-German Catholic—she would ferret all that out of him in a minute—visitor from the big, bad city.

"I am grateful to you, Charlotte, to all of you, that you haven't made me feel I'm intruding," he said to her.

"Intruding? Not at all. I'm grateful you came clear out here to tell me about Mr. Wembly and to inquire about Mother."

Placing his empty plate on the low table between them, he leaned toward her, though she was certain no one was eavesdropping for the first time since he'd arrived. Claus and John were fetching boxes of tree ornaments from the attic, and her sisters were busy in the kitchen. Father, as was his practice in late afternoon, was sitting upstairs with Mother. And Charlotte herself was so thrilled to have Don here that she hardly knew what she was doing or should do.

"I really came to see you above all else," he confided and reached over to the arm of her chair to cover her hand with his big, warm one. "I didn't like the way things ended between us."

"Nor did I," she admitted, but she didn't like the way he admitted they *had* ended.

"I wanted to understand you, and so, I guess, that means understanding your people here in Bromberg and why you changed your name. It wasn't just because it was long or hard to pronounce, was it?"

"No," she admitted, staring down now at his hand on hers. That touch seemed to radiate heat to all of her. She needed to talk to him, but not here in the heart of the family.

"If you want to understand Bromberg, you must see it," she said. "Would you like to take a walk out before dinner, or are you still frozen from the ride?"

"You know I thrive on cold breezes. Let's go."

The business end of Main Street was as she had hoped this crisp, clear, early Christmas Eve—deserted. Both bundled up, her gloved hand tucked in the crook of his arm, they strolled the foot-and sled-tracked sidewalk, peering in store windows, most of which displayed some form of Christmas cheer. A lantern and big-bellied stove burned in the general store, but no one was in view inside. They walked on, each waiting for the other to plunge into deep water.

"It was swell of you to bring the ham and presents," she said.

At the end of the street where the wind made the snow whisper across the crust of itself, he turned her to him. Behind his head and arcing over them were the bright pinpoints of stars in blackest night; snow-deep fields stretched between the few city homes and the closest farms, reflecting their own cold light.

"No more small talk now," he said. His hands held her upper arms tight through her heavy cape. "Were you trying to hide your family from S & R or hide S & R from them at first with that false name? How could you not be anything but proud of these people and who you really are?"

"Because my mother—my father, too—refused to let me live in Chicago when I wanted to so desperately. I was twenty-one at the time. My brother was there, and I lived with him and his wife when I first left, but even that wasn't good enough. I changed my name not to hide, for they knew where I was and didn't approve. It was a moment's rebellion when I changed my name, that's all. I didn't mean to mislead anyone at S & R. And I have suffered so during my estrangement from them. No matter what, I don't want to go back to those sad times again!"

"I can understand. That must have been some family rift. But everything seems so smooth now."

She shook her head. "Only on the surface. I'm here under a temporary flag of truce because Mother thought her illness would make me come back permanently. Besides, you haven't met her nor my sister Edna. Neither has forgiven me, and, even if I came back, those two wouldn't let me forget my . . . the errors of my way."

"Being without your family has made you bitter."

"I said, you haven't met Mother. And even when you do tonight, she's physically weak right now. But inside, she's so different from me, strong and stubborn. She doesn't understand times are different from when she had to leave her family to come clear across the Atlantic. I'm only in Chicago, for heaven's sake! And you can't understand how it was."

"I'll admit I can't grasp how you could leave the bosom of a big family, and the place where you belong—"

"I don't belong here! Not to live. You're out on your own. Surely you champion independence and making one's own way!"

"But at what price? The people you love? Your past and name—your very identity."

"It's all been so painful; why can't I have my family's love but my own life, too?"

She pulled gently away, disappointed he didn't or couldn't understand. Or was it that he really came to get her to stay here so there would be no more complications for him at S & R? He obviously felt she belonged here. Perhaps he had even come to urge she marry Andreas.

She firmly disengaged herself from his hands, and they started back toward the house. As if he could read her thoughts, he asked, "And who really is that man to you—Mr. Kurtz?"

She almost lost her temper then. This reminded her too much of trying to shake Andreas off the other day, in almost this same spot. Only she did not want to shake off this man, at least not until she knew his real motives.

"He's a childhood friend who still believes I should marry him to solve everyone's problems. I've declined his offer. Edna wishes he were her beau, and that hasn't helped my welcome home."

"Charlotte, I'm so sorry about all of this," he said and snagged her arm to swing her to him again. "I hate for families not to get along, especially at this time of the year. It's important at any cost to patch things up, you know."

Through her tumbled emotions, she gazed up into his impassioned face so close. He bent down slightly to her. Thick flakes began to fall again, plopping on her nose and lashes, though the brim of his hat sheltered him. They had stopped between the smithy and the house, on the far side of a fir tree, its branches drooped with snow.

"At *any* cost?" she challenged, her voice shaky now. "I suppose you have some family tragedy that makes you say so, but—"

"No family tragedy. No family at all. I'm an orphan, Charlotte. Worse, I was abandoned. At about one week old on a May morning, I was left in a cardboard box on the very bench in Grant Park where we sat the other day. I was found by two old gardeners with no note, no name, no past, and certainly no future. They took me to St. Mary's where the nuns gave me the name Donald James—the first names of the two who found me—and gave me what love they could. At thirteen I went out to make my way and have been on my own ever since.''

"I'm sorry. I see. I didn't know.''

"I have told no one but Mr. Sears. Too personal, too—as you say, painful.''

She nodded. She gripped his arms at the elbows to hold to him, to comfort him. No wonder he didn't understand her leaving her family. No wonder he worked so hard at S & R, for he evidently felt he had come from . . . from nothing, and maybe it was the only family of sorts he had.

"So different, aren't we?'' he whispered. " But that makes it so alluring and so . . . lovely.''

And then he leaned even closer, bending closer to her. As she went up on tiptoe to meet him, her feet skidded, then wedged between his big boots to tilt her back in his embrace. They held tightly as their lips met. The kiss was gentle at first, then firm, then insistent. His mouth was amazingly warm; his mustache tickled, but she did not laugh. Instead, when he slanted his head to taste her deeper, she opened her lips to feel him. At that his arms went so fast and firm around her waist that her hands were caught against his hard chest. But soon she reached up to clasp his neck as they moved their heads in little circles to prolong the kiss.

He felt wonderful to her. Her breasts flattened against him, her skirts pushed back as his hips and thighs pressed to hers. She clasped him closer and inhaled the manly scent of him: leather, damp wool, his tart pomade or shaving cream. Her head spun with sensations. They breathed harder in unison. It was better than a book by Bertha Clay.

At last he lifted his head and dropped a quick kiss on her forehead, then on her cold nose, both cheeks, a quick peck on her pouted, tingling mouth again. He helped her stand upright.

"I *do* like Bromberg!" he said with a shaky smile.

"Lately, it has some benefits," she admitted. "But we'd best go in before the boys come looking for us. We can't be late for *Christkind* dinner."

"Ja, Fraulein Schwartzmiller," he told her, then grinned at his first attempt at German. He readjusted his top hat where it had been tipped awry, and they swung hands up the walk.

Charlotte looked up at her mother's window and saw Edna's form silhouetted there before she dropped the curtain and turned away. But nothing, *nothing* could ruin this night for her now. She felt she skimmed across a smooth sheet of ice, no longer earthbound. That he had not agreed with her most heartfelt explanations seemed distant and muted now. She had unlocked the secret of Mr. Donald James: he was an orphan who had no one with whom to share Christmas celebrations or the rest of the year. But this holiday he had her love, however hopeless, and she wondered if he knew it.

The family ate the traditional *Christkind* evening meal of stewed fish, potatoes, pumpernickel bread, and special stollen, shaped to recall the baby Jesus' cradle. Everyone finished quickly, for the tree awaited. They had put Don at the end of the table facing Father in Mother's place. Her absence loomed large, though

Father would soon bring her down to the parlor, her first time out of bed since she took ill.

As the four women cleared the table, Claus and John reset it immediately with the traditional soup plates for each child still living at home. In the morning sweets and fruits would fill the bowls if they had been good; a bundle of rods would await the bad child. Charlotte wondered, since they had put out a plate for her living at home this year, if, indeed, the rods would greet her tomorrow.

When Father went outside to clear a patch of snow from the rooftop and scatter corn there to include the birds in the holiday feasting, Charlotte went out to shake the tablecloth. Then she draped it about herself like a huge shawl and traipsed around the corner to call up the ladder, "I can help you."

"Do not catch cold," his deep voice called down. "Two women sick, I don't need that."

"But I climb ladders all the time at work to shelve books."

Otto Schwartzmiller lumbered back down the ladder. "Did you come out to tell me this?"

"No, Father. I hope you like him—Mr. James, I mean."

"Who else?"

"Well, do you?"

"As much as I know him yet, I like him. The thing is you like him a lot."

"When Mother comes downstairs, anything you can do to keep things calm would be a great help."

"It is the holiest night of the year, my girl. Do not think your mother or poor Edna either will ruin that."

He squeezed her shoulder and motioned her in. Like a good daughter, she went.

* * *

Charlotte was grateful when the tree was done and it was time to sing, for by then, by clever interrogation, her mother had already gotten out of Don that he loved Chicago; that he was reared in a Catholic orphanage by nuns and had no idea who his parents or people were; and that he, therefore, had no idea if he had German kin, and knew no Germans until Charlotta. At least, thank heavens, he had not let slip that she had an Anglicized name when he first met her. Still it annoyed Charlotte that in nine minutes her mother had things out of Don that had taken her nine months to learn.

But there was no explosion from Mother, and when at last the family and their guest held hands in a circle around the adorned tree, Charlotte felt almost happy. For these moments of union, there were no family problems and Donald James was hers.

Afraid she would cry if she looked at any of them, Charlotte kept her eyes fixed on the glittering array of blown ornaments and winking glass beads. The familiar wax angel hadn't changed these years Charlotte had been away, though perhaps her once-stiff paper wings looked a bit worn and wilted. Under her lofty heavenly gaze hung the earthly treasures of the tree: gilded fruit, little sacks of nuts, cookies dangling among the boughs on ribbons. And under the tree lay the Old World heirlooms of carved nutcrackers, jumping jacks, and dried fig-and-raisin dolls.

Father then turned down the lamps. In the glow of candles and the heat and light from the old, open-doored stove, they sang the traditional "O Tannenbaum." Though he knew none of the German words beyond that, Don's bass blended with Father's amidst the higher women's and young boys' voices. "O Christmas tree, fair Christmas tree, such happiness you give me. For through the year your joyous cheer remains a mem'ry all too dear. O Christmas tree, fair Christmas tree, your leaves are so unchanging.''

They sang other carols, no longer linking hands, but Charlotte felt adrift in the warm wonder of belonging. They sat around the tree, while Father read the Christmas story in the book of Luke from the big, old Bible. She noticed he glanced once at Mother and stopped reading sooner than he had years ago, for perhaps she was tired. Charlotte helped Anna and Edna serve cups of hot chocolate and pass plates of *pfeffernusse,* anise-flavored *springerle,* and *lepkuchen* cookies, which Don praised heartily.

"Your friend says he likes our town," Mother told Charlotte in German when she passed the plate again to her. "But he says he'll probably always live in the city."

"I wouldn't let it worry you or turn you against him, Mother. Employees where we work are not allowed to socialize—in the city, that is."

Olga rolled her eyes. "So will you both live here so you can socialize like this in the country?"

That annoyed Charlotte. It was her fondest dream, of course, but she did not want Mother either pulling them apart nor pushing them together. Besides, back in the city, he had said it didn't do for them to be seen together. Or was he really here to convince her to stay?

But no, not the way he smiled at her now, the way his eyes followed her, hungry eyes, as Andreas had accused. That expression on his glowing face made Don look as if he could indeed devour her like a Christmas cookie. And she could not help herself, but she smiled back at him with mouth and eyes—and all her heart.

* * *

The next morning it became apparent to Charlotte that Edna had found a special way of tormenting her: chatty and friendly, she did not leave her and Don alone for one minute, unless she was in the kitchen, and then Charlotte usually was, too. Not that she worried that he would prefer her sister—though he was overly kind and polite to her, she thought. But she worried how bitter Edna must really be and that scared her. Was this pretense to make her look like a liar to him because she had told him her sister resented her? Or was it just her way to unjustly accuse—"You kept Andreas's attention from me, and now, how does it feel?"

Edna sat close on Don's other side through the Christmas morning service in the Redeemer Lutheran Church, where everyone, including Andreas's family, stared and whispered about the stranger with the Schwartzmiller sisters. Perhaps Charlotte dared to hope, Edna had aimed all this at Andreas, but she did not even look his way afterward to see how he reacted. And Charlotte fumed as Edna boldly held Don's other arm all the way home, even though he had offered it. Still, Charlotte responded warmly and sweetly to Edna, for she had no intentions of looking like a scold. But wait until she got Edna alone! They needed to clear the chilly air between them permanently.

The *Christkind* gifts on the table had been enjoyed at breakfast. Charlotte was grateful she had received fruits and sweets like the others, but then, no doubt Father and not Mother had doled out the bounty. Now she felt even more nervous as the formal family gift giving approached. Even the wonderful array of roast goose with braised cabbage and potato dumplings, and Elenora's fancy marzipan dessert could not woo her stomach from its overwrought state.

Mother had declared she would not take a present this year unless Charlotte vowed to stay home. Her gift to Father had been returned last year. Would her married siblings who crowded the table with them now be allowed to keep presents she had agonized over? At least, with Don here, Edna would probably accept the lamp, though she would no doubt just as soon break it over her head once Don James set out for home today.

And how she wished she had something for Don— any one of the things she had dreamed of giving him. That iron settee for romantic back-porch stargazing in the summer months, the bow tie, anything. But she realized she had, in a way, given him a special Christmas. How perfectly he seemed to fit in here with her family; how much happier he seemed among them than she did right now with all her worrying.

She helped her sisters clear the table and wash the dinner dishes, then hurried back out to the parlor to catch Don before Edna got his ear again. Claus stood there alone, staring out the window, holding the new sled Father had made for him.

"Claus, do you know where Mr. James went? Did Father go to bring Mother down?"

He turned to her. "Father took him up to see Mother, that's all I know. Do you want to try this sled after presents, Lottie?"

"What? Oh, yes, that would be swell." Her voice trailed off. She stared at the ceiling where the treetop pointed, wishing she could see and hear what was going on directly above. If only that wax angel could fly upstairs to be Don's guardian angel right now!

5

Don James followed Charlotte's father up the creaking wooden steps to Mrs. Schwartzmiller's room. While Charlotte was busy in the kitchen, he had requested to speak with her mother in private—to beard the lioness in her den, as it were—and settle three things before he headed back to the city today. First, sensing Charlotte's father was willing to have him call socially upon his daughter, he needed to know if the mother was also so inclined.

Second, he wanted to see if he had an ally in having Charlotte stay here at home until he could win her hand by visiting and then, if all went well, move her back to Chicago as his wife. How could he court her there without the chance of being caught again and ruining both their futures at S & R? He was not one to revel in rebellion and breaking rules as she had. Besides, if he must, it would give him time to look for other employment, though he'd staked his future on S & R.

Third, he hoped to help patch things up between Charlotte and her mother. Charlotte has said her separation from the family had been painful for her. He felt, above all else, she must be permanently reconciled with them before she could make other key decisions. And, even if it took sacrifice on his part, he meant to help her have that reconciliation—his real gift to her this Christmas, whether she realized it or not.

He found Olga Schwartzmiller, dressed and sitting by the window, waiting to go downstairs for the opening of gifts. He sat on a chair facing her across a small table with a sewing basket on it. As the winter sun slanted in, he saw from the proud lift of the oval-shaped head and piercing blue eyes where Charlotte had gotten her beauty as well as her cleverness and stubbornness.

While Mr. Schwartzmiller went downstairs to see if things were ready, Don came right to his first point: he hoped he had her approval to call upon Charlotte weekends while she tarried here in Bromberg. He would inquire at S & R about her remaining here to tend her mother for a month or so, so the family could be reunited longer.

"You said you like our little Bromberg," Mrs. Schwartzmiller responded in heavily accented English. "You could move here to call upon her for more than a month, get yourself, her too, out of that noisy, dirty city. That gives you time to start a little Sears and Roebuck here."

At first he felt shock she dared to plan his life, but it meant she liked and accepted him, didn't it? "Sears and Roebuck is not mine to start anywhere, Mrs. Schwartzmiller. Such an establishment would need a different place than quiet, little Bromberg. My home is Chicago, and that's where I'll stay."

She began to twist her narrow, gold wedding band. "You are a truthful man. So I must tell you for many years there has been another man in Charlotta's life. Like they say, a childhood sweetheart."

"Andreas Kurtz. But I understand that is over now."

"No, he loves her still. Sometimes I think she went away, because she cares for him, too. But she knows he must live here, in little, quiet Bromberg, near her family. Charlotta thinks she wants to be out on her own. But she is miserable without any of us in her life. He is a proud man, Andreas, waiting faithfully for her when he could have Edna. I think Charlotta would marry him if he weren't a Bromberg farmer. Still, I keep hoping—not that you are not a fine man, Mr. James—that she would stay home for good. Then she will know the truth in her heart. Charlotta loves her family and will return to their arms.''

''And to his?'' he put in, his voice angry when he had meant to be conciliatory.

She nodded, still twisting her ring. ''Forgive a mother for loving her firstborn daughter too much, for wanting her future to be near her family. I was the eldest daughter to my mother. I went away with the man I married. But I suffer all these years that I left my home. If I stayed and Otto came here, there would someday been someone else for me there and without all the pain of losing the family.''

But Charlotte is only in Chicago! he wanted to shout. Still, he knew all too well that distances of the heart were what mattered, and he wanted to spare Charlotte more of that. ''I understand,'' he said and stood. This had not gone the way he intended at all, but at least he saw how things were. For Charlotte to be reconciled to her family she must stay here, at least for a while. And if he dared to hope she could ever be his, he must leave now, and give things more time.

''I'll try to talk Charlotta into staying home for a while longer to . . . to at least be sure about her life,'' he said. ''The last thing I want to do is cause problems in her family, with all those she loves here in Bromberg. I'll write to her about how long she can stay away from Chicago and keep her job. Then, too, she's bright and hardworking, and I'm sure she can find another if she must.''

He was suddenly also angry with Charlotte for leading him on and saying she didn't love Andreas, when perhaps she did. Drat, but he should have known not to fall for a woman who changed her name and fled her family. A woman who went by Charlotte, Charlotta, Char, and Lottie could hardly know her own heart! He wanted to stay and fight for her, but he was not going to help tear her family apart in the process. He would have to give her time to fix things here, and then either she must come to him or he could come here again.

"Maybe Charlotta can work in Reidelbach's store here," Olga Schwartzmiller put in when he hesitated, frowning.

Suddenly Don James knew his country Christmas was over. He treasured it and always would. But he could not bear to sit among them anymore and long for Charlotte if it would make things worse for her. Nor could he bear to wait much longer for what he had been denied and yearned for so desperately—a family, past and present and future—of his own.

"I will be heading back to Chicago—home," he told her. "But I cannot thank you enough for sharing your home and family with me. I don't mean to be rattling on, Mrs. Schwartzmiller, but it gets worse at Christmas, that's all. You see, I miss what I never had, more, perhaps than you miss that family you left behind in Germany. You at least have them in your heart—maybe in letters, in photographs, or memories—but I have none of those things to hold to. Good-bye."

He turned away and was halfway down the stairs before he passed Mr. Schwartzmiller, heading up.

Charlotte saw Don come downstairs and hurried to him. "I heard you've been summoned to Mother," she said low and took his arm.

"Actually, I asked to speak with her," he said, clearing his throat and flexing his shoulders as he gently pulled away to reach for his overcoat on the crowded coat rack. "I wanted to thank her for the hospitality and tell her I must be heading back before everyone opens gifts. The skies look dark again, and I can't afford to get snowed in here. Besides, some friends had asked me for a late dinner this evening, and I don't want to let them down.''

That obviously rehearsed recital of excuses hit her in the belly like a brick. ''You could have mentioned that.''

''And, quite frankly, Charlotte,'' he said, turning to face her at last, ''the longer I stay, the more I want to stay, and that isn't good for either of us. You need to decide some things. If you stay on here, I assure you S & R will give you some time and good severance terms.''

''Well, thank you very much, fourth-floor overseer, company spokesman, and evidently my personal overseer and spokesman now, too! That is a speech I imagine you came to make before you got all caught up in the holiday cheer around here.''

''That's not fair.''

''It isn't fair that S & R doesn't let employees be friends or even more than that on their own time, either. It isn't fair that my brother can go blithely off to Chicago to have a life there, and I cannot. It isn't fair that—''

''Charlotta,'' Edna's voice cut in from just behind her, ''is everything all right?''

''Just fine, Edna, in your life and mine,'' Charlotte said. ''Mr. James is leaving. Would you pack him some food for his trip? Claus, why don't you sled across the yard and saddle Mr. James's horse?''

He spoke to her other stumbling words of explanation and contrition, but she did not even let them sink in. He was leaving here, probably leaving her, despite his insisting the decision was hers as long as she included her family in her plans. So, wasn't he as good as telling her to stay here and marry Andreas?

Father came downstairs for a handshake and fare-well, without Mother. As Don took his leave from the others, Charlotte stood stiffly at the bottom of the stairs by the front door, seething yet stunned at this twist of events. The moments they had shared together—that sky-shattering kiss and the caresses just last night— had they meant nothing to him? They had meant every-thing to her.

She could not bear to go out on the porch with the others when he rode away. She strode to the parlor window amidst the trappings of Christmas—unopened gifts around her feet, the tree they had encircled, the littered remnants of her hopes for a future with him, however great the odds. And then she realized that, although he had requested the interview, one of those odds might have said something to him to make him leave like this. In one quick motion she grabbed her mother's gift and fled upstairs. She knocked on her parents' bedroom door.

"Come in, Charlotta."

"How did you know it was me?" she asked as she entered and closed the door. Her mother's chair was turned to the front window; she had, no doubt, just watched Don James ride away.

"Because I know you better than you realize."

"We're not at all alike, Mother, and that has always been our problem."

That little snort through the nose—then Charlotte saw her mother had been crying. "Stuff and nonsense! We are too much alike, Charlotta, and that is why we argue. And now you came up here to tell me I have wronged you again."

"I came up here to bring you your yearly Christmas

gift you won't accept any more than you ever accepted I was an adult, that I could make my own decisions about where to live or whom to love." She plopped the wrapped gift in her mother's lap. Her mother's hands, trembling now, grasped the package, but made no move to open it.

"Mother, did you say anything to send him away?"

"Sit down, Charlotta. Do not keep hovering over me like the grim reaper." She waited until Charlotte obeyed. "I know I have made some grave errors in life," she went on, "errors I do not want my firstborn daughter to make."

Charlotte gripped her hands in her lap. Her fury partly dissipated as her mother began to cry quietly again. Her shoulders shook slightly, though she did not reach for her handkerchief. Except for the time she was in physical pain this last week, Charlotte had never seen her like this.

"I didn't let your father read all of the Christmas story last night because I knew I could not bear that part where the Virgin Mary rejoices in her firstborn, but knows her joy will later be pierced when she loses Him. I have not let him read it on the other *Christkind* eves you were gone, either. You were always my pride and joy, even above the sons, even more than the later girls, for you were like me, Charlotta, loving, but determined and willful. And when you wanted to leave home—leave me—I could not let you go."

As she spoke, her hands tugged at the red string and bright paper on the box. Charlotte cried, too, as her mother delved into the wood shavings packed around the items, then pulled out the sterling-backed hairbrush and hand mirror.

"So shiny!" Mother said, puffing a bit on the mirror, then polishing it on the sleeve of her dress. "And look, look at you, a girl now grown with her own life to live,'' she went on and turned the mirror toward Charlotte. It was not aligned right, and she saw only Father's Certificate of Citizenship hanging on the wall behind her.

And then Mother held out her arms and Charlotte jumped up to bend into them, holding so tight, despite the wheezing breathing that she heard up so close. ''Oh, Mother, the best Christmas gift of all!'' she murmured through her tears.

''Not the best yet. Listen to one thing more,'' she said and set Charlotte back to perch on the arm of the chair. ''I have done a terrible thing you may hate me for, Charlotta. Maybe you will not come home for Christmas ever again, but I will tell you. I let your Mr. James think there still might be a chance for you and Andreas when he said he wanted to come out here and call on you.''

Charlotte jumped to her feet. ''Mr. James wanted to call on me, not Andreas, you mean?''

''Yes, of course. That dunderhead Andreas must be made to realize Edna is the woman for him. Charlotta, forgive your mother, but I wanted you here among us so much. Perhaps you can convince your Mr. James that you can live here while he comes calling. Or you can find another job so he can come to see you in the city. You just be sure your landlady or that newlywed friend of yours and her husband act as chaperons. I will write to him a letter and say that I was . . . mistaken.''

Charlotte clasped her hand between her breasts, daring to hope. She had almost become the old Charlotte again, angry and argumentative, but she recognized history-making change when she saw it. ''Mother,'' she said, swiping at her tears with both palms, ''you've just given me *my* citizenship paper to adulthood—or at least as much as I'm likely to get until I'm married and with my own family someday. And I don't know if all that will be shared with Don James or not, but I promise you, I will be here every Christmas no matter what. But tomorrow I must go back to Chicago.''

Charlotte saw her mother's mouth set hard, but she did not quarrel. ''George and Eliza can take you back with them,'' she said. ''But you'll come home much more to visit than just Christmas.''

''I will—win or lose with Don James and S & R,'' Charlotte promised and stooped down to hug her just as Father came in and beamed at them both.

''Mother,'' Charlotte said as she and Father walked her slowly downstairs between them, ''what made you change your mind about Mr. James . . . and me?''

''That boy knows the value of family more than any one of us—more than even me. Anna said he liked the family church service this morning, and some of it reminded him of his church. Besides, since he doesn't know who his parents were, he could be German, maybe.''

The first day back at S & R after the Christmas holiday, Charlotte was disturbed to see Mr. James was not in on time. It was most unlike him. She was worried he was sick or had been injured until Mr. Wembly saw her looking up for the tenth time when the door opened, and said, ''He was here bright and early and told me he'd be out of the office till midafternoon.''

''Oh, I see. I just wondered.''

She busied herself with a vengeance; although others had filled in for her while she was away, things were still far behind, and some books were shelved wrong. She made mistakes too, for her mind kept blanking out; she'd just stand for a moment, remembering or planning what she would say to him.

And her parting words to Edna kept barging through her brain: "Go after Andreas, as I am Don, Edna! Mama won't blame you. And if she says you're fast or loose, you just tell me and I'll take care of it with her! Put yourself in his path, smile at him, show him—tell him if you must—how deeply you have always admired him. Don't just fret and fume the rest of your life away and blame me! Men get confused and don't know what they want sometimes, so it's up to us to set them straight! And this time of year with its sentiments and gifts of love is the very best time to do it!''

Brave words, she thought, as she glanced at her watch pinned to her jacket for the hundredth time. She hoped it would work for Edna to win Andreas, but she was so afraid it might be too late for her to win Don.

She hardly touched her lunch; even dear Agnes's concern for her set her more on edge. But when Mr. James did return at a quarter past two and left his office door ajar, she marched to it and knocked.

"Come in."

She entered and closed the door.

"Charlotte! I'm so glad you're back."

"I find that hard to credit after our most recent ending. I do not wish to take company time for personal matters, Mr. James—Don—but I want to tell you I think that S & R is in error not to let people fraternize—you know what I mean. And I wanted to tell you how much I have come to care deeply for you, to admire and respect you, and more than that. Mother and I are reconciled, thanks partly to your efforts, and she wrote this note to you to clarify some of the things she said before you departed. And I don't love Andreas—

the way I do you—and never have, and told Edna to tell him she cares for him. And now that I have said my piece, I will return to my duties.''

She edged close to his immaculately ordered desk and dropped the note there. Suddenly terrified of what he might say—he looked as if he had been hit by a train—she turned and fled, but not before she saw open on his desk what he had been reading, *Love Story* by Bertha M. Clay.

In the valleys of her shelves, she waited hopefully, nervously, to be dismissed from her job. When Don neither came looking for her, nor summoned her, she actually thought it would come to that for her daring. But nothing happened and, when she darted a look at his dark office and closed door at half-past four, dear Mr. Wembly informed her, ''He went to see Mr. Sears, and he never came back.''

''Oh, thank you. Thank you for all your help, Mr. Wembly.'' Her eyes met his. She could tell he felt sorry for her, but that was little consolation. They both knew she had been spurned by Don James now. She had overstepped. Foolish of her and funny, but she longed to have Mother here to tell, to ask what to do next, to hug and comfort her.

And he never came back. Mr. Wembly's words pursued her as she left work promptly at five o'clock. She took the unused strings of stale popcorn and cranberries with which she had meant to decorate the office tree and stuffed them in her handbag and inside pocket of her cape. She would just feed them to the birds and squirrels at home. Thank heavens Agnes was going to the dentist after work, for she could not have borne her questions right now, however kindly intended.

Outside the day was cold, but not windy, with snow

threatening from a lowering gray sky. She decided to walk home so as not to have to face the bustling preparations for Mabel's wedding until she gave herself a good talking to.

But she kept thinking about that starry night when she and Don had walked the little town of Bromberg together. How dear it all was to her now in memory, a toy town under the dark branches of a giant tree of the heavens, lit by candle points of stars. Now memories were all she would ever have of those grand, lost times with him.

"Charlotte! Miss Schwartzmiller!"

She spun around. He had followed her as once before. She gripped her handbag so hard her fingers went numb, but the rest of her felt vibrant and tingling.

"I wanted to be sure you got away from the building."

She could only nod. He had two pairs of ice skates protruding from his overcoat pockets, making them bulge. He looked nervous as she felt. "You're going skating—with Mickey?" she asked.

"Actually I was hoping you would go with me and then stop for supper somewhere. Sears skates, nothing but the best, 'perfectly matched and mated,' as the catalogue says. Will you come along?"

They strolled toward Grant Park, talking but not touching. "I've been with Mr. Sears all morning," he told her. "He was my mentor from the beginning, you know, and always more than fair with me. I confessed about falling in love with you and asked that he reconsider the company policy."

"In love!" she gasped. "You did? Did he?"

"He amended it until they can perhaps review the policy. He's moving me to second-floor overseer next week—Iron Hardware and Farm Implements. It's a bit of a promotion for me, too, and I'll have even more to talk about to your father and brothers. Meanwhile, I think Mr. Wembly—our real guardian angel—will be promoted to overseer and you can keep your job.''

''Oh, good for us all, but I shall miss you!''

He took her arm. ''But—if you are willing—you will not have me to miss. I mean, I want to come calling, both here and in Bromberg, since your mother wrote that you have vowed to visit there more, and that she regrets some things she has said to both of us.''

She stopped and turned to him on the street just before the park began. Several families or businesses had discarded small trees, which lay forlornly abandoned along the sidewalk. But even they looked lovely to her now. And on busy Michigan Avenue filled with carriages and cabs, they fell into each other's arms and just held tight, however much the skates got in the way between them.

''I admire you with all my heart, and love you more than that,'' he whispered in her hair. ''I'd like to hope we can make a family of our own someday, perhaps someday soon, sweetheart.''

His breath was hot on her temple and in her ear. He crushed her harder to him. People went by staring. Someone shouted at them to ''cease and desist,'' but someone else bellowed ''best wishes'' from a passing carriage. A horse gave his belled harness a jangling shake. She was so happy that she was afraid to move or think or breathe.

''Charlotte, I hope you won't mind my adding sweetheart to your panoply of names.''

They moved a bit apart, but still held hands. ''I believe I will take to it faster than I did to skating.''

''I wish we would have had the rest of our country Christmas,'' he admitted. ''But next year we shall not only share one in Bromberg, but have a tree of our own in the city.''

"But look, my love," she said, "there is one for us right here!'' She bounced the branches of the discarded tree with her foot to clear it of snow and slush. "See—I brought the decorations, too."

From her handbag and cape pocket she proudly produced her strings of popcorn and cranberries. He shouted a laugh and dragged the tree—and her by her free hand—down toward the skating pond where they propped the greenery up against their bench. Together they draped the tree, smiling at first, then laughing like lunatics.

He pulled her into his lap on the bench to admire their Christmas tree, but soon they saw only each other again. "One more thing," he said. "My first of many Christmas gifts for you, if you will accept it—and my heartfelt offer for your hand. I took a half day of vacation I dare hope I should have saved for a spring honeymoon. But I needed to go shopping in the first-floor jewelry department of a certain Sears and Roebuck after lunch, and it took me two hours to pick just the right thing."

Her mouth hung open as he fished in his vest pocket and brought out a tiny leather box. Inside, nestled on a blue velvet bed was a diamond betrothal ring. With Agnes and Mabel, Charlotte had spent hours on that page of the catalogue, but had not dared to hope her dreams for one would come true.

"I don't know," he said, his voice gone rough with emotion, "if I can say it quite like those heroes Bertha Clay writes about, but, my sweetheart, will you accept this ring in the good faith and deep love with which it is tendered?''

"Yes," she cried, "Oh, yes!''

"I suppose we should ask your parents."

"We'll tell them together," she whispered as they both admired the ring on her ungloved finger. She hated to cover it again, but she felt it nestled between finger and glove, another Christmas miracle.

Snow began to fall, thick and silent, while the wind whistled a carol from the expanse of frozen lake. But firmly in each other's arms and each other's futures, Charlotta Schwartzmiller and Donald James felt wonderfully warm. As they embraced, crimson cardinals and reddish squirrels came to eat from their first Christmas tree and decorate its branches with themselves in return.